The Good Deed

A novel by
Renee Perrault

Copyright © 2013 Renee Perrault
All rights reserved.

ISBN: 1493654489
ISBN 13: 9781493654482

Chapter 1
Ireland - 1920

E dward O'Brien and Lydia Delaney had not spoken in four years, much to the delight of her younger sister, Myra who had her heart set on the boy. When Edward O'Brien was ten years old his dream was to marry Lydia Delaney. He fell in love with her, and to prove it, he pushed her into a mud puddle. His fate was sealed when she screamed after him, "I hate you Edward O'Brien and I'll not speak to you ever again!"

That proclamation lasted until Lydia was fourteen and suddenly saw Edward through new eyes. The ten year old menace had grown into a tall young man with broad shoulders. His boyish face had become masculine with a hint of whiskers starting above his upper lip. Edwards' contagious smile lit up his face and made his sky blue eyes dance with merriment. His slightly crooked nose kept his face from being too perfect. Lydia regretted ignoring him for four years.

Lydia spent days trying to get in front of Edward, but to no avail. Edward was the tallest in their class. She could usually spot him in the hallway, but he was always surrounded by his friends. She wasn't about to approach him at school.

As punishment from Father O'Reilly for failing a religion test, Edward had to serve early Mass for two weeks giving, Lydia her chance. Edward watched Lydia kneeling at the communion rail. Her beautiful blue eyes closed as Father O'Reilly stood in front of her ready to give the Communion Host. His anger flared as he thought of how she had refused to speak to him for the last four years. *She's a lassie that doesn't forget, stubborn as the day is long.* He mused to himself as he held the silver tray beneath her chin. Father O'Reilly placed the host on her tongue, and Edward watched her full lips curve into a smug smile when she peeked up and saw him staring at her.

He looked down at her clear porcelain skin; the faint smattering of freckles across her nose reminded him of the ten year old he had been so in love with. Her heart-shaped face.

looked innocent as she crossed herself after swallowing the Host. A pretty blush lit up her face, and she glanced at Edward before turning to walk back to her pew. He was thinking how beautiful she looked and a pang of longing hit his heart. Father O'Reilly moved on to the next parishioner while Edward silently followed not noticing the malevolent looks being directed at Lydia by her younger sister from the back of the church.

Every morning Lydia showed up for Mass, taking communion, getting braver each day, opening her eyes and smiling at Edward as the priest put the host on her tongue. She lingered after Mass hoping to catch him as he came out of the church, but Edward always ducked out the rear door to meet up with his friends before school. Neither of them noticed Myra hiding in the back of the church, watching their every move.

He only had three more days of early Mass. He walked out the front of the church after changing into his school clothes. Sauntering out as if he had no cares in the world, Edward saw Lydia dawdling by the door. He passed her without a look and Lydia called after him.

"Edward O'Brien, where are your manners? Are you too good to be sayin' hello to a classmate?" Her tone was huffy and it annoyed Edward.

"You have not spoken to me in four years? Why on earth waste time saying hello to someone who won't respond?" Edward couldn't contain his anger. "I'll be saying hello to you," he continued, "when you can be cordial and let bygones be bygones. It was four years ago that I pushed you. Why haven't you gotten over it by now?"

"Well, most people would have had the courtesy to apologize for pushing someone into the mud for no reason. The manners you are lacking are certainly not my fault." Lydia turned and stomped off.

Edward spent the day at school pondering the situation. Lydia refused to look at him but he was used to it. Being ignored for four years had inured him to her stubbornness, but now, with a chance to make up, he was at a loss.

He walked over to his sister's house after school. Rosie was twelve years older, married with two children, and his favorite sister. As he walked up the stairs to the porch, his head down and shoulders slumped in misery, Rosie looked out the window.

Ah, this should be good, she thought. Her mother had sent word through the family telegraph system that Edward had been acting strangely and feared her youngest child was having trouble at school. Rosie looked at her young brother's handsome face and realized he was growing up, a far cry

3

from the young bairn she used to bathe and change his nappies. He was a burgeoning young man and the look on his face screamed girl trouble.

Rosie was the beauty of the family. Her strawberry blonde hair and emerald green eyes were the calling card of the O'Brien's. At least one woman in each generation inherited those features. Edward looked at his nephew who had Rosie's hair and his niece who had her eyes. Edward laughed in spite of himself thinking, *she'll probably have four or five more. She's bound to get the combination correct at some point.*

What brings you by?" She quickly added, "Not that I'm not overjoyed to see my baby brother, mind you. I could use a little break from my day. Let's have a bit of tea and a biscuit."

Following her into the kitchen, Edward could contain himself no longer. "I should never have pushed her."

Alarmed, Rosie grabbed him by the shoulders. "You pushed a girl? Who did you push?"

"Lydia Delaney. I pushed her into a mud puddle and she hasn't spoken to me in four years, and now she wants to and I want her to, but she got mad all over again, and I don't know how to fix it." His words rushed out in a tumble and Rosie did her best not to smile.

"Why did you push her? And why am I just hearing about it now?" Rosie was the oldest of ten children and by the time Edward had come along, their mother was too exhausted to worry about another child. Rosie had raised Edward until she married four years ago and moved into her own home. "Did you push her because you were mad at me for getting married and leaving you?"

In her mind it seemed logical but logic flew out the window as Edward proclaimed. "I pushed her in the mud because I loved her and knew I was going to marry her someday."

Rosie realized at ten, a boy pushing a girl in the mud was as good as a proposal and bit the inside of her cheeks to stifle her laughter. "All right now. So she hasn't spoken to you in four years? She is one unforgiving young lady. Are you sure this is the love of your young life?"

"Rosie, if you make fun of me I'll leave right now!" Edward's frustration was becoming more evident. It was time to start fixing this mess.

"All right, my sweet Eddie, let me see if I understand. You love her, you pushed her in the mud to prove it, she stopped talking to you, now she wants to talk to you and you want to talk to her, so tell me now, why are you here and not talkin' to the lass?"

"She got mad at me and said I never apologized to her. I didn't see the point since she swore never to speak to me again and now it's too late."

"Well four years is a bit of a delay for an apology, but it looks like an apology is the only thing to get you out of this mess. Eddie, be a man and offer a sincere apology or give up on her altogether."

"But, Rosie, the whole school will laugh at me." Edward was becoming more distressed, thinking he'd look a fool in front of his friends.

"Eddie, go pick her some lovely flowers, put on some clean clothes, go over to her house, and ask her to forgive you. But be warned. If you start with this young girl and she is this stubborn, you'll have to cater to her forever." Rosie was worried helping Edward with this girl might be a big mistake, but the pitiful look on his young face made her hold back further words of warning. *God help me if she breaks his heart someday, it will be my fault.*

The next day was Saturday. With no school and his chores done, Edward proceeded to get cleaned up in his Sunday clothes. Dark hair slicked back, sneaking a bit of his da's aftershave lotion after shaving the fuzz above his upper lip, Edward started off on the long walk to Lydia's home. "Why does she have to live on the other side of the village?" he grumbled as he walked along. "God help me if I run into any of my friends seeing me all dressed up and carrying flowers."

Edward continued his desolate march finally arriving at Lydia's door and making a tentative knock. Then, in a moment of anger at the predicament he was in, knocked loudly. "Lydia, come out. If it's an apology you want, I'm here to make it."

Lydia had been watching his approach from her upstairs window. She could tell by his stride he was working himself into a temper. Descending the stairs, she could hear her ma coming down the hall to answer the door. Not wanting her involved in this discussion, she called out, "It's for me, Ma. I'll get the door."

"And who might be on the other side of this door?" Her mother asked.

"Oh, it's no one in particular, Ma. Go back to the kitchen; I'll take care of it."

"Well, young lady, I'd say 'no one' has a pretty loud knock, but I'll leave you to it."

Holding her breath and wondering what Edward would say, Lydia slowly opened the front door.

"Well, it's about time. You waited four years for this. I guess you're in no big hurry."

"Did you come here to have another fight? Maybe you'd like me to come outside and find some mud to push me into?" Lydia couldn't stop the words from coming out.

"All right, I'll say what I've come to say. I'm sorry I pushed you all those many years ago. You were just so beautiful and all the other boys were looking at you. I knew I wanted you to be mine so I pushed you in the mud to show you how I felt." Edward was stammering but bravely continued. "I thought you knew I liked you. I never thought you could be so cruel and not speak to me for four long years. But if it's an apology you want, an apology you'll get. I'm sorry. I'm sorry I pushed you. I'm sorry I made you so mad. I'm sorry I yelled at you the other day, and I'm sorry your flowers are wilted from my long walk. There, I'm done apologizing."

Lydia smiled, deep dimples creasing her cheeks. "I accept your apology, and I'm sorry I didn't speak to you for four years, but how was I supposed to know you liked me?" Lydia was doing the best she could to curb her tongue and not tell him what an idiot he was. But then, she caught sight of the distress in his face and her heart softened.

"Edward, it's a lovely day. Let me put these flowers in water, and we'll walk down the lane together for a spell."

Edward waited at the door as she took the flowers from his outstretched hand and went to find a vase. Coming back, she grabbed a jumper from the hook by the door and closed it behind her. Lydia shyly took Edward's hand, and they headed down the lane while from the upstairs window, eyes an identical clear blue like Lydia's, turned green with envy as her older sister strolled down the lane with the only boy Myra ever wanted. Going to the closet, Myra picked up Lydia's favorite dress and stabbed it with sewing scissors until it was a useless rag.

Chapter 2

1924 – Three Years later

E dwards dream was to go to America and make a new life for Lydia and himself. He had booked passage on a ship leaving from Queenstown in three days, bound for America. Lydia was distraught. She begged her father for money to go with Edward, fearing once he left she might not see him again.

Mr. Delaney could not be persuaded. His funds were limited and he was reluctant to send his beautiful daughter to America with a penniless husband. Better she wait and, with Edward out of the picture, perhaps a more suitable young man would come along.

Edward was excited to begin his journey but, his heart was breaking with every tear Lydia shed.

"It's our future I'm doing this for. Do you want to stay in Ireland, have a passel of children, and be poor your entire life?"

"Yes, if it is with you. I can't stand the thought of not seeing you every day." Her tearful words tore at his heart and, try as he might, he could not stop her crying.

Mr. Delaney kept a sharp eye on them, not willing to let his daughter out of his sight. He was convinced she had kept her virtue with young Edward, but the last thing he wanted was her to relent now in some fit of youthful passion.

Edward's family assembled to say goodbye. Rosie was overcome with grief. She knew it could be years before they saw each other again. The thought of losing him to America was as bad as if someone had snatched her children from her arms, never to be seen again.

"Don't worry, Rosie. I'll be rich beyond your wildest dreams and successful." Edward's usual maturity was replaced by innocent enthusiasm. "I'll send for Lydia to come live in my fine house. I'll send you a ticket when you've raised the brood you're sure to be havin'."

"A brood you call it? Well since you were the youngest of a brood, I guess you know what you're talking about. I'll miss you, laddie. You've always been my little Eddie and now you're all grown up. Tears welled up in Rosie's emerald green eyes and she looked away before they spilled down her cheeks. Her ruddy complexion was unnaturally pale. She hugged her little brother goodbye and turned away without looking back. She knew in her heart she might not see her brother again.

Edward's scene with Lydia didn't go quite as well.

"I'll wait for you but you don't know what my life is like at home. Without you it will be unbearable. But listen clearly, I won't wait forever."

Edward looked at Lydia and saw the determination on her face. "I will love you for as long as I live Lydia, don't give up on me. I must do this for our future. Just be patient and trust in me.

With that he was gone. It was a long trip to Queenstown and he was anxious to get started. After one last look, he left Lydia sobbing in her living room. Her parents were overwhelmed by her distress, and her younger sister looked on triumphantly. *As long as they're not married I still stand a chance,* Myra thought as she put on a sorrowful face for her parents' benefit. *I need to make sure from now on I get the mail before Lydia.*

Lydia's father surreptitiously studied his youngest daughter; he was not fooled by the look on her face. His only thought was, *If the lad had asked to take Myra to America, I would have bought both their tickets.*

Myra always wanted anything that her sister Lydia had. As a young girl, she screamed when it was Lydia's birthday, jealous of her presents. Myra's parents had to give her a small gift to open, too, or her screaming ruined the entire gathering. Myra learned early how to get what she wanted, and, if she didn't, she destroyed what she couldn't get.

Mr. Delaney was proud of all his daughters, but he had a special spot for Lydia because her baby sister Myra was uncontrollable and demanded all the attention. It made his heart heavy that he was unable to control his youngest child.

Chapter 3

America 1924

The ship President Adams was immense, but Edward did not get to see any of the luxurious staterooms. He was immediately shoved into the third class line. The third class passengers were compliant until they went below and saw the deplorable conditions. Edward looked at the man next to him; he appeared to be in his early twenties.

"I'm Johnny Adams. If you're smart you'll grab an upper bunk. Less likely someone will throw up on you." Johnny's face broke into a wide grin, his blue eyes crinkling at the corners. At six feet tall, he was eye to eye with Edward. Taking off his cap and showing an expanse of brown curly hair, Johnny extended his hand.

Edward looked at him and shook his hand. "I'm Edward O'Brien. Pleased to meet you and, thanks, sounds like good advice."

Just then there was a long racking cough from an older man behind them. Johnny turned on the man and in a loud voice said, "Keep moving, Grandpa. We'll not have you sick people infecting the lot of us. Start coughing on Ellis Island and you get sent back."

The old man started to protest until a couple of other men jumped in and told him to move on.

"Keep away from the sick ones, Edward. You so much as have a runny nose when we reach Ellis Island and all the money you spent on this trip goes for nothing but a lousy two week holiday in the hole of a ship. My uncle wrote me all about it and I'm not taking any chances." Johnny turned his infectious smile on Edward, taking some of the sting out of his words.

Edward hadn't thought of any of this and was glad for the information. Other than Johnny, he stayed clear of the other passengers, worried some illness might infect him before he cleared Ellis Island. Third class passengers were only let out to breathe the fresh air for an hour a day. The weather was miserable but even sitting up in the misty rain was preferable to the stench below. The smell was horrible from so many people with very little air flowing through from the small portholes. Sleep was nearly impossible with all of the noises from the occupants in close quarters. There were late night poker games, but Edward and Johnny didn't join in fearing they would lose what little money they had.

At last land was in sight and thankfully a break in the stormy weather. Excitement ran through the boat like a river, flowing into each corner of steerage. When they finally docked, and the first and second class passengers disembarked, Edward expected steerage to be next. Anxious to hit the streets of New York, he was confused when one of the stewards came down and started lining them up to get on yet another boat.

"Keep it moving. Keep moving. No shoving. The ferry will take you to Ellis Island to go through customs." The porter was trying not to retch at the dank smell of the steerage area.

Johnny grabbed Edward's shoulder. "Hang on, Eddie. They make everyone do it. My uncle wrote me if you're not sick, it won't take too long. You get a physical and, if you're okay, they process your paperwork.

The ferry ride was under an hour and they disembarked only to be in another line. The long meandering line passed through the medical station. Edwards ears were overwhelmed by all the different languages. On the ship the different nationalities grouped together. Listening to the cacophony of voices Edward felt the excitement vibrating through Ellis Island. At last he reached the front of the line. A weary doctor peered into Edward's eyes and ears and gave one thump on his back and listened to his chest.

Three hours passed before Edward made it completely through the line. Finally, a harried customs official looked over his paperwork, inked up his red stamp, and stamped his paperwork "Approved." Welcome to America Mr. O'Brien. Good luck to you.

Edward met up with Johnny, their next step was to take their meager savings and convert it to United States dollars. Johnny pulled money out of the lining in his coat. Looking at Edward, he asked, "How much money do you have? My uncle said to be careful. The money exchangers will cheat you if they think they can get away with it."

"I have twenty five pounds left."

"I'll stand with you. Make sure they give you at least forty US dollars. We need to be careful from here on out. The sooner we get off this island, the better. They'll rob us blind here. My uncle said people have been brought up on charges for cheating immigrants, but it doesn't matter, they still do it. Let's go exchange it, just make sure you count it before leaving the window."

Johnny and Edward stood in another long line waiting to change their money. They watched people with no English exchanging money they had never seen or heard of. When it was their turn, the man behind the cage looked them over and after counting out Edward's twenty five pounds, pushed twenty five American dollars back across the counter.

"I think you need to recount this money, sir. According to your sign up there, I should have forty American dollars."

The man put his cigar down, his dark eyes darting quickly, scanning the terminal. He leaned over to Edward and said, "See the security cop over there? Do you want me to get him over here? You'll be thrown out of the country before you step foot off Ellis Island."

Edward had seen enough bullies on the ship coming over and knew most of them didn't fare too well when you called their bluff. "Aye, it's a grand idea Sir. Let's call the security cop over to help settle this matter." Edward smiled at the clerk, but his eyes were serious. He had toughened up from the voyage and stood his ground.

The money changer knew this mick kid had called his bluff. The Feds had been watching all the vendors on Ellis Island. Complaints about cheating immigrants had become rampant and crackdowns were in place. The barber two stalls down almost lost his shop when he threatened an immigrant with deportation if he didn't get a haircut. The poor immigrant barely spoke English but understood the word deportation and started screaming, bringing the cops. Now they had undercover coppers posing as immigrants trying to catch the scammers. He pushed another fifteen dollars across the counter. "My mistake. Welcome to the United States. You've reached the land of milk and honey, and our streets are paved with gold. Now get outta here."

Johnny clapped Edward on the back. "Come on, Eddie. Like the man says, the bags of money are out there waiting."

Laughing, Edward threw his arm around his friend's shoulder, turning them both around for a last look at the Statue of Liberty. "I want to always remember this moment, our new land, and our new opportunities. May Lady Liberty give us the grand life we deserve."

Chapter 4

Lydia was beginning to become resentful. Her friends were off having fun while she sat at home. The village had seen tough economic times, but the Irish spirit prevailed when it came to the young people. Where there was music, there was dancing and Myra made sure she was at every dance while Lydia sat at home. Most of Lydia's friends were working or married, and she herself had been put to work at her father's bakery. In the evenings she was too tired to go out as she rose for work at 4:30 a.m. Her only distraction from her dull life was getting a letter from Edward.

Writing weekly, Edward described his arrival in New York and looking for work. A great depression was gripping the country, and the Irish immigrants were the last on the list to be hired. He tried working out of the union hall to get day jobs, but they weren't steady, and the hard work and low pay were not helping him get ahead. Edward had quickly realized the city held no appeal for him, and he missed the lush green hills of Ireland.

Lydia was discouraged. She was trying to save money from her weekly pay, but Edward had been gone over a year, and she had not put much aside. When the gaps between letters started to lengthen, she worried she was waiting for a boy who was no longer interested. Lydia began to notice a young man who came into the bakery each morning for a breakfast roll. He introduced himself as Tommy Simon; Lydia remembered he had been three years ahead of her in school.

Tommy Simon had been known in school as a prankster and a favorite of the nuns. Most of the time, they turned a blind eye to his exploits, grateful for a bit of mirth in their dull lives. A natural born comedian, he spread laughter where ever he went. Tommy was slightly built but wiry. He worked for his father as a painter and his curly red hair usually had paint spattering from whatever job he was working on. Tommy made a point of telling a funny story or a joke to make the beautiful Lydia notice him.

Soon she began looking forward to the morning visits. Her father smiled to himself when he noticed her tidying her hair in the mirror before Tommy arrived each day.

Another one to notice was Myra. She was secretly pleased Lydia's attention was being diverted from mooning over Edward. Myra was determined Lydia and Edward would not be reunited. She had her own intentions where Edward O'Brien was concerned.

Edwards' letters chronicled his travels across America looking for work. He tried to be upbeat and funny but Lydia could read the despair between the lines. His last letter held good news. He had finally settled in a town called Little Creek and found work as a logger after a short term job of cooking for the crew. According to Edward, the money was much better as a logger, the work was a wee bit dangerous, but he was managing. Not much longer he promised, maybe another year.

When Lydia read those words, hot angry tears slipped down her cheeks. She was now almost twenty and most of her friends from school were married or engaged with wedding dates set. A couple even had babies, and here she was, wasting her youth on a boy thousands of miles away with a dream that didn't seem as real to her as it did to him.

Tommy continued to come around and was biding his time. He knew the O'Brien boy had a claim on her heart, but he could see it was withering away each day.

Chapter 5

Little Creek was settled in the 1820. The ten waterfalls in the surrounding hills made it not only a place of beauty but prosperity with the gold being mined and the lush forest harvested. For almost a hundred years, two families, ran the town. Asa Parrish and Jackson Brookstone were men cut from the same cloth. Asa established the first bank, general store, and Episcopal Church, and was the first mayor of Little Creek. Jackson Brookstone owned Little Creek Logging Company, the lumber mill, and lumber yard. Both men had a financial hold over the town and ran it as they saw fit. If the sheriff holding office didn't agree, they fired him and brought in another. Asa and Jackson's sons now held the power and ran it much as their fathers had.

After working odd jobs across the United States, Edward found the Pacific Ocean on the West Coast of Oregon with its high cliffs and rainy weather reminded him of Ireland. It wasn't the emerald green of his youth, but it was a deep lush green, just as alluring, that beckoned to him, promising a new life. A few miles inland, he found Little Creek, a logging town in the lush old-growth forest.

They both got hired by Little Creek Logging. Johnny got work as a logger and Edward signed on for the only remaining job available, cook. When the men in camp discovered he only knew two recipes, his mother's stew and a mutton dish, they kicked him out of the kitchen and put him on one of the steam donkeys used for dragging logs down the mountain. Edward was relieved to get out of the cook camp. The pay as a logger was better, and he needed the physical activity. Steam donkeys consisted of a cable and a hoist equipped with huge drums or spools enabling the donkey to move logs from the forest to the trail for transportation to the mill just outside of town. It was dangerous work and there were many accidents, killing or maiming loggers. Edward was twenty years old and had been a logger for eighteen months when a cable off a donkey snapped, hitting Edward in his left leg nearly severing it at the knee. It was the stubbornness and extraordinary surgical skills of the camp doctor that saved his leg.

Dr. Monroe was new to the camp replacing Doc Olsen, who was more interested in drinking and poker than in medicine. All the loggers agreed, if Edward's accident had occurred on Doc Olsen's watch, his leg would have been amputated, especially if the accident had been on poker night. Dr. Monroe was a young surgeon, newly graduated from medical school, and anxious to ply his profession. His skilled surgery saved Edward's leg and his physical therapy helped his patient heal. Dr. Monroe devised a method of exercise to strengthen the leg which he hung small bags of sand on at various points. It was slow going and torturous, but it improved the mobility of Edwards leg.

Chapter 6

Edward had been gone for almost two years. Lydia pulled the box of letters from beneath her bed, reading them again from the beginning. She was searching for any hint Edwards feelings had changed. She had not heard from him in over a month and was beginning to think she should move on and accept a date with Tommy. Hearing the postman, Lydia dried her eyes and headed to the front door. Mr. Jenkins handed her a letter from America that was not in Edward's handwriting,

Dear Miss Delaney,

I am Doctor Monroe and writing this letter to inform you of an accident in Little Creek involving your fiancé Edward O'Brien.

Lydia's heart stopped, her breathing was quickening and she could barely continue.

Edward was seriously hurt in a logging accident. His left leg was nearly severed when a cable from the logging donkey snapped and hit him just above the knee. I managed to save the leg, but

an infection has set in and Edward has been in a coma for the past three days. I have done everything we can do for him; it is in God's hands now. Edward gave us instructions to write you and his family should his condition worsen. He expressed his great love for you and is devastated this accident has compromised his ability to work and earn money for your future together.

Keep Edward in your prayers and I will continue to watch over him.

Respectively,

Dr. Bernard Monroe

Lydia folded the letter and put it back in the envelope. She was sitting on her bed trying to stop her heart from beating out of her chest. Her only thought now was Edward and the fact he needed her. The idea to go to America came into her head and a lifetime of being the responsible trustworthy daughter ceased with her decision to leave. She reached under her bed for the box containing all of her savings and, without hesitation, looked for Myra's stash of money, shocked to find four of Edwards' letters in the drawer. Opening them, she saw that she had never seen these letters before and put them in her suitcase for later. Silently cursing Myra she grabbed the money, and added it to her own.

Lydia started stuffing clothes into her mother's old suitcase. She had no thought of order, just escape, barely packing the essentials. Walking to the train dragging her suitcase posed a problem until she thought about enlisting the help of the young boy next door. Erin was more than happy to help. At twelve, he was stronger than Lydia and lifted the suitcase with ease.

"Erin, you need to take this to the train station and wait for me. Don't talk to anyone and, for heaven's sake, do not tell them who the suitcase belongs to. I'll be there directly."

Erin was bored and more than happy for a little excitement. Taking the suitcase and shiny coin from her hand, he headed down the lane to the depot.

Lydia debated over what to tell her parents. Dr. Monroe had also written to Edward's family. She knew his condition would be known throughout the village by morning. Her father would never allow her to go to America. No matter what, taking the money and leaving would create a chasm in her family. Entering the sitting room, she looked carefully at the family pictures hanging on the wall. A final look brought tears to her eyes, but unwavering in her decision, she ran out the door.

Erin was waiting patiently at the train depot. Lydia hugged him and swore him to secrecy. "Promise me, Erin, you'll not tell a soul you helped me today."

Erin knew trouble was brewing and the thought of incriminating himself was the furthest thing from his mind. He had been smitten with Lydia since he could barely toddle across the floor. She had always been the object of his youthful crush and the thought of her leaving had him near tears.

"I must go, Erin. Edward has been injured and he needs me." Even as she said the words, a tremor shook her. The journey she was about to undertake was frightening for a girl alone and what if Edward died while she was on her way? She pushed the thoughts from her mind and, with a final hug to Erin and the promise of his silence; she forced brave smile and boarded the train.

Knowing she wouldn't be missed for hours, Lydia tried to remember all the steps Edward had taken for his departure. As the train progressed to Queenstown, she was lost in thought when a young couple boarded and sat across from her. She tried not to stare, but they were such a handsome couple, the woman with her blond hair in a topknot and her lively brown eyes, was laughing excitedly with a man Lydia assumed was her husband. The man had dark hair and a wide smile he was bestowing on his wife. It was obvious they were very much in love and Lydia felt a pang of jealousy. Their hands were entwined and Lydia could hear snippets of conversation about America. Lydia smiled shyly at the young woman, got her attention, and asked where they were off to.

Valerie Roark was a newlywed with an infectious smile and reached out to shake Lydia's hand. "My husband, Ronnie, and I are off to America.

Lydia was excited, as she shook Valerie's hand and then Ronnie's. She told them she, too, was off to America.

"By yourself? Have you no one to travel with?" Ronnie asked incredulously.

Lydia burst into tears and stammered out her story of waiting for Edward for two years and the letter about his accident. "I didn't even tell my parents. I just packed and left. I have to get to Edward no matter what."

Ronnie looked Lydia over and, in a kind voice, quietly said, "But, Girlie, you can't go across the ocean alone and then across the country. And they won't let single women off Ellis Island unless they are accompanied by a male relative or have a letter from one living in the States that will promise your support so you don't end up on the dole."

Lydia looked at Valerie. "I don't know what I was thinking. I know it was impulsive, but a voice told me to go and I listened. I love

Edward. I need to be with him. He needs me." The fierceness of her statement shocked even her. Lydia thought back to how she almost gave up on Edward and was momentarily ashamed.

Valerie looked at Lydia. She seemed so young and, although they were close in age, Valerie knew the young woman sitting across from would never make it to America on her own. Lydia was a beautiful girl and it would create a hardship traveling alone. Valerie made a decision. Looking at her husband imploringly, "Ronnie, we must help her…..we will travel together and pretend she's your sister. That will get her to America and through Ellis Island. We'll figure the rest out on the way."

Ronnie looked at his wife. The ink on their marriage license was barely dry, and he knew already, the next fifty years would be very interesting. Slowly nodding his head, he said to Lydia, "Aye, you even look a bit like my younger sister. This means you need to be a Roark from now on and clear customs as a Roark."

Lydia looked at her newfound friends with gratitude. She hadn't thought of any of the complications her impulsive decision would bring and now, for the first time, felt like she truly would see Edward.

As they arrived at the Queenstown station, Valerie and Ronnie informed Lydia they must go to the docks to check on space. Waiting in line, Lydia looked around at the other people hoping to make the voyage. She felt a quiet desperation as they stood silently awaiting their turn at the ticket counter. Lydia didn't know what she would do if she couldn't get on the ship sailing in the morning.

All of a sudden, Ronnie gave a joyful yell, "We're on…we're on, we're all leaving for America in the morning." Ronnie swung Valerie around like a rag doll and, hearing her joyful squeals, Lydia felt a quiver of excitement, not believing it was really happening. Looking at Ronnie, her voice cracking with fear, "Me too? Am I going too?"

"The three Roarks are traveling to America on a ship called The President Adams. We'll be in America in one week."

Lydia gasped, "The President Adams? It's the same ship Edward took to America. It's fate!"

Making their final sailing arrangements, the threesome looked for an inexpensive hotel. Lydia had never stayed in a hotel and was worried about the cost. Summoning her courage, she looked over at her new friend, "Valerie, how much does a room cost for one night?"

Valerie saw the worry on Lydia's face and decreed, "You'll stay with us. We will get you a cot to sleep on."

Ronnie had resigned himself to an imposed celibacy for the entire time aboard ship and was looking forward to one more night with his bride. Reading the look on his face, Valerie blushed and whispered, "We'll have thousands of nights together; we need to look after this girl."

Chapter 7

Making their way to steerage, the newly formed Roark family looked around. Steerage was crowded but the festive mood belied the meager surroundings. Children clung to their mothers as fathers gathered in groups and told of their plans once they arrived in America. Young men looked at the pretty Lydia with a gleam in their eyes. Ronnie, an imposing six footer, made his way through the crowd thankful for the first time the men would be separated from the women and children.

Lydia and Valerie pushed through the crowd to the women's quarters. Finding a room with six bunk beds with barely enough room to turn around, they claimed their space. The bunks were six feet long and two feet wide. There were two and a half feet between the bottom and the top bunk. All the luggage had to fit within that space. Lydia was thankful in her haste to leave, she only had one suitcase to deal with. Valerie had two large suitcases and looked miserable as she contemplated where she was going to store them.

"You take the bottom bunk, Valerie; I'll be fine up here. We can store our suitcases under your bunk."

Just then a woman with three screaming children entered their small space. The harried mother stood squarely before Valerie and Lydia, "I'm not leaving. There's room in here, and I'm taking it for me and the wee ones. I've been pushed out of the last two rooms and I'm here to stay."

Struck by the determination in the woman's eyes, Valerie and Lydia looked at her compassionately. Valerie ruffled the hair of one of the children. "Of course you can stay here. There's room and while it's going to be cramped, it's going to be cramped anywhere in steerage from the looks of it."

"I'm Mary Margaret Allen; this is Connor, Ray, and Robin. Once they calm down, they'll be fine. They got a scare when their Da left for the men's area."

"I'm Valerie Roark and this is my sister-in-law Lydia. My husband is in the men's area, too."

Just then a large man pushed through the door and leered at the three women. "Well, you're the prettiest I've seen so far; I'll be visiting you later."

Mary Margaret squared off in front of him, pushing her children behind her. "You'll do no such thing. There is no one here for you. Be off with you or I'll have my husband box your ears, if I don't do it first meself."

The man leaned down, his face ruddy from all the alcohol he had consumed, "We'll see how much fight you have in you when I come back."

Pushing him out and slamming the door, Mary Margaret leaned against it, her face void of color and her false bravado gone. "Oh my, it's true then."

Lydia, shaken, looked at Mary Margaret, "What is true? What are you talking about?"

"There have been rumors of what goes on in steerage. There have been women assaulted in the most grievous way. Those who resisted were beaten or worse. We had a young woman in our village attacked on a ship. When her husband came to her defense, he was stabbed and died. The authorities didn't do anything. When Christina arrived at Ellis Island, she couldn't even speak; they sent her back on the next outbound ship."

Lydia and Valerie looked at each other in horror. Edward had written about his passage but did not mention the deplorable unsafe conditions for women. Valerie was the first to react.

"I'm going to go get Ronnie….Mary Margaret, we need your husband here too. Lydia, when we leave this room, put the luggage in front of the door. Don't open it until you hear my voice."

Left alone with the three children, Lydia stacked the luggage as best she could in front of the door. She chose a lower bunk and had the children sitting with her. She could hear people going back and forth in the passageway and prayed there would not be another man trying to push his way in. This was going to be the longest week of her life. Blinking away her tears, she realized this might not be the hardest portion of the journey. She still had to make her way to Oregon.

A sharp rap at the door brought her out of her pondering. Valerie's voice came through the thin door, "Open up, we're here with the boys."

Lydia pushed the luggage aside, stacking it on the bunk behind her.

The small room seemed oppressive, the five adults and three children filled every available space. Ronnie was clenching his fists and the anger in his eyes belied his usually agreeable manner. "I'll kill the bastard. You need to point him out to me."

Valerie looked at her husband and knew he would protect her and Lydia no matter what it took. She glanced over at the man she had just met. Mary Margaret's husband, Lee, was almost a head taller than Ronnie. In fact, he was the tallest man she had ever seen. He too had rage in his eyes.

Taking the bull by the horns, Valerie started the conversation, "It seems these ships have a reputation for turning a blind eye to violence or attacks against women. With you in the men's quarters, we're left here to protect ourselves. It is going to be a long crossing….we need a plan."

Lee and Ronnie exchanged looks. They had heard some of the men talking and undoubtedly there was going to be trouble. Ronnie looked at his young bride knew he would do anything for her. "Lee and I will sleep in shifts…..we will sit outside the door at night and during the day. The three of you stick together, there is safety in numbers.

Lee chimed in. "Several other husbands are worried about their wives; we can enlist them, too." He drifted away for a minute, thinking of the poor young widow who came home to his village. "I'll not be sending my wife and wee ones home to the widow's poor house. We need to stick together."

Lydia felt overwhelmed by the situation. She knew if Edward had been here, he would be assisting these two men. Now as the "pretend sister" of Ronnie, she felt she was a burden and started to protest.

Ronnie looked at her, smiled, and quietly said, "Lydia, we will all look after each other. Have no fear. I feel better knowing you will be with Valerie when I can't."

Lydia mustered a smile, put on a brave face, and hugged Valerie and Ronnie. No matter what, she would help them as they were helping her.

The first night was the worst. The single men had smuggled whiskey on board and spent most of the night gambling and drinking.

Occasionally, one would wander the passageways of the women's quarters banging on doors. Ronnie took the first shift, calmly sitting outside their door as the three women stacked all their large suitcases on their side as a deterrent if anyone should get past Ronnie.

Ronnie ended up punching a man in the face and shoving him down the passageway. Bloodied and contrite, the fellow finally fell into a bunk to sleep it off. Lee took the next four-hour shift, and his enormous bulk had the men with dishonorable intentions backing up and returning to their quarters.

The next morning when the women and children went to breakfast, stories of the night before were exchanged. Six women in one room had to fight off an attack from a drunken man. They trounced on him and scratching, biting, and kicking, managed to send him on his way. The women were traveling with husbands, fathers, or brothers who were unaware of the potential danger. After much conversation the women devised a plan to unite their men to help patrol the passageways at night. A sympathetic porter told them they could rely only on themselves. He was severely beaten on a prior crossing when he tried to stop an attack on a female passenger. The porter said he had no support from the shipping company or his fellow workers and, regretfully, would not intervene again if trouble happened.

The turmoil left Lydia without sleep and combined with the retched food and filthy conditions, it began to wear on her.

Looking at Valerie, she whispered, "How on earth am I supposed to last five more days? It's time to go on deck. I just need to be alone for a bit." Finding a quiet corner, she was finally able to contemplate about what to do when she left the ship. Thinking of Edward and praying he was still alive, she was startled by a shrill scream.

"Oh my God, he's going to fall." A slim woman in a white nurse's uniform was ten feet from a toddler standing on the edge of the deck.

Lydia looked up to see a young child holding onto the outside of the deck railing about twenty feet above her. The child had somehow squeezed through and was crying while trying to back up. His small foot slipped and, not thinking, Lydia ran to the spot below him. Just as she reached it the child tried to stand up and turn to his rapidly approaching nursemaid. As his nursemaid put her hands out, the ship rocked tossing the small child away from her. He lost his precarious hold on the railing and fell. Instinct took over and Lydia looked up and moved a few more steps catching the child in her arms. She fell backwards, and when Lydia's head slammed onto the deck, she was knocked out.

Waking up in the infirmary, Lydia was startled to see she was wearing some sort of hospital gown. Anxious and disoriented, she was relieved to see a kindly looking older woman approaching the bed.

"You're awake! You gave us quite a scare. Do you remember what happened?" The woman was dressed very handsomely and spoke with an American accent. Her blond hair was streaked with gray, and her face had an aristocratic look with a slim straight nose and probing green eyes. Her perfectly arched eyebrows were knitted together in a concerned look.

Lydia looked at her bruised arms and remembered catching the child and falling. "The little boy was falling and I caught him. Is he all right?"

"Oh yes, dear, he is quite unharmed. You took the brunt of the fall and that bump on your head must hurt."

"How long have I been here?"

"You've been in the infirmary for a full day. Doctor said I am to ask you some questions to make sure you didn't damage anything. Now, what is your name?"

"I'm Lydia Delaney. I'm on my way to Oregon where my fiancé lives." Lydia was relieved she was not hurt, but the throbbing headache felt like daggers shooting into her head. "Are you the nurse?"

"Oh no, dear. I'm Mrs. Franklin, young Corwin's grandmother, and I'm very grateful to you. The nursemaid says she only turned her head for a second and, well, you know the rest. We are distraught at how close we came to losing Corwin."

Lydia's head was pounding and she struggled to continue. "Is there a nurse here that might give me something for the pain in my head? Are my arms broken?"

Mrs. Franklin looked at the young woman laying there, her face as white as the sheets. "My dear Lydia, I have instructed the nurse to attend to your every need. I just stopped in to check on you. I am quite relieved you appear to have no permanent damage. Your arms probably feel broken. They are badly bruised and sprained, but you will recover. Are you hungry? I'll have a meal brought to you immediately."

Thinking of the deplorable food she had been eating for the two days prior to the accident, Lydia was trying to figure out how to politely decline. Seeing her indecisive look, Mrs. Franklin chuckled and said, "Lydia, your food will come from the first class section of the ship. After saving my grandson's life, you must let me pamper you."

"Where are my friends? Do they know I'm in the infirmary?" Lydia shuddered to think of her two friends and their husbands down in steerage.

"Your friends have asked about you, but they are not allowed to come up to this section of the ship."

"Mrs. Franklin, you have been very kind, but I must return to my friends. You don't know what it's like down there. The women are vulnerable to unwanted advances from the male passengers. The husbands have to stand guard in the passageway, but still undesirables get through and attack the women. The porter said it was our problem to deal with, and I must go do my share to see they are safe." Lydia tried to sit up and sank back down on the bed.

"You're weak from lack of food and your injury. Please, we will have dinner served and then decide how to proceed. Lydia, if it is as deplorable as you say down in steerage, I am not letting you go back there. I will go order your dinner and return once I have spoken to Mr. Franklin." Mrs. Franklin rose from her chair and, and with the bearing of a general on a mission, left the small infirmary.

A nurse entered the room with a tray laden with food on fine china plates. The smells wafting from the dishes tortured Lydia's deprived stomach. The nurse smiled and said, "Let's get this medicine in you, dearie, then we'll deal with the food. Nurse Sullivan handed Lydia two pills and a glass of water. She picked the tray back up and placed it in front of Lydia. "It's a bit overwhelming. How about a sample of each dish and then you can pick your favorite?"

Lydia was overcome with hunger and loneliness. She took a spoonful of pudding and burst into tears. "This tastes just like what my Ma makes."

The nurse looked at the young girl with pity. She had daughters Lydia's age and missed them terribly. As she coaxed Lydia to eat a few more bites, she took a good look at the girl. Something was familiar about her but Nancy Sullivan couldn't put her finger on. Finally she asked, "Where are you from?"

Lydia looked at the kindly nurse. "I'm from a small village west of Tipperary called Gallay."

Nurse Sullivan looked closely at Lydia. "I'm from Tipperary. My daughters are still there and my son Ryan lives in Gallay and is married to my wonderful daughter-in- law, Rosie O'Brien. Do you know her?"

Lydia teary eyes brightened. "I do. I know Rosie. Her brother Edward is my fiancé. I'm going to America to be with him."

"Ah, I knew you looked familiar. Your family owns the bakery. I've been to your shop with Rosie. Well, my girl, you've had quite an adventure and your trip has barely begun. It looks like Mrs. Franklin will be making sure you don't have to return to steerage. That's a lucky break for you."

Lydia smiled at Nurse Sullivan, "Thank you for the food and medicine. I feel much better."

"Look at the time. I best be going or I'll miss my own dinner. I'll be back later to check on you. Try and get some rest."

Ill at ease in the infirmary, Lydia looked around the room for her clothes. As she was plotting her reluctant escape back to steerage and her friends, Mrs. Franklin swept into the room.

"I have been speaking to my husband about what you told me of the problems in steerage. Mr. Franklin and I spoke to the captain. We are appalled by the deplorable conditions you described in steerage and want to keep you safe up here in the infirmary."

Lydia began to protest. "Mrs. Franklin, I appreciate your desire to help me, but you must understand, I cannot leave my friends unprotected. I need to help them."

Mrs. Franklin listened to Lydia's words and a smile spread across her aristocratic face as she called out, "Ladies, please come in... it is time."

As she spoke, Valerie and Mary Margaret, and the three children shyly entered the infirmary. They burst into tears as they saw Lydia and her poor bruised arms. "We were so frightened." Valerie grabbed Lydia's hand and kissed her forehead. "You were so brave and you saved that child's life."

"I can't believe you're here...I was so worried about you and Mary Margaret and the boys. Are you all right? Did anything happen while I was gone?"

Mary Margaret took Lydia's other hand. "Nothing happened. Ronnie and Lee and the other husbands and fathers guarded our passageway. There was less gambling and drinking among the single men. I think they drank all their liquor and lost all their money!"

"Mrs. Franklin said you were not allowed into the infirmary. How did you get here?"

Valerie looked at Lydia with a smug smile. "We are here because we are best friends with a hero."

"A hero? What are you talking about?" Lydia's head was starting to throb again as she looked at her friends.

"You are the hero!" Mary Margaret exclaimed, "How can you not know it? The entire ship is talking about the brave thing you did. It was so amazing. I was sitting out on the deck with the children when I heard a woman scream, and, the next thing I knew, you were running to the spot just as he dropped. You really are a hero!"

Mrs. Franklin watched the young women and their obvious pleasure at being together. The three boys shyly clung to their mother's skirt. The five of them had been in steerage for only three days and the smell in the room was ripe. Spending time below deck in the filthy conditions, with a lack of water, and a rough crossing, it was no wonder Mrs. Franklin was revolted by the smell and their stories of steerage. She waited as long as she could tolerate it and finally cleared her throat to get their attention.

"Lydia has informed me she will not stay in the infirmary with her friends fighting for their honor and lives down below. I cannot in all good conscience return this girl to steerage after she saved my grandson's life. Therefore, I had the captain bring you to the infirmary. Since we only have four days left on our journey, Mr. Franklin has convinced the captain to allow you all to stay here. We are bringing in additional cots for the children and there are two beds. You ladies should finally get a good night's sleep." Mrs. Franklin appraised the situation, noticing the look of exhaustion on the other two women and realized she had done something important. Her heart went out to the remaining women below the deck, but she could only do so much. She would work on these issues with some people of influence once the ship docked in New York.

Spontaneous tears burst out from the three women causing Conor, Ray and Robin to echo their cries until a smiling Mary Margaret cuddled her boys saying, "No, my darlings, these are tears of joy. We're safe."

Valerie turned to Mrs. Franklin. "You'll never know what this means to all of us. The conditions below are intolerable. I know we must smell to high heaven, but we are forced to share bathroom accommodations with the men and we cannot bath. Even changing clothes in our room was risky."

Again, wondering why such atrocities were being heaped on people whose only crime was trying to better their life in a new country, Mrs. Franklin slowly nodded her head. "I imagine all your clothes and belongings are still downstairs?"

"They are, ma'm. When we were brought up here, they didn't tell us anything. We thought we were in some sort of trouble." Mary Margaret exhaled deeply, relieved to be safe with her children. "Our husbands will watch after our belongings, and we will wash ourselves and our clothes in this sink. At least there are a couple of portholes here. We'll let some nice sea air in, and we won't smell up the room too much." Mary Margaret beamed as she thought of her good luck and being away from the foul steerage area.

"What are your plans when you land in New York?" Mrs. Franklin was curious about how one takes on an entire new life in a foreign country.

Valerie, as usual, was the first to speak. "My Ronnie is an architect. He has a fine education and his father had an architectural firm. Ronnie got out of school ready to work and, a month later, his father had a fatal heart attack. There was nothing holding us in Ireland and we felt it was a good time for us to start out for America. Ronnie's mother died when he was a year old and his father never remarried. My own mother died eight years ago, and my father married a widow with a passel of children who was determined to get me out of the house. Ronnie and I were sweethearts for three years and married a month ago. We are hoping he will find a suitable position in New York."

Lydia looked over at Valerie and was shocked to see a tear running down her friend's cheek. Mrs. Franklin noticed it, too.

Mary Margaret shyly looked at Mrs Franklin. "Our dreams are very simple. We just want a chance to better our lives and give our boys opportunities they would never get at home. Lee will work any job he can find. He's a hard worker, and I will find employment. Nothing has ever been handed to us, and we don't expect it to be in America."

Mrs. Franklin took it all in. Her husband was a wealthy man, and she had served on many charitable organizations in New York. What better project could she have than helping people she actually knew and making a difference in their life?

When Mrs. Franklin left the infirmary, the three women began talking at once. They had been slightly intimidated by their new bene-factress and now could talk freely.

Valerie grabbed Lydia's hand and looked into her eyes, "Are you really all right? You're so pale."

Lydia smiled, "I think I am still in a state of shock. I can't believe we don't have to go back to our horrible cabin in steerage. Did you see the look on Mrs. Franklin's face? I don't think the rich people in first class have any idea what goes on down there."

Mary Margaret chimed in. "Aye, I saw the look on her face and, I can tell you, someone's going to hear about this. She is a very formidable woman. It's good she's on our side. I wouldn't want to see her angry."

Just then there was a slight rap at the door. "I've got luggage out here for you ladies."

The door opened and the steward from steerage pushed through with three suitcases. "Your husbands said this would probably be what you would want and they would hold the rest." The steward looked at the three women. "I hope you are not going to be telling tales about what goes on below. I told you no one will do anything."

"We've answered the questions asked by Mrs. Franklin." Lydia sat up as she looked at the steward. "And you should be ashamed of yourself. Have you no sisters or girlfriend? How can you tolerate the atrocities happening and say you can do nothing?" Her anger was palpable. She was relieved to be safe but afraid for the women still below.

"I'm just doing the best I can. I've got a family to support and cannot afford to lose this job." His fear was evident as he backed out of the room, knowing these women now had the ear of one of the richest people on the ship.

Locking the door after he left, Mary Margaret looked at her three boys and said, "You smell to high heavens. Come over to this wash basin, and let's see if we can get you cleaned up."

Mary Margaret looked at herself in the mirror above the basin. "Well, looks like I've no room to talk. I've got a bit of dirt from the trip on me too." A plain girl, Mary Margaret's hair had always been her great beauty. Now it was dull and, when she undid the clip, it hung lankly down her back. "We'll get these three cleaned up and then I'll see what I can do about meself."

Valerie grabbed a towel and started helping her with the boys. Lydia remained in her bed, still trying to control the raging headache that had been plaguing her since she woke. Valerie glanced at Lydia, noting she was lost in thought. "I'm sure Edward is on her mind," she whispered to Mary Margaret.

"Aye, the lass has a big chore ahead of her. How on earth is she going to make her way to Oregon?" Mary Margaret whispered back. "And what if he's dead?"

Chapter 8

Mrs. Franklin continued to visit daily. Her probing questions unnerved Lydia. At first she had stuck with the story of her being Ronnie's sister until she finally confessed when the shrewd Mrs. Franklin asked why her last name was Delaney and her "brother's" last name was Roark. Admitting to their little deceit, Lydia poured out the entire story to Mrs. Franklin.

The next day Mrs. Franklin walked to Lydia's bedside with purpose. Mrs. Franklin took her hands and said quietly, "Mr. Franklin and I have been discussing your situation, and we would like to help you any way we can. We want you to accept this with our gratitude."

Mrs. Franklin pressed a thick envelope into Lydia's hands. "We insist you accept this reward money for your bravery."

"No, Mrs. Franklin, you have already done so much for me."

"Lydia, it is non negotiable. You have no idea how precious our grandson is to us. We insist, and, if it is all right with you, we would like to stay in contact. We want to make sure you get to your Edward safely and all you expect comes true. Because of your injury, you will disembark with me and Mr. Franklin. We would like you to be our guest until we can get you on a train west to your Edward."

Overcome with emotion, Lydia grabbed Mrs. Franklin's hand. "You have no idea what this means to me. Just a week ago, I was working in my da's bakery, waiting and waiting for Edward. Now I'll be able to go to him and help him recover from his injuries. I can't thank you enough."

Mary Margaret and Valerie looked at the two women. They too were overcome by tears when they thought of how close Mrs. Franklin's young grandson had come to death and the changes one selfless act had made for their friend.

Mrs. Franklin looked over at the young women. "Mary Margaret, I believe we can find employment for you and Lee. Our handyman has decided to try his luck at silver mining and has deserted us. You said your Lee is a hard worker. I'm going to hold you to it. I will also need your services from time to time as a helper when we entertain. Please discuss this with Lee and let me know tomorrow morning. We dock at 11 a.m. and, if you are agreeable, we will send a car to Ellis Island to pick you up after you go through immigration.

Mary Margaret was not often dumbfounded, but her capacity for speech momentarily left her. Slowly nodding her head, she smiled transforming her plain face.

Valerie was overjoyed for her friends and relieved their future seemed assured. Of the three women, she was the best prepared for the transition to America. Ronnie had a fine education and she herself had attended a finishing school. She was grateful her father's new wife had used higher education as a ruse to get her out of the house.

Mrs. Franklin looked at Valerie and pulled out another envelope. "This is a letter of introduction for Ronnie. It is for the best architectural firm in New York. Mr. Franklin is well known there, and I'm sure they will be happy to interview Ronnie."

Valerie shook Mrs. Franklin's hand, thankful for her generosity. Mrs. Franklin had met Ronnie only once but was convinced of his character after observing the way he protected his wife and Lydia.

When Mrs. Franklin left the infirmary, Lydia opened the envelope. Much to her surprise, she discovered $500 in the envelope Mrs. Franklin had given her as well as a note.

My dearest Lydia,

I hope you understand what your selfless act of bravery means to Mr. Franklin and me. Realizing how close we came to losing our only grandchild haunts us to this day. Please accept this money as an expression of our gratitude and the opportunities it may open for you and your fiancé. Helping you succeed and prosper in your new country will give us immeasurable peace of mind. Please, my dear, do keep in touch. The time I spent getting to know you have given me purpose to help others in your situation.
Your grateful friends,

Stephen and Beverly Franklin

Stunned at the amount of money Mrs. Franklin had given her, Lydia reluctantly accepted it after Valerie told her she would offend the Franklins. "You and Edward will need this money. Mrs. Franklin is trying to show her gratitude the only way she knows how."

The women rose early and began repacking their suitcases. Grateful the past few days had given them the opportunity to wash their clothing and they no longer smelled like steerage. The infirmary had three small portholes and the women looked out in wonder at the first glimpse of their new country. When their eyes lit on the Statue of Liberty, they were mesmerized by the sheer size of the monument and its meaning.

Lydia was relieved to be back to herself. The bump on the head had given her headaches for three days and only now was she starting to feel well enough to start her journey. She was anxious to get off the ship and start her trip to Oregon.

Mr. and Mrs. Franklin came to pick up Lydia and her meager belongings. Extending his arm, Mr. Franklin smiled at Lydia, "Please, my dear, let me have the honor of walking with you as you set foot in your new country."

Not used to the American accent and such fancy words, Lydia smiled shyly and took his arm. "Thank you, Mr. Franklin. Thank you for everything."

Arranging for a driver to bring Lee, Mary Margaret, and the boys to the cottage, and sensing the other young couple wanted privacy, Mrs. Franklin instructed the driver to take Ronnie and Valerie to a nearby hotel. Smiling, she easily remembered being a young newlywed and chuckled anticipating their surprise when they walked into the honeymoon suite she had reserved for them.

Beverly Franklin was a straightforward woman. She did not often give into sentiment, but even she had to acknowledge how these very special young women had found a place in her heart. The next step was to summon her own physician to examine Lydia. She was not fooled by the brave front the girl was putting on. She could see pain in her eyes and was not about to put Lydia on a train west until she was reassured about the girls overall health.

Lydia's first glimpse of the Franklin's home made her gasp. Surely this was an apartment house, not a home for just two people? It was three stories high and stepping into the marbled entry way with the brightly lit chandelier above, made Lydia's head spin. A large sweeping staircase dominated one side of the foyer. The rest of the room had pictures of what must be Franklin ancestors staring down at her. They looked scary until Lydia spotted a portrait of a much younger Mr. and Mrs. Franklin.

"That was painted shortly after our wedding, thirty-four years ago."

Lydia sighed, hoping a wedding was in her near future, "It's a beautiful picture, Mrs. Franklin. You both look so happy."

"Yes, and I'm blessed that we still are happy. A good marriage is work, my dear girl, but I expect you'll be finding it out soon enough. Come, Lydia, this is Mary. She will show you to your room and help you unpack." Mrs. Franklin's nod brought forward a young woman, not much older than Lydia.

Mary curtsied to Lydia. "Come with me, Miss. I'll get you settled."

As Lydia turned to voice her objection to "settling in," Mrs. Franklin beat her to it. "Now, dear, I know you are anxious to get on with your journey, but I cannot let you leave until you have rested up from your injury. And I want you to see my physician to determine when it is safe for you to travel."

Lydia again opened her mouth to object. As she did, a blinding headache started. Knowing in a few minutes she would feel incapacitated, she looked at Mrs. Franklin. "You are so kind and generous. I appreciate everything you have done, but I must get to Edward as soon as possible."

Mrs. Franklin was relieved and worried by Lydia's easy acquiescence. Then seeing her pale face, she knew her young friend was having another painful headache.

"Take her upstairs, Mary. We'll let Miss Lydia rest. Tell cook dinner will be at seven. Oh, and please see that the kitchen in the guest cottage is stocked. There will be a young family moving in this evening."

Once Lydia was safely resting, Beverly addressed her primary concern of Lydia traveling west alone. She solved the problem by contacting her dear friend George Jay Gould, president of the Great Northern Railroad, who put all her worries to rest and assured her that Lydia would have a memorable trip. Another phone call to Brinks Security finished the plans.

Beverly was taking no chances with Lydia's safety. In early April, the Grand Dragon of the Klu Klux Klan in Indiana, D.C. Stephenson, had been arrested for the kidnapping and sexual assault of a young woman named Madge Oberholtzer on a train. Her injuries from the attack played a part in her death. Beverly abhorred the KKK and all it stood for. The only good thing from this poor woman's tragic death was the awareness of their despicable acts. The tide was beginning to turn; people were beginning to understand the Klan's corrupt dogma.

Mr. Franklin was relieved when his wife told him she was having two Brinks Security men travel on the train with Lydia all the way to Oregon. They were taking no chances with their beautiful young friend traveling unattended.

The evening meal at the Franklins was as sumptuous as anything Lydia tasted from the first class galley on the ship. The long dining table with a white lace tablecloth and starched napkins was intimidating to Lydia. She had never seen a room so posh. Mrs. Franklin looked stunning wearing a simple black dress and a string of pearls. Lydia in one of her everyday dresses felt dowdy by comparison. She was relieved that Mrs. Franklin had thoughtfully included Mary Margaret and Lee. The boys had already been fed and put to bed and were being watched over by Mary who was beginning to wonder how the new handyman and his wife managed a place at the dining room table with the mister and missus.

Ronnie and Valerie were visibly absent at dinner. Mr. Franklin raised his eyebrows when his wife breezily announced she had taken the liberty of sending a lovely meal to their room at the hotel, suspecting they would enjoy some time to themselves. Knowing looks passed between Lee and Mary Margaret. Much to everyone's amusement, the remark went over Lydia's head.

The next day, Dr. Arnold arrived at the house with his little black bag. When he removed his hat, wild grey hair escaped and his kind brown eyes looked Lydia over during the introductions. His large hand enveloped hers and his smile was so genuine, all her fears vanished. Walking to the small study off the living room for the examination, Lydia's nerves took over. She had never been to a doctor; her health had always been perfect. She was shaking as the physician took her arm, covering her wrist with his fingers, and started to take her pulse.

"Oh, my dear Miss Delaney, you'll have to relax. Your pulse is racing so hard I can barely count the beats."

Blushing, Lydia looked at Dr. Arnold. "I've always been so healthy. I've never been to a doctor before."

"What, no childhood illnesses, no broken bones, no cut up knees?"

Laughing, Lydia blurted out, "We had Missus Casey. She was a healer of sorts. We all went to her if we had the need for some of her herbs."

"Well, young lady, I can see you're in fine health. It's these headaches I've been hearing about from Mrs. Franklin we need to talk about." Shining a flashlight, watching her pupil dilate and contract in her left eye, he moved onto her right. A small "hmmm" came out before he could stop himself.

Lydia jerked her head back. "What's wrong? What do you see?"

Dr. Arnold looked at her thoughtfully. "Lydia, when the headaches come, what side of your head hurts the most?"

"Well mainly they shoot across the right side of my head. Honest, they're not as bad as they were at first."

Continuing the examination, he had Lydia squeeze his hand, first with her left and then her right. Then he used a small hammer like instrument and tapped each knee, carefully watching the response.

Lydia was fascinated. She couldn't figure out what he was doing and wondered what on earth her knees had to do with her head.

"Miss Delaney, did the ship's doctor give you any medication for your headaches?"

"Dr. Davison gave me something called aspirin. I'd not heard of it before but it helped a little bit."

"Do you have any pills left?"

"No, when we disembarked the doctor said I could buy them at a pharmacy. I just haven't had a chance."

"Lydia, this is important. Now be honest, did it help with your pain?"

Looking down at her trembling hands, Lydia knew her answer could mean a delay in her trip west, tears dropped onto her lap. In a quiet voice she answered the kind doctor. "It didn't do anything, the pain is unbearable sometimes. I see flashes and dots in front of my face and then all I want to do is get to a dark quiet place to sleep. Please help me. I need to get to Edward. I can't worry about me right now. He could be dying."

"I'm going to try you on something stronger than aspirin, but first I want to talk to Mrs. Franklin."

Leaving Lydia's bedroom, Dr. Arnold sought out Mrs. Franklin. Finding Beverly in the parlor, he sat heavily on the sofa.

"What is it, Kenneth? Your expression is scaring me."

"Beverly, I did a preliminary examination of your young friend. I have some concerns. I can see her right pupil does not react to light like the left one and she has a definite weakness on her right side. I'm very concerned the injury from her fall may have caused a concussion. She is still having severe headaches."

"A concussion? People recover from concussions, yes?"

"I am a family physician. I am not a brain specialist. Given the information of the accident and her severe headaches, I can only draw the conclusion I've just stated. If it is a concussion, the headaches should go away within a few weeks. She has stated the pain is unbearable at times. We need to get her pain under control. However, the drug I want to suggest is very addictive."

"Kenneth, we need to do anything we can to help her. What are you suggesting?"

"I will give her a drug called Laudanum. It's a horribly bitter drug, but, given in small doses, it will relieve her pain. The best thing we can do for the young lady is to get her on a train west to her fiancé. Maybe relieving some of her anxiety will help with the headaches."

Mrs. Franklin put on her best face and walked into Lydia's room with Kenneth. Dr. Arnold took Lydia's hands in his, forced himself to keep it light, and explained he was going to give her a drug to take away the pain when the headaches started. "I believe if you take a small dose when you feel the onset of a headache, the drug will lessen the effect or make it go away. But I must caution you, this drug is highly addictive. You must use it wisely. If the headaches persist after you are finished with this bottle, you must go to a doctor."

"Dr. Arnold, please, I'll do anything. I must travel west to Edward."

A smile creased his face and he looked over at Beverly. "Yes, Lydia, you can travel west. Mrs. Franklin will fill you in on the details. Remember, I want you to take it easy. You need to rest as much as possible before you get on the train. I want you to rest during your trip west also. Your head needs time to recover from the hard hit it took. Please follow my advice."

Jumping up and impulsively hugging Dr. Arnold and Mrs. Franklin, Lydia blushed at her boldness. She was radiantly happy. At that moment, Mrs. Franklin knew what needed to be done. "With all due respect to my dear friend, Dr. Arnold, I will have Lydia rest before the train. However, she is feeling good right now, and, I do believe a short shopping trip is necessary prior to her departure."

Lydia had left Ireland so quickly she had missed packing some of the essentials. She shyly asked Mrs. Franklin where she might get some additional knickers and, perhaps, a dress in which to get married.

Beverly Franklin felt much like the mother of the bride. Trying to be mindful of Lydia's stubborn pride, Mrs. Franklin resisted the shops on Fifth Avenue and took her downtown to Macy's. Having had only one child, and a boy to boot, she was happy to have a girl's day with Valerie and Lydia.

Lydia's eyes almost popped out of her head as she walked into Macy's, seeing counters stacked with merchandise that seemed to go on forever. She had never seen an escalator and summoned all her courage to step on the moving staircase. Looking down at the wood slats she tried to appear as nonchalant as her friends. Valerie's father had taken his daughter to London many times after her mother died. She was used to the fine stores and had ridden on escalators many times. Seeing her friend's eyes widen with fear, Valerie reached for Lydia's hand.

Mrs. Franklin wanted to buy Lydia an entire new wardrobe, but she knew Lydia was stubborn and proud. Finally, after much unaccustomed pleading, Lydia gave in and allowed Mrs. Franklin to buy her two new dresses for her trousseau. One dress made out of a beautiful sky blue silk, and the other, a simple white satin wedding dress with a lace bodice and pearl buttons going up the back. The dress fit Lydia as if it had been made only for her.

Lydia fought tears, wondering if buying this dress was premature. She had not seen Edward in two years. Lydia thought about how she had almost given up on him, and now had no idea if he was alive or dead. She fervently prayed he was alive. She was convinced her heart would know if he had died.

The two days in New York passed quickly. Lydia was pampered and fed wonderful meals. Mrs. Franklin forced her to take an afternoon nap each day. Lydia felt uncomfortable living a luxurious lifestyle not knowing what Edward was going through. The night before her departure, Mrs. Franklin sat alone with Lydia in the parlor.

"Lydia, I think you know how much Mr. Franklin and I care about you. In such a short time, you have become very dear to us, and we hope to be in your life for a long long time. I know you left Ireland rather hastily, and, I suspect, based on our conversations, your mother did not have time to talk to you about married life."

Lydia gasped and stuttered, "No, we never talked about anything between a man and a woman. Sometimes I would hear the women having tea in my ma's kitchen, and they would hint about such things. It sounded like they didn't like it much. I was too afraid to ask my ma anything. With Edward leaving, I didn't want her to think we'd done anything, because we hadn't."

"Dear Lydia, what you are talking about is what makes a marriage complete. It is a wonderful gift from God that two people can make each other so completely happy and fulfilled. Some women complain and call it a marriage duty. The reason is they have not discovered loving and trusting someone so completely with your mind and your body is truly wonderful. You are a beautiful young woman. I can see how full of love you are when you talk about Edward. Just remember to give into your feelings when you are with him. Work together to find your true happiness, and, remember my dear, the bedroom is where much happiness can be obtained. The first time may be a little painful but the pain won't last long. Don't be afraid of your feelings in your marriage bed. Remember, you will be together many many years." As she spoke the last few words, Mrs. Franklin fervently prayed to God Edward was alive.

Lydia looked at Mrs. Franklin, "I'm so happy you talked to me. My ma would have had a fit trying to get the words out. My older sisters always laughed about her talk before their weddings, but they would never tell me what she said. They only told me I'd get the exact same talk, and it wouldn't be a happy one."

"Well then, Lydia, I'm pleased I could offer you a happier outlook for your upcoming nuptials. You and Edward will have a wonderful life together." As she spoke the words, Beverly fervently prayed Lydia's headaches would go away and not be anything more serious.

The day came to board the train. Mrs. Franklin had thoughtfully brought Mary Margaret and Valerie to see Lydia off. Tears were shed but the group was in high spirits as they waited for the train.

Mr. and Mrs. Franklin hugged Lydia. They both realized how very fond they were of this foolish brave girl. Mr. Franklin handed an envelope to Lydia, "You may need this sometime. Don't hesitate to contact us if you ever need help."

Lydia smiled shyly at Mr. Franklin. "Thank you. Thank you both for everything. It's like I've fallen into a fairy tale and have my fairy godmother and godfather looking after me."

Mrs. Franklin laughed at the image. "From what I hear about Mr. Franklin in business meetings, I don't think they'd call him a fairy godfather. More like a tiger on the prowl. We have one more thing to tell you." As she spoke the words, two men wearing suits walked up to Mrs. Franklin. "Oh, here they are now."

Lydia looked at the two middle aged men. She wondered what they had to do with her.

Mr. Franklin cleared his throat. "Lydia, there is not a lot of time to explain, but let me just say Beverly and I cannot have you go to Oregon unaccompanied. Not too long ago a man did unspeakable things to a young woman on a train which resulted in her death. We don't want to scare you, but we just couldn't allow you to be alone. These gentlemen are from Brinks Security. One will be with you during the day and one will be outside your door at night. I'm sorry we didn't talk to you before this. It seems our time together went too quickly for serious discussions. Please know we made this decision in your best interest."

Lydia looked at the concern in her dear patrons' faces, "Don't worry, I understand. I was reading your newspaper this morning and heard about this Stephenson man. I read about the KKK and how they hate Catholics and immigrants. It was quite frightening. I'll be glad to have the company."

Lydia squeezed in several more last minute hugs to the people who had become so dear to her. The security men helped her board the train. Looking at her ticket, the conductor recognized her name and took Lydia to her first class cabin, directing the security guards to the room next door. "We'll be keeping an eye on you, Miss Delaney. We've been instructed to give you anything you need."

As the train started down the track, Lydia marveled at how one simple act can change the course of a life. Ever so thankful to be on her way and praying the rest of her life would be with Edward, she began her journey west.

Chapter 9

Edward was lying in his bed wondering why he had not heard from Lydia. He knew Dr. Monroe had written to her and his family when things were looking dire. Weeks had gone by since he'd last heard from her. Between the accident, a persistent fever, a brief coma, and now, physical therapy, he was exhausted.

Suddenly there was a light knock at his door. When he looked up he saw a young woman rushing across the infirmary. Lydia stopped a few feet short of his bed. She walked hesitantly to his side and promptly burst into tears.

Edward looked at Lydia in disbelief, wondering what she was doing in his room. He decided this must be another one of the crazy dreams plaguing him since the accident. Only when her hand reached out and touched his face, did he look at her again.

"Lydia, how did you get here? Are you real? Am I hallucinating or have I died?" His questions came out in a jumble.

Lydia smothered his face with kisses. Two years without each other melted away as she grabbed his hand. Thinking of the last three weeks and her harrowing trip, Lydia was unsure what to tell Edward or where to start. Looking down at Edward and ready to pour her heart out, she saw his eyes were closed, and he was emitting a soft snore.

When Edward woke, Lydia was sitting by his bed. His head cleared slowly, and he watched her silently until she turned to look at him. He was afraid to speak and break the spell of this wonderful hallucination.

Lydia looked down at his gaunt face, noticing the pallor and dark circles. He looked nothing like the robust youth he was when he left Ireland. His face had matured and the dark stubble of whiskers made him appear years older.

"Oh, Edward, when I received Dr. Monroe's letter I couldn't bear the thought of you being injured and all alone. I had been saving money but knew I didn't have enough. I did a horrible thing. I took Myra's money and what money I had and ran away."

Edward had been in a stupor for weeks, the pain drugs had kept him numb, but listening to Lydia, he knew there was much she was not saying. How could a young woman who had barely been outside their village, manage to travel all the way to America and then on to Oregon by herself?

Edward reached for the glass of water by his bed and took a long drink. "Start at the beginning and don't leave anything out. Do your parents know you are safe?"

Lydia finished her incredible story of her trip across the sea to America and then west to Oregon. She glossed over her head injury. Hiding the pain from a headache she felt coming on, she listened as Edward told her of his life in Little Creek. Edward had been saving money for two years. It was only since arriving in Little Creek he finally felt he was getting close to their dream. Working at the logging camp on the Donkey had been dangerous work.

"I saved and saved wanting to send for you. I knew I needed to have a decent home for you to live in. My friend, Todd Cranston, a manager from the mill, was trying to sell his house. His wife had deserted him, heading back to Boston without a backwards glance at the life they had shared. The little house held nothing but painful memories, and he was anxious to leave Little Creek and head to Alaska. I saw the house and knew we could be happy there."

Edward took Lydia's hand and continued. "It's a small two bedroom with a good sized kitchen and dining room. There's a stone fireplace with a nice hearth. We can have lovely fires in the winter. Todd told me his wife's parents were quite wealthy and mail ordered the house from Sears as their wedding present. The price of the house in the Sears Catalog is $858."

Lydia was listening to the description of the house, but her mind was caught up in the sadness of the story. "Why did she leave him? It's so sad."

"Aye, it is. She said it was too desolate out here and too rough. It was vastly different from the life she knew in Boston. Poor Todd, he bought her fancy furniture to make her happy, but nothing worked. It gave me quite a fright. I kept praying that when you finally got to Little Creek you would love it as I do."

Lydia laughed. "I've only been here a few hours, but I will love any place we are together. I never want to be apart again."

Edward smiled. "I still don't have much strength. Would you mind leaning down so I can kiss you?" Continuing his story, "Like I said, Todd's wife's parents bought the house, but it was in his name and he owned it free and clear. He was angry at his in-laws. They wanted him to sell the house and send them the money. He offered to sell me the house for one dollar. He told me it would give him great pleasure to send them a dollar. Maybe next time they wouldn't cave in to their spoiled daughter's whims so easily. But he said I had to buy the furniture. He needed money to get all the supplies for his trip to Alaska. He wanted $102."

Lydia looked at Edward and could tell he was getting tired. "Edward, you can tell me the rest tomorrow. You need to rest."

"No. I'm almost finished with the story. I didn't have $102, I only had $85. I must have a look of desperation on my face because Todd finally told me to just give him the $85. He said he knew it was crazy but he wanted to leave town. He wished us luck and hoped we will be happier in Little Creek than he was. I knew at the time it was not good to have your dreams come true on someone else's bad luck." He smiled ruefully. "Two days later, I ended up in the hospital nearly dead from blood loss and my leg almost severed. I guess this was my payback."

Now, lying flat on his back and looking up into Lydia's eyes, Edward knew his bad luck was over. He still couldn't believe sweet Lydia, so devoted to her parents, had rushed to his side when she received Dr. Monroe's letter.

Just then Dr. Monroe walked into the room. He was tall and much younger than Lydia had imagined. His handsome features were marred by the slight frown on his face. "Miss Delaney, I'll have to ask you to leave for now. It's time for Edward's physical therapy. Believe me, the words that come out of his mouth are not fit for a young lady to hear."

"Wait a minute, doc. I must make sure Lydia is settled in before your torture begins." Edward looked at Lydia with concern. "Johnny should be here any time now. He will see that you're taken care of."

Lydia was relieved. Her head was throbbing and she wanted to take her medicine and lie down for a bit. Still weary from travel, she told Edward she would see him in the morning.

Grabbing her hand, Edward looked into her eyes. "I still can't believe you're here, it's a blessed miracle. You came all this way for me. I love you, Lydia, kiss me one more time so I know it's not a dream."

Disregarding the shooting pains in her head, Lydia leaned down and planted a soft kiss on his lips. All of the events of the last three weeks had brought her to this moment. She didn't care if the hammers in her head never stopped as long as she was with Edward.

Edward soon realized the stubborn young girl he had left in Ireland had grown into a beautiful and intelligent woman. Lydia had $500 and some thoughts about how it was to be used for their future. She noted the town did not have a bakery. After years of working in her da's, she knew everything about bakeries and was determined to open one. Edward had his mind set on taking over the Black Swan restaurant. His friend Martin Songstad and his wife Patricia were in a hurry to get back to Norway and leave "this godforsaken country." Oregon outlawed liquor in 1916, three years ahead of the rest of the country. Martin started a pub in 1912 and prospered until the cursed prohibition was inflicted on the state. He was tired of running a restaurant and ready to sell. Edward was anxious to stay out of the forest and work for himself.

Two weeks had gone by since Lydia had arrived in Little Creek. She was settled into Edward's little house and came to the infirmary every morning to sit with him. Her headaches were getting better. In the afternoons, when he had his therapy, she would take her medicine and retreat to the darkened bedroom. The laudanum made her sleep but left a bitter taste in her mouth and made her groggy. Lydia knew she needed to tell Edward about her headaches. She just couldn't bring herself to add extra worries while he was still recovering. *It's all right,* she thought, *I'll be right as rain soon, no need to bother Edward.*

Edward's best friend, Johnny Adams, had gone out of his way to make her comfortable and show her around town. He shyly introduced her to Annie Robey, the young lady he had been courting for the last six months. Annie worked at the Black Swan, and although the food wasn't much, Johnny took as many of his meals there as he could to be near her.

Annie and Lydia were about the same age and became immediate friends. Learning Lydia had come halfway across the world to be with Edward, her admiration increased. "I've never done anything so brave! Little Creek is 100 miles from my hometown and the farthest I've ever been. I only came because my aunt lives here, and I was offered a teaching position at the public school in Little Creek. Once they learned I was a Catholic, they refused to allow me to teach at the school. When I first came here in 1924, Oregon had passed a law mandating all children attend public schools. They were trying to get rid of the Catholic schools. They later repealed the law but the nearest Catholic school is thirty miles away. Too far for me to go everyday and still take care of my aunt. Working at the Black Swan is the only job

I was able to get. This town has some prejudices about Catholics and immigrants.

Lydia was startled to hear how much prejudice there was in their small town. She wondered if Little Creek was a good place to settle.

Seeing the hesitation in her new friend's eyes, Annie was quick to tell her, "The majority of the people here are good. They would not resort to the terror tactics used by the Klu Klux Klan. It's only been recently that we've seen issues. I hear there have been huge Klu Klux Klan marches in the larger towns. They wear white sheets and hoods on their heads and preach about the white Protestant's right to everything, and immigrants should be sent home along with all of the Negros. It is ridiculous. These people hiding behind sheets to preach this nonsense.

Lydia stopped with her cup of tea halfway to her mouth. A cold chill ran down her back. "When I was in New York I read a story about the Grand Dragon, D. C. Stephenson. He defiled and tortured a woman on a train. I'd never heard of the Klu Klux Klan. Mrs. Franklin tried to explain, but even she couldn't grasp how someone could be so evil. The Franklins wouldn't allow me to come west by myself on a train. How could such horrible people get a foothold in this wonderful country? Why don't people fight them?"

Annie contemplated the question. "People are afraid. The Klu Klux Klan is a vicious group, terrorizing innocent people. Plus the way they rile up a crowd with the depression going on, it makes sense to some people, especially if they can blame someone else for their plight. It makes some groups handy victims."

For a moment, Lydia was lost in thought. She remembered looking out of the train window and seeing the beautiful country with thousands of farms and ranches along the way. So much bounty to go around. Why did people always have to blame someone else for their misfortunes and not work to make the most of their opportunities? She'd had a lifetime of Myra blaming her for everything and wasn't about to let some men in sheets blame immigrants for their problems.

Lydia continued, "Edward told me of the 'No Irish' signs on the hiring halls when he first arrived in this country. He and Johnny kept thinking if they got away from the major cities it would be OK, but obviously not. I can't believe these dreadful KKK people are in Little Creek."

Annie looked at Lydia and grabbed her hands, "I think Stephenson's trial will show the country how evil the KKK is. Good people are going to realize how dangerous these Klan members are and think twice about supporting them. No one wants to be affiliated with someone who would commit such an atrocity against a defenseless woman."

Lydia looked at Annie. "I can put up with anything now that I am with Edward. These Klu Klux Klan people do not scare me. Scary is leaving your parents' house without a plan and traveling halfway across the world, all the while not knowing if Edward would be alive when I arrived. No, men covered in sheets do not scare me. I'm very grateful to the Franklins for getting me here safely, and relieved Edward is recovering. But I will not bow down to a bunch of cowards in sheets."

Annie marveled at her new friend, knowing there was an inner strength to her that belied her young years. God help the Klan if they try to cross Lydia!

Lydia treasured her time with Annie. She enjoyed telling Edward of all the new things she was learning about America. Slowly the couple rediscovered each other and had long talks about their dreams in America.

Edward looked at Lydia, still unable to believe this slip of a girl had come all the way from Ireland for him. He was wondering how to broach the subject of marriage. It had always been assumed, but he had never officially proposed. On one of his short therapy walks, he held a cane in one hand and Lydia's in the other. Clearing his throat, he laughed. "Well, I'd always dreamed of going down on one knee to propose to you, but I don't think I could get back up. Lydia, I have been in love with you since we were ten years old. I will love you to the end of my days. I know your family is a long way from home, and, given the circumstances, I can't ask your father's permission, but would you consider marrying me?"

Lydia felt the tears fall from her eyes. "I've waited for you my entire life. I'll marry you in a minute if you promise never ever to push me into another mud puddle or teach any of our sons to!"

Edward put a solemn look on his face but couldn't hide the twinkle in his eyes. "I promise. It may be a tough promise to keep. It rains here a lot in the winter, and there is quite a bit of mud, but I'll do my best."

Grabbing Lydia, he kissed her enthusiastically, "It seems like I have waited forever to make you mine. I'll be a good husband to you, that's my promise. I have plans, there are opportunities for us in this town, and we need to talk about them. The Black Swan is for sale, and I think we should buy it. Your reward money would make a good down payment. Think of it, Lydia. We would own our own business."

Lydia knitted her brows. "Didn't you say Martin Songstad was struggling with his business? What makes you think we can make it work? I think we would do better with a bakery, there isn't one in Little Creek."

Edward looked at Lydia. "I know it sounds like a risk, but I think that we can do both. The restaurant will need bakery goods, too.

Lydia looked into his clear blue eyes. She saw her love for him reflecting back and knew her life would be good, for richer or poorer. "We can use the money for a down payment. There is but one thing I need to do before we buy it. I need to send the money I took from Myra back to her. I cannot live with my misdeed, I'm so ashamed of my actions, but I'll never regret doing it."

"Lydia my love, I don't care what it took to get you here. Myra has always been selfish and tortured you your entire life. If it will ease your mind, send the money back to her. Just make it clear there is no place for her in our life here. Your days of pacifying Myra are over."

Lydia had never told anyone, not even her parents, what life behind their closed bedroom door was like. Myra would hit Lydia and push her down without provocation and then whisper "Tell Ma or Da and it will get worse." Bloody bruised knees were common for Lydia. Her ma just thought her daughter was clumsy. One night Lydia woke up with Myra standing over her bed staring at her as she slept. Lydia knew her sister was unstable. She was such a good actress around everyone else it was futile trying to alert her family. She also knew in her heart Myra had wanted Edward. Thwarted by Lydia's bold trip to America, she figured Myra was fit to be tied. Coming to America had freed her of Myra, but it had also separated her from her parents.

Edward didn't notice the far away look in Lydia's eyes. She was thinking of the letters from Edward Myra had kept from her. She knew in her heart Myra wanted Edward for herself. In an odd way, it was a blessing his accident forced her to run away without alerting Myra or her parents of her plans. She probably wouldn't have made it to the train station alive had Myra known.

That night sitting in Edward's kitchen Lydia wrote to her parents.

My Dearest family,

I am with Edward and we are to be married in one month. His health is steadily improving. He still walks with a limp from his injury, but he is much better since my arrival. I have so much to tell you. I am happier than I have ever been. Little Creek is beautiful, and the lush green reminds me of home. I am beginning to meet people and make friends, and soon I will be working with Edward. We are buying a restaurant. I am determined that he not go back to lumber jacking, it is too dangerous. It is a long story but on the ship I met some very influential people. The saints were watching out for me the entire journey. I made good friends, and through a miracle, helped to save a childs life. The grandparents were quite grateful and insisted on sending me on the remainder of my journey to Little Creek on the train at their expense. I am sending back the money I took from Myra. Please forgive me for my thoughtlessness however, there was no other way, I was desperate to get to Edward. Please be happy for us and know we love you.

Your devoted daughter,

Lydia

Lydia sat looking at her brief letter. She longed to tell her parents of her eventful trip on the ship and more about Mrs. Franklin's generosity. Her trip west on the train had shown her sites she had never dreamed of, wonderful mountains, deserts with enormous cacti, and prairies with cattle as far as the eye could see. She knew if she described her trip in detail, Myra would be insane with jealousy. She also guarded the secret of her reward money. With great trepidation, Lydia took her letter, and the money, to the post office. She was comforted by knowing she and Edward would be safely married if Myra were to come to America.

Chapter 10

Myra and her father arrived home to find Mrs. Delaney sitting on the sofa with tears running unchecked down her cheeks. She looked up as her husband rushed to her side. "She's made it safely to America and she's with Edward." Holding a wad of pounds, she looked at her youngest daughter, "Myra, she sent the money back to you."

Trying to grab the money out of her mother's hand, her father was faster. "Oh, no you don't Lassie. From now on, I'll be your banker. One daughter running off and shaming the family is enough."

Myra looked at her father with an expression that sent a ripple of fear up his spine. For a split second, he regretted his decision to hold onto Myra's money. In a flash of introspection he thought of all the turmoil Myra had brought to their family and again wished Edward had chosen her instead of his favorite.

"You can't take my money. I earned it and I want it back. I'm going to America the first chance I get. You can't stop me." She spat the words at her parents, her carefully polished façade of normalcy shattered.

Mrs. Delany looked at her youngest daughter and then her husband. She had overlooked so much over the years. Now, in an instant of clarity, she thought back to all the "accidents" Lydia had experienced during her childhood. *Oh dear God*, she thought to herself, *it was all Myra's doing.*

Myra was pacing the room and muttering. "I can't believe the little ninny made it all the way to Oregon, and they are to be married. I hate her….I wish she were dead." Myra turned on her heel and stormed into her bedroom. She had already taken custody of the dresses Lydia had left behind. She picked up the one she liked the least and systematically shredded it. Each jab of the scissors into fabric was more violent than the last. *The little witch, I could kill her. Now I wish I had helped her along with a horrible accident when I had the chance. Or maybe I should have suffocated her as she slept. Two can play her game. If she can make it all the way to America, so can I. And if Da thinks he's going to hold onto my money he's very mistaken.*

Myra wondered how Lydia had managed to board the boat as a single woman when it wasn't allowed. Now she had to figure out how to get to America.

The answer came faster than she thought. She was working in her father's bakery, and Rosie Sullivan came in with a woman Myra didn't know.

Myra pasted a smile on her face and her flat blue eyes stared at Rosie. "Is there something I can help you with, Rosie?"

Rosie looked at Myra. She didn't much care for the girl— something was a bit off about her. Myra's eyes had no life in them. Looking at the bread, Rosie casually mentioned, "We got a letter from Edward, we're happy Lydia arrived safely. It must be a huge relief to your family."

Before she could answer, the older woman next to Rosie looked at her and exclaimed, "Oh my, you're the spitting image of your sister! You look just like Lydia."

Her comment did not endear the woman to Myra. As she was thinking of her reply, Rosie's companion continued. "I took care of your sister on the ship after her accident. She had quite a bump on her head after saving the little boy. She was a hero. Lucky for her the baby's grandparents took a liking to her. Got her out of steerage and kept her in the infirmary for the rest of the trip so she wouldn't have to deal with the riff raff below deck. They even brought her two friends up to the infirmary, rescued them all from the dreadful steerage section in the ship."

Lydia looked at the woman. "I'm sorry, we haven't been introduced. I am Lydia's sister, Myra. You actually took care of her? My sister is so modest she didn't give us many details of the story. Whose grandchild was it?"

Nancy Sullivan relished a good story, "Well, Lassie, she rescued the grandson of the richest people on the ship. They were ever so grateful. In fact they took Lydia off the ship with them when they arrived in New York City. She didn't even have to go to Ellis Island. They whisked her through customs like a fairy princess. Mr. Franklin owns the Franklin Bank in New York City. I heard Mrs. Franklin talking about it during one of her visits with your sister. Lydia left Ireland and fell right into the pot of gold. The lucky girl."

Myra was trying hard to maintain the fake smile on her face. Her thoughts were racing. She had to figure out how to use this information. "It was so kind of them to look after Lydia."

Rosie watched Myra carefully and saw the scheming look in her eyes. Nudging her mother-in-law she said, "Oh, look at the time. Ryan will be home soon looking for his supper." Rosie paid for the bread and gently pulled her mother-in-law out of the shop. She could feel the poisonous look from Myra as she exited.

Myra stared after them, the wheels in her head already turning, thinking to herself. *Well now, I think maybe I have a way of getting to America after all.*

At home in her bedroom, Myra composed a letter to Mr. Franklin of the Franklin Bank in New York City. She imagined the bank was important enough her letter would get there without an actual street address.

Dear Mr. and Mrs. Franklin,

My dear sister Lydia's has told us so much about you in her letters I thought it would be acceptable to ask for your help. Our parents were in a horrible accident and did not survive. I need to get to my sister to tell her this terrible news in person. I cannot bear to write of it in a letter, I fear the shock would be too much for Lydia.

I have some money saved, and, hopefully, after I have taken care of my parents' estate, there will be enough left for my passage to America. While I am fearful of the voyage, I must come to America to be with my sister and start a new life with her and Edward. I cannot bear the sadness here, and, I am all alone now.

Lydia wrote of single women needing a male companion or a sponsor in America in order to clear customs. I cannot write to her and Edward of my arrival. My sister and I are so close. She knows I would never leave our parents or my life here. Lydia will suspect the worst and I do not want to upset her or cause her undo worry. I was hoping to use your name as my sponsor in America so I can travel to Oregon to be with my dear sister.

I am so sorry to impose on your friendship with my sister but I have no one else to turn to.
Respectfully yours,
Myra Delaney

Rereading her letter, Myra congratulated herself on a card well played. If these people owed a debt of gratitude to Lydia, she was going to collect it. Myra laughed at how shocked her parents would be to know they died in an accident. Now she just had to wait. If this did not work, there were still other ways of getting to America.

Chapter 11

L ydia loved the little house Edward had purchased. She felt bad for being happy from some one else's misfortune, but loved walking through the rooms visualizing their future together. Looking at their bedroom, Lydia had a vision of what she wanted.

Entering the double doors, Lydia was overwhelmed by the amount of merchandise in the Parrish Hardware store. She found the wallpaper area and was deep in thought when a sales clerk approached her.

"May I help you, miss?"

Lydia looked up at the young woman, "Oh my, I've never seen so many beautiful things in one place in my life."

Laughing, the clerk eyed Lydia and retorted, "With that charming accent. I'd say you're not from around here. Yes, we have a lot of product. We have to stock everything or our customers would drive to the next town to shop. We like to think we have a captive audience. I'm Kathleen Parrish. What can I help you with?"

The surprise on Lydia's face must have been evident because the next thing she heard was peals of laughter from Kathleen Parrish.

"Oh my, the look on your face. Do women not work where you come from?"

"Aye, we work, and we work hard. If you forgive me for sayin'. I've just didn't know rich people worked."

"Oh my dear, you have much to learn about America. I want to be valuable to my family's business. It took forever to convince my father. Now he looks on my efforts as something to occupy me until he finds me a suitable husband, as if I would ever allow him to choose a man for me!"

Kathleen Parrish had already rejected all of the young men in Little Creek. A few prominent families in town had produced ambitious male offspring that had tried to court Kathleen and marry into her family fortune. None of the men respected her intelligence or cared about her opinions. Kathleen was a rare combination of brains, beauty, and a tremendous heart. Her face was patrician with vibrant blue eyes set off by perfectly arched eyebrows. She was a pretty young woman and when she smiled it was genuine.

Stunned by Kathleen's revelations, Lydia was momentarily silent. "Well, I am trying to find some wallpaper, can you help me?"

"Of course, what room are you doing?"

Lydia found Kathleen so easy to talk to soon she was pouring out her life story. Kathleen listened attentively. Her life had been one of ease. Kathleen's only challenge was getting her father to treat her as if she had a brain. Certainly traveling across the world for the man you love was far more interesting.

"Edward and I are to be married in two weeks. He is staying at Dr. Monroe's and I'm staying in the house he bought us. I want to surprise him and wallpaper the bedroom." Color rose to her face as she remembered Mrs. Franklin's advice about the marriage bed. Mentally slapping herself to get back on track, Lydia continued, "I was thinking about a rose pattern."

Kathleen was more than helpful. Soon she was procuring rolls and rolls of samples from the back room. After much examination, Lydia finally opened a roll exclaiming, "Perfect, this is exactly what I had in mind!"

After conferring about how big the room was and estimating the amount needed, Kathleen looked over at Lydia's glowing face. "Do you know how to wallpaper?"

"Oh my no. Is it very hard to learn? I'm good at figuring things out if you can give me instructions."

Kathleen looked at the young woman before her. She was at least five years older than Lydia but already in just one adventure, Lydia had accomplished what Kathleen craved— the freedom to do what she wanted with her life. "I'll do better than that. I'll come help you."

"Oh, Miss Parrish, I don't expect you to do help," Lydia stammered. "I can't be inconveniencing you."

"Nonsense, and please call me Kathleen. I would be delighted. You are a breath of fresh air, and I would love to get to know you better. Now let's gather up what you'll need. When do you want to work on this project?"

"I always visit Edward in the mornings and then leave in the afternoon when Dr. Monroe does his therapy."

"Marvelous. I have tomorrow afternoon free. Why don't we meet here at 1p.m. and we'll drive to your house."

Lydia was overjoyed. She couldn't wait to surprise Edward, and realizing she had just made a new friend in the process, added to her pleasure.

The next day, Edward was staring at Lydia as they sat outside in the morning sunshine. "You look like you are up to something. What is going on?"

Lydia turned to Edward, marveling over the fact that after two years apart and only a few weeks together, he could read her mood so adeptly. "Whatever do you mean? I'm just enjoying the morning with you and thinking of our wedding."

Laughing, Edward kissed the tip of her nose. "You're known for being stubborn, not for being a good liar. I guess I'll just see what you've got up your sleeve when you're ready."

Lydia looked at Edward, "I guess it's a good thing I left Ireland so quickly. If I'm so readable, my parents would have locked me away!"

Just as she was about to tease him further, Dr. Monroe announced it was time for the afternoon torture session. Edward groaned and followed him back to the infirmary.

Lydia was thrilled to get started, almost running to the hardware store in her excitement. Arriving breathless, she scanned the store for Kathleen. Kathleen was talking to another clerk, lining up all of the supplies on the counter.

"There you are! I have everything we need and we're in luck. The only thing you have to pay for is the wallpaper and the paste.

Our dear Mr. Johnson has offered to loan us all the tools we'll need."

Lydia looked at the man to Kathleen's left. Mr. Johnson appeared to be about seventy with snow white hair and a face wreathed in wrinkles. The effect when all those creases moved into a smile was stunning. He looked like anyone's favorite uncle.

"Hello, Miss Lydia. I've been hearing about your project. Now here's what you two young ladies need to do…"

A half an hour later, with their heads swirling from all of Mr. Johnson's instructions, Lydia and Kathleen headed to the house.

Lydia imagined as a Parrish, Kathleen was used to only the finest. She knew their modest little home would be a far cry from Kathleen's luxurious home.

Upon entering, Kathleen uttered a cry of pleasure. "This is a Sears Craftsman house. I remember when it was constructed. Look at this lovely fireplace. It's beautiful. I can already see Christmas stockings hanging on the mantle!"

Lydia was caught up in Kathleen's enthusiasm. "I agree. I love this house. I can see many wonderful years ahead for Edward and me here."

Kathleen looked at the sweet smile on her new friend's face. "Lead on, this paper is not going to hang itself!"

It turns out the statement was quite true; it wouldn't hang itself and the two people who were supposed to hang it, were on the floor hopelessly giggling. As they sat there contemplating their next move, a knock at the door startled them. Looking out the window by the front door, Lydia was surprised to see Dr. Monroe standing on the porch. Panicking, she pulled open the door, "What is it? Is Edward OK? Has something happened?"

"Oh, no Lydia, everything is fine. Annie sent me. I stopped at the diner for dinner and she said she hadn't seen you all day. Annie mentioned you sometimes get bad headaches, I came to see if you're OK." Bernard didn't add he had smelled the laudanum on her breath on occasion. He was actually relieved when Annie said Lydia got headaches. At first he had feared Edward was in love with a laudanum addict.

Lydia was aghast. She had not confided her headaches to her friend Annie. Was she so easy to read? "I'm fine, I was trying to surprise Edward and....well, it's just too hard to explain. Come and see."

Lydia led Dr. Monroe into the bedroom. Kathleen was still sitting on the floor, her chestnut hair pulled back into a ponytail. She sat there trying to decipher the notes they took from Mr. Johnson's instructions.

Surveying the room and seeing the look on both women's faces, Bernard Monroe knew he should have stayed at the restaurant.

Lydia smiled at Kathleen, "I'd like to introduce you to Edward's doctor, Bernard Monroe."

Bernard looked at the lovely if not a bit disheveled woman and gently shook her hand. "It appears you ladies could use some help. Mind if I jump in?"

Kathleen looked at Bernard with appreciation. She had heard about the new doctor at the logging camp but had not met him. Now, noticing his brown curly hair and the hazel eyes behind his serious glasses, she was sorry she hadn't made an effort to meet him sooner. "Yes, please, jump in. We thought this would be so easy. We've made quite a mess of things."

Lydia, observing the slight flush on Kathleen's cheeks, thought of the conversation she and Kathleen had earlier. Kathleen didn't have any gentleman callers. To Lydia it sounded like she spent all her time trying to get her father's attention. Maybe Bernard Monroe is exactly the distraction Kathleen needed.

"I worked my way through medical school helping my uncle in the summers. He was a painter and a fine wallpaper hanger. I picked up a few tricks along the way. We'll have this up in no time."

True to his word, three hours later, Bernard had the room done. He was gallant enough to allow the ladies to help, mending their wounded pride.

Surveying the room, Lydia let out a contented sigh, "Edward will be so surprised. He'll love it. The roses remind me of the wild ones he picked when he was apologizing for pushing me in the mud."

"He pushed you in the mud?" Both Bernard and Kathleen commented at the same time.

"Aye, we were ten years old. He finally apologized four years later. He told me it was because he loved me. Aren't little boys silly?"

Kathleen laughed. "That's a charming story, and now you're to be married in two weeks."

"You must come to the wedding. Bernard is giving me away and Annie is helping me get ready. Please say you'll come. We're having a reception at The Black Swan."

Kathleen smiled widely, "I can't think of anything I would enjoy more. Of course I'll be there. You must let me help, too."

Bernard wondered why he had held his breath waiting for her reply. After spending three hours with her, he knew he wanted to see her again but couldn't figure out how to bring up the subject of a date. "Perhaps you'd like to drive to the church with us?"

"Drive to the church. Where is the wedding?" Kathleen was momentarily confused. There were two churches in town. The Episcopalian church her great grandfather had started, and a Protestant church.

"We're getting married at St. Alphonsus in Silverton, it's the nearest Catholic church."

Kathleen laughed, "I've never been in a Catholic church before. There's a first time for everything. I'd love to attend."

Chapter 12

Myra was forced to take over Lydia's job at the bakery. She was angry when her Da made her leave her job in Mrs. Murphy's dress shop. Another reason to hate Lydia for running off to America. She was arranging bread in the display case when the bell on the door chimed. Looking up, she saw two Black and Tans entering the bakery. Her first instinct was fear. Black and Tans were a combination of police and army men sent by the British to quell the Irish Republican Army and their activities. Residents lived in fear of the Black and Tans; they were known to shoot innocent people in retaliation for attacks on them by the IRA. When the British Black and Tans showed up, trouble from the Irish Republican Army usually followed.

The two soldiers looked a few years older than Myra. One was a bit chubby and smiled shyly at Myra. Looking at the array of hot buns, he said to Myra, "I'd-I'd-I'd llliikk…"

The other soldier, tall and well built with a cockiness even Myra found annoying, pushed his companion aside. "Oh Godfrey, do shut up. With all your stuttering this beautiful young lady will be waiting all day to get your order." His clipped manner of speaking was such a sharp contrast to the lilting tone of the Irish, Myra found it even more irritating than his words. For this first time in her life, Myra felt a bit of compassion for another human being. Ignoring the brash young man, she turned back to the stuttering soldier she now knew to be named Godfrey. "It's all right. You can see there are no other customers. I'm happy to help you. Is it the buns you fancy?"

Godfrey looked at her with gratitude, "Y-y- y- yeess, pl-pl-please."

Seeing he was losing control of the situation, the other young man again tried to get Myra's attention. "I'm Byron Yates. Don't pay any attention to him. He's an idiot. I'm more your type." With a leer he added, "I like buns, too. Yours look especially nice."

Myra looked at Byron. He was classically handsome. His dark hair was slicked back, and violet eyes, almost too pretty for a man, looked at her with the expectation she would swoon into his arms any second.

"Actually, you couldn't be further from my type, and I don't appreciate your cheekiness. Now please give me your order or leave."

Byron took a step back as if he had been physically slapped. This was not the response he was used to with women. Godfrey also looked at her with surprise. His tongue was the only thing tied, his mind was agile and quick. This girl was beautiful and usually beautiful girls fell into Byron's arms without hesitation.

Myra also had an unfettered brain and it had just devised a plan. Putting the hot buns in a sack, she looked over at Godfrey and gave him her best smile. "I hope you enjoy these and please come back again. Perhaps you could leave your rude friend behind."

Taking a deep breath, he managed to stammer out, "I'm Godfrey Aldridge…wh-wh what's y-your n-n-name?"

Forcing her sweetest smile, "I'm Myra Delany. It's a pleasure to meet you." Godfrey didn't notice the smile didn't reach her eyes.

Godfrey smiled back as if he had just been handed the moon. Myra knew the hook was set, and now she just had to reel her new fish in. There was more than one way to get to America.

Chapter 13

The day came for Edward and Lydia to meet Mr. Parrish, the president of Parrish Bank. The Parrish name was spread throughout the town on the bank, hardware store, grocery store, and the local theatre.

Mr. Parrish was fifty years old. He was a handsome man who had aged well. For the last twenty years, he had run the family businesses. He had learned from his father fairness and honesty were qualities needed for every business transaction. Stupidity was not. Every loan from the Parrish Bank was fair and honest as long as Harold Parrish felt you were a good risk. He turned down as many loans as he authorized. When he saw the young couple approaching his desk, he looked at his watch. They were punctual, but from their appearance, punctuality was all they could offer. He studied their approach, believing you could tell a lot by the way people presented themselves. The young man walked with a slight limp but carried himself tall and proud. The young woman was quite stunning, walking with an assurance that seemed at odds with her young age.

"Hello, Mr. Parrish, I'm Edward O'Brien and this is my fiancé, Lydia Delaney. We've come to talk to you about purchasing the mortgage on 'The Black Swan.' Mr. Songstad has spoken to you about it I believe?"

Parrish remained seated. Not extending his hand, he motioned for them to be seated. "I've heard of you, O'Brien. You've been here almost two years, and you've stayed out of trouble. But how do I know you too won't get the urge to return home and walk away from the restaurant, leaving my Bank with a defaulted loan? You immigrants are not a steady group. In fact, we don't make many loans to newcomers."

Edward's face flushed with anger. "Mr. Parrish, I have travelled across this country and have seen the unfair treatment of immigrants. I find it odd a country formed by immigrants should have this prejudice. Your family may have been here for over a hundred years, but they too came from somewhere. I'll not be treated like a…"

Suddenly Lydia put her hand on Edward's arm. "Mr. Parrish, I have a letter of recommendation from Mr. Stephen Franklin of the Franklin Bank in New York City. He suggested I give it to you for review prior to our business discussion."

Harold Parrish was usually not given to surprises, but a letter of recommendation by Stephen Franklin from this little slip of an Irish girl was quite out of the ordinary. Scanning the letter, he glanced up at Miss Delaney. "Young lady, Mr. Franklin says he is personally acquainted with you and holds you in the highest regard. He further states his bank guarantees any loan you and Mr. O'Brien contract with our bank. This is highly unusual, but, I must confess, while I am intrigued by this letter, we still must treat this loan as we would any other. We will discuss your plans, your financial obligation, and your experience."

Reaching into his pocket for his pipe, he slowly tapped the tobacco into the bowl. Making a production of lighting it, he finally spoke. "My family founded this town and the Bank. I have an obligation to both. I don't make loans because someone in New York City tells me to. I make them based on ability to pay back and the character of the applicants."

Edward looked at the banker and realized he was trying to save face. Oregon was still a bit of the Wild West. Even thought the Parrish family was respectable and powerful in their town, Parrish was smart enough to know granting a favor to a New York banker might be a useful card to hold. However, Edward knew he did not want to appear as if he were being bullied into doing something at the orders of an East Coast banker.

Parrish lit his pipe and asked Edward, "What makes you so certain you can succeed?"

"I came to this town and my first job was cooking at the logging camp. My fiancé's family owned a bakery in Ireland. She knows her way around a kitchen. We've a down payment of $400 and we are no strangers to hard work."

Parrish hid his surprise at the size of their down payment and wondered how they accumulated so much money. "I'll loan you the money to buy out Songstad, not because some fancy banker in New York City tells me to. Come back tomorrow at 3 p.m. and we will have the loan papers ready. One more thing, this Bank will own you body and soul until the loan is satisfied. Payments are made on the first of the month, every month. If you are late, we will start foreclosure. Look around town, do you see how many businesses are named Parrish? There have been many before you that thought they would be successful, and the Bank had to take over. Be careful your restaurant doesn't turn into the Parrish Restaurant."

Edward looked at Mr. Parrish, the hard glint in his eyes a sharp contrast to his earlier demeanor. Parrish was a shark who profited by others' failures. The fact that half the businesses in town were named Parrish had not escaped Edward's notice. Edward looked at the man behind the desk knowing he loved power and making people squirm was a ritual he enjoyed. With no other alternatives for a loan, Edward swore to himself he would get through this for Lydia's sake.

Parrish finally looked at Edward. "I will see you tomorrow at 3 p.m., don't be late."

Lydia's smile was dazzling. She turned to the banker and extended her hand, "Mr. Parrish, people talk about your honesty and fairness. I am most thankful those qualities entered into your decision.

Clearly charmed by Lydia, Mr. Parrish smiled at her, enjoying the adulation.

As they made their way to the entrance, Edward glanced over to see the owner of Little Creek Logging walking in. Edward didn't miss the look of appreciation that crossed the man's face as Brookstone looked Lydia over. Holding her close, Edward passed by Brookstone without a second look. He had nothing but contempt for the man and the shoddy equipment in his logging company. Edward's injury could have been avoided if the equipment had been maintained. He was not the only logger who had been maimed by Brookstones' company but, at least he was alive. He knew three families who lost their men from logging accidents. He smiled wryly to himself thinking, *ironically, if it hadn't been for that man's greed, I'd still be working at his logging camp trying to scratch out a living, and Lydia would still be in Ireland. Perhaps I should be grateful.*

Barely able to contain their excitement, Edward and Lydia exited the Bank with much less decorum than when they entered. Outside,

Edward hugged Lydia closely. "Thank God you had that letter. I could tell he was looking forward to refusing our loan request. He was clearly impressed that you know Mr. Franklin. The old bugger, he'll not be happy until he owns everything and everyone in this town. Well, he'll never own us. We'll work hard and be successful in this country and then we'll help other 'undesirables' like us!"

"Oh, Edward, how can a dreadful egomaniac like him have such a lovely daughter? His ego will be his downfall. But right now, I'm just grateful we got the loan. We will be successful; I can't stand the thought of that despicable man getting our restaurant."

It didn't occur to Edward to wonder how she knew Parrish's daughter. All he could think about was they had succeeded in their first step.

Thus became the auspicious beginnings of "O'Brien's Family Restaurant."

Calvin Brookstone III sauntered over to Parrish's desk. Dressed in corduroy pants and a flannel shirt, he looked more like a logger than the second most successful man in town. His salt and pepper hair was combed straight back and his wide unlined forehead looked younger than the rest of his face. Deeply etched frown lines marred each side of his mouth, and his green eyes bored into Parrish's as he approached the banker's desk. Jerking his thumb towards the door, Brookstone said, "What did the micks want?"

"The 'micks,' as you so charmingly call them, wanted a loan."

"You didn't give it to them, did you? I thought we were going to start weeding these immigrants out of our town."

"I was all set to refuse when the young lady pulled out a letter of recommendation from the Franklin Bank in New York City, one of the most influential banks in the country, and the letter was signed by Stephen Franklin himself." Parrish could barely contain his exasperation. "How on earth did she come to know him?"

"So you gave them the loan?"

"Calvin, it isn't a wise idea to make enemies in the banking industry. Of course I gave them the loan. I didn't see any other option. There is no way Songstad will sell to us. He's current in his payments and I can't foreclose. I saw no other recourse."

"How about if we burn them out? I can make a suggestion to our local Klan leader. We could kill two birds with one stone or maybe three. Songstad is leaving, and you can bet O'Brien and his girl would leave too. He can't be a logger with his bum leg. What other options do they have?"

Parrish's face turned bright red. "You keep your cowardly hooded Klu Klux Klan friends out of this town. I've warned you about it before."

Brookstone gave a derisive laugh. "You know the Klu Klux Klan is in Portland. Are you really so naïve you think we don't have members in our own town?"

Parrish looked at Brookstone. Their great grandfathers had started this town. The families had virtually been in each other's pockets for over a hundred years, but he had never understood Calvin. His family had more money than they knew what to do with but neither, Calvin or his father had ever satiated their thirst for power. The Klu Klux Klan had been lining up politicians and local government officials all over the state. Marches were being held and hundreds of Oregonians had been joining their "cause." There was even a branch for women and a Junior Order of Klansmen for teenagers.

Parrish reminisced on the simple days of his youth when their fathers ran the town. Thinking how O'Brien had pointed out "the entire country had been formed by immigrants" Parrish now pondered his words. The first immigrants came for religious freedom. Now the Klu Klux Klan was seeking to remove anyone who wasn't a Protestant? Carefully selecting his words, he turned to Brookstone, "You leave your Klu Klux Klan out of our town, or I will take a very close look at the mortgages I'm holding for anyone I deem as a member."

Brookstone stood up, his tall body bent over Parrish's desk. "You do and you'll start something you won't be able to finish. I'll see to that. Standing to his full height, Brookstone slammed his fist on the desk and turned away without another word. As he stormed off he thought, *the boys and I will pay these two a little visit. Let's see how long they want to stay in town after a visit from the KKK.*

Chapter 14

Lydia was spending her last night alone in the house she would soon share with Edward. Unable to sleep, she was sitting in the kitchen having a cup of tea when she heard what sounded like several cars stopping in front of her house. Glancing at the kitchen clock, Lydia knew no good comes from a visit at 2:00 a.m. Her first thought was something happened to Edward and started to run to the front door. Common sense kicked in, and she realized if there had been a problem, Bernard would have called her immediately. Turning off the kitchen light, she crept to the front window of the house. Concealing herself behind the lace draperies, she was able to see at least 10 men standing on her lawn. Anger surged through her when she realized they were wearing white sheets. Suddenly a fire blazed in the front yard. Lydia's heart stopped as she saw the fire was in the shape of a cross. Lydia knew there were no weapons in Edward's house or she would have gone out to the front porch and done some target shooting. Her father had taken her bird hunting many times and she was more than a fair shot. The men stood in their robes and hoods staring at the cross as if mesmerized by the flames. Lydia stood twenty feet away, hidden behind the drapes shaking with righteous anger. It looked like the men did not have weapons but she couldn't be sure. Remembering the stories she had read, she willed herself not to do anything foolish like confronting them. Finally, the cross started to burn out and the men retreated to their cars and drove off into the night.

Lydia took a bucket off the back porch and filled it with water. Walking to the cross she extinguished the remaining embers and kicked the cross over. She would dispose of the rest of it in the morning. She'd not have Edward see evidence of their bigotry. Little Creek was now her home and she was not going to be intimidated by men in sheets.

After a restless night, Lydia awoke early on her wedding day. Laying in the bed she and Edward would soon share, she put the prior night's horror behind her and smiled in nervous anticipation. Staring at the beautiful rose covered walls, she wondered what Edward was thinking at that very moment. He had officially been discharged from the infirmary, but for the sake of propriety, could not sleep in the same house as Lydia until they married. Dr. Monroe, or Bernard, now that he was a friend and no longer taking care of his reluctant patient, insisted Edward stay with him in his bachelor quarters until the wedding. Weeks of having Edward under his care had created a close friendship between the two men.

Bernard kept telling her Edward's recovery was due to her. Each time Edward would quietly remind him, "If you hadn't been such an excellent surgeon and torture master, Lydia would likely have been taking my broken body back to Ireland instead of getting ready for our wedding."

Lydia marveled at the beauty of Oregon in June. The lush green forest was accented in pink and white as the wild rhododendrons blossomed. Daffodils and tulips lined the walkways of the small houses and the streets were defined by rows of flowering cherry trees.

The restaurant had been decorated the night before by friends picking colorful flowers from their yards and scattering vases around the dining room. Candles were ready to be lighted when the bride and groom arrived.

Bernard drove Lydia, Annie, and Kathleen to St. Alphonsus. He was going to escort Lydia down the aisle. Annie had insisted Lydia not see Edward before the wedding. "It's bad luck. You need to follow tradition!"

Bernard drove up to the church and the women rushed into the rectory. Lydia changed into her wedding dress and Annie helped with the multitude of pearl buttons. The dress fit like a dream. When Annie finished with Lydia's hair and placed the veil, she stepped back and gasped. "Lydia, you are a beautiful bride. You look like a picture."

Lydia's eyes filled with tears. "I'm missing our families and so sorry they couldn't be here, but you are already like a sister to me, Annie. I'm so grateful for your friendship!"

Annie looked at her friend. "I never had a sister or a brother. My only remaining blood family is my Aunt Mildred, and she is...well, she's not a very loving person. I too feel like we are family Lydia and it is a wonderful feeling."

Lydia shyly looked at Kathleen, "You are such a dear to be here. I am also glad to have you as my friend."

"Oh Lydia, if you only knew how special you are. It's hard not to be your friend. I've brought you something. We have a tradition, 'something old, something new, something borrowed, something blue.' I thought you could tuck it in your sleeve."

Lydia opened the package. "Oh my, Annie, look at this. It's a lace handkerchief with a beautiful blue ribbon running through it. Something new and something blue all in one! Thank you, Kathleen. It's beautiful. I know I will be wiping away tears of joy with it."

Lydia heard footsteps and looked up. She was shocked to see Mrs. Franklin approaching with her arms extended, a smile lit up her face as she hugged the beautiful bride.

"Oh my dear, you look radiant. I couldn't miss seeing you in your wedding dress!

"I'm so happy to see you. I never expected you to come so far for our wedding."

"My darling Lydia, you still have no idea how much you mean to Stephen and me. As it turns out, Stephen had a business meeting in Portland. It was perfect timing. Looks like I'm just in time for 'something borrowed, something new'!" She laughed merrily at the look on Lydia's face, handing her a small velvet box.

With trembling hands, Lydia opened the box to discover a magnificent strand of pearls. "They're beautiful. They match my dress perfectly. How did you know?"

"Lydia, you don't have a deceptive bone in your body, but, fortunately, I do. I simply asked the salesclerk at Macy's to find me some pearl necklaces to choose from while you were changing. We were able to match everything, and you were none the wiser! I so love a good surprise!"

"Oh, Mrs. Franklin, the necklace is lovely, I've never owned anything so beautiful. I'm so pleased you're here; I can't wait for you to meet Edward, he has heard so much about you. But first tell me how Corwin is. I think of him so often."

"Corwin is very good. He follows Mary Margaret's boys everywhere. I fear when he starts talking it will be with an Irish accent." Beverly smiled as she thought how grateful she was to the young woman in front of her. "Now, I am looking forward to meeting the young man who caused you to come halfway across the world. But, really dear, after all we've been through, don't you think it's time to start calling me Beverly?"

Hugging Mrs. Franklin, Lydia whispered, "You are like a mother to me. I am so thankful to you for all you have done." Taking a small breath Lydia added "Beverly."

Annie and Kathleen excused themselves to give Lydia and Mrs. Franklin some time alone.

"You know Mary Margaret and Valerie are extremely disappointed. They so wanted to be here for your special day."

"I miss them but I know it's a very long trip. Mary Margaret couldn't leave the boys, and I don't think Valerie could stand being away from Ronnie.

"Valerie came by before we left. She said you would need something to borrow to complete the tradition. This is her great grandmother's rosary. She wanted you to use it today. She carried it for her own wedding, and now you have your something borrowed."

"Oh, it's beautiful and so very special. It's an honor to carry it with me down the aisle."

Annie was the maid of honor and Lydia had asked Kathleen if she would be a bridesmaid. Bernard was going to walk her down the aisle, but when he saw the obvious affection the Franklins had for Lydia, he asked Mr. Franklin if he would step in to give Lydia away. Bernard said he would escort Mrs. Franklin to the front row, and then stand up at the front of the church with Edward and his best man Johnny.

Beverly Franklin fell into her new role as "mother of the bride" with enthusiasm. Lydia was a beautiful bride, the dark circles she had in New York were gone and the fresh Oregon air had given her a healthy glow. She was relieved when Lydia informed her that the headaches were very infrequent, but puzzled when she begged her not to mention them to Edward.

"Lydia, did you not tell Edward about your injury on the ship?"

"I mentioned I fell but didn't really talk about the headaches. I didn't want to worry him, and, they're getting fewer and fewer. I didn't want anything to distract him from his recovery."

"It's time for the ceremony; I hope you don't mind, Stephen would like to walk you down the aisle. And, please, call him Stephen!"

"It's lovely you came all this way. I would be honored to have Mr. Franklin, I mean Stephen, walk me down the aisle."

Right on cue there was a soft knock at the door. "Is our girl ready?" Stephen Franklin's wide smile showed his pleasure at seeing Lydia again. "My dear Lydia, you look wonderful. I'm proud to walk you down the aisle."

Bernard came in to take Beverly to her seat and then joined the men at the altar. Edward turned, his eyes misting over as he looked down the aisle at Lydia. He couldn't remember a moment in his life that he hadn't been in love with her. As she got closer, a tear dropped down Edward's cheek. She looked radiant, and while he had only met Mr. Franklin briefly, the look on his face was of genuine affection for Lydia.

Holding her hand out to Edward, she turned and shyly planted a quick kiss on Mr. Franklin's cheek whispering, "Thank you." With a slight hesitation she added, "Stephen."

Edward's last thought before taking his bride's hand was to wish their families were present to witness this magical day. Then, looking around, he took stock of his new family and knew they would always be together.

Taking Edward's hand, Lydia took her place by his side, a place where she knew she belonged. She had no regrets for all it had taken to get there.

Kathleen stood by the altar and watched the magic of the Catholic ceremony. The Mass said in Latin held her interest. She had taken the ancient language in college and could make out some of the words. Thinking of the dinner table conversation last night, she remembered her father and brother's talk about the Klu Klux Klan, and Catholics. Why would people be so opposed to something so beautiful? At the end of the Mass, the wedding vows began. Kathleen cried when Edward and Lydia said their "I do's." She had only known Lydia for two weeks, but already felt if anyone threatened her new friend, they would have Kathleen's wrath to deal with.

After the ceremony, the joyous bride and groom walked up the aisle. Smiling at the small crowd of friends, they walked out the church door into the brilliant spring day.

There was quite a bit of horn honking as the three cars made their way to the restaurant. Bernard and Kathleen sat in the front seat smiling at each other as the newlyweds in the back seat were laughing and kissing.

Kathleen, reflecting on the Mass and wedding ceremony, looked at Bernard and asked, "Are you a Catholic too?"

"No, I come from old Boston Episcopalians. I really haven't been attending church since I came out west."

"If you had, I would have met you sooner. Wouldn't that have been nice?" Kathleen looked over at Bernard with a wistful smile on her face.

"Yes, but I think we've been making up for lost time."

Since meeting two weeks ago, Bernard had endeavored to see Kathleen as much as possible, asking her out for walks, and Sunday drives, and even being invited to the Parrish home for dinner.

"I've been meaning to ask you, did I pass inspection with your father? He was giving me some pretty scrutinizing looks at dinner last Sunday."

"Oh, it's not my father you have to worry about. It's my brother Douglas. Thank God you have doctor in front of your name, or he would have made you eat in the kitchen. He's a dreadful snob. He won't even date any of the young women in town. He feels they are inferior. He's impossible to deal with and keeps telling me it is scandalous that I am working at Dad's hardware store."

"I love the fact you are working at the hardware store. I may not have met you if it hadn't been for your, ah, well let's just say amazing wallpapering skills."

Just then there was a giggle from the backseat. Lydia smiled at the memory of Kathleen and Bernard's first meeting. "Bernard, we would have figured it out eventually. We're just happy we didn't have to. You did a fine job with the wallpaper."

It was Edward's time to laugh. "Well at least being bossed around by these two gave you a taste of how you'd been bossing me for weeks!"

Before Bernard could reply, his attention was diverted by a group of people lining the streets, "Oh my God, it's the Klu Klux Klan. Look, they're marching."

Kathleen was appalled. "Oh, Bernard, please take a different road. I can't bear to look at these idiots. It's hardly a reflection of the entire town."

Edward was incensed, spitting out his words. "It's a reflection of too much of the town. Look at these cowards marching under the cover of their hoods and carrying the cross. Do they honestly think 'their' God is so different from anyone else's? This country continues to baffle me with their class system. I thought the English were bad."

Lydia looked out the window, silently wondering how these people could call themselves Christians. Remembering the Franklins in the car behind them, she was mortified they would see this vulgar display.

Arriving at the restaurant, they were greeted with a shower of rice and the merry shouts from Edwards logging friends and their families. The Klu Klux Klan was momentarily forgotten.

Edward and Lydia looked at the smiling faces of their friends. Clutching Lydia's hand, Edward was pleased to see Annie and Johnny had already taken charge of the reception, pouring lemonade for their guests.

Johnny cleared his throat and whistled for everyone's attention. "Well, I love my new country as much as the next man here, but, I do have to admit this prohibition throws a wrench into a good party. Let's raise our glasses to our dear friends Edward and Lydia." Looking at the happy newlyweds, Johnny went on, "I am so glad this day has finally come. Edward has nearly driven me mad in the two years I have known him. It was always 'Lydia, Lydia, Lydia,' day and night. Lydia, I'm pleased I finally met you before I went stark raving bonkers. You are every bit as wonderful as he constantly told me. I raise my glass to you and my dear friend Edward, and as my ma always said on such happy occasions"

> *"May you have love that never ends,*
> *lots of money, and lots of friends.*
> *Health be yours, whatever you do,*
> *and may God send many blessings to you!"*

Lydia smiled, "Aye, God has already blessed me. Just being here with all of you and my Edward is a blessing."

Edward looked at Lydia with loving eyes. "We will always remember this blessed day, and we are thankful to you all for being here. Our special thanks to the Franklins for coming all the way from New York."

Kathleen looked over at the Franklins. She remembered her father talking about how surprised he was to see a letter of recommendation from Stephen Franklin. She couldn't wait to tell her father she actually met the famous Mr. Franklin. Douglas had thrown a fit when she informed him and her father she was going to the O'Brien wedding. She laughed to herself, remembering how she had called him an incredible snob and a brat. Honestly, sometimes her brother was as bad as the KKK. Kathleen worried about him. He was young and sometimes spouted the ideology of those ignorant people and how they just want to keep immigrants in their place. As she and Douglas shouted at each other, her father had walked in and stopped the argument. At least he hadn't forbidden her from going. Looking at the joyful bride and groom, Kathleen knew if he had, she would have disobeyed.

No one missed the absence of alcohol. The music was so enticing soon the entire room was dancing. Stephen and Beverly Franklin danced together, their eyes meeting, and satisfied smiles lighting up their faces.

"Stephen, I'm ecstatic you had a conference in Portland. I wouldn't have missed this for the world. Lydia looks so radiant and, I like her young man. I can tell she will be in good hands and happy in her new life."

Franklin looked at his wife, "I would have thought so too if I hadn't seen those Klu Klux Klan people out on the street. What do they hope to prove? I almost wish they hadn't bought this restaurant. We might have had a chance to entice them to live in New York where things are much more civilized. Lydia told me the bank manager was being rather difficult until she pulled out my letter of recommendation. The small minded buffoon!"

"Shush, the small minded buffoon's daughter is right over there dancing with the handsome Dr. Monroe."

"She's a Parrish?" Stephen was uncharacteristically at a loss for words.

Beverly glanced over at Kathleen, "Yes, she seems like a nice girl. I wonder what Kathleen's father thought of her attending the wedding?"

"I'm sure he was upset but something tells me Kathleen knows her own way, and her father doesn't interfere much. Now let's go cut in on the bride and groom." Stephen twirled his wife and politely tapped on Edward's shoulder. "My turn, old man, you'll have her for a lifetime and we're leaving in the morning."

Lydia graciously released her new husband to the clutches of Beverly. She implored Beverly with her eyes not to tell Edward about the headaches.

"Edward before I met you I knew you were a lucky man. We are quite taken with your wonderful wife. My fear was you wouldn't deserve her. Now, I can see you are well suited for each other." Beverly laughed when she saw Edward's shock at her statement. "I'm known for being outspoken, but truth is truth."

"Mrs. Franklin, when Lydia told me of meeting you on the ship, how you got her and her friends out of steerage, and the captain was taken to task for the deplorable conditions, you became my heroine. Lydia told me you are a formidable woman, and you get things done. I can't tell you how much it means to me that you took Lydia under your wing. I remember well the conditions on the ship and trying to help some of the men guard the women's areas."

Beverly Franklin looked up into Edward's eyes. "You are a decent man, Edward. You will do well in this country."

Just then Stephen danced close by. "Edward, I'm ready to return your lovely wife. I have been bending her ear with unnecessary advice, just as I'm sure Beverly has been bending yours."

Both Edward and Lydia laughed good naturedly. "With our families so far away, I'm forever grateful you stepped in and became my parents for the day." Lydia looked into both of their faces and realized they truly did care for her. Somehow, their feelings of gratitude over her saving Corwin had turned into genuine friendship.

Just then Kathleen approached Lydia. "What a wonderful party! And, Edward, this restaurant has so much potential."

"You're right, Kathleen, if by 'potential' you mean there's a fair amount of work to be done to bring the shine back to it. The previous owner lost hope when prohibition was thrust upon the people of Oregon. As you probably know, it was opened as a bar. Songstad really didn't want to own a restaurant. It actually makes it better for Lydia and me. We can put our own signature on the place."

"Edward's right. I'm very excited about the bakery goods I am going to create for our restaurant. I think we might do a fair amount of business with those items as well. It should keep us going until Edward learns some new recipes."

Edward's face broke into a grin. "She's making fun of me now! I'll have you know, Mrs. O'Brien, my stew is legendary in these parts!"

Johnny and Annie walked up at the right moment. "Legendary!" Johnny bellowed, "Legendary? We had to put him to work in the forest before we all died from too much mutton. We were starting to grow wool on our bodies. We begged him to serve something else!"

Annie nudged Johnny. "Behave yourself. Edward and I have been talking about a new menu. I'm going to help with the cooking while Lydia does the baking. O'Brien's will be the talk of the town soon!"

"I'm sure it will. Stephen and I will have to come again. We'll look forward to sampling the menu!"

Stephen took his wife's arm, "It's time for us to head to our hotel room. It's going to be a very long day tomorrow."

Hugging Lydia closely, Beverly whispered mischievously into her ear. "Remember our talk in New York!"

Lydia's face turned bright red. Edward threw a curious look at Mrs. Franklin but thought it was wiser not to ask.

It was time for the newlyweds to start their honeymoon. The guests stood in front of the restaurant and waved as Bernard pulled away from the curb with the O'Brien's in the backseat. He drove them home and gallantly jumped out of the car and opened the back door for Lydia and Edward.

Edward and Lydia were alone at last. Climbing the five stairs to the front porch of their home, Lydia took Edward's hand. "Can we just sit and look at the stars a bit? This is the first time we've been in your house together. I just want to savor it for a moment."

"You mean our house, my sweet bride. Everything here was done for you." Edward looked at his blushing bride and assessed a bit of nerves on her part. He was just as nervous. He had never looked at another woman the entire time he was away from Lydia. His inexperience worried him.

They sat on the porch looking at the stars and listening to the sounds of the night. Lydia was relieved she had removed all the evidence of last night's KKK visit and prayed there would not be an encore performance. Finally, Lydia reflected on the advice Beverly Franklin gave her in New York. She loved Edward with all her heart and trusted him implicitly. Taking his hand, she walked into their house and led him back to the room with the wild roses, the start of everything.

Chapter 15

Kathleen sat at the breakfast table recounting her day with the O'Brien's and the wedding. Her father was not thrilled that she went, but had given up years ago trying to inflict his will. He was barely listening when all of the sudden, two things caught his attention.

"And then as we approached the restaurant, we had three cars full of people, including the Franklins from New York, and the entire street was lined with Klu Klux Klan. It was horrifying. They just stood there and watched us get out of the cars and go into the restaurant. I was so embarrassed the Franklins had to see it. Father, can't you do something about them?"

"The Franklins came to those people's wedding, all the way from New York?"

"Father, 'those people' have names, Edward and Lydia O'Brien. You've met them!"

"Yes, yes, yes. When are the Franklins leaving? I'd like to meet them."

Kathleen looked at her father. I think you're missing the point Father...the Klu Klux Klan are on our streets. Why would they try to ruin such a lovely day? What have the O'Brien's done to them?"

"I'll deal with that situation later. Right now, I'm calling the hotel and inviting them to lunch. I don't want to miss the opportunity to meet Stephen Franklin. We'll see if they're available before they depart. I need you here, you can introduce us."

Stephen Franklin was less than pleased when a call came through from Harold Parrish. He bristled at the suggestion of lunch, but while Beverly waved at him frantically, he asked Parrish to hold for a moment.

"Stephen, we simply must go. I want to get a look at this man, and you need to find out how dangerous the Klu Klux Klan is here. I didn't get a chance to tell you what they did last night. Lydia confided to me they burnt a cross on their yard. She swore me to secrecy not to tell Edward."

Stephen knew Edward would not leave this place and Lydia was firmly attached to his side. Nothing could dissuade them from staying in Little Creek. Rather than argue with his wife, he agreed to meet Parrish for an early lunch. "Will your charming daughter be with you? We would love to see her again."

"I would be honored if you would come to my home for lunch. Of course Kathleen will be joining us as well as my son Douglas. I'll send a car for you at 11:30."

"Very well, we'll be in the lobby." Stephen put the phone back in the cradle and looked at his wife. "Well, we're stuck now. He's sending a car for us so we won't even be able to make an early exit. At least we can find out how dangerous the KKK is here. It terrifies me Lydia was home alone when they came. Thank God nothing worse happened."

"We can't leave Lydia unprotected in a town teeming with KKK people. I want to hear what Parrish as to say about this."

At precisely 11:30 a.m. a car pulled up in front of the hotel. Whisked away to the Parrish home, Stephen kept giving his wife a pleading look. Inwardly laughing, she returned a look only a couple married for many years can exchange. Stephen sighed, knowing he was stuck being sociable to a backwoods banker.

As the car pulled up to the stately home, Parrish himself walked out the front door, extending his hand to the Franklins. "Pleasure to meet you, Mr. and Mrs. Franklin, please come in. I know we're a little short of time so we'll go directly to the dining room."

As she stepped into the room, Beverly observed the surroundings. Finely crafted furniture decorated the bright sunny room. A beautiful lace tablecloth covered a long table set for four.

Catching her eye, Parrish explained, "My daughter Kathleen will be joining us. She so enjoyed meeting you yesterday. My son Douglas is out for the day. I wasn't able to catch him before he left. I know he'll be sorry to have missed you."

At the mention of her name, Kathleen walked into the dining room, "Hello, Mr. and Mrs. Franklin. It's nice to see you again. Welcome to our home."

Beverly extended her hand and smiled at Kathleen. "You've saved me, my dear. I thought I would be spending the next hour listening to bank talk. It's lovely to see you again."

Kathleen smiled and looked over at Stephen, "I'm sure my father will manage to interject a few banking topics into the conversation, but, actually, he can be quite entertaining when he wants to be."

Parrish smiled good naturedly at his daughter. "Don't listen to her. She's trying to charm me out of something. I'll know about it when she's ready to lower the boom. Come in please and have a seat. The cook has prepared a lovely lunch."

Stephen was starting to relax, when all of the sudden, Beverly got her 'look.' It was the look she always got before she tackled something distasteful. He sighed as she turned to their host.

"Mr. Parrish, I really must ask you. I was quite shocked to see your local Klu Klux Klan parading in the street yesterday. Was this a protest of our dear friend's wedding or is there something else going on in your town?"

Parrish was momentarily deflated. "My family has been in this town for a hundred years. My great grandfather was a founding father. We have always tried to maintain an open mind on immigrants. In fact, your young friend Edward O'Brien reminded me a couple weeks ago this country was founded by immigrants. Something I'm afraid we third and fourth generation Americans seem to forget."

Before Stephen could stop Beverly, she looked Parrish in the eye, "Well, the Klu Klux Klan were a novel touch. People in New York are more tolerant of immigrants. It was rather shocking to see the KKK lining the streets of Little Creek. I understand they also paid a visit to the O'Brien house and burned a cross on their yard."

Parrish was seething inside. He kept himself in check. "I'm so sorry you had to witness the Klu Klux Klan trying to flex their muscle. You must think we are quite a backwater town."

Stephen looked at the banker and knew a tense situation was quickly escalating. "Beverly, let's drop the subject, you're making our host uncomfortable. Mr. Parrish, it is regretful your town has this problem. My bank owns a cement company in New York City and several other cities around the country. The State Highway Commission created by your former Governor Olcott, opened an opportunity for us to expand into Oregon. We're looking for a company with a rock quarry. My meetings in Portland disclosed the company I was interested in doing business with had Klu Klux Klan involvement. It looks like I will have to continue my search in other parts of the state. It's a shame you're faced with the Klan problem. I would have considered your city as a location."

Beverly smiled to herself and thought, *well if that moron Parrish didn't see the carrot he's a bigger idiot than I thought. He'd be a fool not to grab the opportunity Stephen just dangled in front of him.*

Harold Parrish looked at the Franklin's and accessed the situation. He didn't give a rat's ass about the Klu Klux Klan. That was Brookstone and his goons' pastime. Now an opportunity to create more jobs, and make a fortune, was presenting itself. To get rid of the Klu Klux Klan he would have to give Brookstone a piece of the action. With his mind calculating what a new industry would mean to the infrastructure of Little Creek, he addressed his guest. "Mr. Franklin, I'm not sure if you are aware of our natural sand and gravel pits just outside of town. I would be interested in working with your company to provide materials. I know you have a bad impression of our town, but, I assure you, I will make certain the Klu Klux Klan situation is handled."

Beverly could almost see Parrish with the hook in his mouth as he swallowed the bait her husband had so accurately cast out. Looking at Stephen with amusement, she watched the two men.

"Parrish, I would consider doing business with you, if certain conditions are met. I will have Timothy Smyth, my VP of Operations, contact you. My interest in having the Klu Klux Klan out of your town is personal. We think the world of Lydia and her husband. Knowing the Klan paraded purposely on their wedding day is disconcerting, and burning a cross on their front lawn is frightening."

"Franklin, I will handle the Klan. My bank holds the mortgages on almost every house and business in this town. It won't take long to send a message to the offenders."

Kathleen looked at the antique clock above the buffet. "Look at the time. We must get you to the train depot. I'm sorry our visit was so short."

Beverly looked at Kathleen. "You're a very gracious hostess, my dear. It was a pleasure getting to spend more time with you, and, our compliments to the cook."

Parrish folded his napkin and placed it by his plate. Carefully choosing his words, and trying not to look too eager, he stood up, extending his hand to Stephen Franklin. "Thank you both for taking the time to come to our home. I look forward to meeting Mr. Smyth, and I'm confident we can do business together. Mrs. Franklin, I wish you a pleasant journey home."

Beverly looked at Parrish. "Lydia and her husband are very dear to us. Regardless of whether you and my husband do business together, we will be back in Little Creek."

Harold Parrish looked into Beverly Franklin's eyes and knew she would hold him personally responsible if anything were to happen to the O'Brien's. He could tell she swayed her husband on business matters and was not someone to have as an enemy. "Mrs. Franklin, I will look forward to the day you grace our town with your next visit."

Stephen Franklin saw the light glean of sweat along Parrish's brow. It was not the first time his wife had intimidated someone in his position. He thought back to an evening at the White House when she even got the President to sweat a little.

Chapter 16

Stephen Franklin stared at the letter in front of him. Rereading the words he knew he would have to go home and share the letter with his wife. Sadness overtook him as he rose from his desk and buzzed his secretary. "Hildy, cancel my afternoon meetings. I am going home and will not be back until tomorrow morning."

Stephen put the letter in his briefcase and walked out his office door.

Mrs. Hildebrand or Hildy to her boss and friends, had been Stephen's secretary for twenty years. At sixty two she showed no signs of slowing down. Her husband had died years ago, and she had no children. Her gray hair was perfectly coifed and glasses hung on a chain around her neck. Her face was smooth except for the crow's feet around her eyes, caused by her philosophy that laughter made the world go around. As Stephen walked by her desk she raised an eyebrow. "Yes, sir, is everything all right?"

"No, Hildy, but there is nothing you can do to fix it. Mrs. Franklin will have to figure out this problem."

"Sir?"

"Hildy, I'm sorry to be so cryptic. Once I discuss this with Mrs. Franklin, I'm sure she will enlist you to help with the details. Call my driver. I'll be out front."

Thirty minutes later, Stephen Franklin opened his front door and was startled to see his wife on the other side. "Hildy called. She said you were coming home early and you needed me."

"Damn that woman. She is too efficient for her own good. I didn't want to alert you and give you extra time to worry."

"Stephen, what is going on? Spill the beans, now."

Stephen put his briefcase on the credenza and pulled out the letter, handing it to his wife.

"It's from Ireland?" Beverly quickly pulled the letter out of the envelope and walked to the parlor sitting in the sofa. "Oh my, no, this can't be. Both of Lydia's parents were killed? Her sister says an accident but, as you can see, she doesn't elaborate. Lydia hasn't talked much about her family. I know she was sorry they were not at her wedding, but we don't really know much about them or her sister."

Beverly sat deep in thought. "Well, Myra is correct. Had she written to Lydia about their parent's death, the letter would have arrived right about the time of the wedding. What a horrible way to start a new life. Stephen, we must help Myra travel to the United States and then her get to Little Creek. This kind of news will be devastating to Lydia."

"How do you propose we do it? Wire the money?"

"Let me think about it. Knowing the horrors of steerage we need to get her a first class ticket. Darling, when's the last time Hildy had a holiday?"

"No, no, no, you are not taking Hildy. I can't survive without her, and if you ever tell her it will be my undoing."

"Stephen, I can't have this young woman traveling to New York all by herself. We can send Hildy over to Queenstown, meet Myra, and accompany her back here. See, darling, it's very simple."

"Simple for you. I will be two weeks or more without Hildy and my life will be hell. The last time she took a holiday it took her weeks to repair the damage the temporary secretary did. She won't go, Beverly. You'll have to think of something else."

"Nonsense, darling, once the situation is explained, she will be on the next ship."

Stephen resigned himself to the fact his wife was an organizer, and protesting would do no good.

"Now, Stephen, should we telegraph Myra or send a letter?"

Chapter 17

Myra was walking home after a long day at her father's bakery. Her shoulders were slumped in defeat. It had been six weeks since she had sent the letter to Lydia's patrons. Coming up to her house, she saw the postman with a big smile on his face.

"Well, missy, you have a big important looking letter from New York. Is it from your sister?"

Myra grabbed the envelope and ran into the house. Sitting on her bed, she ripped open the letter to see a first class ticket and a letter.

> Dear Miss Delaney,
>
> We are so sorry for the loss of your parents. Our hearts go out to you and Lydia. It was considerate of you not to write your sister with this sad news. Upon our return from her wedding, we received your letter. I'm so relieved the tragedy did not mar her wedding day.

Myra let out an angry shriek, "Damn her, I would loved to have marred her wedding day."

A first class ticket is enclosed. The ship will sale on July 17th. If you have not concluded your parents' estate and need more time, please telegraph immediately. If not, we will meet your ship in New York on July 24th. While you will be perfectly safe in First Class, it is simply not acceptable to us for you make this journey alone, in light of your recent sorrow. We are sending our trusted employee and friend, Mrs. Hildebrand, to chaperone your trip. She will meet you on board the ship. We will help you make your travel plans to Oregon. Our thoughts and prayers are with you during this difficult time.

Sincerely,
Stephen and Beverly Franklin

Myra finished reading the letter and her face lit up in glee. She laughed and thought how easy it had been to collect on Lydia's good-will with these people. Now she had to figure out how to leave her parents' home without their knowing she had deceived the Franklins. She had two weeks to figure it out.

The next day, Myra put her plan into action. She had thought carefully and realized she needed to get her parents out of the way. Her father was a fool if he thought she didn't know where he hid her money. Myra knew her father would be happy to get her out of the house, but there was no way he would allow her to go to America and possibly ruin Lydia's happiness. With her ma giving her cautious sideways looks and her father stepping lightly, she knew her final plans had to be carefully set.

Myra had been cultivating Godfrey as her dupe. It was child's play actually. He would come to the shop and sit on a stool, watching Myra wait on customers. He always waited to visit after Myra's father had left for the day. Mr. Delaney started baking at 2 a.m. every morning and at noon went home for lunch and a nap. Myra realized after the second visit, having a Black and Tan hanging around the shop was bad for business and word would eventually get back to her da.

"Godfrey, it's dangerous for both of us for you to sit in the shop while I work."

Devastated, Godfrey looked at Myra with imploring eyes. "I-I-I-I li-li-like seeing y-y you."

"Oh Godfrey, I like seeing you too. We must be careful. My parents can't see me with you. Meet me after work down on the corner and you can walk me home."

Smiling, Godfrey walked out of the shop with a spring in his step that almost made Myra laugh out loud.

Myra let Godfrey walk her home every night for a week. It was easy enough to get away from her neighborhood, and Godfrey had the sense not to meet her wearing his uniform. On the eighth night, Myra burst into tears. Startled and confused, Godfrey stammered out "M-m-m-myra, wh-wh-wh-whatever is w-w-wrong?"

It was the opening she needed. "Oh, Godfrey, it's terrible and I can't tell you. They will hurt me."

Godfrey was worried and wanted to help Myra. He was already smitten with her. "Y-y-y-you mmmust te-te-tell mm-m-me. I'll d-d-do any th-th-thing f-f-f-or you."

Myra bit her smile back. *Of course you will.* She turned to him, big tears running down her cheeks. "Oh, Godfrey, I'm so afraid. My parents are monsters and they are consorting with very unsavory characters. I fear for my safety. I haven't slept well in days. They have meetings all night long and sometimes these fellows try to get in my room."

"F-F-fellows? Wh-wh-what f-f-fellows?"

"My parents make me leave the room. I've tried to listen. They keep talking about getting their revenge on the British. I'm so scared. I don't want to be part of what they're doing and those men scare me."

Godfrey had been a soldier in His Majesty's Army for almost five years. He knew all about the politics in Ireland and had served there for two years, most recently assigned to Myra's town. Despite his speech problem, he had a clever mind and was a highly valued soldier. Listening to Myra, he knew something big was happening. A plot was afoot and he had to solve it.

"Do y-y-you h-h-have a pl-place to go to? A r-r-r relative?"

"No, I can't trust anyone in the village. My parents have too many connections. I just need to get away before they do something terrible and I'm blamed, too. I worry so much that you'll be hurt, Godfrey. I'm scared for you and all the British soldiers. I have a cousin in Queenstown that I trust, but I can't pay for a ticket. My da takes all of my money. He's afraid I'll run away like my sister did to get away from them."

Godfrey, emboldened by her declaration of worry for his safety, pulled her close. He whispered into her ear words of comfort. He would save her. "M-M-M-Myra, I h-h- have s-s-s-some m-m-money sa-sa-saved. I ca-ca-can buy y-y-you a r-r-rou-rou round trip t-t-ticket to Que-Que-Queenstown. I'll ma make su-su-sure th-th this pr-pr problem is fi-fi-fixed, I pr-pr-promise. Wh-wh-when can you be r-r-ready to g-g-go?"

"Oh, Godfrey, you would do this for me? You hardly know me." Adding more convincing tears to her act, Myra clutched him close. "I knew there was something special about you the minute I saw you, I'm so grateful."

Godfrey swelled with pride. He had a beautiful girl in his arms, and only he could save her.

"C-c-can you p-p-pack y-y-your cl-cl-clothes wi-without you're p-p-parents seeing you?"

"Oh yes, Godfrey." She favored him with a smile as the tears glistened in her icy blue eyes. Knowing her mother and father would be playing cards on Thursday evening and her ship sailed on Saturday, she looked at him. "I don't have a suitcase. I'll have to see if I can find one. It will take a couple days. Someone might tell my parents."

Godfrey looked at her, noting the worry lines streaking across her forehead. "I h-h-have a su-su-suitcase, you ca-ca-can bo-borrow it."

"You are too good to me. Can you bring the suitcase tomorrow night? I can pack and sneak it out. Then I can catch the train to Queenstown to my cousin Mary's."

Godfrey knew he had to save her. He also had surmised, based on the information she had given him, the young men meeting with her father must be IRA. It was his duty to save her and to stop the IRA from future strikes against the British Army.

The next day, Godfrey went to his superior officers alerting them there was an IRA plot afoot. After three hours of discussion, a raid was planned for the following evening. Based on the Intel Myra had given him, Godfrey knew her parents would be gone from six to eight, and the hoodlums they were working with usually showed up at 9 p.m. He planned on getting Myra on the evening train to Queenstown before the raid, knowing if everything went off as planned, the British Army would quell another IRA cell. Once her parents were under wraps, it would be safe for Myra to return, and he would be there to help her.

Myra walked into her parent's bedroom. Her da had no imagination when it came to hiding things. She rifled through his dresser drawers until she found a sock stuffed with her money. Digging a little farther, she found another sock heavy with money. Grabbing both, she raced to her bedroom, stuffing the suitcase Godfrey had loaned her.

Casting a final look at her childhood home, she hurried down the lane without a backward glance.

Godfrey was waiting with a car. Rushing out to put her suitcase in the boot, he gave her a fast hug. "A-a-are y-y-you OK?"

"Oh, Godfrey, I'm so scared. Please hurry. Let's get out of here before we're seen."

Godfrey put the car in gear and drove to the train station. He was bereft that it would be several days before he saw her again, but knowing she was safe was all he cared about.

"I bo-bo-bought you a r-r-r-round tttt-trip ticket. A-a-are y-y-you s-s-sure your cousin Mary w-w-will let you stay with her?"

Myra smiled to herself. Imaginary people were the easiest to manipulate. "Yes, I know she will. I sent her a note two weeks ago letting her know there were problems in the village. I'll be safe and will return once you write me everything is alright. I just feel so terrible to be imposing on Mary. My da keeps all of my money, and I won't be able to help Mary with expenses."

"D-d-don't worry. H-H-Here."

Myra took the envelope from his hand. Inside was a wad of pounds. Looking into his trusting eyes, she smiled. "Oh Godfrey, you're just too good to be true. Thank you so much."

Arriving at the train station, they timed it so Myra would go from the car to the train to minimize the chance of her being observed. It was dangerous for her to be seen with a British soldier. Myra turned to Godfrey and graced him with a kiss on the lips. "Thank you so much." She handed him a slip of paper. "Here's Mary's address. You'll let me know when it is safe to return?"

Flustered by the kiss, Godfrey could only nod. Tears were starting to glisten in his eyes.

Myra squeezed his hand. "I must go Godfrey. Please pull my suitcase out of the boot. I can carry it to the train."

One last hug and she was off without another thought of the man who had facilitated her escape. She was looking forward, already anticipating the surprised look on Lydia's face.

Myra boarded the train and sat in the first class seat Godfrey had purchased for her. It was almost too easy to get him to help dispose of her parents. Detaining them would make it easy for her to get away. It never occurred to Myra her parents might be relieved at her departure.

Arriving in Queenstown, Myra hired a cab to take her to a hotel downtown. So far she had spent none of the money she had saved, and Godfrey had added another thirty pounds to her pot.

Checking into the hotel, Myra luxuriated in her room, touching the bedspread, feeling the fabric, and testing the lush bed. Until Lydia had run off, the sisters had always shared a room and this hotel room bore no resemblance to their mismatched one at home.

Lying in her bed, her fists clenched, she thought to herself, *Lydia will be paying a pretty price for marrying Edward. If I had gotten there first, he would have married me. She'll be sorry to see me.*

The next day Myra woke with purpose. She had to have some decent clothes, or she was going to look very out of place in her first class cabin on the ship.

The streets of Queenstown were crowded. People were arriving early, queuing up to board the ship for America. Myra looked dismissively out her window at the people who were obviously passengers in steerage. When she asked at the hotel about boarding time, the clerk gave her the once over and was about to remark she should already be lining up for steerage when his eyes widened at the first class ticket. "Miss, the ship sails at 4 p.m. First class can board any time. Normally, checkout for the hotel is 12 p.m. However, we have no bookings for your room if you would like to stay a bit longer." Puffing up to his full height of 5'6, he continued, "I'll authorize it."

Looking at the clerk, Myra realized she did not meet the image of a first class customer. Myra batted her long lashes, "I've a bit of shopping to do before I check out. Please hold the room. You have been ever so thoughtful."

Myra walked along the streets lined with stores. There were so many to choose from, not like home. Finding a ladies' dress shop, she tentatively opened the door with a sign proudly stating in gold letters, "Mrs. Anita Bonner, Proprietor."

A woman Myra presumed was Mrs. Bonner sat behind a sewing machine, her mouth full of straight pins. She eyed Myra, noticing the bone structure and her perfect figure. Seeing that the young ladies clothes was not what her regular customers wore, Mrs. Bonner sighed, thinking this was going to be a waste of her time. Pasting a smile on her face she addressed Myra. "Good afternoon, how can I help you?"

Myra could read the boredom on the woman's face, "I'll soon be boarding the President Adams for America. I need some proper dresses for a first class passenger."

Mrs. Bonner gave the girl a closer look. "Well now, I usually do custom dresses for my clients, but I do have a small assortment of dresses we could look through. You look to be a standard size. Let's take a look, shall we?"

Taking Myra to the back of the store, she started pulling dresses off a rack. "This color would match your eyes. It would be good for day wear. Here's a lovely dress that would do for dinner. What do you think?"

Looking at the dresses, Myra was overwhelmed. It was if the designs in her head had been sewn. The dresses were beautiful, but far too dear for the money she had to spend. "They're lovely, but I'm afraid these might be a little more than I can afford."

"Oh now, dearie, you must think of this as an investment. You will be meeting all sorts of upper crust people on the ship. You'll need to look your best."

Myra did some quick calculations. She was money ahead with what Godfrey had given her and what she took from her da, plus her own nest egg. So far she had only spent money on the hotel. Once she reached Oregon, she would be on her own. She held no illusions Lydia would welcome her. She would need to have money to support herself if necessary. Then, in a moment of clarity, Myra knew she could always find someone to look after her. Godfrey had shown her how easy it was. Mrs. Bonner was quite correct. These dresses were an investment in her future.

The dress was made of sky blue silk with a drop waist, bell sleeves, and a slim silhouette. Being on the thin side, Myra tried on the dress and was amazed at what the style did for her figure.

"Oh, miss, it's like the dress was made for you. This is the latest style from America. I read all the magazines and copy the dresses. These haven't sold because the women here are too traditional, but Miss, you were born for this style."

Myra looked at her reflection. She, too, had looked at magazines to imitate their style, and she knew her hair was all wrong. It was long and in a top knot. If she was going to America, she would need to change from the little Irish girl to a woman of the world. Looking at Mrs. Bonner, she turned her back to the woman. "Help me out of this one. I want to try on the evening dress." The dress was elegant but understated. It was trimmed in lace and the lush emerald green was cut to emphasize a woman's hips. The material didn't just move it flowed. Myra stood transfixed in front of the mirror. *Well if this doesn't turn a few heads, nothing will.*

"I'll take both of these. I'll wear the blue one now. Please wrap my dress and the green dress."

Mrs. Bonner beamed with pleasure. For a moment, she considered offering the girl a discount but caught a calculating look in Myra's eyes and decided against it.

"Well, lassie, you will be the bell of the ball. I pity the man who falls under your spell, he will be helpless."

Myra got a shrewd look on her face. "That's the plan, Mrs. Bonner.

Leaving the shop Myra walked straight into the hair salon on the corner by the hotel.

"I want my hair bobbed. Is there someone who could do it now?" Myra peered down at the woman behind the reception desk. Her hair was in a sleek bob with bangs that emphasized her big brown eyes.

"Hello, my name is Brenda. I have some time before my next customer."

Guiding Myra to a chair, Brenda wrapped a barber's cloth around Myra and pulled the pins out. Myra's hair was long and sleek.

"Oh, Miss, your hair is perfect for a bob. It has just the right texture, and it is nice and straight."

Myra had always envied Lydia's beautiful curls, but now she was going to be the one envied. "Cut away, Brenda. I've a ship to catch."

As Brenda made the first cut, Myra let out a gasp as a twelve-inch lock of hair fell to the floor. Steeling herself, Myra watched Brenda cut away.

An hour later, Myra emerged from the salon looking like a fashion model. Her hair was feathered with bangs around her eyes and the bob fell just below her perfect jaw line. Her eyes looked twice as big, and Brenda had suggested a light brow tweezing, shaping her eyebrows into perfect arches above her blue eyes.

Surveying the results in the mirror, Myra smiled broadly. "Oh, this will do just fine."

Brenda looked at the young woman she had transformed. "Miss, I wouldn't know you as the same person."

"Well that will certainly come in handy, too." Myra chuckled as she got up from the chair. She paid Brenda, and, collecting her packages, she waltzed out of the parlor heading to the hotel.

When she walked up to the desk clerk to retrieve her key, the desk clerk looked up. It took him a second to realize this was the same little Irish girl who left two hours ago.

"Well, Miss, as they say in America, Va Va Va Boom!"

Laughing, Myra said "Va Va Va Boom! What a wonderful saying! I've a lot to be learning about America and all their lovely phrases."

Collecting her key, she told the clerk to have someone come get her luggage. She was ready to board the ship and meet the waiting Mrs. Hildebrand.

Myra smoothed her hair and climbed the gangway to the first class section as a well groomed older woman approached her.

Hildy had been studying the young woman as she walked up the gangway. She certainly resembled Lydia, but this young woman looked more like a model than someone from a small village suffering from the recent loss of her parents. Her face was radiant and a smug smile curved her lips.

"Myra Delaney I presume? I'm Mrs. Hildebrand. I will be your chaperone for the crossing to New York."

Myra took a moment to look the woman over before she replied. Now was not the time to alienate this woman. Especially when she did not know how she was related to the Franklins.

"Tis' a pleasure to meet you, Mrs. Hidebrand. It is so kind of you to be my chaperone."

"Ah, dear girl, I am happy to be here. I've been in need of a little holiday and this was a fine opportunity. Although the fact it comes due to your family tragedy saddens me greatly. My condolences on the untimely loss of your mother and father."

An odd look crossed over Myra's face before she replied, "Thank you, Mrs. Hildebrand. It has been quite a trying time." Myra managed to muster up a smile, but it did not reach her eyes.

Hildy looked the girl over. She did not seem to be in the throws of grief. Her complexion was smooth and unwrinkled. She looked well-rested and, while a bit thin, did not appear to be suffering any anxiety. Her dress was stylish and obviously new.

"What a beautiful dress, my dear. It becomes you."

Myra had the decency to blush and instantly realized her mistake. This woman was expecting a poor little Irish girl devastated by grief. "Thank you very much. I didn't have much left over from our parents after things were settled and I was so sad. I bought this dress and another to wear at dinner. I was worried I would be an embarrassment to the Franklins." Myra managed to muster up a couple of tears making her opening act complete.

"Oh, my dear, don't you worry about a thing. In fact, Mrs. Franklin anticipated you might need to add to your wardrobe. You'll be happy to know there is a wonderful store on board the ship. We'll go visit it after we get you settled."

"Mrs. Hildebrand, you are too kind. I am forever indebted to you and the Franklins for helping me get to my dear sister. Do you know how she is doing?"

"Mrs. and Mrs. Franklin attended her wedding last month. They were pleased with her husband Edward and told me it was a perfect match. The O'Brien's are doing very well."

If she hadn't been looking right at Myra, as she said the words, Hildy would have missed the reaction. Myra's eyes turned cold and, for an instant, her look was murderous, then she carefully schooled her face back to the angelic look she had first presented to Hildy.

"I'm so anxious to see my sister and dear Edward." Myra's voice was flat and her eyes were dead.

Hildy looked at Myra and knew there was more going on than was obvious. Wondering what she was really seeing in this young woman, Hildy smiled at Myra and said, "Let's go our stateroom and get you settled in. Then we can see what items you'll need from the store to complement your wardrobe."

Myra smiled sweetly and did her best to look like a complacent, grief-stricken young woman. Her only tell was the shrewd look in her eyes calculating just how much she could take the Franklins for.

Hildy studied Myra. The young woman looked like a Cheshire cat. Her smile was self absorbed, and her beautiful face looked chilling as the women sat reading in the parlor of their stateroom. *Myra couldn't be more the opposite of her sister if she tried.* Hildy thought to herself. *She sure doesn't look like someone whose parents have just died.*

Myra smiled at Hildy, "Thank you for taking me shopping today. It is very generous of Mr. and Mrs. Franklin to pay my way to America and to buy me clothes. I don't know how to thank them."

"You can thank Lydia. It is their debt of gratitude to your sister that has been extended to you."

"Mrs. Hildebrand, our Lydia is so modest. She never fully explained how she saved the child. In fact, she barely mentioned it to us."

"Well, dear, you'll have plenty of time to hear about it. I'm sure Mrs. Franklin will tell the story, and when you reach Oregon, you'll have to pry the story out of Lydia. As you said, she's such a modest girl."

Myra bristled at the compliment for her sister. She was sick to death of constantly hearing about Lydia, Lydia, Lydia. "I think I'll take a quick nap before it's time to dress for dinner, Mrs. Hildebrand."

"Yes, dear, I'm sure you're exhausted after all you have been through the past few weeks. This is your time to rest and recuperate."

Myra smiled and walked into her bedroom. She couldn't believe her luck, "I've fallen into the lap of luxury. I'm not about to give this up if I can help it."

Looking at herself one more time in the mirror, she fingered her short hair. She loved her new look. Striking several poses, she smiled at herself in the mirror. She was ready for a new life.

Two hours later, Mrs. Hildebrand and Myra walked into the dining room. The self assurance Myra felt only hours ago evaporated instantly. The room was filled with elegant men and women dressed in their evening finery and chatting with one another. A maitre de showed them to their table, pulling out the chair for both Mrs. Hildebrand and Myra.

Myra's look of fear actually endeared her to Hildy. Placing her hand over the girl's, she gave it a quick squeeze whispering, "Don't worry, dear, they don't bite. Just be your charming self and you'll be fine."

Myra glanced down at the table setting. She had never seen so many utensils by a plate before. She had no idea what to do.

Hildy saw her look and whispered, "Just watch what everyone else does and copy them." She was actually relieved to see Myra's hard shell of self confidence crack a little.

The table seated six people. Two men, one older and the other in his early thirties were introduced as Mr. Marcus Vautrin and his son James, who was seated next to Myra. *Well, maybe this trip will be more interesting than I anticipated,* James thought as he gave Myra a quick appraising look.

For once in her life, Myra was tongue-tied, blushing furiously and looking down at her plate. The last two diners were a couple returning from their honeymoon abroad. Justine Driscoll was a plain little thing who reminded Myra of a bird. Her nose was a bit beaked and her arms moved in fluttery motions. Her brown eyes darted from person to person as she spoke. Myra was amused to notice her husband hung onto every word and his fingers continually touched his wife's arm in some sort of marriage Morse code. Mrs. Driscoll would look over and smile at her husband and, for a moment, her plain face was almost pretty.

Myra realized everyone at the table was American and her accent stood out like a sore thumb. She sat quietly and absorbed the conversation, the nuances of words, and how Americans gestured a great deal when they spoke.

James Vautrin did his best to engage Myra in conversation. She politely responded to his questions but only spoke when spoken to. James thought it was charming that she was so shy, not realizing Myra was a changeling busy absorbing the language.

Mrs. Hildebrand was nobody's fool. Her late husband had been a cop, and she'd seen and heard a lot during their ten year marriage. His death had not stopped her fascination with people. Because he respected her instincts, Stephen Franklin never failed to introduce her to a new client. Her read on people had saved him many times. She could never explain how she knew. It was something in their eyes. The way their mouth turned with certain words. Sometimes it was a simple gesture, but her instincts were never off. Stephen relied on her, and he was not going to be happy when they landed and she reported her observations.

She joined a long string of people that knew something wasn't quite right with Myra. At times her eyes would go flat, almost dead. Hildy observed this whenever she mentioned Lydia or Edward's name. At other times Myra's laughter was just a little too gay, almost maniacal.

What fascinated Hildy the most was the transformation of the seemingly shy little Irish girl. The first night at dinner, Hildy watched with astonishment as Myra mimicked how people held their forks and how they interacted with the waiter. By the second day, Myra's Irish lilt had started to change into a barely distinguishable accent. Her ability to copy dialects was uncanny.

Hildy watched and waited, never letting on that she saw anything amiss. Trusting her instincts, she sent a telegram from the ship to her employers.

"Something is not right stop Are you sure her story is true stop Worried for Lydia and Edward stop"

Hildy knew how dear Lydia was to the Franklins, and her employer was dear to her. She was determined to get to the bottom of this little charade before the ship landed in New York.

While Myra was languishing aboard The President Adams, her parents were in a British prison. Mr. Delaney had been subjected to intensive questioning. He had hours and hours of people screaming at him, occasional punches to the face, and water thrown on him. He had lost weight, his hair was starting to fall out from stress, and he was in fear of his life. He couldn't understand what had brought this all on.

"I haven't done anything. Please you have to let me know if my wife and daughter are all right."

It had been nearly a week. He had no idea where his wife and Myra were. He was confused and losing control. He wept, "Please, I haven't done anything. Why are you holding me?"

"We have it on good authority you are a member of the IRA and are plotting against the British government." The clipped British accent of Captain Withers spat out the words. Withers was in his early forties and tired of this backwater assignment. He wanted to be where the action was. Breaking this prisoner and getting information was his ticket out. Withers mopped his brow and balding head.

"I don't even know anyone in the IRA. I'm a baker."

"Well you can just sit in prison and rot until you decide to tell us who the others are. Who are the young men you meet with nightly?"

"What men? What are you talking about? Ask my wife or my daughter. There are no meetings."

Withers was starting to smell a rat; most prisoners would have broken by now. Delaney kept asking about his wife and daughter.

He obviously didn't know his daughter was safely tucked away in Queenstown.

"Get Aldridge in here. Something doesn't smell right."

Withers spent an hour painfully going over the information that Godfrey Aldridge had given him. Aldridge was driving him mad with his stuttering. He was ready to beat the man about the head to get the words out faster. Finally, he decided to have Godfrey sit in while he interviewed Mrs. Delaney.

Mrs. Delaney was hollow-eyed. After almost a week of not knowing the fate of her husband or daughter, she had retreated into silence and shook uncontrollably in her chair. She tried to ignore the two men who stood over her. They sat staring at the woman who had aged ten years in just days.

"Mrs. Delaney, you can save yourself and your husband. Give us the names of the men your husband has been meeting with every night."

Staring silently at the men, her lips cracked, she struggled to form the words. "There are no men. Where is my daughter?"

Godfrey couldn't stand seeing the pain in her eyes. "Myra is safe with her cousin Mary in Queenstown."

Mrs. Delaney turned and looked at the two men. Tears streamed down her face. "It looks like all of us have been played by the girl. She doesn't have a cousin in Queenstown. I'll bet she's on her way to America."

Godfrey turned white. Based on the interviews of the Delaney's neighbors, and the fact neither of them had deviated from their story in a week, he suspected she was right. Godfrey slumped in his chair. Myra was gone and he knew in his bones she had played him for a fool.

Withers looked over at the young officer. He knew what he suspected was correct. These people had been thrown to the British Army as a diversion so Godfrey's little tart could run off to America. Heads were going to roll on this one. Withers had to make sure his was not one of them.

Chapter 18

L ydia settled into Little Creek with an ease that surprised Edward. He expected her to be homesick for her parents and family, instead, Lydia relished the freedom. The burden of always pleasing her parents or trying to protect herself from Myra had been lifted. She was experiencing profound joy and happiness in starting her new life with Edward.

Lydia's years working for her father benefited the O'Brien's Restaurant. Word of the homemade buns and other savory items spread. Annie and Edward had revamped the menu creating a home-style cuisine that was affordable and delectable. Soon their business was booming with loggers as well as families filling the tables.

People were drawn to Lydia. Her good nature and humor endeared customers and Edward stood in awe at the transformation. The stubborn young girl with the wicked tongue had grown into a self-assured young woman with a keen head for business. After listening to the stories of her childhood with Myra, Edward realized the 8,000 miles separating them was a security blanket for Lydia. Her fears were abating, and he was grateful for her peace of mind.

Edward found Lydia kneading dough in the corner of the kitchen she called her headquarters. He stood behind her, wrapping his arms around her waist. "You smell like sugar."

Laughing she turned to face her husband. "You're just now realizing how sweet I am, are you?"

Edward looked into her eyes. He could tell when she had one of her headaches. He could see the pupil in one eye was slightly larger. Lydia had never told him of her injury aboard the ship. Beverly Franklin had pulled him aside and said how worried she was and insisted he make sure Lydia rest frequently and not overdo. What she didn't tell him was how to persuade a headstrong woman, who didn't know he knew about her headaches, how to rest often.

"You look tired, love. Why don't I make you a nice cup of tea and you can put your feet up for a bit."

Lydia looked up at her husband. She had sworn both Bernard and Annie to secrecy about her headaches. She did not want to add worries to Edward's already full plate. Starting a new restaurant, buying a house, and getting married were enough of a change. Thinking to herself, *Edward needn't know about my headaches. I'm getting better. I must, I'm almost out of my headache medicine.*

"Edward, my darling, I'll just put the finishing touches on these rolls and we can both take a few minutes."

Seeing the smile on his face and the warm kiss he bestowed on her, she giggled a bit. "Oh, I see, were you thinking of taking tea at home?"

Beverly Franklin had been right. Her advice to trust her instincts and her husband in their marriage bed was the best thing she could have said. Lydia smiled to herself and the memory of her honeymoon night only four weeks before. The shyness they had experienced lasted only minutes, and every day the comfort of each other's body reached a new height.

One night while lying in Edward's arms, Lydia giggled. "Beverly Franklin is a very wise woman."

When questioned by Edward, she repeated Beverly's words. To her astonishment, her husband had a tear fall down his cheek onto her naked back as he hugged her close.

"Aye, she is a wise woman. I bet if you had asked your ma you would have received a much different answer. Mr. Franklin gave me a word or two at our reception, much of it the same as his wife. They are a wonderful couple, and, from what I observed, have a good strong partnership marriage. Then after he gives me the tender advice, he tells me to be sure not to break you. I thought he meant physically, and, for a moment, it scared me that such a thing was possible. He must have seen the look on my face because he laughed and said, 'No, Edward, don't break her spirit. You have a fine woman with thoughts and ideas. She is incredibly brave. Don't take such a woman for granted. Make sure you appreciate her mind as well as her body'."

Remembering that night, Edward tipped Lydia's face up to his and whispered, "I'm blessed. I'm blessed and now I need you to rest for just a bit my darlin'. I don't want you working so hard."

Looking into Edward's eyes, Lydia saw them tinged with worry. She suspected he knew of her headaches, but this is one area of total honesty she was determined to ignore. "I'll sit down for a cup of tea and I'll write a quick letter to Ma and Da. I haven't had a letter from them in two weeks.

Edward had never kept a secret from his big sister Rosie in his entire life. So it was with reluctance he skirted the issue of Myra and her treatment of Lydia. Lydia had sworn him to secrecy, and he did not want to betray her trust. However, in his heart he felt the business with Myra was far from over. Soon after Lydia's arrival, Edward had written Rosie to ask her to keep him up on the news of the Delaney family. He was totally unprepared for her telegram.

"Lydia's parents are in jail **stop** Accused of aiding the IRA **stop** Myra is missing **stop** Believed she made her way to Queenstown **stop** Mailman said she received thick envelope from New York **stop** Thought the name on envelope was a bank **stop** Will let you know if I hear more **stop** Keep Lydia safe **stop** Love Rosie **stop**"

Edward read the last part and knew his older sister had read between the lines in his letters to her. When he started courting Lydia, she had said, "Better her than the younger sister. There's something not quite right in the head with that one."

Now he had to figure out how to break the news to Lydia, and also find out how the Franklins had become involved with his wife's sister.

Lydia was in the kitchen of the restaurant making dinner rolls when Annie walked in the back door. Looking up Lydia stopped kneading the dough and broke into a big dimpled smile. "Annie, you're up to something, and I actually believe you are walking on air. You'd best tell me right now!"

"Johnny asked me to marry him. It was so wonderful. We were out strolling in the park. He had me sit on the park bench, and he got down on one knee. He told me I was the love of his life and would I please be his wife."

Lydia hugged her friend, "We've a wedding to plan! Have you set a date?"

Annie's face clouded over. "I'm having a problem. Johnny's not a Catholic, and I don't know if Father Murphy will marry us in the church. My aunt will have a fit if we don't have a Catholic ceremony."

Lydia understood her friend's dilemma. "You know, Annie. I've heard of people getting married in the sacristy instead of the church. It's still a Catholic wedding and should satisfy your aunt. Johnny would have to promise to raise your children as Catholics."

"Lydia, that's a fabulous idea. Johnny and I will go talk to Father Murphy before we break the news to my aunt. In fact, maybe we'll bring the priest to my aunt's house. At least when she tries to kill Johnny, Father Murphy can give her absolution!"

The two young women started giggling, and when Edward walked in his mood lifted to see his wife having a lighthearted moment. "What kind of mischief do you two have going on?"

Annie impulsively hugged Edward. "I think I have you to thank. My Johnny proposed last night."

Edward let out a yell. "It's about time. He told me he was going to, but he wouldn't say when. After all this time, does that man of yours not believe I am capable of keeping a secret? I'll have to give him a smack on the head when I see him."

Annie grabbed his hand, "He knows you can keep a secret. He just didn't think you should keep one from Lydia."

Edward and Lydia both looked guilty. Working side by side with the young couple, Annie knew there were some things they needed to discuss, and now was the perfect time. "I have some things to attend to out in the dining area." Annie made a quick exit.

Edward looked at his wife and saw tears in her eyes. He couldn't hold his tongue. "Darlin', I know about your headaches. I've been waiting for you to tell me yourself. Why are you keeping them a secret from me?"

Tears were coming down Lydia's face. "I was trying to protect you. With your injury, taking out a loan with the bank, and all the preparations for getting the restaurant ready, I didn't want to add to your burdens."

"Oh, Lydia, you are not a burden. I just want you to let me take care of you." Holding his wife close, he kissed her hair. He was not expecting her next words.

"Edward, you need to tell me about the telegram."

Edward pushed back. "How do you know about the telegram?"

"Because the Western Union boy came to our house first and wouldn't leave it with me. I sent him to the restaurant. I've been waiting two days for you to tell me what was in it."

Edward looked chagrined, "I could take a lesson from Johnny on not keeping secrets. I was trying to protect you, just like you were trying to protect me. I've kept it in my wallet all this time. I was trying to get up the nerve to show it to you, but first I was working on getting some answers."

"Give it to me. It must be horrible news judging by the look on your face."

Edward reached into his pocket, pulled out his wallet, and extracted the dreaded telegram. Handing it to his wife, he grabbed her other hand. "We will get through this. I will do whatever it takes to keep you safe."

Lydia unfolded the telegram. When she finished reading it she looked at Edward. "Oh, dear God, what has she done now? How could you not tell me? Edward, how could you not?"

"I called Beverly and Stephen. They said she sent a letter to the Bank. It was around the time we got married. She claimed your parents had died in an accident and she needed to tell her 'dear sister' in person. She told them the news was too terrible to write in a letter. Myra wrote how close the two of you are, and how she was going to start her new life with us in Oregon."

The color drained from Lydia's face. "But why would they help her? They don't even know her?"

Edward had cursed the Franklins a thousand times since getting the news. Then he realized how much they loved Lydia and thought they were doing the right thing for her. "Ah, Lydia, we can't blame them. I've tried, but Stephen and Beverly did it because they thought they were helping you."

"Will I never be rid of her? I thought we would have our lives together in America free from her insanity. And my parents, oh dear God, what has happened to them?"

149

"I called the Franklins two days ago. When I explained the situation to them, they had one of their European banking partners send a security man to British headquarters in Tipperary where your parents were being held. He got there just as they were being released. I wanted to wait until I had actual news before I told you. I heard from Stephen this morning. Your parents are home and they're badly shaken up. They were interrogated for almost a week, but finally the Black and Tan's case against them fell apart. One of their officers finally admitted to giving Myra money to go stay with her cousin Mary in Queenstown."

"Cousin? We have no cousins in Queenstown and no cousin named Mary."

"Yes, once the British figured they'd been duped, they released your parents."

"Edward, what do we do now? Where is Myra?"

"Myra is on a ship heading into New York harbor. She arrives in two days."

"She could be here in another ten days."

"Stephen told me his secretary, Mrs. Hildebrand, is traveling with Myra. He received a telegram from her three days into the cruise alerting them something was not quite right with Myra's story and to check it out."

"Saints preserve us. My sister is on a mission and it is to get to me. She's dangerous and, based on what she just did to our parents; Myra is showing she has no conscience. At last my ma and da will see what I've seen in her all these years. I met Mrs. Hildebrand when I was in New York. She's a dear lady. The Franklins must make sure she's safe!"

Edward looked at his wife, her despair was evident. "We'll call the Franklins. We'll get her stopped at customs. I'm sure the British would like to get their hands on her."

Lydia looked out the back window of the kitchen. A far away look was in her eyes. "Valerie said on the ship how one incident had a domino effect and could change lives. At the time, we were marveling how saving the Franklin's grandson had changed all of our lives. Now I can see it's like a rock thrown in the water. The rings just keep going farther and farther and changing people's lives. Stephen told me a banker friend, a Mr. Andrew Mellon, always used to say, 'No good deed goes unpunished.' It's a frightful thought isn't it? Is Myra going to be my punishment for saving the Franklin's grandson?"

"They'll get her, I promise. Or I'll get her myself. Meanwhile, we're going to start being a little smarter about locking doors and making sure someone is always with you." Edward walked to the back door and locked it. The need to physically ward off danger was a primal response.

Lydia straightened her shoulders and looked her husband in the eye. "Myra bullied me my entire life and I let her. I was so afraid of rocking the boat and not being the perfect daughter, but I'm under no illusions I will be the perfect wife. I will take your strength and use it, but I am not going to alter our lives for her. I'm not hiding behind locked doors. I'm not going to shut out our friends and neighbors."

Edward looked down at his hands, and thought about how he would like to put them around Myra's neck. It frightened him that he could actually contemplate killing someone. Listening to the stories of his wife's childhood and all the "accidents" Myra had arranged for Lydia enraged him. Edward knew in his heart if she came to Little Creek, he would do anything to protect Lydia, and if it was murder, so be it.

Chapter 19

Harold Parrish never ceased to be amazed at how money was such a guaranteed motivator. After Stephen Franklin dangled the concrete contract under his nose, Harold was determined to make good on his promise to eradicate the Klu Klux Klan from Little Creek. Knowing Brookstone would be a problem, he devised a plan to partner up with him and kill two birds with one stone. He and Brookstone owned the two quarries outside of town. Their fathers had purchased the land for a song thirty years ago and had done nothing with it. Now, with the new highway contracts and bridges being built in Oregon, these two quarries were a key element in Parrish's plan.

Calvin Brookstone was an intelligent man, but his biggest flaw was his bigotry. It would take some fancy footwork to get him on board with stopping the Klu Klux Klan activity in their town. Dangling the concrete contract and the projected money they would make was the first step. Calvin's other major flaw was his greed, but, in this case, it would work in Parrish's favor.

Parrish invited Brookstone to dinner at his home. These conversations were best held in private. Sending his daughter and son out for the evening proved to be easier than he thought. Kathleen was excited to spend time with Bernard, and Douglas had a poker night with friends. The help was dismissed for the evening and the two men were alone. As they sat at the dining room table, Brookstone slammed his hand on the table. "I won't be blackmailed by that son of a bitch. It's none of his concern what we do in this town."

Parrish took a deep breath, "For the last time, Calvin, it is his concern. He and his wife have some sort of connection with Edward O'Brien's wife. They have more money than you and I have ever dreamed of, and God knows the influence they have in government."

"Don't be ridiculous, Harold. The Klu Klux Klan owns the government in Oregon. I don't care what you say."

"Calvin, haven't you been paying attention? The Klu Klux Klan has been losing ground. The Grand Dragon in Indiana really messed things up for the entire organization. You and your thugs are losing. The sooner you face it the better off you and this town will be. We have to look to the future, not terrorizing some immigrants because you don't like their religion. This contract with Franklin is worth millions."

Brookstone did not like to admit defeat, "OK, but I'm meeting with this Franklin. I don't care if I have to go all the way to New York City. I'll take Daniel and we'll do the negotiations."

Parrish held back a smile. Actually this played right into his hands. With both Brookstones out of town, he could work on the list of Klan names he purchased from a client that owed him a favor. The $500 he spent was worth every penny to get the names of all the Klan members in Little Creek.

"Damn it, Calvin, you drive a hard bargain. You win. It would probably be better if you negotiated it. I don't think I hit it off with Franklin."

"I don't give a rat's ass if he likes me. I want a good price for our sand and gravel. We have the largest pit in the state and we're close to the train. He'd be a fool to buy elsewhere and pay the transportation costs."

Harold looked at Calvin. "I'll set up the meeting. How soon can you get to New York?"

Calvin thought for a moment. "It will take three days on the train, and I have some things to prepare before we go. Set it for the second week of July. I'll spend a few extra days in New York sewing some wild oats with Daniel. Daniel has been all work no play since he graduated college. It's time for a holiday."

Harold Parrish was not a religious man but he muttered a silent prayer, hoping God would take pity on the prostitutes in New York and save them from the Brookstones. Neither man was known for being gentle with the ladies. The whores in New York would be brutalized if the past repeated itself. There was a long history of Brookstone men abusing women.

Three weeks later with the Brookstones out of town, Harold Parrish was in his office staring at the list in front of him. He hit the intercom and called his secretary in.

Mary Hanson was in her late forties and a divorcee. While the bloom of youth had left, she was still considered a handsome woman and dressed to show her figure. The fact she occasionally slept with her boss was no one's business but hers and Harold's. She was a woman who could hold secrets, and Parrish was aware she had never exploited their relationship. Basically, she had physical needs and so did he. To her it was a perfect partnership.

Mary entered and took a seat in the chair in front of his desk. Harold looked across his desk and thought what a striking woman she was. At this stage of his life, Harold had no need for a wife but, as his mistress, Mary held a small portion of his heart. Nonetheless, business was business and he would enjoy the private side of their relationship later.

"Mary, this is very sensitive, I don't want you discussing it with anyone. Here is a list of the Klu Klux Klan in our town. I want to know how current every single one of them is on their mortgages with Parrish Bank."

"I see Brookstone and his son are at the top of the list. What do you propose to do about them?"

"They've already been dealt with. I think when they return from New York we will find a change in their attitudes towards immigrants and Catholics."

Raising her eyebrow with a quizzical look, Mary stood. "I'll start on this immediately. I'll have your information by tomorrow morning."

"Thanks, Mary. By the way, I haven't had` a home cooked meal in quite a while."

"Well, Harold, it seems I'm in the mood to cook. Shall we say tomorrow night?" Mary smiled demurely at Harold as she exited his office.

The next morning Mary Hanson had finished a precise recap of the debts owed by the Klu Klux Klan members on the list. Taking it a step further, she had requested a list of the accounts receivable from both the Parrish Hardware Store and the Parrish General Store.

Knocking softly on Parrish's office door, Mary entered and presented the list to her boss. "I took the liberty of adding other Parrish owned businesses debts to the ledger."

"Good work, Mary. As usual you are a step ahead of me." Parrish smiled at his secretary. "Now I have to figure out how to proceed. Some of the people on this list are riff raff the town could do without. Others hold respectable positions in the community. I need to have a conversation with these people. Let me study the list for a bit, and we'll figure out a meeting time."

"Yes, Mr. Parrish." Mary smiled and walked out of the office. She was overjoyed the Klu Klux Klan was going to be disbanded. As a divorced woman, she had been snubbed by some of the so-called Christian women of Little Creek. Now many of these women's husbands were on this list and some of them would be run out of town.

An hour later, Parrish called Mary back into his office to give her instructions. "Mary, send letters of foreclosure to these eight men, and I want these twelve men in my office tomorrow morning, 9 a.m. sharp. Make sure they know being late is not an option."

Mary looked at her boss. "I will let them know, and, Harold, dinner is at 7 p.m. tonight. Oh, and being late is not an option." With those parting words she gave him a dazzling smile and walked out the door.

Harold watched her walk away. She was a stunning woman. Her first marriage had been turbulent, and Mary was not willing to go down that road again. Harold really didn't care to consider marriage either so their relationship worked out perfectly for both of them.

Smiling to himself, he thought he'd better leave early and pick up some flowers. Women enjoyed those types of gestures, and he got a kick seeing Mary's face light up when he brought them.

The next morning Mary Hanson was typing the foreclosure notices for the Klu Klux Klan members. Of course the letter did not refer to their membership. Word would reach them from the twelve men on the list who were deemed worthy enough to stay in town.

At 8:50 a.m. the first of the twelve people summoned to Parrish's office arrived. Within seven minutes, the other eleven had assembled. Looking around at each other, they saw the connection they all had. Fervent whispering took place among the men.

Forcing a pleasant non committal smile, Mary walked over to Harold Parrish's office and lightly knocked on the door. "They are all here."

"Send them into the conference room."

Mary walked back to the waiting area. "Gentlemen, if you would please follow me."

Directing the crowd to the conference room, Mary got them seated and offered coffee. All but one declined. Nervous looks flew across the room, but no words were spoken. After making them wait ten minutes, Harold Parrish entered the room.

"Good morning. I trust by now you might have a hunch as to why I have asked you here." Harold looked around the room as he spoke.

"Parrish, I don't have a clue and time is money, so spit it out. I've got a business to run." Al White decided a good offense was a good defense.

"Certainly, Al, that's the point. You all have businesses benefiting Little Creek. And, you all have business loans with this Bank for said businesses. Here's another little coincidence I just couldn't ignore. You're all members of the Klu Klux Klan, terrorizing our town, and making us look like a bunch of ignorant rednecks. Not exactly the image my great grandfather envisioned for his town and not one I want to see either."

"We have a right to assemble. We haven't broken any laws. There's Klu Klux Klan all over the state. What's your problem, Parrish, too soft?" Al White had appointed himself the voice of the twelve. It hadn't occurred to him to wonder if the other eleven held the same arrogant views.

"Miss Hanson, could you please pass out the personal financial information for each of these gentlemen?"

Mary knew all of them from their patronage of the Bank or from shopping in their businesses. She quietly went from man to man with a sealed envelope.

White looked around and saw only half the men were looking at him. The other half were looking down at their financial report weighing their options, realizing they owed the Bank and other Parrish businesses plenty of money.

After giving them all a few minutes to review their financial statements, Parrish stood up at the head of the table.

"You'll notice eight of your compatriots are not here. They are leaving Little Creek. The Bank has foreclosed on their home mortgages. There is no place in this town for small-minded bigots. This town is going places, and we will not be hampered by the backward bigotry of the Klu Klux Klan. Your random attacks on immigrants are laughable. Burning crosses on yards is despicable. I'm giving every man in this room an opportunity to walk away from the Klu Klux Klan. Cease activities now, or I will call in every debt due the Parrish Bank or any of my family's businesses. Then, if you survive that, I'll make sure all of the people in town know who you are. We have good citizens who don't share your prejudices. How long do you think your business will last?"

Parrish looked at each man seated before him. He saw sweat break out on a few foreheads. A couple still had defiant looks.

Al White was still flexing his muscle. "Parrish, you can't do anything to us. I may owe you money, but I'm current on my loans. I'm not going to be threatened by you and your self-righteous spiel. What does Brookstone have to say about this?"

"Brookstone is behind me 100 percent. In fact, he is in New York closing a deal that will bring jobs and opportunities to this town. He has seen the big picture, and the Klu Klux Klan is not going to bring money into this town. Gentlemen the choice is yours. Keep the Klan going in this town and your business loans, home loans, and, the debt due to the various Parrish businesses are due by the end of the week."

There were several murmurs from around the table. Al White looked as if he was going to start up again when suddenly, Mike Johnson, the owner of the only car dealership in town stood up. "I got my start in this town from your bank. You've always been fair and have sent business my way, which I appreciate. I don't know why I got involved with the Klu Klux Klan in the first place. My business and my family mean more to me than the Klan. I would suggest the rest of you do some soul searching."

Parrish looked at the crowd of men. "If you're conflicted about doing what is right, perhaps this town can do without you. Parrish Bank will buy your businesses immediately."

Most of the men in the crowd had families and were longtime residents. Silently cursing, Kevin Wiggins stood up. "Mr. Parrish, I've lived here my entire life, as have my wife and her family. It seems like us regular people are always being pushed one way or another by your family or the Brookstone's. Now to me, it appears Brookstone has had a change of heart if you say he's now against the Klu Klux Klan. For most of us here, he's the one who strong-armed us into joining. How do we know he won't change his mind?"

Parrish was glad for the question and, while he knew Brookstone was unhappy with being pressured to disband the Klu Klux Klan, he also knew Calvin valued money. "Wiggins, I can assure you Calvin Brookstone is through with the Klu Klux Klan. As I said before, this town is going places. There will be new jobs and opportunities for a better life here. Brookstone knows it is better than anything the Klan can offer Little Creek.

"Yeah, but what kind of people are going to be coming here? More of those god damned immigrants?" Al White was so angry he had spittle coming down his chin.

"White, you are an ignoramus, and if you want to keep those narrow-minded views, then we'll see who lasts longer. You own the only insurance company in town. This Bank has been sending business your way for twenty five years. All the homes we loaned money on have insurance with your company as a requirement to getting a loan. Do you honestly think I can't get a new company in here? Do you think I would hesitate for a moment to pull business from you and put it with a new company?"

All of a sudden, Al White brightened, "You can't threaten me. I could go to Governor Pierce with this information. As you know, he supports the Klu Klux Klan. Hell, he even threw a big fancy dinner party for the Grand Dragon last year. He called it a "patriotic dinner"

Parrish looked around at the men at the table. Despite Al White's blathering about the Governor, he saw most of them had the slumped shoulders of defeat, and a few of them looked relieved. "Gentleman, is there anyone in this room with any doubt the Klu Klux Klan is no longer welcome in this town? Is there anyone who doesn't believe I have the power to foreclose if I deem you undesirable for this town? The cards have been played. You can go out of here a loser or a winner. The choice is yours. And, it's not just Little Creek that is sick of the bigotry of the Klu Klux Klan; other towns are going to be following our lead. Read the newspaper, Governor Pierce may have gotten elected because of his Klu Klux Klan support but good people are starting to push back."

Parrish sat back and watched their faces. He knew all of the men. Some he even played poker with on occasion. They knew he was not a man to bluff.

Finally, Richard Weeks stood up, "I got a business to get back to. I've been in this town my entire life, all my family and friends are all here. I joined the Klu Klux Klan because I thought I was protecting them. Listening to you, I have to admit that my grandparents came from England. At one point in time, they were the god damned immigrants. You're right, Parrish, in the light of day you can see straight into the situation. But you put a sheet on and have a snort or two seems like the other side makes sense." Chuckling, he added, "Guess my wife will be glad that none of her sheets will go missing again. I'm out of it, I got more to lose by stayin' in, and I would bet the rest of you do, too."

There was the general sound of assent. Al White was still red faced. He had expected support from the other members. Al was a hothead but he was pragmatic and knew that Parrish was not giving him an idle threat. He needed to think things through and now was not the time. Pulling out a handkerchief, he mopped his bald head. Trying his best to look contrite, he glanced over at Parrish. "OK, you win. I just hope to hell you and Brookstone know what you're doing."

Parrish had the good grace not to openly gloat. Having made his point, he walked out of the conference room, leaving a contrite group of men exposed to the light of day, naked, without their white shroud of anonymity to protect them.

Chapter 20

C alvin and Daniel Brookstone cut imposing figures as they walked into Franklin Bank. Heads turned as the two men made their way to Stephen Franklin's suite of offices.

The temporary secretary taking Hildy's place was a young woman who was easily intimidated. Brookstone walked up to her desk and, in a superior tone, announced "Tell Franklin that Calvin and Daniel Brookstone are here."

Elaine Ellison was just out of secretary school. At nineteen, she was a chubby, plain, mousey thing and scared of her own shadow. She knew the etiquette of bringing visitor's coffee and making them comfortable during their wait. "Sir, can I bring you both a cup of coffee while you wait?"

"I don't expect to wait young lady. We've travelled over two thousand miles for this meeting. Let your boss know we are here." He showed his perfect teeth in a forced smile that scared Elaine to death. She rose from her desk and scurried into Mr. Franklin's office.

"Sir, Misters Calvin and Daniel Brookstone have arrived for your 2 p.m. meeting." Her face was flushed and her palms were sweaty.

Looking at her in amusement, Stephen tried to hide his grin. He wondered how the unflappable Hildy would have handled the Brookstones. He wished she were here now to size the two men up. Her uncanny ability to read a person had become Stephen Franklin's secret weapon. More than once she had warned him away from a business deal because the principle negotiating the deal had seemed "off" to her. On two of those occasions, Stephen was grateful for her gift when the men had later ended up in federal prison for racketeering. He trusted Hildy absolutely and again wished his long time secretary was at his side.

"Elaine, give me a minute to get Smyth here. Show our guests into the conference room."

Elaine walked back out to the Brookstones. Steeling herself, she smiled sweetly. "If you gentlemen would please follow me, Mr. Franklin will be joining you momentarily." She guided them to an opulent meeting room with the mahogany table that seated at least twenty people. The view of Manhattan was stunning.

"Hmm, this Franklin guy must think we are country bumpkins and this sort of thing is going to impress us." Calvin Brookstone was out of his element but not willing to admit it.

"Calm down, Dad. You're going to get yourself all worked up before the meeting even starts." Daniel Brookstone knew poker and now more than ever it was time for a poker face.

As he entered the room, Stephen Franklin did a quick read and could sense that the older Brookstone was uncomfortable. "You must be Calvin Brookstone, a pleasure to meet you. I'm Stephen Franklin, and this is my business associate, Tim Smyth." Reaching out his hand he turned to Daniel. "Good to meet you Daniel."

Brookstone did his own appraisal of Franklin. He saw a man about his age, grey hair and intense brown eyes that didn't miss a trick. He also felt power emanate from the man running the largest bank in America. Brookstone was no fool. It was time to lose the attitude and bend a little.

"Pleased to meet you, Franklin. We've heard a lot about you from Harold Parrish."

"We were surprised that Parrish didn't accompany you to the meeting. However, I have looked into your business interests in Little Creek and admire the tenacity with which you've built your empire. Little Creek Logging is a respected name and I appreciate a good reputation."

"Thanks, Franklin. Parrish couldn't join us because he is attending to one of the matters you discussed during your visit last month. We intend to clean up Little Creek. There is no place for the KKK in our town."

Daniel Brookstone almost lost his poker face. Staring at his father he had to admire the glib way he was dismissing the Klu Klux Klan, especially since he started the particular branch that was intimidating some of Little Creek citizens. Realizing the amount of money that could be lost if this deal went south, Daniel nodded his assent to his father's statement. "I'm relieved Harold is taking the bull by the horns. Of course, my father and I will back him up."

"Let's be seated, gentlemen. We have some issues to go over, and I'd like to hear your proposal." Stephen Franklin chuckled to himself.

An avid poker player, he was amused by the two men's feigned horror over the Klu Klux Klan. Stephen's investigators had uncovered the fact that both men were members and high officers.

Several hours later, an agreement was pounded out, and a lawyer brought in to write it up. Stephen played his hand well. He conceded on items he didn't care about and had only brought to the table so the Brookstones would feel they won a hand or two. Stephen looked at the two men thinking, *these two will need to be watched. They've turned over their new leaf a little too quickly to be believed. Good thing I've got a man planted right in the middle of their business. Did these fools really think I'd trust them with a deal of this size?*

Stephen Franklin put on the smile of a man that has been bested. He carefully looked at both Brookstones and extended his hand. "You gentlemen drive a hard bargain. The lawyers will write up the agreement, and we can sign it in the morning."

Calvin Brookstone puffed up and clapped Stephen Franklin on the back. "Well, when you put two Brookstones together, no one can beat us. It's been a pleasure doing business with you Franklin. We're going out to celebrate, see you in the morning."

Normally, it was a standard business practice for negotiating parties to have dinner together. Franklin was relieved he did not have to participate in their festivities. They had already made several veiled suggestions about hiring some girls for the night. Stephen pitied the unfortunate women hired by the Brookstones. He was anxious to get home to his wife and tell her the Klu Klux Klan situation in Little Creek was under control. The fact that he was now tied to these buffoons for the next few years was an insignificant consequence.

The two Brookstones strutted out of the Bank and headed to their hotel. Calvin was not unfamiliar with the ways of New York and knew maitre de' or concierges could hook them up with escorts for the evening. It was time to initiate his son into the world of power.

Approaching the concierge, Calvin grabbed his arm, "Hey you, my son and I are interested in some female companionship for the evening." As he slipped him a $5 bill, the concierge palmed it and stuffed it into his pocket.

"Sir, we have some lovely ladies that are visiting our fair city. I would be happy to ask them to join you in your suite."

Calvin laughed. "Visiting your fair city, that's a good one. Just make sure they're here in a half an hour. We're celebrating, and I want them pretty."

"Yes sir. Let me see what I can do."

Brookstone stood toe to toe with the concierge, "Do it and make it snappy or I'll take my business to another hotel."

Exactly thirty minutes later, there was a discreet knock on the door of their suite. A tall redhead with a curvaceous figure smiled as Calvin opened the door. "Mr. Brookstone, I'm Ellie Mathers. I understand you're looking for a little entertainment this evening. My sister May and I would love to join you and your son."

Brookstone gave her the once over—pretty face, great figure, and fiery red hair. Her "sister" had blonde hair cut in a bob. She was pretty and her shy smile made her look like the girl next door instead of a prostitute.

"Sure, ladies, come on in. We can talk about the details later. This is my son Daniel."

Ellie looked at Daniel. He looked harmless enough, might as well let the kid have him. She'd take on the old man. She hoped that he was as harmless as he looked. She was in no mood for trouble.

Brookstone had slipped the concierge an extra twenty to get him some booze. Prohibition was cramping his style. He would have preferred to be out at a speakeasy, but decided that having it sent in would be easier. This would give him more private time with the hookers. He was looking forward to that. It had been a while since he'd had the kind of fun he really enjoyed with a woman.

Another light knock at the door, Brookstone looked at his son. "Get the door Daniel and don't forget to tip."

Daniel walked back into the living room of the suite with a bottle of scotch in each hand. "Ladies, can I interest you in a drink?"

Ellie looked at Daniel. He was a handsome young man. He didn't have the cruel look around his eyes that the father had. Ellie knew in her gut she was going to have to watch herself tonight. "Sure, that'd be swell, doll. I just need to use your facilities first."

Once inside the suite's bathroom, she glanced at herself in the mirror. At thirty, she looked at least ten years older. The life she had dreamed of when she came to New York was long forgotten. The small town farm girl had turned to the streets after she almost starved to death when she couldn't find work. Growing up in Iowa had not prepared her for life in the big city. Little education and no skills other than being pretty had led her to this profession. She was street smart and trying to teach her friend May the ropes. Hooking for a living wasn't a great way of life, but if a girl was smart, she could live pretty well. Ellie had learned to tell bad johns from good ones after she got her nose broken. By the time she had been kicked in the ribs and burned with cigarettes from another john, she was a pro. She had worked this hotel for eight years and trusted Louie, the concierge. When she caught a look in the older Brookstone's eyes, she got a bad fluttery feeling in her stomach.

Finishing in the bathroom, she went back into the suite's living room. She looked over at May and gave her a smile and a slight shrug of her shoulders. Daniel was talking to May and the older Brookstone was opening a bottle. He looked over at Ellie. "What are you doing lurking around?"

"I was using the little girl's room. Now where's that scotch you promised us?"

Brookstone smiled showing white teeth that looked like a wolf's, "Right here. Let's see how well you can hold your liquor."

Pouring a full glass of scotch, Brookstone shoved it at Ellie, "Drink it down."

"Oh, honey, I like to savor my scotch like I savor my men. Let me just sip this while we get to know each other."

Brookstone's slap was as quick as a snake's bite. "I'm paying you, and you'll do as I say. Drink it down." Looking over at his son he lashed out, "Daniel, this is how you treat a whore. Don't confuse sex with love. If you give them an inch they'll take a mile. That goes for whores and any other female. Including the woman you marry someday."

Daniel had heard this speech his entire life. He looked over at the redheaded hooker.

The red hand mark on Ellie's face was vivid. Her face had paled as his open hand hit her. She'd been hit before, but never this early in the evening. Brookstone had not even taken a sip of his scotch. Fear snaked through her belly. She had to get herself and May out of there.

"Come on May, we're leaving. This ain't worth the money."

Calvin Brookstone grabbed her wrist, crushing it in his large hand. "No one leaves me. You're not going anywhere but where I tell you, and that, girlie, is the bedroom."

Brookstone dragged her down the hall. He shoved her through the double doors into his bedroom. Tossing her on the bed he started to undo his pants. Ellie steeled herself for the blows she knew were coming.

Whimpering she looked up at Brookstone, "I'll do anything you want. Please don't hurt me. I'm just a working girl."

In the living room of the suite, May looked fearfully at the door. She wanted to run through it, out the lobby doors, and never look back. The sounds coming from the bedroom were frightful. She looked at Daniel and gauged her chances of making it to the door.

"Don't even think about it, you whore. I'm not as vicious as my father, but I won't hesitate to hurt you if you try to leave before I'm finished with you."

"Please don't hurt me. Please….I'll do anything."

"You've got that right, bitch. Now finish that drink. We're going to have a little fun." Looking at the fear in May's face, Daniel laughed, "Or maybe I'll be the only one having fun."

Ellie Mathers could hear Calvin Brookstone getting dressed. He whistled a jazzy little tune like a man without a problem in the world. She was bruised and battered from her night of terror. There wasn't a part of her that wasn't in pain. What he hadn't hit with his fists, he hammered at internally. He loved the feeling of power when he forced himself deep into her, not for sexual pleasure but just to watch the pain in her eyes. Ellie learned quickly that if she screamed in pain, it excited him all the more. She had laid there with her eyes clenched shut praying for it to end. Now twelve hours later, she was pretending to be asleep. She was afraid to ask if she could leave. Her plan was to find May and get them both out of this chamber of horrors. She prayed fervently that May had fared better.

"You whore. I know you're not asleep. Look at me when I talk to you." Calvin Brookstone wanted to wrap up the business with the whores before he and Daniel left for their meeting.

Pulling out a wad of bills from his wallet he told her, "Get up and get out. I'm sick of the sight of you."

Ellie wrapped the sheet around her battered body and, grabbing her clothes, headed for the bathroom. She dressed as quickly as she could. Her stiff body screamed in pain as she tried to hook her bra. Looking at her naked breasts she cried at the bruises and bite marks. Mumbling, "I'm alive. At least I'm alive."

Suddenly Brookstone beat on the bathroom door. "Get out here now."

Ellie zipped up her dress, putting her arm behind her back was agony. He had twisted it behind her numerous times during the night. "Just a minute, please, I'm dressing." Coming out of the bathroom Ellie hugged the side of the wall, trying to get as much distance between her and Brookstone as the space would allow.

"Get out of here, and don't even think about sending cops. Who are they going to believe, me or a whore? Now get your 'sister' and get out of my suite."

Ellie ran out of the room. The living room was empty and she frantically called out. "May, May, where are you?"

A door opened and Ellie gasped. "Oh May. Come on. We have to get out of here." Looking at her friend her heart was breaking. May had two black eyes, and it was obvious her nose had been broken.

"Why, Ellie. Why did he do this? I did everything he wanted." Tears streamed down May's face. "Why was he so angry?"

"Quick, we've got to get out of here now. Come on, lean on me."

Making it out of the suite to the elevator, the ladies of the evening faced the new day. Exiting the elevator, the harsh sunlight streaming through the lobby showed the damage to their faces. The look in their eyes showed the wounds that were deep beyond the surface.

Louie Mahoney had been sending girls to rooms for eight years, and he had never seen anyone brutalized like the two girls he sent to Brookstone's suite. He was just coming on duty as the girls exited the elevator barely able to walk. Thankfully, Mahoney spotted them before the house detective did. He was able to get them out of the hotel and into a cab. He instructed the cabbie to take them to the hospital.

Ellie protested. "We don't need no god damned hospital, we need the cops. Those two are crazy. They almost killed us."

"You're nuts, Ellie. Cops aren't going to arrest those two men. You know that it'll never stick, and then they'd come after you for prostitution. If you don't want to go to the hospital go home, lie low, and don't take any new jobs. I'll check in on you tomorrow."

"Louie, look at us. Do you think anyone would want our services looking like this? Are you blind? Don't you see what he did to us? You should see what the clothes are covering. Those men are crazy and depraved."

Tapping on the roof of the cab, Eddie signaled the cabbie to take off. Going back into the hotel, he knew that it was fruitless. The

"Have's" always beat out the "Have Not's." The only think he knew for certain there was no way he was sending anymore "dates" to room 1241.

Slightly hung over, Daniel Brookstone looked at his father. "Well, dear old Dad, you certainly know how to throw a good party. I don't know when I've had such a great time. That little whore was quite entertaining."

Calvin looked at his son with pride. "Just remember what I said, whores are for fun, don't confuse sex with love. Basically, all women are whores. Some of them just demand a ring on their finger before you see their true nature."

Walking out of the lobby, the two men didn't notice the murderous look the concierge sent their way.

Calvin and Daniel Brookstone met with Stephen Franklin looking none the worse for their evening. They dropped hints about having a fine time with two ladies and not getting much sleep. Stephen did his best to ignore them. Shuddering to himself, he wondered what kind of women would associate with these two boorish men.

"So you'll be heading back to Little Creek soon?"

Calvin raised his head from the papers he had been pretending to understand. "We're leaving in four days. We still have business to attend to here." It was none of Franklin's concern what they did. He had made it more than obvious he and his wife would not be socializing with them.

"Well, we certainly have a diverse city with so much to offer visitors. Please let me know if there is something you want to see, and I'll try to make arrangements for you."

"Thanks, Franklin, but we'll be fine. I know how to find the kind of entertainment that my son and I enjoy."

Franklin cringed at the leering laugh that followed Brookstone's statement. He abhorred doing business with these two men. But, when it all boiled down, he had bought the rights to their sand and gravel for a price far less than he had been willing to pay. The Klu Klux Klan was being dealt with which would help to ensure Lydia and Edward's safety. And, he had a man planted in the town to keep an eye on things. All in all, it was a successful deal.

"Gentlemen, I will be back in Little Creek towards the end of the year. I'll look forward to seeing you two as well as Parrish." With that he pointedly looked at his watch and stood to leave.

Taking the hint, Brookstone rose and looked at his son, "Daniel, let's get out of here. I want to go spend some of Franklin's money."

Laughing uproariously, they walked out of the office.

Chapter 21

M yra had been on the ship for five days. With only two days left, she needed to get to work on her future. James Vautrin had mentioned he loved to walk on deck early in the morning when there were few passengers about.

Myra smiled and placed her new sun hat on her head, walked to the door, and quietly let herself out. Making her way to the promenade deck, she glanced down at the people in steerage two levels below taking their hour on deck. Myra knew if she not had the smarts to contact the Franklins, she, too, would have been down there.

As she stood at the railing, a deep voice behind her said, "Poor buggars. Look at them. One hour a day and the other twenty three stuck in that hole they call steerage."

Myra turned to look up at James Vautrin. He was the tallest man she had ever met. Her head was barely up to his chest. He exuded masculinity, but with an innate grace, a handsome man with a long straight nose and full lips that gave him an aristocratic look. Myra blushed as she looked into his deep-set grey eyes.

"I can't look at them. It's too depressing. I want to enjoy this beautiful morning. Look at the sun coming up on the water. The way it's shimmering, it looks like a pathway to the promised land."

"Well, Miss Delaney, that's the most I've heard you say in five days." James Vautrin was fascinated with this young woman. He knew there was story to her, and he was watching with interest as it unfolded.

"How are you enjoying your trip across the ocean? Is it everything you expected?"

"Oh yes. It is that and more. I'll be sorry to have it end." Myra looked up at James with a sincere look adding to her feigned look of distress.

James Vautrin was thirty-two years old, and worked for the *New York Daily News*. He relished a good story and had been observing little Miss Delaney knowing there was more to her than met the eye. It had only been five days, and he had watched her transformation. He clearly remembered hearing her charming Irish accent on the first night of the cruise when she spoke in hushed tones to Mrs. Hildebrand. Now there was barely a trace of an accent. *Curious,* he thought, *why is this young woman reinventing herself? And who is Mrs. Hildebrand? What is she to this girl?*

Myra stole a glance at James. She loved to listen to him and his father talk at dinner. She was fascinated by his accent, his fine manners, and the ease in which he conversed with the other people at the table. She absorbed every little detail, mentally mimicking the inflection of his words and all the Americans at her table. His laughter would bubble up when he told funny stories. Myra hung onto his every word. His eyes were intelligent and she often caught admiring glances aimed at her.

"I think father is quite taken with Mrs. Hildebrand. She's quite a lady." James threw the line out casually to see what information he could reel in.

Myra saw his lips moving but paid little attention to his words. She loved to watch how his moustache would lift and his bright white teeth flash as he spoke. Finally grasping what he was saying, Myra laughed. "Mrs. Hildebrand is her own woman. From what she's said, her husband passed away almost thirty years ago. She's been on her own for a long time and is very independent."

"I think that's what attracts my father. He appreciates strong women. I think we should work on getting them together. We still have two more days. We could make a lunch date for the four of us. Then you and I could cancel, leaving just the two of them together."

"No, James. That would never work. Mrs. Hildebrand would never allow me to go off with you alone. I'm lucky I managed to get away by myself this morning. She watches me like a hawk. Her employers are so worried I will be 'compromised' aboard ship. It may look like she's my sweet guardian, but she's not. Mrs. Hildebrand is my jailer."

"Employers? Jailer? What are you talking about?" James looked at Myra. He had been a reporter for ten years. He had interviewed hardened criminals and was street smart. He was right. There was definitely a story behind Myra's transformation. He was about to ask her more when suddenly he spied Mrs. Hildebrand approaching.

As Mrs. Hildebrand got closer she appraised the situation. Five days in Myra's company had alerted her to the girl's many faces. She could see the protective way James Vautrin was standing by Myra as she approached.

"Myra, there you are! I was worried when I awoke and you weren't in the suite. What a beautiful morning for a walk, and I see you've found some pleasant company. Good morning, Mr. Vautrin. I trust you're enjoying the wonderful sea air?" Mrs. Hildebrand looked from Myra to James with a guileless smile on her face.

James' reporter's intuition was working overtime. Nothing was what it seemed. Myra's distress and fear had evaporated as suddenly as it had come on. Mrs. Hildebrand was the same sweet woman he dined with every evening, hardly the sinister character that Myra was insinuating moments ago.

"Mrs. Hildebrand, lovely to see you, I was just trying to persuade Miss Delaney to have lunch with me this afternoon. I'm having a hard time convincing her that I am harmless. Perhaps both of you would join my father and me for lunch?" James looked at her with a sincere look and flashed a charming smile.

"Lunch would be lovely. Myra and I have been taking it in our suite. I would quite enjoy getting out of our cabin. Myra dear, is that suitable for you?"

Myra looked at Mrs. Hildebrand and thought, *what is this old bird up to?* Looking at James she smiled coyly. "It would be lovely to join you and your father for lunch."

"Marvelous. It's settled then. I'll leave you two ladies and go inform my father of our lunch plans."

Hildy watched as James departed. "He's a fine looking young fellow isn't he?"

Myra, too, looked at the back of James as he walked away thinking to herself, *If I'd had a few more minutes alone with him, he would have walked through fire for me. If only the old busybody hadn't interrupted us. Well, I've still got two days to reel him in.*

Hildy looked at Myra's face and noticed she looked a bit peevish. "Dear, are you all right?"

Myra turned on Mrs. Hildebrand and snarled, "I would be if you would give me some time away from you. Why are you always spying on me?"

Mrs. Hildebrand was taken aback. She had expected Myra to maintain her mask for the duration of the trip. Getting a look at the real Myra was a bit unnerving. "I was not spying on you. I was concerned because you left without leaving a note. I would hardly call it spying." Hildy squared her shoulders and looked directly into Myra's face. The charming smile Myra had bestowed on James Vautrin was long gone, replaced with a look of malice.

"I don't need you watching me every moment of the day. I can do as I wish on this ship. I am a guest of Mr. and Mrs. Franklin while you are merely their employee." The sweet little Irish girl was dead and buried. She had been replaced by a woman with an indistinguishable accent, sleek new clothing, and a superior attitude.

"Yes, it is true I am an employee of Mr. Franklin's. I have been instructed to make sure you arrive at New York safely and that your trip is comfortable. I do believe being cooped up in the cabin with an old woman has taken a toll on you. Please, Myra. I have no wish to see you upset. By all means, do as you wish. We will be docking in two days, and this should be a pleasurable cruise for you." Hildy continued, patting Myra's hand, "My dear, you've had a dreadful blow. Losing your parents and all you've been through. Perhaps I've just been a little overzealous in my desire to take care of you."

Myra resumed her former demeanor of the sweet, compliant, little Irish girl. "Oh Mrs. Hildebrand, I'm so sorry. I don't know what came over me. It's just so much to take in. All of the fine people, with their grand manners, and trying to understand all the American slang. I'm afraid I took it all out on you. I'm ever so sorry. Please forgive me."

Hildy was not fooled one iota, but forced herself to smile at Myra and give her a hug. "It's all right. I understand. Now let's be friends again, and you've got a lunch date with that fine young man to get ready for."

Myra returned Mrs. Hildebrand's hug. Taking a step back, she looked at Hildy and in an odd voice said, "Thank you. Thank you for everything."

Hildy could not help but notice that Myra's blue eyes had gone flat and lifeless. Her apology sounded wooden, and, for a moment, she felt as if someone had walked on her grave. A slight shudder went through Hildy.

She had been on this earth for sixty two years and had seen enough evil to recognize a threat. Myra was definitely a threat to Lydia and possibly even to herself. If Myra had any inkling she had sent the Franklins a telegram asking them to investigate her story, Hildy had no doubt her own life would be in danger. Watching Myra walk away, Hildy thought to herself, *I think it's time for me to start sleeping with one eye open. That girl is not to be trusted.*

Chapter 22

Elaine Ellison buzzed the intercom. "Mr. Franklin, I have Mr. Bernard Wilkes on line one."

Franklin grabbed the phone. "Wilkes, how are you. What did you find out?"

Bernard Wilkes was an international banker with friends in high places in British Intelligence. In his mid sixties, he still had a strong voice and his keen mind was in tip top shape. "Franklin, I don't know how you know this girl, but I can tell you from what I've heard, she has absolutely no conscience. She framed her parents as IRA members and they were arrested. Their house and business were totally ransacked as Scotland Yard looked for evidence. They were interrogated for nearly a week and kept in deplorable conditions. This is actually an embarrassment to our government. The idiot Black and Tans were convinced of their guilt." Wilkes paused for breath. "Finally, they realized that things just weren't ringing true. Neighbors came forward attesting to the Delaney's innocence and their character. The postman even testified the daughter had received a letter from a bank in America. Finally, the interrogating officer put two and two together, especially since Mr. and Mrs. Delaney had both been separated and their stories were identical. A young officer, Godfrey Aldridge, fessed up that he had given Myra money to stay with her cousin. Her 'cousin', who didn't exist by the way, conveniently lived in a port city with a ship sailing for America the next day. I believe that's where you come into the story, old chap."

"Yes, Bernard." Sighing deeply, Stephen continued, "Her sister is a very dear friend of Beverly's and mine. Lydia, the sister, saved our grandson's life, and we've grown very close. We received a letter from Myra Delaney saying her parents had been killed in an accident and she needed to join her sister in America. My wife and I fell for it hook, line, and sinker. We sent a first class ticket to her for a ship that is arriving in New York in two days."

Bernard interrupted Stephen. "Cheer up. That's a bit of good news for Scotland Yard. They want her back. She's going to be prosecuted for all that she's done. No one makes a fool of the British Government and gets away with it. No one that is, unless you're a Member of Parliament. God knows they've botched a few things over the years." Wilkes chuckled at his little joke.

Stephen was relieved they wanted Myra returned and she would face charges. The thought of this creature getting close to Lydia was frightening. His phone conversations with Edward had been most enlightening. "I will see she is met by Immigration. They'll make sure Scotland Yard gets her back. You'll need to have your people talk to them. I'm sure they won't take my word on something like this."

"No worries, old friend. We'll keep her out of your country. I'm sure she won't be met with open arms in her own. From what I hear, her parents have written her off. She really has nothing to return to. Even the nit wit she duped into helping her has seen the light."

"I owe you one, Bernard. Keep in touch. I'll let you know how this plays out." Stephen was anxious to get off the phone and send a telegram to Hildy.

Hanging up the phone, he buzzed Elaine. "Please come in. I need something done immediately." Stephen sat at his desk deep in thought, his hands laced together. He stared straight ahead. Finally he looked at Elaine. "I've got it. I need a telegram sent to Hildy and make sure it is worded exactly this way."

> You were right as usual **stop** Shipment will be returned **stop** Client grateful for the product information **stop** The merchandise is very flawed. You saved our client **stop** Have a safe trip **stop** See you in two days **stop**

Satisfied the telegram was cryptic enough if it fell into the wrong hands, Stephen instructed his temporary secretary to get it to Western Union immediately. Now he just had to wait for Immigration to contact him and arrange to meet when the ship docked.

Chapter 23

Hildy smiled at Marcus Vautrin. He stood and, giving her a slight bow, pulled out her chair. Seating herself, she noticed that Myra was not yet at the table. Her thoughts were dark, *waiting to make an entrance I'm sure*. Hildy had figured out that Myra was working on James Vautrin. To what purpose she had no idea, but while she was waiting, she tried to learn what Myra was up to.

James looked at Mrs. Hildebrand. Her face was relatively unlined for a woman her age and her smile was genuine. "And where is your lovely companion, Mrs. Hildebrand?"

"I believe she may be doing a little shopping. We only have two days left!" Her eyes twinkled and her little laugh showed her tolerance of her young charge. Thinking to herself, *Myra, you're not the only actress on the ship, and I wonder what bills you've rung up for the Franklins to pay.*

Just then Myra arrived in a flurry of activity. The boxes she had been balancing started to slip. James jumped up immediately to help her.

"Sorry to be late. I was shopping and lost track of time. I didn't want to go all the way back to our suite. Can we put these on the table behind us?"

Marcus Vautrin jumped up to help his son. "My goodness young lady, is there any merchandise left in the ship's store?"

Giggling, Myra looked at James and Marcus Vautrin. "Oh you men are all alike. Really, I just picked up a few essentials that I'll need in New York."

Hildy heard New York and was curious about the omission of traveling on to Oregon. She decided to be quiet and see what story Myra would tell.

Hildy was surprised when Myra looked at their companions. "Gentlemen, please, I so want to hear about life in America. James, what's it like living in New York?"

James smiled at Myra and started talking about taxi cabs and crowds and soon had the entire table laughing at his stories.

A waiter appeared with an envelope on a silver dish. "Mrs. Hildebrand, I have a telegram for you."

Thanking the waiter, Hildy took an unused knife from the table and sliced open the envelope. "It's from my employer, Mr. Franklin." Scanning the telegraph she read between the lines and knew that she needed to watch herself. "Mr. Franklin has a client that was about to make an investment that I cautioned him against. Our client backed out of the deal just in time, and it appears that the president of the bogus company will be going to jail."

James saw this as the perfect opening, "Who is your employer, Mrs. Hildebrand?"

"Mr. Stephen Franklin, president of Franklin Bank."

"I've heard of Mr. Franklin. He and his wife are quite philanthropic. They give to quite a few major charities in New York. My newspaper wanted to do a story about them, but Mr. Franklin refused."

Hildy looked at James. "Mr. and Mrs. Franklin do not like to take credit for their good deeds. They prefer to stay in the background."

"What a shame, they'd make a good story. Maybe you could put in a good word for me." James looked at her inquiringly.

Mrs. Hildebrand smiled and artfully changed the subject.

James watched her and thought how protective she was of her employer. *So what is this evil plot Myra hinted at? This just gets more and more interesting. I need to get Myra alone.*

Before Myra knew it, lunch was over. She looked at her chaperone, "Mrs. Hildebrand, would it be acceptable if James helped me back to our stateroom with my packages? I don't want to disturb you. Please enjoy your coffee with Mr. Vautrin."

Hildy looked into Myra's eyes and saw the challenge. "Well dear, you certainly have a lot of packages and can't possibly manage them all yourself." Looking at James, she added. "You look like you could make quick work of such a task, James. Myra, I'll see you at dinner."

She didn't miss the look of triumph that shot through Myra's eyes. Hildy looked at their backs as they walked away. *Let her think she won this one. We'll see who wins in the end.* Taking a sip of her coffee, Hildy looked at Marcus Vautrin. "The young have so much energy. It's a pleasure to watch."

Marcus Vautrin looked at Mrs. Hildebrand, "So, dear lady, how did you go from corporate advisor to babysitter?"

"Oh, I would hardly call Myra a baby, maybe just a little wet behind the years. Mr. and Mrs. Franklin are friends of Myra's sister. Myra will be joining her sister, Lydia, and brother-in-law, Edward, in the States. Mr. and Mrs. Franklin were well acquainted with the horrors in steerage from some of their charity work. I was long overdue for a holiday so they asked me if I wouldn't mind accompanying Myra on her voyage." She smiled brightly at Marcus. "I've had the pleasure of a voyage on this luxurious ship and meeting new people."

Marcus smiled back at her and fancied that she might be flirting with him.

"Myra certainly is a lucky young woman to have such a well-connected sister."

Hildy looked Marcus right in the eye. "I would say luck had nothing to do with it." Briskly changing the subject she turned to her lunch companion. "Marcus, I would love to take a stroll around the ship. Would you like to accompany me?"

Marcus was charmed. He was fascinated by Mrs. Hildebrand and the cool efficient way she handled everything. While he was curious about Myra, especially since his son seemed so attracted to her, he respected the fact Mrs. Hildebrand was not given to idle gossip. "It would be my pleasure, dear lady."

Myra and James left the dining room and, as he carried all of the packages back to her stateroom, he wondered what he was seeing. The carefree girl at lunch was gone. They were barely out of the dining room before Myra started crying.

James was alarmed. "Myra, what on earth, what is wrong, why are you crying?"

"I can't keep this deception up any longer. I just can't. She tells everyone that they are bringing me over to America to join my sister, but it's a lie. Mrs. Hildebrand finds young brides for old men, and, I think the Franklins are in on it."

"Myra, that's preposterous. They are well-respected people in society. There has never been a hint of misconduct with them, ever."

Myra looked at James. She knew he wanted a story, and she was going to give him one. "James, do you honestly think a couple I have never met, would give me an open account at the ship's store? Allowing me to buy anything I want? Mrs. Hildebrand calls it my trousseau. She says I have to look proper for my new husband. I don't think they even told my sister I was coming. This is a sham. Mrs. Hildebrand says my sister slipped through their fingers, but they'll make sure I don't. I'm so confused and scared. I'm just trying to get to my sister. Our parents died in an accident, and she is the only person I have in the world. I have to get away from Mrs. Hildebrand."

James looked at her beautiful face streaked with tears. Her big blue eyes looked at him with terror. The reporter in him wanted the story. The man in him was overcome by a surge of protectiveness for this terrified woman. "Come, Myra, let's get rid of these packages and go find a place to talk. We need to get this sorted out before we dock and time is drawing near."

Myra looked at him, her teary eyes filled with gratitude. The tall man stood straighter, his sharp reporter's instinct dulled by his desire to protect a poor, defenseless young woman.

As he hugged her close, her face was pushed into his chest. Myra's lips curved into a satisfied smile, and a plan was formulating in her shrewd brain.

She was absolutely giddy. As Myra disembarked the ship, walking down the gangplank reserved for employees, she looked the crowd over. James had promised he would find the Franklins and stand by them so she could get a look from a distance. True to his word, he stopped near them with his father at his side and nonchalantly pulled a cigar from his pocket. He fumbled with a cutter and match, giving her plenty of time to get a look at the couple who had set her plan to get to Lydia in motion.

Myra chuckled to herself thinking, *won't they be surprised when they discover their precious Mrs. Hildebrand hog tied in the bathroom. Who did the old biddy think she was fooling with her sweet and innocent act? And hiding a gun under her pillow? Why was a woman her age carrying a gun?*

James gave her an imperceptible nod and started to walk to the edge of the pier. Following from a safe distance, Myra shadowed James and his father to the cab stand. With no luggage, she walked easily through the crowd. James had a porter with a cart carry all of their suitcases, including her two large ones, now in James' possession. Thankfully, his father didn't seem to notice the extra luggage, or perhaps he thought it was some other passenger's. James had promised to send her bags to the hotel by taxi so she could check in with luggage.

As instructed, Myra walked past them. At the street, she looked up to notice the signs. James had been very specific about paying attention and had given her explicit directions to the hotel where they were meeting in two hours.

Myra was amazed as she looked at the tall buildings and the hustle and bustle of the streets. She backed up to the front of a store, just to take a moment to absorb it all. Observing the stylish people, Myra felt a little dowdy wearing the oversized coat James had loaned her as part of her disguise. He cautioned her to keep it on until she was safely away from the pier.

Myra continued to make her way to their meeting place. She looked in a store window at her reflection, patted her hair, and smiled at what she saw. *Why I look just as American as any of these people. I'll pass, that's for sure.*

As she got farther from the pier and closer to the hotel, she took the bulky coat off. Her stylish dress and flapper figure turned quite a few heads as she walked down the street. Myra smiled as she sauntered through the crowd. She didn't have a care in the world. For once, she held no malicious thoughts of Lydia. She was simply enjoying her first taste of freedom. Myra walked towards the hotel James had told her to go to. In her pocket she had $200 cash the duped James had insisted she take as a "loan" for her trip west. She had played her cards perfectly, crying about her sister and telling him Mrs. Hildebrand had taken all her money to make sure she didn't try to run away.

The money was going to have to last awhile, but she still had all of the money she had left Ireland with. Spotting a bank, she walked in. Stopping to study the chalkboard posting the exchange rate, she calculated her money thinking, *another $100 to add to the pot. That's a fortune.* As she exchanged her money, she casually asked where a quality hotel might be found. Myra had already figured that James was an unnecessary complication. With his cash in hand, she needn't continue her ruse.

The bank teller looked Myra over, saw an expensive dress and modern haircut, and decided she was a lady of quality. He leaned over the teller's counter. "Miss, you'd fit right in at the New York Biltmore. It's over on Madison Avenue and Forty Third Street."

Myra's accent was no longer Irish, but she couldn't figure out the bank teller's strong New York accent. "Could you please write it down? Is it far from here?"

"No, miss. It is only six blocks from here."

Myra walked out of the bank with money in her pocket book and a plan. She needed to go to the Hotel Pennsylvania to pick up her luggage.

Standing on the street corner, she marveled at the cars and people. Everyone had some place to go, and were rushing to it. Watching the cars, she took a tentative step off the curb.

Myra walked into the Hotel Pennsylvania. The opulence of the lobby took her breath away. She faltered for a moment, and then thought of the first class passengers she had spent a week with. Their mannerisms, speech patterns, and the way they carried themselves were now part of the new Myra.

Standing to her full height of 5'4, Myra approached the concierge. "Excuse me, I'm Martha Vautrin. My cousin James was sending my luggage here. It should have arrived within the last hour."

The concierge looked her up and down. Nice looking young woman, dressed in expensive clothes, modern hair, but something about those beautiful blue eyes gave him pause for a moment. "Yes,

Miss Vautrin, your luggage has just arrived. Have you checked in? I can take the bags to your room immediately."

"No, actually, there has been a change of plans. I'd like my luggage taken out to a cab. There's been a family emergency, and I won't be staying here." Her words were clipped and brooked no rebuttal from the concierge.

"Certainly, miss. If you'll just wait here a moment, I'll call a cab."

"Oh, and one other thing, I have my cousin's overcoat. I haven't had time to get word to him of my departure. I'd like to leave it here. I was to meet him for dinner, but now that's not possible." Myra put an appropriate amount of distress and distain in her voice as she held out a dollar bill.

Mike was used to dealing with the upper crust. They always wanted something and he was just the guy to do it. Smartly pocketing the dollar bill, he added, "Yes, miss. I will be happy to hold his coat in the concierge's room behind my desk."

"Thank you. Now please, I'm in a hurry, if you would be so kind as to call a cab."

Chapter 24

Stephen and Beverly Franklin insisted Hildy be taken to the hospital to be checked over. Stephen looked over at Hildy. "We'll never forgive ourselves for putting you in danger."

Hildy's face was ashen, but she managed to smile and tried to soften her words. "You may be my boss, but don't be an idiot. How on earth could anyone have known Myra isn't right in the head? I'm to blame as much as anyone. I realized how dangerous she was, but slept with a gun under my pillow and an unlocked door. I was the idiot. Now she has the gun my dear husband gave me, and my pride has been severely wounded. I guess the good news is my little Derringer can only hold two rounds and she has no other bullets. Let's pray Myra is a bad shot."

Beverly looked over at Hildy. "Oh my dear, dear friend, I understand how you feel. Our pride is a little worse for the wear, too. We have endangered Lydia by bringing that deranged young woman to America."

Hildy took Beverly's hand and gave it a squeeze. "Mrs. Franklin, if you are feeling bad now, just wait until you see the charges Myra rang up on the ship. I tried to cut her off, but she would sweet talk them into charging it to our room."

Beverly had the good grace to laugh. "Well, truly, it is the least of my worries. In fact, a well dressed con artist may be easier to find than a poor little Irish girl."

"Well she is no longer a poor little Irish girl. She managed to erase any trace of an accent during our seven days on the ship. It was amazing to watch her transformation. In fact, at one point she very pointedly told me I was merely an employee and she was a guest." Hildy was still peeved at the memory.

Stephen was taking it all in. He was trying to figure out their next move. "My biggest fear is now for Lydia. In my conversations with Edward, it is obvious Myra means to do harm to her sister. Luckily, I have a man planted in Little Creek."

Hildy arched her eyebrow at her boss. "He'd better be ready to meet the femme fatal. Little Miss Myra has turned into quite the gun moll. I'm convinced she had help, and my guess is James Vautrin. He was quite taken with her on the ship."

Stephen pondered the information. "We need to get the police involved. She is now a wanted international felon. I'll make a few calls after we get you looked at. We can track down this Vautrin fellow and see what shakes out."

Hildy tried to remember everything she knew about James Vautrin. "He's a reporter for *The New York Daily News*. I don't know what part of the city he lives in, but we can start there. And I'm not going to the hospital. We need to find Myra before she heads west. You may be my boss but on this I stand firm. Myra is a chameleon. If we don't find her soon, she will adapt into her new surroundings and no one will be the wiser. I've never seen anyone change so quickly. She can mimic any accent and she's very smart."

Stephen exchanged glances with his wife, "OK, Hildy, you're right." Leaning over he told the cab driver. "Get us to the *Daily News* and step on it."

Stephen, Beverly, and Hildy descended on *The New York Daily News* offices, demanding information on James Vautrin. When Stephen threatened a lawsuit and demanded to see the managing editor, they were led to the executive offices.

"See here, man, you must get me in touch with James Vautrin immediately. It truly is a matter of life and death." Stephen was red faced and Beverly was seriously worried about his blood pressure.

"Mr. Franklin, we respect the urgency of this matter. If you'll give me a few minutes, my secretary will get the number, and we'll call Vautrin."

"We need to see him. We believe he helped a young woman wanted by Scotland Yard get away today."

"Wanted by Scotland Yard? What on earth did James run into on his holiday?" Robert Banks was staring at Stephen. Banks was trying to grasp the fact that one of his best reporters had aided a criminal. "This isn't possible. James will go far for a story, but he is not one to break the law. Whatever help he gave this young woman I can state positively that he would not aid a criminal."

Beverly looked at Banks, "Any of the reporters I've ever met would sell their mother for a story. How can you be so sure of James Vautrin?"

"Mrs. Franklin, I have worked with Vautrin for eight years. I hired him and I know his values. And, yes, he will go far for a story, but he will not break the law."

Renee Perrault

As Banks was speaking, his secretary walked in with a slip of paper. Banks rose from his chair, "All right, here's his address, but I'm coming with you."

The four people in the cab racing to West 91st Street were silent. Robert Banks smelled a story. He had no doubt that his best reporter had caught the scent, too. "Franklin, why is this young woman wanted by Scotland Yard?"

"She implicated her parents in a terrorist plot with the IRA. She also defrauded an officer in the British Army."

"Well now, that's quite interesting, but she doesn't sound like someone that could dupe an experienced reporter. I'm sure that James is working on the story, and we'll get to the bottom of this." Robert Banks felt somewhat relieved this Myra woman wasn't an armed killer or worse.

Stephen Franklin let out an exasperated breath, "She brutalized Mrs. Hildebrand and left her tied up on the bathroom floor all night, and now has a gun in her possession."

Mrs. Hildebrand broke into the conversation, "I spent seven days with her. I believe her to be mentally imbalanced. My late husband was a policeman and he would tell me of people that had no conscience or felt no remorse for their actions. Myra fits the description. She has one purpose in mind which is to destroy her sister. To do that, she will use anyone she can, and has no problem discarding them when their usefulness has expired."

Banks was intrigued with the story, "Here we are. That's the address. Look, there's James coming down the steps."

The cab pulled to the curb and Banks jumped out. "James, James…. over here."

James saw his boss and, for a moment, was taken back, "Robert, what are you doing here? I'm still on holiday for another day. Are you trying to put me to work? I'm running late right now. What's going on?"

Robert Banks stood aside as Stephen and Beverly Franklin exited the cab. "James, I don't believe you've met the Franklins. For the sake of expediency, please get in the cab, we can make our introductions as we go meet your Miss Delaney."

The look of shock that passed James' face was fleeting and a deep fury took its place almost immediately. "You are not going to let those people get anywhere near her. Do you know what they plan on doing to her? This is a huge story and I'm going to break it."

It was Robert Banks turn to be shocked. He valued James for his fine writing and good judgment. This young woman was very proficient at running a con.

Beverly Franklin assessed the situation. "Mr. Vautrin, please forgive my bluntness but you have been duped and you are not alone. My husband and I fell for her con as well. In fact, I believe we were her first victims. She sent us a letter telling us her parents had been killed, and she needed to get to her sister in Oregon. We are very close to her sister Lydia and agreed instantly. We sent her the ticket for her passage. You've met our dear friend and employee, Mrs. Hildebrand. She saw through Myra immediately and sent us a telegram to check her story. Mr. Vautrin, we really don't have time to waste. Myra is trying to make her way to her sister. We believe she intends to do her harm. We must apprehend her post haste. Scotland Yard is looking for her and now, of course, Immigration will be getting into the act. She needs to be returned to Ireland and prosecuted for her actions."

James looked at Beverly in amazement and felt like a fool. "I couldn't quite believe her story, but her distress was so real, I felt I had to help her. Plus, I was thinking the brides for sale story sounded plausible."

"Brides for sale? If this situation was not so dire, I would laugh. We're running out of time. Where are you to meet Myra?" Mrs. Hildebrand's voice was stern and caught his attention.

"The Hotel Pennsylvania, we're to meet in half an hour. She's checking in as my cousin, using the name Martha Vautrin."

Franklin turned to the driver, "Hotel Pennsylvania. Hurry."

Traffic was at a crawl. The cab driver was doing his best to go around cars, but it had taken fifteen minutes to get to West 70th Street, and they still had thirty blocks to go. James was to meet Myra at 5:30 p.m. and it was 5:10.

James kept running everything through his mind. Embarrassed, he kept thinking, *I haven't been duped like this since the first story I worked on as a cub reporter. All her tears and histrionics, she's a first class actress.*

Traffic started moving again. There was a collective "Thank God" from the group.

The cab finally turned into the Hotel Pennsylvania, the five of them rushed out as soon as it stopped. Stephen spotted a policeman near the front door. Rushing over to the cop he said, "Officer, I'm Stephen Franklin of the Franklin Bank. We need your help. There is a young woman staying in this Hotel that is wanted by Scotland Yard, and she must be apprehended."

The policeman looked at the group. He recognized James and called out, "Hey, Jimmy boy. Is it true what he's sayin'?"

"Officer Dugin, pleasure to see you. Yes, it's true. Looks like you're going to be famous for making a big arrest."

James went to the front desk and asked for the room number of Miss Martha Vautrin.

The desk clerk smiled. "I'm sorry, sir, Miss Vautrin is not registered. According to our concierge, she cancelled about an hour ago."

"What? Where is the concierge?"

The desk clerk rang a bell and the concierge walked over from his stand.

"Mike, this gentleman is looking for his cousin, Miss Vautrin. I understand you spoke to her earlier today."

"Yes, sir, I did. She left your coat here and wanted to express her disappointment that she had to leave abruptly due to a family emergency."

James' mouth was hanging open. He was still hoping that some part of her story would be true. "Where did she go? How long ago did she leave?"

Mike was beginning to realize he should be selling this information, but he was standing too close to the front desk to start wheeling and dealing. "About an hour ago. She left your coat and asked me to call her a cab."

"Did you recognize the driver? If we find him we'll know where he took her." Beverly was losing patience at James' inability to grasp the situation.

Mike actually felt remorse, "No, ma'm, I didn't look at him too closely. He was out front and his trunk was open. I helped her into the back seat and put her luggage in the trunk. I didn't hear the conversation between the young miss and the driver."

Hildy walked up to James. "See what you've done. If you hadn't helped Myra, she wouldn't have eluded the authorities. Whatever happens is on your head. A grown man duped so easily and a reporter to boot. You should be ashamed."

Stephen Franklin took his secretary's arm. "Hildy, it's time we had your injuries looked at. Plus we need to figure out our next move."

Chapter 25

The Brookstones had four more days in New York before taking the train back to Oregon. They were in good humor as they walked into the New York Biltmore Hotel. They had no appreciation for the fine art in the expansive marble lobby, the only thing on their mind was dinner and finding a speakeasy.

As they walked to the front desk to retrieve their room key, Daniel spotted Myra at the window next to them checking in.

Myra decided that her best course of action was to assume Justine Driscoll's identity. Then, realizing that Justine conveniently had a "mousey" unmarried sister, she decided to become her instead. "I'm Miss Martha Driscoll. I believe you have my reservation?"

The hotel clerk looked through the reservations and could not find a reservation for Driscoll. Looking at the stunning young woman he said regretfully, "I'm sorry, miss. We don't have a reservation for a Driscoll." As he said the words, Myra's eyes clouded with tears. Quickly, to avoid a scene, the clerk hastened to add. "Fortunately, we are not full. I have a lovely room with a view of the park available."

Myra gave the desk clerk a dazzling smile. "I don't know how the mix-up happened, but I'm grateful you have a room available."

The clerk was enchanted, such a beautiful woman, and so gracious. Most of the guests yelled first, and then blamed him for any problems. "I'm happy to help, Miss Driscoll. Here is your room key and, if there is anything else, you have only but to ask. We are at your service."

"Thank you for your assistance. Can you possibly give me a recommendation of a good restaurant for dinner?"

"Oh yes, miss. Our own hotel restaurant, The Palm Court, is excellent. You'll be quite pleased with the cuisine. I'll be happy to make reservations for you. Will anyone be joining you?"

Myra had just had a week of first class cuisine and now considered herself to be quite an expert. "Please make reservations for me for 7 p.m. for one."

As she turned to walk to the elevator, she felt someone staring at her. Looking over, she saw a handsome young man devouring her with what could only be described as a ravenous look. Smiling shyly and looking down, she continued her walk across the lobby to the elevators.

"Pop, we still have some scotch left from last night. Let's have a drink upstairs and eat dinner in the hotel tonight."

Daniel was still following Myra with his eyes. He had never seen anyone so beautiful.

Calvin looked at his son and noticed the young woman he was eyeing. "Son, I've told you a hundred times, all women are whores. Some you pay in advance and others you pay for your entire life. Don't get taken in by some little gold digger."

"Did you see her? She has the face of an angel. You do what you want tonight, but I'm having dinner in the hotel." Daniel rarely defied his father, but there was something about the young women's vulnerable smile and innocent face that melted a bit of the ice around his heart.

Calvin stared at this son. "Do whatever the hell you want. I'm celebrating with or without you."

Daniel looked at the desk clerk, pulled out a $5 bill, and told him, "Dinner reservations at The Palm Court and see to it my table is next to the young lady's."

"Yes, sir, consider it done." The desk clerk blessed his good luck, but knew he'd have to split part of it with the maitre de to get the best table.

The bellhop took Myra's suitcases and escorted her to her room. Using her key, he opened the door and pushed his cart through the entry. Myra preceded him into the room; thankful the bellhop was behind her and couldn't see the look of amazement that passed over her face.

"Is the room acceptable, miss? Shall I have a maid come in to unpack your bags?"

"Yes, it will do nicely, and no, I do not need anyone to unpack." Pulling a dollar out of her pocket book, she tipped him as he left her room.

Myra pulled out her new clothes. She had enjoyed spending the Franklin's money. The shabby suitcase Geoffrey loaned her was long gone, replaced by two large matching leather bags. The two dresses she had purchased in Queenstown still looked good, but the new evening wear she bought on the ship was far more elegant and suitable for this hotel. Myra walked into the plush bathroom and started drawing a bath. The hot steamy water turned her pale skin a healthy pink glow. Luxuriating in the bath, Myra thought of the past few days with James.

He was such a handsome man, witty and with a fine job, but so gullible. Myra laughed to herself at how much easier it was getting to hook the fish and cutting them loose was effortless. She would have loved to have seen the look on his face at the Hotel Pennsylvania when he came to rescue his lady in distress.

The clock on her mantel chimed. It was 6:30, time to get dressed for dinner. Myra fluffed her hair and added a little color to her eyelids. She used only a light touch of make up, enough to accent her big blue eyes, and a light dusting of powder on her face. Selecting her most elegant dress, she put it on and appraised herself in the full length mirror. "Not bad. Not bad at all for a poor little Irish girl."

Taking her shawl and a small jeweled handbag, Myra exited her room. Riding in the elevator, she got off at the first floor crossing the lobby to the hotel restaurant.

The maitre de watched Myra approach and, before she opened her mouth, said, "Miss Driscoll, we have your table prepared. Please follow me."

As he pulled out her chair and placed the white linen napkin on her lap, Myra noticed the young man who was at the front desk when she checked in, seated at the table next to hers. She pretended not to notice and scanned the menu.

"I hear the beef dish is quite good." Daniel turned to her with his most winning smile.

"Thank you. I'll take it under consideration." Myra's voice was a bit cool. She really didn't need another fish so soon after James.

Undaunted, Daniel tried another approach. "Please forgive me for being so direct, but I have never seen anyone as beautiful as you in my entire life."

Myra tried to resist, but her brain started calculating four days in the hotel and a train ticket to Oregon, maybe one more fish. "Sir, you are entirely too forward."

"You're right. I haven't even introduced myself. I'm Daniel Brookstone. I'm here on business. I actually live in a town just outside of Portland, Oregon, called Little Creek. My father and I have quite a few business interests in the town. Actually, we own half of the town."

Myra schooled her face into one of indifference. "You're a very long way from home, Mr. Brookstone. Half the town? That's impressive but half is always relative to the size of the whole." As she spoke she surreptitiously looked him over. His raven black hair intensified the color of his startling green eyes. Prominent cheekbones and wide lips gave his face an exotic look. The entire effect was ruggedly handsome, and a quick second glance told her he was well aware of his effect on women.

"And if I may ask, where are you from? You don't sound like a New Yorker." Daniel was doing his best to be engaging. He puffed up with pride and added, "By the way, owning half of Little Creek is a sizeable amount."

Myra thought back to some of the people she met on the ship and decided that she could retell some of Justine Driscoll's stories if need be. "You're correct, Mr. Brookstone, I am a Midwesterner."

"What brings you to New York?"

"Really it's a story I don't care to share with a stranger." Myra forced some tears to her eyes. "I'm so sorry. I would prefer to enjoy my dinner alone."

Daniel's heart stopped. The tears in her eyes and her fragile demeanor called out to a protective instinct he wasn't even aware of.

"Miss Driscoll, I'm so sorry. I can see that I have distressed you. Please forgive me. Of course, I will give you your privacy."

Just then the waiter intervened, "Miss, have you decided on your entrée?"

Myra looked at the waiter, still trying to figure out how to reel in the fish next to her. "Yes, I hear the beef is quite good." With that she cast a small smile at Daniel.

Daniel Brookstone always got what he wanted, and had never backed away from a challenge. Little Miss Driscoll had turned into one. He had watched her covertly throughout dinner. He saw her dainty bites and her aristocratic bearing. He woke up the next morning determined to know this young woman. She seemed different from other women. His father was wrong, not all women are whores. The beautiful Miss Driscoll was a lady.

At the same time, Myra woke up laughing. She'd heard it was a small world, but to actually meet someone who was from Little Creek? The saints were not only smiling on her, they were laughing, too. Myra was trying to figure out how to work this to her advantage when she noticed an envelope had been slipped under her door. Picking it up Myra opened it and smiled. It was from Daniel Brookstone.

Miss Driscoll,

   It is going to be a lovely day for sightseeing. I would be honored to take you on a tour of the city today. Please meet me in the lobby at 10:00a.m.

I assure you I am a gentleman and in a city as crowded as New York, you will have constant chaperones. Wear comfortable shoes, the best way to see the city is on foot.

Sincerely,
Daniel Brookstone

Myra wanted to be on her way, but Daniel was throwing himself at her, and it would be entertaining to hear about the town Lydia and Edward live in. She dressed carefully, wanting to maintain her illusion of wealth. She had picked up some nice pieces of costume jewelry on the ship. They looked expensive and complimented her stylish dress perfectly. Looking at her face in the mirror, Myra was pleased with what she saw. She looked like an aristocrat and carried herself as one. If only the Franklins knew what they had created with their first class ticket.

Seeing Daniel near the revolving door, she approached him. 'Mr. Brookstone, I really am not in the habit of spending the day with people I do not know. I'm sorry, but I will have to refuse your gracious invitation."

Daniel was used to getting his way and would not to be deterred. "Miss Driscoll, I can assure you I am a gentleman. I'll take you on a tour of Central Park. I promise you there are hundreds of people in it at all times. And, I will dangle dinner at Delmonico's as an enticement. No one should come to New York without visiting the oldest and most famous, restaurant in the country."

Myra smiled to herself. Pausing as if she were thinking it over, she gave him a stern look. "Mr. Brookstone, I will accompany you today, but, be warned, if you try anything unseemly, I will return to the hotel."

She watched as a wide smile lit up his face. She thought *reeling in this egotistical fish will be very entertaining.*

Just then Calvin Brookstone stormed across the lobby. "I need a word with my son."

Myra was a little taken aback by his abruptness and watched the exchange between them. She heard the end of the conversation.

Daniel spat out the words. "Father, you don't know what you're talking about. I'm going."

Calvin Brookstone whirled around and stared at Myra. He'd caught a quick look at the young lady in the lobby yesterday, but had not fully appreciated how beautiful this Miss Driscoll was. Looking at her now, he could see what had his son in such a heated state. "Miss Driscoll, forgive my rudeness. I'm Calvin Brookstone, Daniel's father."

Myra appraised the situation. It was obvious the elder Brookstone was unhappy his son was going out for the day. She studied the older man, noting his piercing green eyes were identical to his son's. "Mr. Brookstone, I hate the thought of taking you away from your son for the day. Perhaps you would like to join us?"

Brookstone looked at her carefully. She seemed guileless. Her clothes and jewelry were tasteful and obviously expensive. Her face held a slight touch of cosmetics, but was not overdone. Instinct told him she was as she appeared, but experience left some room for doubt. He had a healthy distrust of women and would hold that opinion until proven otherwise. "That is a very kind and generous offer, Miss Driscoll. I wouldn't dream of imposing on your sight-seeing. Go and enjoy your day. My son is quite well versed in the history of New York City. I'm sure he'll prove to be an entertaining guide."

Daniel looked at his father. His demeanor seemed harmless. It was the hard glint in his eyes that belied his affability. For the thousandth time, Daniel cursed his mother for running off and leaving them. Calvin had never recovered and had punished numerous women for his wife's misdeeds.

"Miss Driscoll, let's get started on our tour. I see you've worn sensible shoes. That's marvelous. Walking is truly the only way to see New York."

Myra smiled. "I agree. From what I've seen of the city so far, on foot is the only way to enjoy the ambiance. Shall we go?"

Turning to Calvin Brookstone, Myra smiled. "I do hope we meet again. Thank you for the loan of your son."

Calvin watched them depart. There was something different about this Miss Driscoll. Something he couldn't put his finger on, but looking into her shrewd eyes was almost like looking into his own.

Myra's look of wide-eyed amazement was not faked. Touring New York with Daniel showed her a world she had never dreamed of. Edward had written to Lydia about his stay in New York, the tall buildings, and all the skyscrapers being built. Skyscrapers indeed! They were aptly named. Myra stood back and tried to see the top of the buildings. It looked as if they really did scrape the sky.

Daniel was thrilled to show her New York. He and his father had been here twice before, and he was familiar with the city. He was pleased Myra wanted to walk rather than view the sights from a cab.

"Daniel, I want to feel the pulse of the city. I can't do that from a cab."

And feel it she did. She listened to the people, heard all the accents, and smelled the peanuts roasting on the vendor's carts. New York was a cacophony of sounds, sights, and smells. Myra thought it was a shame she had to leave such a wonderful, vibrant city to go to a backwater town like Little Creek. She was already bored to tears listening to Daniel go on and on about his fair city and how he and his father were so influential.

"Oh, I'm sorry, Daniel. You were saying?"

"New York City is exciting, if that's the sort of thing you're after. In Little Creek, we have lush forests, and mountains and ten water falls. Our town doesn't have this huge influx of immigrants."

At the word immigrants, Myra's ears perked up. "Why Daniel, it sounds like Oklahoma. Oh not the lush forests, but the fact that true Americans live there like we have in Tulsa."

Daniel flashed a brilliant smile. "Oh, Martha, I knew you were a refined woman. We work very hard to limit the amount of immigrants in our fair city."

"How do you manage that?"

"We have our ways. You've heard of course of the KKK?"

Fortunately, Myra's dinner companions had covered a wide variety of topics in their week together. "Of course, we actually have a group of those brave Americans in Tulsa."

Daniel was amazed. Martha understood everything he and his father stood for. "My father would be so pleased to know you feel the same way as us on topics of such importance."

Myra was in no hurry to spend time with Daniel's father. She hadn't missed the hard look he had given her in the hotel lobby and the cruel look in his eyes. Shuddering she did her best to smile at his ignorant son. "Yes, my family has been here for three generations. We don't want to have people in our town that don't share the same values or religion."

Daniel was elated. Martha was a woman of sophistication, beauty, intelligence, and, apparently, personal wealth. He fancied himself quite a catch and felt he had finally met a woman who could be an asset to a man like himself.

"It was very generous of you to invite my father along today."

Myra smiled, knowing full well the elder Mr. Brookstone wouldn't have called her bluff. I hope he finds something entertaining to do today."

Daniel smiled to himself. His father was going to talk to the concierge about some afternoon fun with a female. Daniel didn't think he stood much of a chance. He saw the hard looks Louie, the concierge, kept throwing their way. Daniel could care less what he thought. Those women deserved what they got. In his opinion they were the lowest life form on earth. His dad is wrong though. All women aren't whores, but he's right you don't have to worry about what you do to whores. Turning to Myra, he smiled. "I'm sure we don't have to worry about my father. He'll find something to do."

Myra was fascinated with the activity in New York City. They walked by an enormous crater in the earth that was soon be the home of the new Chrysler Building. It was projected to be the tallest building in the world. Heading uptown, they walked by huge construction areas. Myra thought back to Edward's letters about how hard it was for the Irish to find work. "There's so much construction going on in this city. I'm sure there's no shortage of men to work them."

"Oh, there's no shortage. In fact, there are so many men the construction companies can afford to be picky. You'll see that most of them have signs saying no Irish or Italians need apply."

Myra was incensed at the blatant discrimination, but kept her face neutral.

"These Catholics think they can come over here and push their religion on our country. It's not going to happen. We've taken care of the situation in our town."

"Really? How did you accomplish that?"

"It's against the law in our town to have a Catholic church. We make it very inconvenient for the immigrants. The nearest church is twenty miles away and Catholic schools are against the law in Oregon."

Myra hadn't really cared about church as a child, and the only school in their village was Catholic. Obviously a thought she wasn't going to share with Daniel. "That's very interesting. Look, is that Central Park?"

"Oh, we're here already. I was so busy talking, I hadn't noticed how far we've walked. Yes, this is Central Park. It stretches two and a half miles, and it's a half mile wide. When the city fathers first decided they wanted to make this area a park, used eminent domain to take over the property from some Irish Pig farmers and some German farmers. I think it was worth it. Don't you, Martha?"

Myra was looking at the expanse of park in front of her. She saw a zoo to her right, and, turning to Daniel, she couldn't contain her enthusiasm. Her mask cracked a bit, but she managed to keep her voice unaccented. "Oh, Daniel, please. Can we go to the zoo?"

Daniel laughed with eagerness. "I love zoos, too! Let's go get tickets."

Myra was surprised. She had a marvelous day. Daniel started off a bit boorish, going on and on about Little Creek and how everyone bowed down to the Brookstone's wishes. But once Myra and Daniel were in Central Park, a fun-filled young man emerged, and the rest of the day was lovely. They toured the zoo, went on a boat ride on the lake in Central Park, and ended the day with dinner at Delmonico's.

Daniel looked at Myra. "Martha, you have a wonderful smile on your face. Did you enjoy the day?"

Myra was spooning a bit of caviar onto a piece of toast. "Oh, Daniel, I don't know when I've had so much fun."

Looking around Delmonico's, she felt a déjà vu from the ship. Everyone was dressed in evening clothes and the waiters hovered around each table. The food was French, and there were so many wonderful items on the menu, Myra found it hard to select. "Daniel, I simply cannot make up my mind. You order for both of us."

Daniel looked at Myra. They had stopped at the hotel for a brief rest and to change for dinner. The two hours he was away from her seemed like forever. He was totally captivated with the woman he thought of as Martha. She had been an enjoyable companion all day. Her humor and intelligence kept him on his toes. He was not used to a woman who had opinions, and she was so interested in his life.

"Martha, it occurs to me I don't know very much about you. All we've done is talk about me and Little Creek. Please, tell me about yourself. What are you doing in New York? When will you be going back to Oklahoma?"

"Daniel, please, I don't want to talk about this now. I've had such a lovely day. It's the first time in months I've been able to forget about the sad things in my life. As to going back to Oklahoma, there's no point. My parents are dead and my sister and her husband have the house. I decided to come to New York to start a new life, but after a week here, I realize this city is just too big for a little gal from Oklahoma. Please, I'd like to enjoy this dinner with you. We have so little time left together before you head to Little Creek."

"Of course Martha, this has been such a wonderful day. We can talk tomorrow." Daniel was happy to have the conversation turned back to him.

Daniel described every street, all the businesses, and even mentioned the "Mick owned" restaurant in town. She could almost see her sister sweating behind the stove in the kitchen.

Myra was pleased. She had gleaned information about Little Creek that would be useful in the future. Her plan was to make it to Portland and look for work. Playing cat and mouse with her dear sister and Edward appealed to her. She would enjoy prolonging their anxiety.

Myra was sitting in her hotel room when there was a knock at her door. She didn't expect company. She had made it clear to Daniel she was a lady and expected to be treated as such. Opening the door, she was shocked to see the elder Brookstone standing there with a scowl on his face.

"Mr. Brookstone, is there something wrong? Is Daniel all right?" Myra could see he was very agitated.

Brookstone started to push his way into the room. Myra shoved the door into him. "Mr. Brookstone, if you wish to speak to me we can do so in the hall or in the lobby. You are not coming into my room. This is very improper."

"Who are you trying to kid, I'm on to you with your big airs and high fullutin' ways."

Myra could smell liquor on Brookstone's breath. She wondered what he was up to. She knew there was no way that Brookstone had figured out anything about her. Myra hadn't given Daniel enough information to put together any sort of check on her.

"Mr. Brookstone, I do not wish to be rude, but you are not coming into my room. If you wish, we can continue this conversation over coffee in the lobby." Myra gave the surprised man a gentle yet firm shove backwards, and slammed the door. "I will meet you in the lobby in fifteen minutes, Mr. Brookstone."

Myra sat on her bed. She was shaken by his words, but she recognized a bully when she saw one. Daniel had confided to her the reason they were in New York and talked about the meetings with Franklin. He hinted his father had been intimidated by Franklin but put up a good front. The one thing Myra had learned about Americans is they like to win at all costs. "Well, we'll see who puts up a good front now."

Exactly fifteen minutes later, Myra walked into the lobby. She stood with her back straight and her head held high as she surveyed the room, looking for Brookstone. Spotting him in the corner, she strode purposely across the lobby and greeted Brookstone with a smile. "Mr. Brookstone, what is it you wish to discuss?"

Brookstone looked her over. She was not shaking in her boots or apologizing for their earlier encounter. She didn't berate him for his boorish behavior nor did she seem intimidated. This woman was puzzling. He could understand his son's attraction to her.

"I want you to stop seeing my son." Brookstone stared at Myra, daring her to disagree.

"Mr. Brookstone, your son and I have spent two days together touring New York and having dinner. I would hardly consider that a relationship to be concerned about." Myra smiled as she faced off with Calvin.

"I have plans for my son. They don't include marriage to someone like you."

"Someone like me? Exactly who or what do you think I am? Please tell me, I'm curious." Myra stared him down. She was actually enjoying this little encounter.

"Daniel is not ready for marriage, and it is all you women want."

"Marriage is the farthest thing from my mind. I have been the dutiful daughter and now that my parents are deceased, I would like a bit of freedom before I tie myself to some man for the rest of my life. If your only concern is I've decided to marry your son, your fears are unfounded and extremely premature. I truly see no need to further this discussion."

Brookstone was dumbfounded. This was contrary to all he knew about women. They were all manipulative bitches looking for a meal ticket. He wasn't used to a woman standing up to him.

"What are your plans, Miss Driscoll? Are you staying in New York?"

"Mr. Brookstone, my family owned several stores in our small town. I was in charge of the dry goods, and it bored me to tears, but

I'm good at business. My sister recently married and, with our parents' death, I decided to leave Oklahoma and go out on my own. I've decided to open a women's dress shop with upscale merchandise. Now, before you start to worry, I will not be relocating to your quaint little town. While the East Coast has some qualities that would go well with what I have in mind, I find I don't care for New York. I've had offers for opening a store in Seattle and Portland. The West Coast appeals to me. I have distant relatives in the area and would consider relocating there. Two East Coast investors are fighting to be my business partners. As you can see, I'm certainly not after any Brookstone money."

Brookstone watched Myra closely. He prided himself on being able to detect a bluff. Nothing in her demeanor alerted him to any deception. "Why in the hell would you be making East Coast investors richer than they already are? I'm so sick of East Coast bankers and their goddamn ways. You should be offering West Coast investors the opportunity to make the money."

Myra hid her surprise. She really hadn't planned on Brookstone falling for her pretense of opening a store.

"Mr. Brookstone, I have spent much time working with these bankers. In fact, I'm considering The Franklin Bank as one of my investors. It's much too late in the process to be offering it to other investors."

"God damn Franklin Bank and that arrogant Stephen Franklin. Whatever he is offering I'll double as long as you open your business in Portland."

"Mr. Brookstone, really, I'm not prepared to…."

Brookstone cut her off. "Miss Driscoll, where I come from, we put our money where our mouth is. How much is Franklin investing?"

Myra was momentarily perplexed. She had no idea what to tell Brookstone. She threw out the first number to come to her mind. "Five hundred dollars."

She thought Brookstone was going to have a heart attack. "What the hell kind of shop are you opening? Are the dresses spun with gold thread?"

"Mr. Brookstone, I've told you I intend to sell high end merchandise. It takes capital to stock a store. Obviously, this business investment isn't the kind you are familiar with. I believe I will continue my business with Mr. Franklin's bank."

"The hell you will. I will have a cashiers check drawn for one thousand dollars. It will be ready by 9 a.m. tomorrow. For that kind of an investment, I want to have input on where you'll set up shop. You don't know Portland but I do. Daniel and I are leaving town on Thursday. You'll travel with us. We'll stop in Portland and find you a suitable store front."

Myra maintained her detached demeanor and paused as if she were considering his offer. She hated this arrogant man, and now he had backed her into a corner. However, on the upside, he was paving the way for her to head west. "Mr. Brookstone, since you obviously have connections in Portland; perhaps you would be the best choice as an investor."

Brookstone puffed up, proud to have bested Franklin again and that he had forced Martha Driscoll to take him on as an investor. He didn't like the arrogant way she had dismissed his son. "You've made a smart decision. Hopefully, the rest of your decisions are good. I'll be watching you and my money."

Myra looked at the man who had just paved her way to the Promised Land. "Mr. Brookstone, I did not anticipate this change in my plans. However, I must say I look forward to the challenge of working with you."

She stuck her hand out and shook Brookstone's, then turned and walked out of the lobby to the hotel elevator. Once inside, she started to laugh until tears ran down her cheeks thinking, *if all the Americans are as easy to manipulate as James and Brookstone, this isn't the land of milk and honey. This is the land of fools.*

Myra spent the last two days in New York visiting clothing manufacturers. Daniel was ecstatic at the thought of her being in Portland and had insisted on taking her down to the garment area. Myra placed four purchase orders with women's dress manufacturers in the garment district, knowing she probably would not be around to take delivery on any of them.

When they requested money down before they would work on her product, Daniel was quick to take out his checkbook and make a show of paying for her. Myra had convinced Daniel, she wanted to open her bank account in Portland and, therefore, had no checks available. Daniel was only too happy to pay. Myra promised to reimburse him. She thanked him profusely for his help while suggesting he not tell his father. "Daniel, I don't want your father to know you paid the down payment on my orders. My finances are all tied up right now with the settling of my parents' estate. Your father will lose confidence in me if he finds out you fronted the money."

"Martha, rest assured we both have complete confidence in your abilities." Daniel looked at her intently. His mind was actually was wondering about her bedroom abilities.

Myra was astute at reading faces and when Daniel's face changed to a look of lust, she studiously ignored it. This was getting very complicated. She knew Daniel was falling in love with her, and while it was to her advantage to play along, she didn't want things to go too far, thinking to herself, *I have business to take care of and, it's not the business the Brookstones are investing in. Although if I'm successful, I'm sure they'll be thankful to have two less 'micks' in their precious town.*

It was finally time to head west. Myra accompanied the Brookstones to the train station. She had been in New York five days and thought if the railway station was being watched, they would have given up by now. Anyone looking for her would be looking for a woman alone. Myra felt confident she would slip by unnoticed.

Once she was in the possession of Calvin Brookstone's thousand dollar check, she no longer worried about spending her own money. The three of them boarded the train and headed to the first class compartments.

Calvin Brookstone watched her every move. He was still suspicious of Martha Driscoll and how she had bewitched his son. Daniel hung onto her every word and made a great show of telling amusing stories and entertaining her on the three day trip. Myra was fascinated with the countryside but tried to maintain a blasé look.

Every evening the men went into what was formally known as the bar car. With Prohibition, the car was now just a place where the men gathered to smoke cigars and swap stories.

Myra was grateful for the respite from their company. Two Brookstones were two too many as far as she was concerned. It had never been her intention to be joined at the hip with them. With money involved for her alleged business, she had no choice. When she thought about it, opening a fine ladies store sounded rather intriguing. She worked in a dress shop at home until Lydia ran off and she had to help in her da's horrible bakery. She was good with numbers and had an eye for fashion. Maybe, after she took care of Edward and Lydia, she really would open a store somewhere. Myra was looking out the window smiling in anticipation when the conductor walked by.

"Why, Miss Delaney, how nice to see you again."

Myra almost fell out of her seat. She looked at the conductor and, in her American voice, said very coldly. "Sir, you have mistaken me for someone else. I'm Miss Driscoll."

Thomas Best had been a conductor on trains for thirty five years and never forgot a face. Looking at his passenger list he realized that indeed, this was Miss Driscoll. "I'm so sorry, Miss. You reminded me of a passenger we had a couple of months ago. Really, the similarity is amazing. You're a dead ringer for Miss Delaney. You could be long lost twins."

"I hardly think so. Now if you'll excuse me, I'll be retiring to my sleeping compartment." Giving the conductor a scathing look, Myra walked off with the bearing of a queen.

Best watched and realized that he was getting old. How could he have mistaken this woman for Miss Delaney who had been sweet and friendly? Miss Driscoll was acerbic and quite impressed with herself, nothing like Miss Delaney. Noting her name, he remembered hearing the porters talk about what a difficult passenger she was. Still, the resemblance was startling.

Myra reached her sleeping berth and couldn't stop her heart from racing. What if the Brookstones had been with her when that old fool called her Miss Delaney? The chances of them knowing her sister were unlikely, but this was a close call. She knew she couldn't venture a trip into Little Creek without someone putting two and two together.

Chapter 26

Edward walked into the restaurant and straight back to the kitchen. Lydia usually went to the restaurant at 5 a.m. to get the baking started. Edward was in the habit of staying home and doing whatever book work needed to be done. Stephen Franklin had called their home at 8 a.m. with the information about Myra.

Looking at his beautiful wife, Edward saw a smile light up her face when she saw him entering the kitchen. It faded when she looked at his grim expression. "Edward, you look as if you've seen a ghost. What has happened? Did you get word of Myra?"

Edward grabbed her hands and led her to the kitchen stool to sit. "Aye, I've word. I talked to Stephen this morning. The ship was met by Stephen and Beverly yesterday as planned. The custom agents were to apprehend Myra the minute Mrs. Hildebrand walked up to the Franklins. All of the first class passengers disembarked. The Franklins waited and waited. Mrs. Hildebrand was nowhere to be seen. When the last of the first class passengers came down the gangplank, the Franklins demanded that her cabin be checked. After the custom agents burst through the cabin door, they found Mrs. Hildebrand gagged and tied up in the bathroom. She was badly bruised from the rough treatment and very upset Myra had gotten away. Myra snuck into Mrs. Hildebrand's room in the very early hours. She shoved a gag in her mouth and bound her hands. Mrs. Hildebrand's eyes were covered so she had no idea if Myra was working alone. It was a frightful experience and spending hours on the cold bathroom floor was hard on her. Fortunately, she seems to have no permanent injuries."

Edward swallowed hard and continued, "Darlin', there is some bad news. Apparently, Mrs. Hildebrand travels with a gun, a small Derringer her late husband gave her when he was working nights as a cop. He was worried about her being alone. Once she got word Myra could be dangerous, she kept it under her pillow."

"Oh, Edward, please don't tell me Myra has it." Lydia's eyes were huge and her face had gone a deathly white.

"Yes, the gun is missing, and we can only surmise Myra has it. Stephen and Beverly are horrified. They are taking all the blame and have made it their mission to find her.

"Edward, I must talk to Stephen and Beverly. I can't bare the distress this has caused them. They mustn't be so hard on themselves."

"We can call them this afternoon. Stephen figured you'd want to talk to both of them so we've set up 4 p.m."

"Well, right now, I have work to do. Knowing it's impossible for Myra to get here before next Tuesday is a small measure of comfort. Maybe, as I pound down the dinner rolls, I'll picture her face." She slammed down the bread dough and kneaded it with vigor.

Edward walked behind his wife and quietly held her. "Lydia, I know this is hard. I am praying it will soon be over."

"Oh, Edward, she tries to destroy everything I care about, and I'm not going to allow her to succeed. Look what Myra has done to the Franklins. They are lovely generous people and she has used them, harmed Mrs. Hildebrand, and she's running around the country on money she's taken from other people. At least my parents are now home and safe. How could she do this?"

Edward hated to see Lydia distraught. "She's never been right in the head. It was obvious to some people in the village. She had few friends, and those she had were very easy to manipulate. She managed to hide her rages from everyone because she used you as a punching bag. I'll kill her if she comes near you again."

Lydia thought for a moment and very carefully said to her husband, "I know you are trying to protect me, but I'm not stopping our lives for her. I won't waste another moment living in fear. We are having an engagement party for Johnny and Annie tomorrow night, and I don't want to hear the word 'no' come out of your mouth, Edward."

Edward looked at his bride and noted the set of her jaw. He knew she would not back down. He also realized Lydia needed a good distraction. In the time-honored tradition of men who want to please their wives, Edward said the five words that made her smile for the first time in three days. "Tell me what to do."

Lydia was glowing. Her friend Annie had no idea there was a surprise engagement party scheduled for tonight. The restaurant was decorated with flowers and candles, much as their friends had done for them on their wedding day. She had baked a large sheet cake and decorated it with flowers, their names, and Congratulations was written on the top.

She was quite pleased with the effect. When Edward came in to ask a question he looked at the cake in amazement. "Lydia, my love, it's beautiful. I didn't know you knew how to decorate cakes."

"I didn't either. Maybe all those years of watching my da did some good. I remember he never let us touch his decorating utensils. He said he couldn't afford to have us make mistakes and have to redo it." A wistful look passed over her face, and Edward knew she was thinking of happier times with her family.

Just then, one of the customers poked her head in the door. "You'd better get out here. Looks like Johnny and Annie are coming down the sidewalk."

About thirty friends and customers were gathered in the restaurant. The tables had been arranged to form a U shape with a spot for Annie and Johnny at the center. Edward had asked Johnny to come tonight with Annie to help watch Lydia while he secretly called the Franklins for an update. It was a reasonable ruse. They were very worried about Lydia. Edward hated to take advantage of the situation, but he wanted to see the look on his friend's faces when they discovered the party was for them.

The door opened and at first they didn't register anything was going on. Both Annie and Johnny focused on Edward and Lydia, looking for any signs of distress. When the crowd finally broke out with a loud "Congratulations," they realized the party was for them. Annie cried when she saw her aunt in attendance. She knew Lydia must have worked her magic to get her aunt to come.

"Thank you everyone. Thank you so much for coming!" Annie and Johnny beamed at the crowd.

Johnny puffed up. "I've chased this girl for months. Our engagement won't be too long. I'm anxious to make her my wife before she comes to her senses."

The crowd laughed as Annie playfully cuffed him on the arm. "It's me that's worried about you coming to yours!"

Edward and Lydia raised their glasses of lemonade and proposed a toast.

"Johnny, you're the first friend I made when I left home. We've been through much together, and we've always watched out for each other. I'm grateful for your friendship. I'm also grateful for the lovely woman you will soon call wife and Lydia and I will always call friend. May the years be kind to you and your life together be blessed."

Johnny looked at Edward. "Well that was a mouthful. I, too, am thankful we have stuck together and made a life for ourselves here. It's a good place to raise a family." Johnny looked pointedly at Annie's aunt and continued, "A Catholic family that is. I will cherish my Annie to my dying day and bless my lucky stars she said yes."

There was a loud cheer and many glasses clinking together. Edward and Johnny exchanged looks, both reading the other's mind. It was good to have a lighthearted moment and to be surrounded by friends.

Chapter 27

Stephen and Beverly had marshaled all their best resources. Security officers from the Bank had combed through the city. There was no one named Myra Delaney or any of her known aliases, Martha Vautrin or Myra Vautrin, registered in any of the hotels in town. Myra had literally disappeared.

Bank Security had the train stations under surveillance. They were ready and willing to deal with any situation. The Franklins made sure all modes of public transportation to Little Creek were watched.

Mrs. Hildebrand returned to her desk and was the official command post coordinating all of the efforts and regulating the shifts at the train station.

Immigration could not spare the manpower, and there had been no official word from Scotland Yard. In their eyes, Myra was just another immigrant who got through the system, not a big enough crime to order the manhunt Stephen Franklin was demanding.

Stephen Franklin had used every favor he could. He finally got the mayor to put a sketch of Myra in the police station, and she was the subject of all the shift meetings. When Stephen and Beverly looked at the sketch Hildy had drawn, they saw the eerie resemblance to Lydia in her lips, nose and the set of her jaw. It was only when they looked into Myra's dead eyes that they could see a very different person.

Beverly walked into Stephen's den. "I just got off the phone with Lydia."

Stephen turned towards the door. "How is she? Did you speak to Edward, too?"

"Yes, I spoke to them both. Lydia is upset, but I think she's handling it very well. Edward's tone was murderous. "Myra would be smart to just disappear into America and leave her sister and Edward alone."

"I blame myself. I should have realized she was very crafty and would pull a disappearing act. James Vautrin is not a stupid man and look how he, too, was pulled into her fabrications."

Beverly sat in the chair opposite Stephen. "Waiting is the hardest part. I just wish the other shoe would drop so we could deal with it and let Lydia and Edward live their lives."

"I've got a man at the Portland Terminal as well as the Little Creek Terminal. We'll keep him meeting trains until something breaks."

"Stephen, please come to bed, you've exhausted yourself with all of this. Being sleep deprived is not going to help Lydia and Edward."

"You're right. I'm not doing any good sitting here brooding. Come, my dear, let's get some sleep."

Stephen and Beverly Franklin realized at the same moment the search was fruitless. Myra had given everyone the slip, and, after four days, they stopped surveillance of the train and bus stations. Stephen already had a man in Little Creek to look out for his business investments, now he would have to have him slip into Edward and Lydia's life as an extra set of eyes.

Stephen looked at his watch. Michael Tucker would be home now from his job at Brookstone's mill. He reached for the phone and had the operator place the call.

Tucker answered on the third ring. Stephen wasted no time. "Tucker, I need to extend your duties a bit. I want you to start eating at O'Brien's restaurant. Get close to them and see if you can keep an eye out for the crazy sister we believe is heading to Little Creek."

"Crazy sister? Mr. Franklin, I'm going to need more details."

"Lydia O'Brien has a sister named Myra Delaney. From what I understand, they look very much alike. Myra has a modern flapper-style haircut, something that should stand out in Little Creek. The sister assaulted my secretary, Mrs. Hildebrand, and she's wanted by the British government. She's quite the con artist. She managed to convince my wife and me she needed to come to America to tell her sister their parents had died. We sent Mrs. Hildebrand over to escort her to the States. The parents, by the way, are alive and well. Myra's intent all along has been to get to her sister and do harm. From all accounts, she's very intelligent and quite the chameleon. She is able to assimilate into her surroundings like a native. Lydia O'Brien has become like a daughter to us, we're trying to keep her safe. Her husband, although well meaning, thinks he can handle this on his own. Mrs. Franklin and I would feel better with another set of eyes keeping watch."

Tucker pondered while he processed the information he was just given. "Mr. Franklin, I usually eat at O'Brien's a couple of times a week and have gotten to know Edward and Lydia. I've noticed a tension the past few days, and this certainly explains it. You can count on me to watch over them."

"Good. Keep me informed."

Stephen hung up the phone feeling slightly better. It was a bad omen Myra had eluded all their search efforts.

Chapter 28

Myra was in a panic. Seemingly calm on the outside, she was doing her best to figure her way out of business with the Brookstones while still keeping their money. This was the second day of being dragged around Portland to look at storefronts, and Calvin Brookstone was starting to get antsy.

"This building is located in the best retail area of Portland. The rent is reasonable, and it's the sixth place we've looked at. You've managed to find fault with all of them. I thought you were excited about opening a store, it looks to me like you're making excuses and dragging your feet."

Myra was about to come up with a sarcastic retort when she spied a beauty parlor next door to the empty storefront. Thinking back to the day before she sailed to America when she bought new stylish dresses and got a fashionable haircut, she loudly exclaimed, "This is it, this is the perfect location."

Expecting another rebuttal, Calvin was caught off guard. "Why this place? What's so special about it? It looks like all the others."

"Mr. Brookstone, you must understand location is everything. Look at the surrounding shops. There's a jewelry store, a hair salon, and a millinery store. Everything screams for women to come shopping."

Calvin had to admit, looking at it through her eyes, she was on to something. "OK, Miss Driscoll, this is where we are going to make money selling women's dresses? This is the type of business Franklin was so eager to invest in?"

"Mr. Brookstone, we will be in the business of selling dreams. We're selling beauty and we're selling transformations." Myra turned on her heel and walked into the store area again. Somewhere between accidently conning Brookstone out of his money and looking at six potential places of business she had no intention of renting, this shop spoke to her. Myra knew she really could make a go of it if she put her mind to it.

"So when will you be able to get stock in here and set up shop?"

Myra thought about the orders she had already placed. "I can have stock here in three weeks, and the shop ready to go a week later."

Brookstone nodded and looked at his son. "Daniel, I'm going to Little Creek. Handle the rental details, and I'll see you at dinner this evening. Miss Driscoll, I expect you will be on schedule and have this shop opened in thirty days."

Myra felt a surge of relief that Brookstone was leaving. His presence was oppressive, and she had to be on her toes with him around.

Watching him leave, Myra turned to Daniel. "I plan on staying at the hotel until the end of the week and then look for suitable lodging."

Daniel smiled. "I'm pleased this is working out. The thought of you being just an hour away from Little Creek makes me very happy. I'll come see you as often as I can."

Myra was wondering how she was going to get transportation to Little Creek to nose around and see what her sister was up to. Myra smiled and looked pleased, all the while thinking she'd really stepped in it this time. "Yes, Daniel, and I look forward to visiting Little Creek and seeing your lovely town." *And,* she thought to herself, *getting even with my sister.*

Myra wanted to leave the hotel. While she had plans to eventually take all of Brookstone's money, she wanted to save some of her own cash. She asked the concierge about boarding houses and was directed to Mrs. Rogers' home.

Mrs. Rogers was at least seventy with her white hair carefully twisted in a bun that sat on top of her head like an apple waiting for an arrow. She was small and round, but her brown eyes looked sharp behind her glasses. She offered only one room, and it had just become available. Giving Myra the once over Mrs. Roger noted the young woman's expensive clothes were at odds with hands that looked as if they had seen work. Myra did her best to seem amiable to Mrs. Rogers, smiling and looking sincere at all the right times. It was her eyes she had trouble masking.

Mrs. Rogers was a little apprehensive until she saw the wad of cash Myra laid out for her first month. Money was tight, and she didn't want to be long without a renter. "All right, Miss Driscoll. The room is yours. Rent is due on the first of each month. I serve breakfast and dinner. You are to tell me if you won't be coming home for dinner. I'm not a rich woman. I can't afford to be wasting food."

"Of course, Mrs. Rogers, I will make sure to let you know if I will not be home for dinner. I'm grateful to stay in your lovely home."

Privately, Myra was thinking, *the old battle-axe is going to be a pain, but her home is close to my alleged shop. I'll be quite comfortable here while I figure out how I'm going to get to Edward and Lydia.*

"Where did you say you are from, Miss Driscoll?"

"I'm from Oklahoma, Mrs. Rogers, but I'm relocating to Portland and opening a ladies dress shop."

Mrs. Rogers was concerned. She may have been too hasty in agreeing to rent the room. Girls from good families don't just up and leave their home unless they were in trouble. Pointedly looking at Myra's slender waist, she decided the young woman didn't look like she was in the family way and, with her figure, probably hadn't had a baby recently. There was a story with this girl, and Mrs. Rogers knew she'd find out sooner rather than later.

"I've never been out of the state of Oregon. I don't like to leave my home. My late husband was the traveler. He was a salesman and went everywhere. By the time he came home from a trip, he was in no mood to travel for fun."

Myra breathed a sigh of relief. She was always worried about people asking her questions about Oklahoma. She had details she had absorbed from Justine Driscoll endless prattle aboard ship, but was at a loss for the finer nuances of the state. Determined to make a good impression on Mrs. Rogers, she smiled and said with all sincerity, "Oregon is a lovely state, and, from what I have seen of Portland, it is very beautiful. Who would ever want to leave a place like this?"

Mrs. Rogers warmed up immediately. "Oh dear, you are so right. Perhaps you would like a cup of tea before you settle in?"

Myra smiled her best smile and thought to herself, *Americans are so easy to fool.*

Chapter 29

C alvin Brookstone walked into the Parrish Bank looking for Harold. He wanted to him tell about the deal he'd cut with Franklin and how he'd one-upped him in business. Strutting to the back of the Bank, he walked by Mary Hanson as if he owned the entire town. "No need to announce me," he said as he gave her a quick leer.

Mary watched as he pushed open the office door and saw the look on Harold Parrish's face. *Oh to be a fly on the wall,* she thought.

Calvin sprawled out on the sofa and put his feet on the coffee table. "Well, Harold, I got us a hell of a deal with that pompous ass Franklin."

Harold frowned at the feet on his antique English table and looked at Calvin. "Yes, I've received the papers. It looks to be in order and I'm happy with the deal. I thought Franklin was okay. He seemed like an amiable sort of chap. What was the problem?"

"The problem was he treated me like a backwoods hick. He thought he was better than us. I could tell he was ready to try and pull one over on us." Puffing up, he added, "I showed him. I nailed him on some details and got us more than he was ready to pay. You should be glad I went there to negotiate."

Harold looked at Calvin. "I'm sure you did a fine job, but, meanwhile, I had to clean up your KKK mess. I've disbanded your so-called Klan, and, after my discussion with your group, I don't think they will be a problem. I foreclosed on eight of your members' homes. As far as I'm concerned, they were more undesirable than the immigrants your KKK was protecting us from."

Calvin shrugged his shoulders nonchalantly. "That's another thing about that insufferable prig Franklin. He looked at me like I was a communist or something. All I was trying to do was to keep this town safe for decent Americans."

"Calvin, I'm not going to get into it with you again. We're going to make a fortune on this deal with Franklin. Just keep your nose clean and stop that KKK nonsense before you jeopardize our entire operation."

Brookstone had already had a long conversation with Al White about the KKK and their future efforts to keep the town "pure." He looked at Harold and said, "I own half this town. I employ who I choose to employ, and there are others that do the same. So, no, we won't be marching in the streets. This contract means too much money to me, but I won't have Franklin telling me what to do in other areas of business." Brookstone failed to mention his foreman, Sam Shaw, had hired two micks a few months ago. He'd almost fired Shaw, but then one mick got hurt and the other one was a damn good worker. Brookstone laughed to himself. *I'll have to remember to tell Franklin how open-minded I am, one immigrant employee out of the hundred and twenty men in the mill.*

Parrish sighed deeply. "Calvin, the portion of the business we do with him stipulates there be no discrimination of hiring. Do what you want in the logging and lumber end of the business but any of the sand and gravel workers better not be denied employment based on their religion. Word gets back to Franklin, and he'll figure out getting rid of the KKK did not solve the problem. I'm certainly not willing to lose money for your ridiculous prejudices."

Parrish stood up to make his point and to get Brookstone out of his office. "Franklin will be back out here in a few months to check on things. I'd suggest we both live by the contract he sent."

Brookstone stood up and spat out, "You can bow to his wishes, but I'm still man enough to take him on if he interferes with this town." Storming out, he slammed the door behind him. He was so intent on leaving, he forgot to give Mary his customary leer, much to her relief.

Mary went to Parrish's office door and gently knocked before she entered. "Are you alright? It didn't sound like it went too well."

"It went as well as could be expected. Brookstone had to save face. He won't admit it, but he was intimidated by Franklin. He was out-classed and it irked him to no end. He'll do something rash to strike out and assert his superiority over the town. I'll just have to be ready to pick up the pieces."

Mary looked at Harold Parrish and felt a surge of protectiveness over her boss and lover. She had always hated Brookstone and his leering looks. There were rumors around town about the life his wife had led before she escaped. Mary had women friends who whispered about Mrs. Brookstone and the bruises she had tried to hide. They said she had the most haunted eyes they'd ever seen. She must have been in fear of her life, or she never would have left four-year-old Daniel all alone with that monster. Mary believed every word she'd ever heard about Calvin Brookstone and fervently wished he would disappear in a puff of smoke. "Too bad there's not an organization similar to the KKK to get rid of the white undesirables. I'd put him on the top of their list."

Harold Parrish looked at her in surprise and laughed out loud. "Leave it to you to come up with a novel solution. I'm sure there are many who would agree with you."

Chapter 30

Edward was tired of the stress of waiting for Myra to make an appearance. Lydia wasn't sleeping well, and they were both out of sorts. He was sitting at the counter of the restaurant when Annie and Johnny came in.

Johnny looked at his best friend and saw the slump of his shoulders and grim expression. "Edward, you are driving us all crazy with worry. It's time for you and Lydia to take a break. You need a couple days off, and I have just the plan for you."

Edward looked up and saw the smiles on their faces. "What plan might you be hatching? You both look like you've swallowed the canary."

Annie clapped her hands together. "It's so exciting. The Queen of Romania is coming to Oregon! There's going to be parades in each city as she travels through, The Dalles, Hood River, and Multnomah Falls! Then she's going to Portland. That's the most exciting part!"

Edward was a little bewildered. "How can the Queen of Romania going to Portland be exciting to Lydia and me?"

Johnny broke in. "Because, you idiot, you and Lydia are going to Portland for the parade and two nights away from Little Creek. The parade is on Wednesday. You can leave Wednesday morning, see the parade, and come home on Friday morning. Think of it, two days away from the stress of waiting for Myra to appear."

"And just who is going to mind the restaurant while we're gone?"

Annie piped in, "I am, Edward. My faithful assistant here is going to help wait tables. We have it all worked out. Michael Tucker is going to loan you his car. A hotel he worked for owes him a favor and is giving you two nights for free. See, it's all worked out!"

In a short time, Michael had become a good friend to the O'Brien's, showing up for dinner at the restaurant three or four times a week. He had no family in the area and was lonely. Lydia and Edward had adopted him and often sat with him to eat their own dinner. The fact it was supposed to be work never crossed his mind.

"It's very generous of Michael and you two. You've got me thinking now. I never took Lydia on a proper honeymoon. This could be a nice break for us, and we'd be back in time for the weekend business."

Realizing Edward was agreeing to it, Annie and Johnny exchanged relieved looks.

"It's settled. Go tell Lydia so she can start thinking of what clothes to pack." Annie was elated her friend was going to get a break from all the stress.

Annie and Johnny stayed out in the dining area and watched Edward walk back to the kitchen to talk to Lydia. The next thing they heard was a squeal of delight and Lydia saying, "Really? A parade and two days in a hotel! Oh, Edward, it all sounds lovely."

Just then, the co-conspirator, Michael Tucker, walked into the restaurant. "Did you tell them?" As he said the words another excited squeal came from the kitchen. "No need to answer. Sounds like it went well."

Michael was relieved. Stephen Franklin had come up with the idea and was paying for the hotel. He felt a little guilty telling Johnny and Annie the manager owed him a favor, but he knew Mr. Franklin would give the hotel a plausible cover story. Michael was relieved his friends would get a bit of a respite from their worries. He, too, was beginning to get a little edgy, looking around corners waiting for this alleged mentally ill sister to jump out.

Little Creek was driving Michael crazy. He was keeping an eye on the Brookstones by working in their Mill office. Daniel Brookstone was strutting around grinning like an idiot since his return from New York. Michael knew through Mr. Franklin the business deal had gone well for the Bank and the Brookstones thought they had "won" the negotiations. Still, it was no reason for Daniel's recent behavior. He was leaving work early whenever he could. It could only mean there was a woman involved somewhere. From the local gossip Michael had picked up, the Brookstones were notorious in Little Creek. Calvin's first wife was known to have been abused by him, and there wasn't a woman in town that would date him. His son proved early on the apple hadn't fallen far from the tree. So chances are, whoever he was seeing, wasn't from town. Michael thought to himself, *if even half the rumors are true, the young lady should run in the opposite direction before it's too late.*

Lydia was on cloud nine. She couldn't believe they would be spending two nights in a hotel and see a parade with the Queen of Romania. She was thankful for any excuse to get out of Little Creek and all the worry. Watching Edward drive Michael Tucker's car, she smiled with amusement. "When did you become such a good driver?"

Edward laughed and looked at his wife. "I've done many things since I've come to this country. Johnny actually had to teach me. We worked as delivery drivers at one job. I think they paired us up for brains and brawn."

Lydia giggled. "Well, you are a bit taller than Johnny, so you must have been the brawn."

"Aye, and sometimes the brains, too. It's hard to get a truck loaded well so the load doesn't shift, and you can take it out in the proper order. We were doing very well until the owner said to get rid of the micks."

Lydia bristled and touched Edward's arm. "I'm sorry. I know it was hard trying to earn a living and deal with all the prejudice."

"Well now, it all worked out in the end, and we're in a position to help others. And now we're on this wonderful holiday. Everything happens for a reason and we're together.

It's the only thing that matters." Edward reached for Lydia's hand and gave it a squeeze. "All that will ever matter."

Lydia sat back in her seat. For the next two days, she was going to live in the moment and not think about Myra. She would enjoy this wonderful reprieve and everything Portland had to offer.

"I think the hotel is down this street." Edward made a right turn and, in the distance, they could see a grand hotel.

"Oh my, are you sure this is it? What kind of work did Michael do there? It's awfully posh!" Lydia's eyes were as big as saucers.

"I think by the time our two days are up, we are going to owe Michael quite a few free dinners." Edward, too, was a bit struck by the grandness of the hotel.

They pulled up to the front door and a valet came out to park their car. Edward, unaccustomed to such service, was reluctant to give the man his friend's car.

Laughing, Lydia looked at her husband. "It's OK, Edward. He is the valet. It's his job to park and watch over the car."

"Well I've never heard of such a thing. What if he takes it?"

By now Lydia was in a fit of giggles. "Edward, the Franklins took me to a restaurant that had a valet. They'll take good care of Michael's car. Come on. I'm anxious to see the inside."

Edward had not had the advantage of spending time with rich people in New York, but was determined not to let his lack of knowledge spoil his day. "Lydia my love, you never cease to amaze me by how easily you fit into America."

Lydia and Edward went up the stairs to the lobby. Struck by the ambiance of the hotel, they walked over to register, feeling a little overwhelmed.

Edward cleared his throat to get the attention of the desk clerk who eyed them and figured they didn't have the type of money needed to stay at the Multnomah Hotel. "Yes, what can I do for you?"

"We have a reservation. Mr. and Mrs. Edward O'Brien," Edward told the clerk.

Lydia smiled. She was still getting used to being a missus.

Looking through the reservations, the clerk's eyes widened. "Oh, excuse me, Mr. O'Brien. Yes, of course, we have you right here. It says you and the missus are in the bridal suite." What he didn't mention was the note attached stating these two guests were VIP's and to treat them with kid gloves.

"The bridal suite!" Lydia was beaming from ear to ear. "Michael reserved the bridal suite for us? It must be a huge favor he's owed."

"All I know Mrs. O'Brien is you're to have our best room." The clerk rang a bell and the bellman came over for their bags.

"Jonathan will escort you to your room. Please do not hesitate to ask if there is anything I can help you with."

Looking at the clerk's name badge, Edward shook his hand. "Mr. Wills, I do believe everything will be absolutely wonderful. Oh, one thing. Can you tell me when the Queen of Romania will be parading by? What street will it be on?"

Wills smiled; happy he could be of service. "The parade will be right outside the hotel. Your room is on the opposite side, so you'll need to go out our main doors. I will have someone hold a spot for you on the street. Just be there in one hour. It's when we estimate the Queen will arrive."

"Arrive? I thought she was just parading by."

"Mr. O'Brien, didn't you know? She's staying at this hotel. It will end here so we will hold a spot for you on the corner so you can get the full effect of the thirty cars making up the entire parade.

"Well, I'll be darned. This is turning into quite an experience." Taking Lydia by the elbow, he followed the bellboy to the elevator. Anticipating having his wife to himself for an hour, he was already smiling as the elevator doors closed.

Lydia saw his smile and a shiver of anticipation went through her. "Edward, you better never try to play poker. You're much too easy to read." She snuggled beside him and gave what she hoped was a seductive look.

Chapter 31

Mrs. Rogers was very excited. She was rushing Myra through breakfast and had just spilled tea on the white table cloth.

"Oh my, look at what I've done. Haste makes waste."

"Mrs. Rogers, what are you doing today? You are in such a hurry. I can clear the table and do the morning dishes if you'd like."

In the last few days, Mrs. Rogers had actually developed a soft spot for Myra or the woman she knew as Martha. She decided the poor girl was trying to leave all the sadness of her parents' passing. And, Mrs. Rogers suspected Martha's sister had married the man she had wanted for herself.

"Martha, haven't you heard about the Queen of Romania coming to Portland? There's going to be a huge parade. You must come!"

Myra was so tired of her charade of opening the store she was excited to take a day off. "Who could say no to a parade and a Queen? I'd love to go with you."

Mrs. Rogers was elated. "This is so very exciting. We've never had a Queen visit before. We must hurry so we get a good spot along the street."

Myra went to her room to change clothes. She had been dressed in a casual outfit suitable for a woman who was allegedly preparing a shop. Everyday she went to her "shop" and made a show of dusting and looking at paint colors. Brookstone had dropped in once unannounced and berated her for the lack of progress. "I'm investing my hard earned-money into this shop, Miss Driscoll. You'd better make your promised opening date. Why has no stock arrived?"

Myra had made appropriate excuses but damned the day she had gotten into this mess. Who knew Brookstone's competitiveness with Franklin would make him so stupid? She wanted to attend to her business with her dear sister and brother-in- law, and then be off to see the rest of America on Brookstone's money.

Mrs. Rogers's excitement was contagious. Myra changed clothes and headed back down to the parlor. Mrs. Rogers had her coat on and was waiting.

"Take a warm coat, dear. Do you have any gloves?" The landlady had become quite motherly in the last day or so, which almost endeared her to Myra. At least it guaranteed the old lady wouldn't be left bound and gagged like the meddlesome Mrs. Hildegard.

"Oh, let me run up and get my gloves. I'll be right back."

Mrs. Rogers took advantage of the time and opened Myra's handbag. She found nothing of note. In fact it was rather empty, only a checkbook, some cash, and a mirror and lipstick. She shut it quickly when she heard Myra's footfalls on the stairs.

In a rare moment of affection, Myra linked her arm with the older woman's. "Let's be off, Mrs. Rogers. I can't tell you the last time I saw a parade!"

Myra and Mrs. Rogers walked briskly down the street heading for the parade route. After walking ten blocks Myra was losing patience. Mrs. Rogers had rushed her out of the house and now they found out the parade wouldn't be starting for two more hours. She was about to abandon Mrs. Rogers when she saw the look of rapture on the older woman's face. Myra's frown softened as she thought, *oh my, I may be a poor Irish girl, but I've seen a bit of the world. This one hasn't even been out of Oregon. I might as well resign myself to a wasted day.*

Mrs. Rogers was ecstatic. She had been talking to people in the crowd and learned the Queen of Romania would be staying at the Multnomah Hotel, almost a mile away. Turning to Myra she exclaimed, "Martha, the Queen of Romania will be staying at the Multnomah Hotel! It's not very far away. I thought it would be grand to try to get close to it and watch the parade end at the Hotel. Please, will you walk with me so we can get a good spot?"

Myra looked at the gray-haired woman in front of her. Mrs. Rogers's plea was in her eyes as she silently beseeched Myra to go with her. Laughing, Myra looked at Mrs. Rogers and exclaimed, "I can't think of anywhere I'd rather be. Lead on, Mrs. Rogers. I'll be right behind you."

Mrs. Rogers bravely faced the crowd and made her way through it, walking almost a mile before she found the perfect spot on the corner by the hotel. They could see the majestic structure in the background, but also could look up the street and see the entire parade advancing.

Myra was grumbling as she followed Mrs. Rogers through the crowd. She could care less about the Queen of Romania as her feet started hurting in her stylish shoes. *Ah the price American women pay to look good. Give me a good old pair of Irish shoes any day of the week. No wonder*

American women have such pinched looks on their faces. But look at Mrs. Rogers now. The old bird is ecstatic, might as well keep trudging on.

Pushing her way through the crowd with Myra behind her, gave Mrs. Rogers a little time to reflect on her new boarder. So far she had been a mystery. After spending a day with her and seeing what a wonderful companion Martha was, Mrs. Rogers was pleasantly surprised.

"Martha, this looks like a good spot. Let's stand here. The parade will be by within the hour, I think."

Myra stopped. Looking around, she saw the Multnomah Hotel which was the place the Queen of Romania would spend the night. She mentally compared the exterior of the Multnomah Hotel to the Biltmore. The building before her was quite large and similar to the Biltmore. However, she was sure it wasn't as opulent as what she had experienced in New York and wondered what the Queen of Romania would think of it. Turning from the Hotel to her companion, she said, "This does look like a good spot, Mrs. Rogers. What a beautiful hotel."

"It's the largest hotel in the Northwest. It has 600 rooms. Can you imagine that many rooms in a building? It was built in 1912 and twice they've had a plane take off from the roof! It was a plane with a propeller at the back. Mr. Rogers called the plane a Pusher. He brought me here to watch it take off. It was back in 1912. He died in 1920." Mrs. Rogers warmed up to the story. She loved an enthusiastic audience. "See the three buildings that rise up like a palace? The bottom two floors are all restaurants and ballrooms stretching out for the entire block. I had tea there once. It was quite a treat. My husband liked to surprise me sometimes with special outings."

Myra noted the look of wistfulness on Mrs. Rogers face. "You must miss him very much."

Mrs. Rogers sniffed and dabbed at her eyes. "A love like that only comes once in a lifetime. My husband was a good man and we had a good life together. Married forty years when he suddenly keeled over one night after dinner. Dead before he hit the floor."

Myra took Mrs. Rogers hand and gave it a gentle squeeze. "You're so fortunate you had forty good years together." Now it was Myra's turn to have a wistful look on her face.

Myra held Mrs. Rogers hand for a moment longer, and then looked across the street. An involuntary gasp came out as she saw her sister and Edward. Her eyes were wide with shock. She watched them smiling and laughing with each other as they waited for the parade. Edward's arm was around Lydia's waist. His body language was both protective and adoring. Even Myra could see the love the two had for each other. She couldn't keep her eyes off them. Her feet were frozen in place and her breathing was becoming labored.

Mrs. Rogers was chatting away about the Queen of Romania when she noticed Myra's expression and saw her staring intently across the street. "Oh my, what a handsome young couple, they remind me of when my husband and I were young. What a good looking pair. You can see from here how much in love they are."

With a gasp, Myra choked out the words. "Yes, any fool could see it just by looking at them." Myra felt a tear slip down her cheek. How could she have been so blind? She had loved Edward for so long. She had known Lydia wanted him and it made him all the more enticing. Lydia and Edward were obviously happy and in love, she could feel venom seeping out of her pores. She hated her sister, her own flesh and blood. Myra wondered, *what kind of monster am I?*

Mrs. Rogers looked at Myra. "My dear, are you all right? You're absolutely white. Is something wrong?"

"I'm not feeling very well. I have a horrible headache. I need to go back to my room and lie down. Please forgive me, Mrs. Rogers. You've been so lovely to invite me to share your day. I'm so very sorry."

"Martha, you look dreadful if you don't mind me saying. We need to get you home."

The last thing Myra wanted was a prolonged conversation or Mrs. Rogers hovering over her. "Please, Mrs. Rogers. I will feel worse if you miss your opportunity to see the Queen of Romania. I'll just walk to the other street and catch a cab."

Myra took a final look at Lydia and Edward. She watched as Edward leaned down and planted a soft kiss on Lydia's lips and saw him hug her close. Her heart felt like a dagger had been shoved into it. She walked unsteadily through the crowd and made her way to the first street off the parade route. A cab pulled over to the curb as she waved her hand in the air.

She sat in the back seat with her head back and eyes closed. She couldn't get the image of them together out of her head. Myra's fists were clenched, and all she could think was thank God she didn't have Mrs. Hildebrand's gun with her.

Edward was enjoying himself. He was enjoying the sunshine and watching Lydia's excitement. Suddenly the crowd started screaming, "They're coming, they're coming." Edward looked around, there were hundreds of people as far as he could see and knew more were on the long parade route. The cars were in view. Horns were honking and the dignitaries riding in the cars were waving at the spectators. In the middle of the parade, was the Queen of Romania. Dressed in a long fur coat, she was wearing leather gloves to stave off the chill of the November air. Large jeweled rings were on the outside of her kid gloves, and she used both hands to wave at the crowds lining the street. The radiant smile on her face made her seem much younger than her years.

Lydia was smiling and pulling on his arm. "Look, Edward, look. Here she comes!"

The Queen of Romania was fifty-one years old and quite stunning. Lydia followed the car with her eyes, clutching Edward's hands. "She married her husband when she was seventeen. She had been in love with King George V of England before he was King. He wanted to marry her, but her mother wouldn't allow it. So her mother searched all the royal families in Europe until she found Prince Ferdinand of Romania and forced Princess Marie to marry him. They say since she has been married to King Ferdinand, she has had at least two affairs, and her last two children weren't even her husband's! She's deliciously scandalous."

Edward turned to his wife. "How on earth do you know all this?"

"Annie and I did some fast reading at the library. Plus, I called Beverly to tell her about the trip, and, of course, she knew quite a bit." Lydia giggled as she thought of how Beverly described Queen Marie as a very complex woman. "During the war she actually volunteered as a Red Cross nurse. Can you imagine being treated by the Queen?"

"You've clearly done your homework. Oh look, the parade is stopping."

The cars began to stop one by one and unload their passengers who proceeded into the Hotel. Edward and Lydia were right at the end of the parade and had a close up view of Queen Marie.

Lydia nudged Edward and whispered, "Look, there she is. She's going to walk right by us! She's quite beautiful."

Edward looked in the direction Lydia had indicated. He was impressed by the Queen's regal presence as she exited her vehicle on the arm of a man who looked important. "Who's the gentleman she's with?"

A man directly behind Edward answered the question. "That's Sam Hill. He built the mansion that is now the Maryhill Museum of Art. She came all the way from Romania to dedicate the building. Ain't that something? All the way from Romania!"

Lydia turned to the gentleman and smiled. "Thank you for the information. We're so fascinated with her. My friend told me she volunteered as a nurse in the Red Cross during the war! Can you imagine, a Queen wearing a nurse's outfit? I wonder if she wore her Crown.'"

Just as Lydia said the words she heard a woman's laughter right in front of her. To her chagrin, the Queen of Romania was laughing. "No dear, I didn't wear my crown, just a small daytime tiara, and, of course, the white nurse's shoes to complete the outfit." The Queen and her entourage all burst into laughter and proceeded into the hotel. Lydia's face was scarlet and was made redder when Edward joined in the good natured laughter.

"Now, Lydia, it's not everyone who can say they got a Queen to laugh. Think what a great story this will be for our grandchildren and great grandchildren. I think it will get better with each telling!"

Even Lydia had to laugh. "I didn't know she would hear me. Thank God the hotel is huge. At least we won't run into her."

Edward wiggled his eyebrows at her and said with a leer, "For sure we won't be running into her if we spend the rest of the day in our luxurious room and in our big fluffy bed."

Lydia swatted him on the arm but her eyes were merry. "I think you may be right. Let's go see if the bed is as soft and fluffy as it looked."

Arm in arm, the couple turned and walked into the hotel. They were unaware a shrewd pair of brown eyes had taken note of the close resemblance of her newest boarder and the lovely young woman who made the Queen of Romania laugh out loud.

Chapter 32

Myra barely made it back to her room before she broke down, emitting a keening sound. Her body was wracked with sobs. A voice not been heard in weeks, decisively Irish, kept repeating, "Why didn't he love me? Why?"

Seeing Lydia and Edward together, so obviously in love, was a devastating blow. Myra was trying to calm down enough to think of her options. She didn't hear the front door open and Mrs. Rogers quietly making her way up the stairs.

Standing in front of Myra's door, Mrs. Rogers stood and listened to the words the anguished girl kept repeating. Thinking to herself, *what a strange turn of events the day has taken. In the three weeks the self-possessed Miss Driscoll has lived here, this is the first time the girl has shown any sort of emotion. Martha is so stilted and proper in her behavior, the façade of calm had finally cracked and, my oh my, it will be so interesting to find out what all this fuss is about. And why is she speaking in an Irish accent?*

Rapping softly on the door, Mrs. Rogers said, "Martha, are you all right? Are you ill?"

Myra snapped out if her stupor as if cold water had been thrown on her. Wondering how long Mrs. Rogers had been standing there, she replied, "I've a very bad headache. If you don't mind, I think I will forego dinner this evening. I hope it doesn't inconvenience you."

"No, my dear, you rest. I'll check on you later."

Descending the stairs, Mrs. Rogers couldn't wait for her boarder to go to her shop the next day. She wanted to get a closer look at the girl's personal possessions. Chuckling to herself, *nothing like a little snooping to uncover the truth about someone.* Mrs. Rogers had no guilt about snooping. She was within her rights. It was her house, and a woman her age had to be careful.

By the next morning, Myra knew what she was going to do. Whatever plan she had of seeking revenge on her sister and Edward was over. In the darkness of her room, after hours of sobbing, she finally admitted to herself Edward had never been interested in her. Myra realized she only wanted him because Lydia loved him. It was pointless to kill Edward for not loving her. Truth be told, she was more in love with the idea of taking him away from Lydia. She had never really loved him.

Carefully dressing in her best outfit, Myra looked at herself in the mirror. She saw a woman with slightly puffy eyes and a deathly pale face. *Oh now, this won't do. I need to put on a good show for the bankers.* Adding a little more powder and some light color on her eyelids, she stared at her image in the mirror and thought, *I've certainly looked better but this will have to do.*

Her suitcase was packed. She would return for it after going to the bank. Going down the stairs to breakfast, Myra tried to act as if this was an ordinary day.

"My, you look pretty this morning. Your headache must be gone." Mrs. Rogers noted Martha's puffy eyes. "Did you manage to get any sleep?"

"Not much I'm afraid. But yes, thank you, my headache is gone. I'll just have a bit of toast and be off. I am meeting with the bank this morning."

"I'll go get the toast, and you must have a bit of eggs, too. You had no dinner last night. You need to keep up your strength, especially with all the hard work you've been doing getting your shop ready."

The hard work statement almost made Myra choke on her tea. "It is very kind of you, Mrs. Rogers. Yes, eggs would be lovely."

When Mrs. Rogers went off to the kitchen, Myra looked around the dining room thinking, *this is the last time I will have breakfast in this house, and even if she is a meddlesome old lady, she has been kind to me these last three weeks.*

In the kitchen, Mrs. Rogers was plotting her search of Martha's room. *Those puffy eyes don't fool me. Headache indeed, the girl cried her eyes out all night. If I'm right, it has something to do with the handsome couple at the parade. She looked like she'd seen a ghost yesterday.*

Coming out with the toast and eggs, she told Myra, "I'll be playing bridge today at my friend Elizabeth Dougherty's. Our group has been playing bridge together for forty years."

Myra was relieved Mrs. Rogers would be out of the house when she returned for her suitcase. She wanted to be on her way, and she was paid through the end of the month. "Have a lovely time, Mrs. Rogers.

I have a busy day planned, and I'm meeting one of my investors for dinner. I don't expect to be back until late."

Gathering her purse and coat, Myra impulsively hugged Mrs. Rogers. Marveling at how sentimental she was becoming, Myra looked at her landlady. "Thank you for checking on me last night. I'm so sorry I couldn't stay for the parade."

"Well I'm relieved you're better now, dear."

Myra walked out the door and turned to take one more look at her landlady. Then walking briskly to her shop, she gathered up some of her personal items and headed to the bank. She had insisted the bank account be in her name only. She wanted easy access to Brookstone's money. As she opened the door to the bank, the bank manager was exiting. Myra got in line. When it was her turn, she asked the teller for the balance in her account.

"Miss Driscoll, you have $850 in your account."

Writing the amount on the withdrawal slip, she pushed it across the counter to the clerk.

"Oh, Miss Driscoll, I don't have that amount of money in my till. The bank manager just walked out the door for a meeting and won't be back for two hours. I'm sorry. Can you possibly come back at 1 p.m.?"

Myra was upset her plan to leave town quickly and quietly were being thwarted. "Isn't there an assistant manager who can open the vault?"

"No, miss, and, for a withdrawal of this size it must be approved by Mr. Barrett."

"But it's my money. Why would he have to approve it?"

The clerk started to answer, but before he could, Myra lost the last of her patience. "I'll be back at 1 p.m. and Mr. Barrett had better be here with my money ready."

Turning on her heel and stomping out of the bank, she didn't notice the clerk immediately picked up the phone and dialed the number on the account card. "Mr. Brookstone, you asked to be notified if any substantial amounts were being withdrawn from Miss Driscoll's account. Sir, she was just here to close the account."

Myra went back to her shop and dawdled for two hours. She was anxious to be on her way with Brookstone's money in her pocket. She had done much soul searching during her sleepless night. She was jealous because Lydia was the favorite daughter, a position Myra felt she deserved, being the youngest. It had finally dawned on her only a monster would want to kill her own flesh and blood. She was ready to move on to California where her talent for acting and blending in would be best served.

It was so easy to get money from men in America. She wasn't about to stop now. There would be plenty of new opportunities in California. Looking at the large clock on the wall, she realized it was time to go back to the bank.

Breathing in the cool November air as she walked down the street Myra thought to herself, *Yes, it's time to leave this area. It's chilly and I'm ready to see California and fee the warmth of the eternal sunshine I keep hearing about.*

Stepping into the bank, Myra didn't notice the sheriff standing in the corner. As she approached the teller, she saw him do a slight nod of his head. Still not understanding, she stood in front of his cage. "Is Mr. Barrett back from his meeting?"

"Yes, Miss Driscoll, he is. He has asked to see you to complete the transaction. His secretary is over at the desk to your right. Check in with her and she'll escort you to his office."

Annoyed such a simple transaction was taking so long, Myra stepped out of line and walked to the secretary's desk. "I'm Martha Driscoll here to complete my withdrawal transaction with Mr. Barrett."

"Yes, Miss Driscoll, please come this way."

Opening the door to Mr. Barrett's office, the secretary directed Myra to walk in. Mr. Barrett rose from behind his desk. "Miss Driscoll, I understand you want to withdraw all of your money and close your account?"

"Yes, Mr. Barrett. I've had a change of plans and will be relocating to California."

Suddenly there was a motion from behind her. "You're not going anywhere with my money, you little thief. Get Sheriff Smith in here, Barrett. I want her arrested and thrown in jail. I have a copy of the contract she signed when the loan was drawn up. She's a thief and a con artist and she's going to jail."

Myra's knees buckled and she started to sink to the floor.

"Oh no, you don't. None of your helpless female play acting." Brookstone jerked her arm up and roughly pushed her into a chair.

The sheriff walked in with handcuffs in his hand. "Miss, you'll have to stand up and put your hands behind your back."

Myra felt as if she was at the bottom of a deep well. She could see their lips moving, but could barely make out the words. Sheriff Smith took her arm and pulled her up from the chair. He was instructing her, but she couldn't understand him or what had happened. She could see Brookstone. His face was beet red and spittle was coming out of his mouth as he shouted and shouted. It was like the English language had abandoned her brain. She was thinking in Gaelic, and, no matter what language, she was in deep trouble.

Handcuffed, Myra walked out to the paddy wagon with the sheriff who placed her in the back. She sat on the bench, thankful to be alone, trying to gather her thoughts. It didn't matter. There was no way out of this mess. She should have stayed with her original plan to go to Little Creek and kill her sister. Myra muttered to herself, "See what happens when you have a change of heart?"

The paddy wagon smelled like vomit. Once, when she and Mrs. Rogers were out, they saw one pass by on the street. Mrs. Rogers had informed her, the paddy wagons were usually reserved for raids on speakeasies. She laughingly told her only the slow drunk people got caught. From the smell of the wagon they must all have gotten sick. Myra was getting queasy and prayed the ride was not a long one.

Arriving at the police station, Myra was pulled out of the paddy wagon and brought into the station. All of the men stopped what they were doing to take a long leering look at the pretty woman in handcuffs.

"What'd she do? Is she a prostitute? I wouldn't mind breaking the law for a roll with her." Each comment got worse, and Myra was in tears by the time they lined her up to take her picture.

She still hadn't spoken when all of the sudden a man yelled "Look this way," and a flash of light blinded her. "Turn to the right." And then another flash went off.

The sheriff put her in a room with a table. "I need to take your statement. Brookstone will be here soon to fill out the criminal complaint."

Myra looked at Sheriff Smith. He looked to be about forty with grey hair at the temples of his otherwise dark brown hair.

His face was lined with years of seeing the underbelly of human behavior. Regaining the use of her voice, Myra looked plaintively at Sheriff Smith. "I don't know what I was thinking. I didn't want Mr. Brookstone as a business partner. He pushed his way into my business and threatened to ruin me if I didn't let him control everything. He badgered me and verbally abused me at every opportunity. He knew my personal accounts were frozen because my sister is disputing the distribution of our parents' will. I mailed him a letter this morning acknowledging my debt to him and my intention to pay him back. I wasn't trying to run out on my debt to him. I swear I wasn't."

"Miss Driscoll, if what you say is true, then hopefully we can clear this up. Unfortunately, we will have to keep you in jail until he receives your letter of intent. If there is no such letter, and, for your sake, I hope there is, you will be formally charged and a court date will be set. We haven't had a lot of female criminals so the jail conditions are not very pleasant. Right now, I'm going to put you in a cell as far away from the male population as possible. We don't have sequestered areas for men and women."

Myra thanked God while waiting for the bank manager to return, she had written a letter to Brookstone swearing that she, Martha Driscoll, would pay him back. Sad for Calvin Brookstone, but Martha Driscoll would soon be dead to the world. Myra would no longer need that persona when she arrived in California.

"Right now, we do have one female employee who will come in and search you. Then she will escort you to a cell where you will wait until this can be sorted out."

A large woman wearing a plain grey dress walked into the room. She was in her mid thirties and homely. The Matron looked at Myra's expensive clothes, stylish hair and beautiful face with distain. Myra knew immediately the woman hated her.

"OK, Sheriff Smith. I can take it from here." The Sheriff got up from the table and walked out the door softly closing it behind him. Myra thought of running after him and begging for mercy. She could feel the hateful gaze of the matron. "Let's get this over with. Take off your clothes."

Myra looked at her beseechingly. "Please can I have some privacy?"

The matron gave Myra a dismissive laugh. "Well who do we have here, the Queen of Romania? No, you can't have any privacy. Start stripping or I'll rip your clothes off you, and you'll be sitting in your jail cell trying to keep your body parts covered."

Myra lowered her head and started unbuttoning her dress. The popular flapper style had numerous buttons going down the front. Her hands were shaking so badly she could barely make any progress.

"Hurry it up. It's almost time for my shift to be over. I don't have all day."

Finally, Myra was naked, standing in front of the matron. She shut her eyes so she wouldn't see the woman's triumphant look.

"All you pretty girls think you're so special. Well let's see how special you are in jail, you bitch. You better hope someone saves you from prison. There are lots of male guards who just love to break in pretty little things like you. Plenty of women too, if you get my drift."

Myra didn't have a clue what she was talking about, but could tell from the woman's tone of voice it was bad, all bad.

The matron forced Myra to turn slowly to make sure she wasn't hiding any weapons. At that moment, Myra wished fervently for Mrs. Hildebrand's gun. She wanted to kill this heartless woman.

Satisfied it was safe to put her in a cell, the matron searched through Myra's clothes and instructed her to put her dress back on. Then she roughly grabbed Myra by the arm and took her to the jail section to be processed in.

Listening to all the men screaming at her, yelling obscene things, Myra was shaking by the time she was locked into her cell. She was actually grateful to be as far away from them as possible, not realizing how vulnerable she was to the whims of the male guards.

Every half hour, the same guard walked by, stood in front of her cell and leered at her. "You sure are a pretty one. Bet you smell real good, too. Later tonight, I'm going to find out for myself. Just you wait, pretty lady. You're going to get an up close inspection from Tom here."

Tears streamed out of Myra's eyes, *Oh what kind of hell have I gotten myself into?*

Just then she heard a commotion at the end of the aisle. Daniel Brookstone was making his way towards her accompanied by a man in a suit and Sheriff Smith.

"Martha, oh Martha, are you all right? You are as white as a sheet. Sheriff, open this cell immediately."

"Now, Mr. Brookstone, we talked about this, I said you could see her, I didn't say nothing about going into her cell."

"Which is precisely why I brought my lawyer, this woman should at least be granted bail. This is all a horrible mistake."

"Daniel, can you get me out of here? I'm so frightened." Myra looked at him imploringly, and Daniel puffed up with pride at his ability to save the fair maiden.

"Martha, we need to talk. Gentlemen, please, give us a few minutes."

The three men walked a few feet away to give them privacy.

"Martha, my father said you were running away with all of his money. How could you do this to me?"

"Daniel, I wanted to tell you, but I knew you'd never believe me. Your father has been badgering me at every opportunity. He kept telling me I wasn't good enough for you, and I'd better not set my sights on you. I think he knows how much I care for you and didn't want us to see each other. It was horrible. I finally wrote him a letter of intent to pay him back and tried to withdraw the money. The rest you know. He had me arrested and told me I would be going to prison. Oh, Daniel, how could this have all gone so horribly wrong?"

"Martha, do you care for me really?"

Martha saw the hope in his eyes and knowing her other option was jail or prison, looked him in the eyes and formed a lie to guarantee her survival. "Daniel, I know I'm a rather reserved person, and I'm hard to read, but I care for you very much. I was beginning to hope we might have a future together, but I knew your father would never allow it." Warming up to her role, she added, "It was so painful to see you and know we couldn't be together. I thought it would be better if I left town. Can you understand how I felt? Now it's too late, he's ruined everything."

"No, Martha, he hasn't. In fact if he doesn't stop this insanity he may recover his money but will lose his only son. Martha, I am hopelessly in love with you. Marry me. Marry me and we can make this whole problem go away. My father would never prosecute you. In fact, he needs to stop this mess now if he doesn't want to be a laughing stock."

Myra swallowed and struggled for control. Marrying Daniel had never occurred to her but, given the alternative, she smiled at him and reached for his hand through the bars. "Yes, Daniel, yes, I will marry you. But how will you ever get your father to accept me?"

Daniel knew more than anything his father wanted to make sure the Brookstone name continued. He had told Daniel repeatedly all women were whores but a necessary evil to continue the Brookstone name. "I'll take care of everything. First we need to get you bailed out of here."

"Daniel, please hurry. The guard has been saying things to me, and I'm so afraid of what will happen here tonight." Real tears flooded her eyes and ran down her cheeks. Myra had never been as afraid as she was in the jail cell. She'd marry the devil himself if it would get her out of there.

"I went to college with the son of a Portland judge. Once things are explained to him, I know we can get you released."

Daniel left to confer with his lawyer and to make a call to Jonathon Parker, his friend from college. He knew Jonathon could be persuaded to help him convince the Judge.

Two hours later, Myra looked up and saw Daniel and two men coming towards her cell. Again the Sheriff was accompanying them.

"Martha, this is Judge Parker. I've told him everything, and he is going to release you to my custody." Daniel's eyes looked mischievous. "However, under one very important condition—if you marry me."

"Daniel, yes, I would love to marry you."

"Well, young lady, you're in luck. Daniel has been very persuasive, as has my son. My son Jonathon says Daniel has never gone back on his word, so I am holding him to it. I will release you to Daniel's custody. I have been informed by Daniel that in order for his father to drop this charges, it would be better if you two were married. I don't understand the logic in this, but since it is the desire of both of you to be married, and it is within my power to do so, I suggest we adjourn to a more suitable room. Somehow, I don't think it is every woman's dream to have her wedding in a jail cell."

Myra's head was spinning. She had agreed to marry Daniel to get out of jail but never expected the marriage would take place this quickly. Looking around her jail cell, sitting on the edge of a badly stained mattress and the putrid smell in the air, she realized marriage to Daniel was her only recourse. Thinking of the leering guard and the thought of prison brought her reality in focus. Putting her best face on, she stood as the sheriff unlocked her cell. She held her hand out to Daniel who grabbed it and put an arm around her shoulder as they walked out of the jail area.

Judge Parker shepherded them into the interrogation room. He looked at Myra with his piercing blue eyes noticing her bewildered look and her expressionless blue eyes. "Daniel, I think this poor young lady is in shock. Miss Driscoll, are you sure you want to marry Daniel Brookstone?"

Again, Myra pondered her options. She had none. At this point, marriage was her only solution. She was actually looking forward to seeing the look on Calvin Brookstone's face. "Yes, Judge Parker, I do."

"Very well then, let's get on with this. The honorable Sheriff Smith will be a witness as will Daniel's lawyer, Sam Jones. Miss Driscoll, would you like a few minutes to freshen up?"

Myra nodded and the sheriff walked her to the bathroom. "I'll wait out here for you, Miss Driscoll."

Standing in the windowless bathroom, Myra looked in the mirror and noted her pale face and the dark circles under her eyes. The sheriff was thoughtful enough to bring her purse. She opened it, took out her cosmetics, redid her makeup and combed her hair. Trying one more time to come up with another plan, and realizing escape was impossible, she thought, *Well now, this is as good as it's going to get and marriage is much more attractive to me than jail.*

She squared her shoulders, opened the bathroom door, and walked back to the interrogation room with Sheriff Smith.

Daniel smiled broadly. "You look beautiful. Here, I picked this up for you," handing Myra a small bouquet of flowers. Myra didn't see Daniel's smug look of triumph.

"Thank you, Daniel, it was very thoughtful." Myra smiled at him. Daniel didn't seem to notice that the smile didn't reach her eyes.

Twenty minutes later, she was Mrs. Daniel Brookstone. The Judge required that Daniel fill out bail forms and pay for bailing out his bride. He assured the couple it was just a legal formality and as soon as her letter of intent was found either at the post office or at Calvin Brookstone's home, the charges would be dropped.

The sheriff looked at them both. Daniel's expression was one of joy, Martha Driscoll looked shell shocked. He had seen many criminals and con artists in his twenty plus years with the force. He felt something was off with Martha Driscoll. There was more there than met the eye.

Daniel finished signing everything and left a check with the clerk. "Well now, Mrs. Brookstone, you have been officially released into my custody. Let's get out of here and go to the hotel to start our honeymoon."

Myra's eyes grew wide. She hadn't thought beyond her quick wedding. Her mother had never talked of such things. She had only overheard hushed comments when the local neighborhood women had tea in her parents' kitchen. Seeing the undisguised look of lust on Daniels face, she was more frightened than when she was in jail.

Chapter 33

While a terrified Myra was sitting in jail, Edward and Lydia were languishing in their large feather bed after a day of sightseeing. They had room service deliver their dinner and were enjoying their honeymoon suite.

"Edward, promise me you'll bring me back to this hotel for our twenty-fifth wedding anniversary."

"My love, I will bring to you back to this hotel long before our twenty-fifth anniversary. Someday we'll be rich and own a fancy restaurant and hotel, maybe the hotel next to our restaurant. After all, we're in America, where dreams come true."

Lydia demurely pulled the sheet up to cover her nakedness. She still hadn't gotten used to the look of absolute joy on Edward's face when he looked at her body.

"Why are you covering up? I love looking at you. We don't get enough time off to just enjoy each other."

"Edward, if we enjoy each other much more I won't be able to walk tomorrow."

A huge guffaw of laughter escaped from Edward's mouth. "Lydia, there are times you can be quite shocking!

Waking up in the luxurious hotel room, Lydia nudged her husband awake. "Edward, how on earth can you sleep when we are at this fabulous hotel and city? We have more to see before we drive back to Little Creek tomorrow."

"Maybe it's due to the fact my insatiable wife kept me up half the night making demands on my worn out body."

"Edward!" Lydia slapped his arm in mock anger. "How can you say such a thing?"

"I can say it because I'm a very happy man and because it's true!"

"Well I'm starved, and if you want me to be a very happy wife, you'll get out of bed and get ready for breakfast."

Edward got out of bed, and then turned to his wife, nibbling on her ear. "Are you absolutely sure it's breakfast you want?"

Lydia giggled. "Yes, and then we'll see how the rest of the day goes. It's our final night in this hotel, and I want to see more of the city."

Dressed and standing by the elevator, Edward and Lydia saw the doors open but a man quickly stood in front of the door. "Please take the next elevator."

Edward looked inside and saw Queen Marie of Romania and what he assumed were her bodyguards and entourage. Just then, the Queen looked out at him and Lydia. "Oh Jorrard, it's the lovely young couple from the Parade yesterday. Do let them in."

Lydia automatically curtsied. "Thank you, Your Majesty." Stepping into the elevator as the man called Jorrard moved aside.

The Queen turned to Edward and Lydia. "You are a beautiful couple and so obviously in love. Are you on your honeymoon?"

Lydia was momentarily speechless. "In a manner of speaking, yes, we were married four months ago but didn't have time for a honeymoon. We came to Portland from Little Creek to watch the parade. I mean your parade, and a friend helped us get a room at this lovely hotel."

"Your accent is charming. You must be Irish. Am I correct?"

"Yes, Your Majesty. I've been here six months, and my husband has been here almost three years."

"And how do you find America so far? Is it all you dreamed of?"

"Yes, we have been luckier than some and we're hard workers. We have a grand life here, that's for sure."

The elevator doors opened and the Queen looked at Lydia. Taking a small jeweled pin off the front of her jacket, she said, "It's not often a Queen gets to laugh at herself or meet a charming young couple on their honeymoon. Please, accept this as a wedding gift."

She leaned over and put the pin on Lydia's lapel. Smiling, the Queen walked out of the elevator as a dumbstruck Lydia looked after her. Looking at her lapel she saw a small round brooch with a center diamond surrounded by sapphires. Lydia gasped, "It's beautiful. I can't believe she just gave it away to a stranger."

"I wish I could afford to give you gifts like that, my darlin'. Some day we'll find the streets paved with gold. The only ones we've been able to find are those paved with hard work. Not that I mind. Our life is still better here than at home."

"Oh, Edward, this is a magnificent brooch and it will certainly add to the story we tell our grandchildren about the Queen of Romania. But it's not fine jewelry I want out of this life. It is you, only you, and the brood of kids you're wanting."

Edward laughed. "I always said my sister Rosie would have a brood of kids and now my words will haunt me."

Edward and Lydia walked into the restaurant for breakfast. With 600 rooms in the hotel there were two restaurants. The Arcadian Room was the largest dining room and the beautiful pillars were decorated with the insignia of the Multnomah Hotel. Despite the earliness of the hour, all of the waiters were wearing tuxedos.

"Edward, I don't think we're dressed properly. This is very posh."

"Lydia, with that brooch on your lapel, the waiters will be falling all over you. They'll think you are a princess yourself."

They proceeded to their table, and a waiter came over and asked for their room number. When Edward said room 526, the waiter smiled and said, "Oh, the bridal suite. You must be Mr. and Mrs. O'Brien. Congratulations on your marriage. I hope you are enjoying your stay with us."

Edward and Lydia both smiled and nodded their heads, "It's wonderful. This hotel is magnificent."

The waiter looked at Lydia and smiled, "Yes, it is, we're very proud of our hotel and the prominent guests that stay here. Did you see the Queen of Romania?"

Edward laughed. "Yes, we've had two encounters with her, and today in the elevator she gave my wife a brooch as a wedding present to us both."

The waiter's eyes widened. "The brooch you're wearing now?"

Lydia preened a bit and smiled as she looked down at the wonderful piece of jewelry. "This will be my favorite reminder of our stay in Portland. I'm overwhelmed a perfect stranger would be so generous."

"My, how fortunate you were in the right place at the right time. Now let's see about getting you two a delicious breakfast before you start touring our town."

Edward and Lydia spent the next two hours eating the most marvelous food they had ever seen, pastries and Eggs Benedict and exotic fruits. They were stuffed but couldn't bring themselves to stop eating. They sipped their coffee and watched the other people in the restaurant. "They're so fancy," Lydia whispered to Edward. "I feel a little out of place, but I'm enjoying watching everyone so much I wouldn't think of leaving."

"Lydia, my love, you are clearly the most beautiful woman in the room. Every man here is envious of me. It's a wonderful feeling."

Lydia blushed and touched her husband's arm, "And haven't you been noticing the looks some of the women have sent this way? Even the Queen of Romania was giving you quite a wide smile in the elevator."

"Well, perhaps we should be on our way before one of these wanton creatures throws herself on our table."

Lydia snickered behind her hand as an older woman looked over at Edward and smiled. "Yes, Edward, get moving. I'm not in the mood to fight off all the adoring women."

Many eyes followed the handsome young couple as they exited the restaurant, smiling in anticipation of the day before them; and carefree for the first time in weeks.

Chapter 34

M yra and Daniel stopped by Mrs. Rogers to pick up her previously packed suitcases. Mrs. Rogers had long returned from her afternoon bridge game and was startled to see Martha walk in with a young man.

"My, who do we have here?"

"Mrs. Rogers, this is Daniel Brookstone."

Daniel laughed and turned to Mrs. Rogers. "I'm her husband. We were just married today."

"Married, married you say?" Mrs. Rogers jaw had actually dropped. "Why she's never said a word about having a gentleman friend. Martha, you've given this old woman quite a shock. I'm happy for you both."

Myra looked at Mrs. Rogers. "It's been a rather interesting day. I can't go into detail right now. I've come to collect my things. Daniel, why don't you visit with Mrs. Rogers, I won't be long."

Ascending the stairs, she heard Mrs. Rogers invite Daniel to sit in the parlor. Opening the door to her room, Myra immediately smelled Mrs. Rogers' lavender sachet perfume. *So the old bird's been snooping has she?* Myra had carefully packed her bags, planning on returning for them when Mrs. Rogers was playing bridge. She was sure Mrs. Rogers had tried to open her two suitcases, but she had left both bags locked. *I won't be coming back here. Let the old bird think what she wants.*

Myra walked to the top of the stairs and called down to Daniel, "I'm ready. Would you come and help me with the bags?"

"Of course, Martha, I'll be right up."

Daniel was anxious to get out of the house and on with the honeymoon. Picking up the bags, he got a very hungry look on his face. "Come, Martha, it's time to go to the hotel."

Myra looked at him and a sliver of fear worked its way down her spine. She hadn't seen that ravenous of a look before and she had no idea what lay ahead.

The Multnomah Hotel had a honeymoon suite in each of the three towers. Thankfully, Daniel and Myra had been assigned to the third tower. Edward and Lydia were in the first tower. In the elevator, Daniel eyed his new bride. He had waited for this moment since first meeting Martha Driscoll. Her beauty initially attracted him and her reserved nature intrigued him. He could sense her nervousness as he led her down the hall to the honeymoon suite.

"Here we are." Daniel surprised her by sweeping her up in his arms and carrying her over the threshold of their room.

Uncharacteristically, Myra giggled. "Daniel, you can put me down now."

"I have some connections in town, and I was able to get a bottle of champagne. Come sit here and I'll open the bottle."

Myra had seen champagne on the ship. There was no Prohibition in international waters, which grateful Americans celebrated nightly.

Handing her a glass, Daniel looked at the expression on her face. "Drink up. It will help you relax."

Sipping the champagne, Myra grew increasingly uncomfortable. "Daniel, my mother died two years ago, she never talked to us about wifely duties." Embarrassed, she was speaking quietly, willing herself to get through it.

"Martha, you can relax. I've been around the block a time or two. Maybe you'd like to change into something more comfortable?"

Myra reluctantly opened her suitcase and pulled out a nightgown. As she changed in the bathroom she could hear Daniel refilling his glass. "Don't keep me waiting too long. I've been looking forward to this for weeks."

When she finished, she opened the bathroom door. Daniel looked her over. "That's a pretty old fashioned nightgown, but it doesn't matter. You won't be in it long. Come over here."

Myra stood in front of Daniel. The affable young man had been replaced with a starved madman. He grabbed her and pressed his lips to hers in a crushing kiss. As he kissed her, Daniel walked her over to the bed and pushed her down on top of it. He broke the kiss and quickly took off his shoes. Impatiently pulling off his pants and the rest of his clothes, he stood naked in front of her. Look at me Myra. This is what you do to me."

Myra looked at the huge erection and almost screamed. She had never seen a naked man. Daniel didn't wait for a response. Stretching his long body on top of her, pulled her nightgown up, pinning her arms down and plunged into her without warning. She could feel her tissue tearing and the warm blood on her inner thighs. Hot tears stung her eyes and she could feel him pounding into her. Each thrust brought more pain and anger.

Like a tsunami, hatred for her new husband flooded every corner of her being. Daniel's brutal attack turned the tide of Myra's plans of revenge. It was the Brookstones' fault she was in this mess and they would pay for it dearly. The old man should never have forced her to go into business with him. *Whatever happens now is not my fault*, she thought to herself. Her eyes closed and to block out the look of rapture on Daniels face.

Daniel was relieved to find his bride was a virgin. He suspected she would be, but knowing for sure would make it easier to sell his dad on the idea of their marriage. He had never felt this way with any of the other women he had been with. He whispered into her ear, "It's so good, Martha, it's so good. Did you like it?"

The blood was rushing through her ears. She thought she was going to pass out. It only lasted five minutes and finished, Daniel rolled over next to her. She lay there already plotting her escape. Finally, sitting up she started to get out of bed. Daniel grabbed her arm. "Where are you going, we're not done."

"I need to wash off, I have blood and…and.." Myra was so innocent she didn't know the word for the sticky liquid between her legs.

"Semen, darling. The word is semen. And you'd better get used to it."

Shutting the bathroom door behind her, Myra bit into the washcloth to quiet her sobs. She remembered now how the wives in the neighborhood would gather around the kitchen table and grumble about doing their wifely duty. A couple of them said the only reason to get pregnant was to get a break from the old man for a month a year. Oh God, what had she done?

Daniel knocked on the bathroom door. "Come out, Martha. I miss you."

Myra opened the bathroom door. She had washed her face and cleaned up as well as she could. Daniel pulled her by the hand back to the bed. "I know I was a bit rough for your first time. I just wanted you so badly I couldn't slow down. I'll try to be better this time."

"This time? You mean people do it more than once a night?"

Daniel laughed at her naïveté. "I'm a young virile man. I'd never stop at just one time."

There were two more times, and each time lasted longer than the last. While Daniel wasn't as cruel as his father, years of association with working girls had made him a rough, selfish lover. His attempts to be gentle were clumsy and for an innocent young woman who had never had more than a quick kiss, it was rough and painful and degrading.

Daniel finally finished and fell asleep instantly. His soft contented snores annoyed Myra almost as much as his lovemaking. She was sore and tired. The assault on her body had left her too weak to get out of bed. Forced to lie next to Daniel, she fell off to a troubled sleep dreaming of Mrs. Hildebrand's gun hidden safely in her suitcase.

Chapter 35

E dward and Lydia slowly packed their bag. Taking one last wistful look at their beautiful room, Lydia broke the comfortable silence. "Edward, I'm missing home. Hurry, let's be on our way."

"Lydia, you're not a very good liar. In two short days, this is the closest I've ever been to the lifestyle of rich people. While I don't think it's for me, it was a pleasurable experience."

"I'm not lying. I do miss home, and I miss my kitchen at O'Brien's. Let's be off. Our life is waiting."

As they waited for the elevator, Edward leaned down and gave her a quick kiss on top of her head. "Thank you my lovely wife for two fabulous days I will always treasure." The elevator doors opened. "Look, no Queen of Romania in the elevator this time, how very disappointing."

Lydia looked down at the lapel of her coat. The brooch was pinned near her heart and gleaming up at her. It would always remind her of their honeymoon.

At the front desk, they encountered the same clerk who had checked them in. "Mr. and Mrs. O'Brien, did you enjoy your stay with us?"

"Yes, it was wonderful. Everything was perfect." Lydia was beaming and once again the clerk thought how pretty she was.

"We'd like to settle our bill for our meals and room service." Edward was reaching for his wallet.

"Just a moment, Mr. O'Brien, let me pull your card." Going through the guest cards he found O'Brien. "Your charges are all covered, Mr. and Mrs. O'Brien, courtesy of our management. We hope you enjoyed your stay and will come visit us again."

Lydia and Edward were speechless. Edward turned to his wife, "Michael Tucker will never pay for another meal at O'Brien's."

Neither of them saw the young couple making their way to the Arcadian Room. The young man was strutting proudly as he walked next to his wife who took careful steps beside him. Trying to mask the pain, she walked slowly pretending to look at the art work on the walls.

Chapter 36

E dward and Lydia had been back from their honeymoon a week when Michael Tucker walked in for dinner. He had been trying not to come around as often. He was in a quandary. He couldn't tell them his boss, Stephen Franklin, had paid for their time at the Multnomah Hotel, and he was feeling guilty about all the free meals they had been giving him. He finally told them he wouldn't come back again if they wouldn't let him pay. Because they valued his friendship, and he insisted so wholeheartedly, they agreed to let him pay. Instead, they gave him larger portions.

"Have you heard the latest Little Creek gossip?" Michael was smiling like the cat that swallowed the canary.

Both Edward and Lydia shook their heads.

"Daniel Brookstone got married! He's been in Portland at the Multnomah Hotel on his honeymoon all week and won't be back for another week or more."

Lydia laughed. "Well now, it seems the Multnomah Hotel is a very popular honeymoon place for people from Little Creek! I haven't met

Daniel Brookstone, but I've seen his father in town. Acts like he owns the town and all of us in it."

"Oh, he believes it all right. If serfs were allowed in the United States, we'd all be working for him for free. His son's not much better. Has a real sense of entitlement. From what I've heard, there's not a woman in town who will have anything to do with father or son. Seems the way they treat ladies is none too gentle."

"Who did he ever find to marry him? Obviously she's not a local girl." Edward was only half listening. He had disliked Brookstone on sight and was grateful the man was too snobby to come into their restaurant.

"Old man Brookstone was bragging about his new daughter-in-law just the other day. Guess she's from some rich family in Oklahoma. He says she's very beautiful."

Michael Tucker had obviously been doing his homework where the Brookstones were concerned. "They say when old man Brookstone was married he never let his wife go anywhere without him. Hear she ran off when the boy was about four. It was over twenty years ago and he's never remarried."

"Well if their reputation is so bad, no wonder he married a girl from so far away. Poor thing, she probably doesn't know what kind of man he is." Lydia felt an instant sympathy for the poor young woman who would be so far away from home and married to what sounded like a bad man. "I hope the poor girl makes some friends here, it sounds like she'll need them."

Chapter 37

It had been two weeks and Myra was growing weary. Daniel was two people. By day, he was reasonably considerate and attentive. He enjoyed showing off his beautiful wife, and seeing the envious looks from other men. At night he was a different person. His love-making was becoming increasingly aggressive. After the initial assault on her body, he tried to please her, but when Myra would just lie there enduring his thrusting, he became frustrated. Daniel was used to prostitutes who at least pretended to enjoy sex. His lifeless young wife was making him angry. He gave up all pretense of trying to make sex enjoyable for his young inexperienced wife. Instead, in his desire to get a reaction, started biting her breasts until she cried out in pain and begged him to stop.

Daniel rolled off her. "I just don't understand why you don't enjoy sex. There's something wrong with you."

Myra bit her tongue. She had no experience, but she instinctively knew relations between a husband and wife shouldn't be like this. For the first time, she missed her sister. She knew Lydia was not experiencing the same problems based on the loving looks she had seen on the faces of her sister and brother-in-law. She was trying to think how to escape. Calvin Brookstone had stormed into their suite three days after they had married. He had her letter of intent, and, after a private conversation with his son, decided to accept her into his family.

"I knew you had designs on my son from the moment I saw you smile at him." Calvin gloated at being right. "You're just lucky I didn't have you thrown in prison. I would have had a jail bird for a daughter-in-law." He threw his head back and laughed at his own joke.

"Hey, Pop, I want to enjoy our honeymoon for another couple of weeks."

With a sly look, Calvin spoke to his son but leered at Myra, "Sure, son, I can see how you'd like to enjoy this tasty little morsel. Two weeks, not a day longer. We have a business to run."

Myra's face was flushed and some of her fire was coming back, "I am your son's wife. I'm not a 'morsel' and won't be treated like some tart."

Daniel looked at his wife, leaned over and slapped her across the face. "Since we'll be clothing and feeding you, I think it would be wise for you to keep a civil tongue."

Myra jerked away from him and ran to the bathroom. How could this have gone so horribly wrong? Her avenues for escape were closing in on her. Daniel had taken any cash she had on hand a few days ago. Did he suspect she would run given a chance?

The two weeks crawled by. She was never out of Daniel's sight and was scared to talk to anyone. If she paid too much attention to the waiter, Daniel would grab her arm and make her leave the restaurant. The carefree Daniel she had met in New York was replaced by a sex crazed, jealous, insecure man, with a hair trigger temper. Myra felt like she had aged ten years in two weeks. Now she had to worry about going to Little Creek and her house of cards tumbling down.

The day finally came when Daniel announced they would be going home. Myra realized any chance she had for escape would be long gone when they went to Little Creek. Daniel told her to stay in the room; he was going downstairs to settle the bill. "I'll send a bellhop for the bags."

Seizing the moment, Myra grabbed her smallest bag, stuffed some additional items in it and opened the hotel door. Daniel was standing by it with a menacing look on his face. "I told you to wait here. You're not trying to leave without me, are you?"

Myra panicked and tried to think on her feet. "Of course I'm not trying to leave. I must have misunderstood. I thought you said to get my small bag and meet you in the lobby and the bigger bags would be taken care of by the bellhop."

Daniel grabbed her wrist and squeezed it hard. "You'd better never try to leave me, Martha. I will always find you, and I will always own you body and soul."

Wrenching her arm away from his she looked down at the red mark his hand had left on her small wrist. She was getting used to his roughness and found it ironic before, when she played damsel in distress, there was always a man ready to save her. Now that she was in real danger, where was her knight in shining armor?

"I'll wait here, Daniel. I'm anxious to get to Little Creek and see my new home."

"Just remember one thing. My father and I own the house. You own nothing." After giving her a crushing kiss on the lips he walked down the hall whistling a peppy tune.

Myra turned and walked back inside. He was right. He would find her no matter where she went. She was a prisoner and, in hindsight, prison would have been much, much more pleasant.

Daniel opened the car door for her and helped her into the car. After two weeks of married life and his mercurial mood swings, the small display of kindness shocked her.

"You'll like Little Creek. It's not fancy like Portland, probably more like Oklahoma."

Daniel was in a chatty mood. She knew a response was called for but couldn't muster up one. The two weeks of sleepless nights had worn her out. She was so tired she felt like she could sleep for a week. She felt a pinch on her arm. "Wake up. You're missing all the scenery."

Myra forced herself to keep her eyes open. Daniel said Little Creek was one hour away. If she could just stay awake for another hour, maybe he'd let her have a nap when they arrived at his father's house.

"Lovely, the scenery is lovely, Daniel. I'm very excited to see Little Creek."

"Well, you won't be seeing much of it for a while. My father is anxious for me to get back to work at the mill. You're not to go to town unless I'm with you."

"Yes, Daniel." Myra was tired of arguing with him about the long list of rules he had been giving her. Not leaving the house was rule number one hundred. Prison would have been an improvement over her present situation.

Little Creek had a canopy of trees on the main street of town. The leaves were gone and the bare branches reached out to each other meeting in the middle of the road. Myra could visualize how beautiful it would be in the spring when the leaves reappeared. Daniel slowed the car and made a left turn into a long private driveway with a large expanse of mowed lawn, edged by large oak trees. The ground was littered with gold and orange leaves. When the house came in view, Myra was startled by the ugliness of it. Several architectural styles were all melded together and, even to her untrained eye, it was hideous. Two big columns were by the front entry. They were oversized and above them was a rounded balcony. To the right there was what appeared to be an addition to the home. It was faced in rough brick and expanded the home about fifty feet. It was two stories and butted up against what must have been the original wood structure.

"What do you think of Brookstone Manor?" Daniel puffed up with pride looking at the home he was born and raised in. "See the brick portion on the right? That's where our rooms are. My dad's is on the other side of the house. Good thing, too, with as much crying as you've been doing lately."

Myra looked at the brick structure which now reminded her of a prison. At least she would be far away from the senior Brookstone. "It's lovely, Daniel." Myra had already learned to agree with him to avoid anything unpleasant.

"Come on. You need to see the rest of the home to truly appreciate all my family has done to it in the last one hundred years." Daniel leapt from the car and again, walked around to her side to help her out. "Oh, and you'll meet Mrs. Miller. She basically raised me after my mother was gone. She's been with our family forever."

Myra cheered slightly at the thought of another woman in the house. Maybe there was hope for escape yet.

As they entered the front door, Daniel grabbed Myra and carried her over the threshold. She grimaced, remembering the last threshold he carried her over had become a chamber of horrors. God help her. From the look of things, she was going to be here a lot longer than two weeks.

Laughing to keep Daniel's mood light, Myra forced a giggle as he ceremoniously put her down in the living room. Looking around, she saw several animal heads mounted on the walls. "Oh my, look at the poor creatures."

Daniel laughed. "Martha, if you want to eat, not everything gets to live. How did your family get meat in Oklahoma?"

Myra thought about Tom McNeil, the butcher in her village, and momentarily wished with all her might to be home. "We went to the butcher shop and bought it."

"Well, we have a butcher shop, too. Mrs. Miller buys meat when hunting season is over and we are out of venison."

Just then a female voice called out. "Mr. Daniel. You're home! Let me see the woman who managed to marry a Brookstone man!"

A tall thin woman walked into the room. Her dress was old fashioned but the fabric was beautiful blue cotton that fit her rosy coloring perfectly. Her hair was brown with a fair amount of white invading her top knot. Her face was lined, but her age was hard to read. Myra estimated anywhere from fifty to sixty. Her posture was erect and her hands were work-worn.

Daniel walked over to Mrs. Miller and hugged her. "This is Mrs. Daniel Brookstone, formally, Martha Driscoll of Oklahoma."

Mrs. Miller gave Myra a good once over. Noting Myra's flapper hairstyle and modern dress, Mrs. Miller frowned a bit. She had hoped Daniel would marry a more traditional woman. She looked at Myra's smile and noticed it did not meet her eyes. Thinking to herself, *her eyes look like a trapped animal. She looks scared to death.* Extending her hand to Myra, she said, "It's been a long time since we've had a Mrs. Brookstone in the house. I am very pleased to meet you."

Myra gave her a real smile as she said, "Mrs. Miller, I'm so happy to meet you. It will be nice to have another woman around to talk to."

Mrs. Miller saw the eagerness in her eyes and then noticed the bruise on the girl's wrist. *So it's started already. The apple doesn't fall far from the tree in this family. I hope she lasts longer than the last Mrs. Brookstone.* Smiling, she gently squeezed Myra's hand and said, "It will be nice for me, too."

Daniel looked over to his wife. "Come on, Martha. I'll show you the rest of the house."

Mrs. Miller started to grab the bags. "I'll be happy to unpack these for you."

Remembering she still had Mrs. Hildebrand's gun hidden in her suitcase Myra said, "Oh no, I don't want to trouble you. I'll unpack our bags. It's time I take on some of the duties of looking after Daniel." She said it with such sincerity Daniel gave her a quick hug.

"Keep talking like that and we'll never have a problem, Martha."

Myra thought to herself, *if I wait on you hand and foot, never speak to another man and, be available to have sex twice a day, your life will be perfect and mine will continue to be a living hell.*

Daniel proceeded to show her each room in the house and explain in great detail which ancestor had built the room, or the addition, or the piece of furniture. Her head was spinning with all the details, and she knew Daniel expected her to smile and nod with each new piece of information.

Finally, he brought them to their portion of the house. "This is my room, now, of course, our room. I see Mrs. Miller has already moved some clothes around to make room for your things. I need to go over to the mill. Why don't you unpack while I'm gone and get better acquainted with Mrs. Miller."

Myra was relieved. In two weeks the only time she had been out of his sight was when she went to the bathroom. "How long will you be gone?"

"Only an hour or two. Are you going to miss me?"

Ever the liar, "Of course, I will. We haven't been apart for two weeks!"

Daniel smiled and gave her one of his lip-crushing kisses.

Closing the door behind him, Myra started looking around the room for a hiding place for her gun. Once she unpacked her suitcases they would probably be stored somewhere and she wanted the gun close to her. She finally settled on tucking them into the homemade pads she had for her monthly period. No man would dare touch such an item.

After unpacking her and Daniel's clothes, she couldn't resist snooping through his things. There were some college pictures in his dresser drawer and a group photo of what she assumed was a sports team of some sort. She really had to familiarize herself with American sports. There was nothing exciting in any of his personal items. No diary or skeletons in his closet.

Tiptoeing down the stairs, she heard Mrs. Miller in what she assumed to be the kitchen. Tentatively pushing open the swinging door, she saw Mrs. Miller cleaning vegetables at the sink. "Oh, you startled me, I'm used to being alone in the house. Please come in and sit down. Can I make you some tea or coffee?"

"Tea would be lovely. I have so many questions, I'm happy we have some time alone. Daniel's told me almost nothing of his childhood. What kind of little boy was he?"

"Oh dear, this is not a conversation to have on your first day in this house, but maybe it will help you understand Mr. Daniel a bit. His mother left when he was barely four years old and he cried for days. The only word he would say was Mama. His father couldn't stand it and, before I could stop him, Mr. Brookstone slapped the poor motherless boy across the face. I was horrified. Mr. Brookstone shook him and said, "I never want to hear you crying for your mother again. She's gone and good riddins.""

"I thought the boy was too young to understand what his father was saying but that was the last time he ever said mama, and he never cried for her again. Mr. Brookstone's always been heavy-handed with Daniel, but he loves his son. He's been both hard on Daniel and he's spoiled him. Daniel has always gotten anything he's wanted."

"She left?"

Just then the kitchen door was pushed open and slammed into the wall. Calvin Brookstone walked up to Myra and loomed over her. "Well, Martha, you certainly didn't waste any time questioning the help did you?"

Before she could reply, Mrs. Miller stepped in. "Now, Mr. Brookstone, it's natural for her to be curious about her new family. She didn't mean anything by it."

Almost cowed by Mrs. Miller, Brookstone turned and walked out without another word.

"Mr. Brookstone isn't a bad sort. He's just used to running half the town and two big businesses. Don't get me wrong. You don't want to be on his bad side. It's fierce. I stay clear of most of their arguments, but this being your first day, I stepped in."

"Thank you, Mrs. Miller. I'll try and curb my curiosity."

"Well now, finish your tea and go get some rest. You look worn out and dinner is served at six."

Myra drank the last of her tea and headed back to her new room. Lying on the double bed she thought about the demands Daniel would be making on her poor tired body. Sighing, she drifted off to sleep. What seemed like only moments later, Daniel was trying to push her dress up and pull off her underwear. "Daniel, please, let me sleep for just a few more minutes."

Daniel pinched her hard and pushed his body into hers. "Feel this? Does it feel like I can wait a few more minutes? Come on, Martha, act like you enjoy it for once."

Myra wasn't given the opportunity to respond. Daniel pulled off her underwear and rammed himself inside of her. Pounding and pounding until at last he was spent. She lay there afraid to move until he was finished. At last he rolled off of her and said with a sardonic laugh. "The honeymoon continues my dear little wife. At some point you'll either like it or realize I don't care if you do or not."

"I'm your wife not some dirty little whore you can mount whenever you want."

"Oh you're wrong Martha. You're my wife and a dirty little whore. You were going to run away with my father's money. Your little letter of intent really didn't fool anyone. It just made it easier to get you out of jail and scare you into marrying me. And speaking of money, what ever happened to your family money? Another big whopper of a lie I'll bet. I just wonder what other little secrets you have, Martha. I guess time will tell. My father was right. All women are whores. Some you just find out about after the ring goes on"

Myra bit her tongue. She knew the matter of her family money would come up at some point. She almost wanted to end the charade but he found out she had a sister in town, he'd never let her out of the house, fearing her family would help her escape. If Daniel only knew how much her family loathed her, he would know there was no worry of a rescue.

"Daniel, please let me up. Mrs. Miller said dinner is at 6 p.m. and I need to tidy up."

Moving off the bed Daniel took one more look at his beautiful wife. No matter what lies she had told or that she seemed to hate sex with him, Martha was still the most exquisite woman he had ever seen. He'd keep her on a short leash. She'd already proven to be quite resourceful with her phony letter of intent.

Chapter 38

It had been two weeks and Daniel Brookstone's new bride still had not been seen in town. Calvin Brookstone made a point of talking about his new daughter-in-law and the fine society family she came from. Never one to admit a mistake, he made sure everyone knew his son had married well, despite the fact he knew she was penniless and had conned him out of money. Forgetting he had forced her to accept his investment money in his haste to beat the Franklin Bank out of the opportunity. Yes, the girl was clever. He and Daniel both kept their eyes on her to make sure she didn't try to run off.

Michael Tucker walked into O'Brien's. "Well, still no sighting of the mystery bride. Daniel is strutting around like he's the only married man in the county and brags about his wife constantly."

Lydia looked at Michael. He was a handsome young man with blonde curly hair and big brown eyes with dark lashes. When he was a child, Michael's mother always said a girl deserved those eyes and lashes, not a rough and tumble boy who didn't appreciate them. He stood as tall as Edward and was only a couple years older but was very serious. His job at the Brookstone Mill was his main focus. He worked long hours in the office doing the accounting and overseeing the payroll.

"Michael, you look tired. You've been working too hard. What can I get you for dinner tonight?"

"Lydia, you're a mind reader. I am tired. Do you have any of your famous pot roast?"

Lydia went to the kitchen to fix Michael's plate. Michael sat there reflecting on his situation in Little Creek. He got the job because he had a college friend who knew Daniel Brookstone. Daniel didn't know the recommendation from his friend was a payback for a favor due Stephen Franklin.

Franklin was happy to get an employee on the inside to keep an eye on the Brookstone operation and the O'Brien's. Stephen Franklin was convinced of Michael's ability. He had done his research before hiring Michael and knew he had been raised by an abusive stepfather. He had defended his mother and little sisters the best he could, starting at age nine, when his mother received the first brutal beating from her new husband. Michael had a penchant for fighting for the underdog. Steven thought those qualities would serve him well in his attempt to protect Lydia and Edward.

Lydia returned from the kitchen. She placed a plate laden with pot roast, mashed potatoes and gravy in front of Michael. His mouth watered as he picked up a fork and continued his story. "Daniel says she's from an affluent family in Oklahoma. He hinted they own oil wells, but it could just be him exaggerating. If she's as rich as he says, she must not be much to look at. Money and beauty never mix!" He threw back his head and laughed showing perfect teeth.

Lydia smiled at Michael. "Kathleen stopped by just yesterday. Mr. Brookstone asked her to help put together a party for the newlyweds. She's helping their housekeeper, Mrs. Miller, order food and organize everything. She asked me if I would make a cake for the event, something similar to what I did for Annie and Johnny's engagement party. The party is this Saturday. Edward and I will deliver the cake. Maybe we'll get a peek at her. I've only seen the Brookstone home at a distance. It will be interesting to get an up close look."

Edward looked at his wife, "I thought all the small town gossip would end when we left Ireland. I honestly think it is worse in Little Creek"

"Oh, never you mind. This is a small town and, just like home, people love to talk."

Michael laughed. "You should hear the men at the mill. They're all dying of curiosity, too. What kind of woman could capture the black heart of a Brookstone? Too bad they're such dreadful snobs. No one in the office is invited as far as I know."

"Well it's not surprising. Everyone says they stick to their own kind. Sounds like his son has the same traits, I hope this young woman knew what she was getting into." Lydia thanked God she was married to Edward.

Chapter 39

Myra was going stir crazy. She had not been out of the house since she arrived over a month ago. Mrs. Miller told her Daniel had requested she not leave the premises. Mrs. Miller was kind, but firm. She would not disobey the instructions of her employer. Myra was stymied. She was much better at manipulating men and could not charm the housekeeper into letting her out of the house.

She spent her days reading books from her father-in-law's extensive library. She was happy to see he had a book with maps of the United States. It gave her time to study up on the state of Oklahoma, in case any questions came up.

Daniel came home for lunch every day and expected her to be waiting with a smile. He ate lunch and then pulled her up to the bedroom for sex. Afterwards, she would lie in bed and nap. She was exhausted from the nightly thrusts and his afternoon delight as he liked to call it. She was far from delighted. Her body felt battered and, after six weeks of marriage, her thoughts were consumed with trying to form an escape plan.

At lunch one day Calvin announced, "We're having a party. People are wondering about the new Mrs. Brookstone. You are quite the mystery, Martha. It's time to introduce you to some of the better people in Little Creek."

Relief filled Myra as she calculated the odds of meeting someone to rescue her. "A party would be wonderful. I would like to make some friends here. It's been a bit lonely."

Daniel looked at his wife, the rejected little boy striking out. "I don't see how you can be lonely. I devote every moment to you when I'm home. I do everything for you. You don't need friends you have me."

Myra had learned her lessons well. It was harder to manipulate Daniel now that he could demand sex whenever he wanted, but she had learned to use a conciliatory tone. "Oh, Daniel, I didn't mean it that way. I love being with you, but it would be nice to meet some women friends."

Brookstone interrupted. "I've asked Kathleen Parrish to invite some young married couples and some quality people who are important to Little Creek. We'll have about twenty guests. Kathleen is working out the food with Mrs. Miller. Martha, I'm sure you have something suitable to wear."

For a brief moment Myra thought about saying no a trip to town would be needed, but she saw the stormy look in Daniel's eyes. "Yes, I've a few dresses suitable for a party."

Myra had become adept at defusing Daniel. He still slapped her on occasion and wasn't above a painful pinch to make his point, but it hadn't escalated as she had feared in the beginning.

"I'll ask Mrs. Miller if there is anything I can do to help with the party."

Daniel looked at her. "You'll do no such thing. Mrs. Miller is paid to run this house. She knows what she's doing and can do it better than a spoiled little heiress from Omaha."

Daniel reveled in needling her about the elusive Driscoll fortune that had yet to be seen. When he brought her to Little Creek, she had spun a great story about how her sister married a man who took all their money. She mustered up a tear when she talked about their housekeeper, who, like Mrs. Miller, had been a beloved family member. The story she wove still put her in the grandiose lifestyle that was attractive to the class-conscious Daniel.

Brookstone looked at his son. "You just make sure your wife is on her best behavior. Important people are coming to your party. See that neither of you embarrass me."

Daniel shrugged his shoulders. "We'll be fine. Now if you'll excuse us, I'd like a few minutes with my wife."

Myra's face froze, Daniel grabbed her wrist and non-too-gently pulled her out of the chair. Taking her to their room he pushed her onto the bed and proceeded to roughly thrust himself into her. When he was finished, he slapped her in the face. "Maybe next time you'll show a little enthusiasm for your husband. Martha, making love to a mannequin is getting very tedious."

Putting her hand up to her cheek Myra woodenly nodded her head. "I'll try, Daniel."

Chapter 40

There had been no word of Myra in weeks. Lydia was beginning to believe she had moved on and they were safe. On Saturday morning, Lydia was in the kitchen putting the finishing touches on the cake. Kathleen walked in just as Lydia pronounced with relief, "Finished."

"Oh, Lydia, it's beautiful. They'll be so pleased. Daniel and Martha didn't have a real wedding. They eloped and a judge married them. It sounds so romantic. Mr. Brookstone said he knew they would end up together the moment they met in New York. He said Martha Driscoll was the most beautiful woman his son had ever seen, and he couldn't keep his eyes off her. I guess she played a little hard to get. When he proposed and she said yes, he insisted they get married immediately. Her parents are deceased so she agreed to a small wedding. At least now they'll have a reception, and everyone will enjoy your beautiful cake!"

"You certainly are a wealth of information regarding the new Mrs. Brookstone after weeks of having nothing to share. Have you met her yet?"

"No. It's so very odd. Mr. Brookstone comes to our house to discuss details. He's asked me to give Mrs. Miller a list of things to do, but everything else he wants me to handle. I have offered to go over to their home and discuss the details with the bride, and he keeps saying it's not necessary. It's odd but who am I to question the goings on at the Brookstone house, they've always been a strange lot."

"What time do you want the cake delivered? Edward is out right now. Michael Tucker is loaning us his vehicle to make the delivery."

"Can you come at 5p.m.? Guests will be arriving at 6 for dinner. We'll get the cake set up in the dining room so it's on display during dinner. I have to rush off. Mrs. Willows is putting the finishing touches on the dress I'm wearing tonight. I'm hoping it will drive Bernard wild!"

"You naughty girl, you know he is wild about you already."

"Yes, but it's been five months; and I'm hopelessly in love with him. I'd like a spring wedding and if he doesn't hurry up and ask me, I won't have time to plan one!"

Lydia hugged her friend. "You two are perfect together. It's wonderful to see how happy you are. I suspect a proposal is not too far off in the future. I can't wait to see your dress."

Kathleen left and Lydia found herself with a few minutes alone. She sat down to write a quick letter to her parents. The letters she had been receiving from them were filled with worry about Myra and how they both forgave her. Lydia was at a loss as to how anyone could do what Myra had done and still be forgiven.

Saturday was a busy time at O'Brien's and, when Edward returned from his errand, he had Michael Tucker in tow. "Lydia, my love, Michael is going to take you to deliver the cake. Two of us can't be gone from the restaurant when the dinner crowd comes in. Annie and

I will hold down everything. It shouldn't take you more than an hour to go there, set up, and get back here, right?"

"I can't believe your curiosity hasn't gotten the best of you. All right, Michael and I will go make the delivery. We'll have all the details, but knowing how you detest local gossip, we'll just keep it to ourselves."

Edward playfully swatted at his wife with a kitchen towel. "So that's the game you're going to play? We'll see how long you last. It's you who has been dying to know about the mystery bride. You won't last an hour when you come back."

Lydia stood as tall as her 5'4" would allow. "Well, we'll see who lasts longer. I know you're dying to know the details and won't admit it." Taking her apron off she turned and kissed Edward, "I'm going home to tidy up a bit. I can't be going to the swanky Brookstone house looking like the scullery maid."

Edward hugged his wife. "You'd be the prettiest scullery maid they have ever seen."

Lydia loved her husband beyond reason. She thanked God everyday that she had found him alive and well. Now she added Myra to her prayers, hoping she was far far away and would not be coming to Little Creek.

Chapter 41

Kathleen arrived at the Brookstone's home at 4:30 p.m. She wanted to be there when Lydia arrived with the cake and also have some time to make sure all the details on her list were done. Mrs. Miller greeted her at the front door. "Miss Parrish, please come in. I assume you're here to see to all the final details."

"Hello, Mrs. Miller. I'm sure everything is perfect. I came early because the cake will be delivered soon, and I would like it set up in the dining room. And I was hoping to meet Martha Brookstone before the other guests arrive."

"Let me go upstairs and see if she's ready. I told her you'd be coming early and she's anxious to meet you. Poor little dear, she doesn't know a soul in town, and that rascal Daniel has kept her marooned in the house. He claims he's not ready to share her with the world."

Kathleen laughed. "Well, he'd better be ready tonight. There are quite a few guests who can't wait to meet her. She's been the talk of the town, and everyone is curious about the woman who married the most prominent bachelor in Oregon." Secretly Kathleen wondered what kind of woman would willingly marry a Brookstone.

Mrs. Miller went up the stairs to fetch Martha. Kathleen stood at the doorway of the dining room and surveyed the room. As she requested, there was a large sideboard with a beautiful lace runner waiting for the arrival of the cake. The long dining room table was set for twenty guests. Silver candelabras were ready to be lit and the sterling silver place settings gleamed in the late afternoon sun. There were three small rose flower arrangements on the table. The blood red roses stood out against the white lace.

Just then Kathleen heard a discreet knock at the back door. Leaving the dining room and going into the kitchen, she opened the back door for Lydia and Michael. Lydia walked through and whispered, "Where is everyone? Are we too early?"

"No, you're right on time. Mrs. Miller went upstairs to get the guest of honor. I told her it would be nice to meet the new Mrs. Brookstone before the party starts. If you would like to get the cake and follow me out to the dining room, we can set it up."

Kathleen opened the swinging door for Michael. As he was carrying the multi-tiered cake, Lydia walked behind him into the dining room.

"Put it right here, Michael. Lydia, what do we need to do to set it up?"

I've brought some flowers I thought would look pretty around the base. When you're ready to have the cake cut, they can just be moved to the side."

As she started to arrange the flowers, she heard a woman say, "You must be Kathleen. I'm Martha Driscoll Brookstone."

Lydia looked up into the mirror over the sideboard, anxious to finally get a look at the bride. She almost fainted when she saw her sister standing behind her conversing with Kathleen. Steadying herself by holding onto the sideboard she took several breaths.

Michael was looking at the new Mrs. Brookstone and didn't notice Lydia's distress. He saw a thin young woman with the face of an angel. She had tormented eyes tinged with dark circles reminding him of how his mother looked before the beating that killed her. Her cultured voice and tentative smile belied the nervousness Michael could sense was just below the surface. Knowing all the rumors he had heard about the Brookstones, he felt sad for the beautiful young woman before him. Fading to the background, he watched her carefully. He thought of his mother and the years of abuse from his stepfather. Her mouth always held the secrets that her eyes betrayed; the same as the new Mrs. Brookstone.

Kathleen was also oblivious to Lydia's distress. "Martha, you must meet the woman who made your cake. She and her husband own a restaurant in town and are very dear friends of mine. This is Lydia O'Brien."

Lydia turned and faced Myra. She saw a stricken look matching her own on her sister's face. With an unperceivable shake of her head, Myra's eyes implored Lydia to silence. Lydia looked into eyes identical to her own and saw the terror in her sister's.

Lydia extended her hand. "I'm pleased to meet you, Mrs. Brookstone. I hope you enjoy the cake and your party."

Myra reached out and grasped Lydia's hand with both of hers. Giving it a gentle squeeze, she looked her sister in the eyes and mouthed the word "Help."

There was a slight cough from the corner of the room. "How rude of me, this is our dear friend Michael Tucker who helped me transport the cake." Lydia squeezed her sister's hands and looked in Michael's direction.

Michael was bright red, a blush colored his neck and entire face. He managed to bow his head slightly and, with a quick, "Pleased to meet you Mrs. Brookstone," he looked into her eyes and felt like he was being swallowed up by memories of his childhood and the sounds he had heard in the night.

For a moment, Myra forgot where she was. The soul searching look from Michael Tucker's eyes was so intense she had never experienced anything like it. She had to force herself to turn away and take a final look at her sister.

"Kathleen, I must be getting back to the restaurant. Is everything to your satisfaction?" Lydia was anxious to leave before her composure crumbled in front of everyone.

"Lydia, it is beautiful as usual. I'll stop by next week for lunch." Kathleen looked at her friend and was concerned at the sudden change of mood. The stiff formality was unlike Lydia. As Kathleen turned from Lydia to Martha Brookstone, she immediately saw the resemblance. The flapper haircut was so opposite of Lydia's curly topknot and the new Mrs. Brookstone was terribly thin but it was obvious, looking at the facial features of both women that this was the long lost Myra. Fighting for self control, she said goodbye to Lydia and Michael. Taking Martha's arm, she suggested they retreat to the living room to get to know each other before the other guests arrived.

As Lydia left, she heard a man's voice in the living room. "There's my bride. Now, Kathleen, don't try and pry information out of her. She's a very private person. Aren't you dear?"

Even from a distance, Lydia could hear the threat in Daniel Brookstone's voice.

As Lydia walked out to the car, she needed all of her self control to not shake into a million pieces. Her sister was married to Brookstone? How on earth could her sister have ended up in this unholy union?

Myra was relieved Daniel had not seen Lydia. She could sense Kathleen had picked up on the resemblance of the two sisters, but Daniel had come in before they could talk.

Daniel looked at Kathleen and gave her a sly grin. "I hate to interrupt this little gab fest. I just can't bear to be without my wife, even for a few minutes."

Myra forced a smile at Daniel. It was clear that he was not going to allow her to talk to anyone without him. "Oh, Daniel, I think women's talk will bore you to tears, but please stay."

Kathleen watched the exchange between the newlyweds. There was something menacing in Daniel's tone, and, Martha, who had looked excited only a few minutes earlier, had retreated into a shell.

Daniel turned on the charm and soon had Kathleen laughing about things that had gone on when they were children. Myra observed and hardly recognized the man she had married. She had not seen the light-hearted Daniel she had met in New York for weeks. Myra had never been in love with him, although she had liked the Daniel in New York. Now she loathed him. Myra was trying to figure out a way to get to her sister for help.

Calvin Brookstone walked into the living room. "Hello, Kathleen. Good to see you. Is everything ready?"

"Yes, Uncle Calvin, we're all set. All we need are guests. I invited Bernard Monroe to be my date." Kathleen blushed as she said the words.

"Well look at Kathleen blush!" Daniel hooted with laughter. "I heard you were seeing our young doctor. He seems a little timid to me. You need a strong man to keep you in line."

"Daniel, what a ridiculous statement, women do not need to be kept in line by their husbands. You are positively barbaric." As Kathleen said the words she saw the stricken look on Martha's face. The entire situation became clear to her instantly. When they were children, Daniel was always the bully. Now it appeared he was bullying his wife.

Daniel laughed. "I have not met a woman yet that didn't need to be kept in line, and you Kathleen, need to know that men control everything a woman's life. It's our job as the breadwinner." Looking at the two women dismissively, knowing he was right said, "Let's change the subject. Can I get anyone a drink?"

Myra shook her head. "I'll wait until the guests arrive. Thank you."

As if on cue, the doorbell rang. Moments later, Mrs. Miller showed Kathleen's father and Bernard Monroe into the living room. Kathleen rose to greet her father and gave Bernard a quick hug and kiss on the cheek, whispering, "Thank God you're here."

Bernard gave her a quizzical look and then was distracted by Calvin Brookstone's loud declaration of, "Hello Bernard, it's not every day one of my employees comes to dinner."

Even Harold Parrish was taken aback by the boorishness of the statement. "Well, Calvin, since Bernard is a friend to me and Kathleen and practically a member of our family, I'll ignore your rudeness. Now make yourself useful and get us a drink."

Kathleen was thankful for her father's intervention. "Daniel, are you going to introduce your lovely bride?"

Daniel rose from his chair and pulled Myra up with him. "This is my lovely bride. Everyone, this is Martha Driscoll Brookstone."

Myra smiled and shook hands with Bernard and Harold. Harold had a puzzled expression on his face, "Martha, you remind me of someone, but I just can't put a finger on whom. It will come to me."

Kathleen and Bernard exchanged looks. She knew he would see the resemblance to Lydia and a slight shake of her head quieted him.

Soon the rest of the guests arrived, and the new Mrs. Brookstone met what her husband and father-in-law thought of as Little Creek's leaders and upper crust. Her head was swirling with names and faces. Daniel never left her side. Many of the men were giving her the eye, and Daniel puffed up with pride. He was drinking whiskey at an alarming rate. Calvin had a connection for booze and deemed Prohibition as a law for the little people and not for him or his family. The men had whiskey before dinner and ample wine was served with the meal.

After dinner, Kathleen announced it was time to cut the cake. Myra and Daniel stood up and walked to the sideboard. Myra took a long look at the cake. It was beautiful. It reminded her of her da's cakes. Daniel took a forkful of cake and fed it to her. It was delicious and tasted like home. For a moment, real tears came to Myra's eyes. She took a forkful and fed Daniel, smiling through her tears. "Such a beautiful cake, and a lovely dinner. Thank you all for coming to celebrate our marriage."

There were smiles around the table. Myra, looking worn out and frail had charmed Calvin and Daniel's friends. Little did they know charm was her survival technique and her manipulations to escape were being put in place.

Chapter 42

Michael Tucker's head and heart were in turmoil. He had been so taken by Mrs. Brookstone's beauty and fragility; he failed at first to notice resemblance between her and Lydia. When he saw the color drain out of Lydia's face, and seeing the women side by side, he put two and two together. Watching Lydia and her sister reach out to each other was contrary to everything he had heard about Myra. When he looked into her eyes, he saw a haunted woman. "She's quite a looker, isn't she?"

"Yes, Mrs. Brookstone is very pretty. I hope they enjoy the cake."

She did not confide in him as to the identity of the new Mrs. Brookstone. Realizing Lydia was not going to talk about it, the rest of the short drive to the restaurant was very quiet as Michael tried to sort out his feelings. He had felt such a connection with Lydia's sister. He could see the pain in her eyes and knew she was suffering like his mother had suffered with his stepfather. When he looked into her eyes wide with fright, Michael knew he had to help Mrs. Brookstone. He couldn't reconcile the information Mr. Franklin had relayed to him and the woman he just met. Michael kept his thoughts to himself and waited for Lydia, to confide in him. As he pulled his vehicle up to the sidewalk in front of O'Brien's, Lydia hastily thanked Michael for his help and jumped out of the car.

Michael drove away wondering what he had gotten himself into. The angelic face of Mrs. Brookstone haunted him. Knowing he could not stand by if she was in danger from her husband, he sensed this would not be the last time he saw her. He was a boy when his mother was brutalized by his stepfather and was powerless to help. He was now a man and would help the new Mrs. Brookstone. The rumors about the Brookstones gave him reason to believe the poor woman was in danger. He would do what he could for her, disregarding any privileged information he received from his East Coast employer.

Entering the restaurant, Lydia immediately went up to Edward. The tears she held back were now falling from her eyes.

"Lydia, what's wrong? Come here, and tell me what happened." Opening his arms Lydia fell into them.

"She's here. Edward, she's here. Myra is in Little Creek. She's married to Daniel Brookstone." Lydia started shaking uncontrollably and Edward walked her back to the kitchen.

"Sit down. Let me get you some tea. You're shaking like a leaf." Edward turned away so his wife wouldn't see the murderous look on his face. As he reached for the tea kettle, he tried to get his emotions under control. He almost snapped the tea cup in half his grip was so tight. Edward turned around, his face belying his anger. He put a cup of tea in front of Lydia. "Now tell me what happened."

Once the words came out, Lydia couldn't stop. "She's got a modern haircut and she speaks like she was born here, not a trace of accent. But, Edward, something's wrong. She's scared to death. She has dark circles under her eyes and she's so thin. Edward, she mouthed the word "Help." I keep thinking about all the rumors we have heard about how cruel those two men are."

"Aye, and you above all people know how manipulative your sister can be."

"No, Edward, you didn't see her. She's very frightened. I can sense it."

"Tomorrow we'll have Kathleen come over and tell us everything she knows. Lydia, I know you're frightened for her, but please don't forget all that's happened, what she did to your parents, Mrs. Hildebrand, and the mental anguish you've been through. Please don't let your soft heart take over common sense."

Lydia cocked her head and set her chin at an angle. Edward knew she was about to be stubborn. "I want to talk to her. I want her to be safe, and, most of all, I want her out of Little Creek. We are not going to tell the Franklins until I get to talk to her."

Edward sighed. He knew his wife would not back down.

Chapter 43

The guests left at eleven o'clock and Myra dreaded being alone with Daniel. He had barely left her side all night. By the end of the evening, Daniel was quite drunk. He grabbed Myra by the hand and as they walked up the stairs to the bedroom he was shouting at her for talking to men at the party.

"But, Daniel, you were with me every minute, I only talked to people in your presence. I didn't do anything wrong." Myra knew better than to argue, but she was exhausted and in no mood to talk to her drunk husband.

She didn't see his arm snake out and punch her in the face. It was so fast she didn't have time to duck. He caught her in her right eye. The pain was excruciating, and she could feel it starting to swell. Myra curled up into a ball and prayed he wouldn't hit her again.

"You bitch. I saw you looking at all the men. I saw you." His speech was slurred and, before he could strike out again, Daniel fell onto the bed and immediately passed out. Myra got up and walked down the hall to the bathroom. She ran some cold water and held a compress to her eye. It was almost swollen shut.

In a fit of blind rage, she stumbled back to the bedroom and opened the drawer containing her monthly pads. As she reached for the hidden gun she sat down hard. Myra realized she hadn't used her pads since at least two weeks before her marriage. That was over six weeks ago. Gasping for breath, she felt as if she had been punched in the stomach. "Mother of God, please make it not so. I can't be pregnant." The tears came, and Daniel was too deep in his drunken sleep to hear. The anguish wasn't for herself but for the baby inside her that she wanted as much as the black eye she had just received.

There was no way she could run now. Daniel had taken all of her money, and she had no idea if Lydia would help her. Living in the house for a month had taught her one thing. These men were ruthless and would stop at nothing to keep what was theirs. Daniel considered her his property, and now with a baby she would be nothing but a brood mare to him. The only good news was if she were pregnant maybe the nightly assaults on her body would end. Myra knew she was stuck, but perhaps being pregnant would serve a purpose until she could figure a way out of this situation.

The next morning Daniel woke up with a dreadful hangover and was in a foul mood. He looked at Myra's eye and asked, "What the hell happened to you?"

"You hit me, Daniel. Don't you remember?"

"Martha, if I hit you, you probably deserved it. Now leave me alone. My head is killing me. Go get me some breakfast and bring it up here. Be a good wife and don't make me ask you twice."

Just then Myra was overcome with nausea, and rushed to the bathroom to throw up. With very little left in her stomach from the night before it was more of a dry heave. Walking back into the bedroom she was nauseous again. It was the odor of the whiskey Daniel had consumed the night before. The room stank of it. Turning on her heel she left to go get his breakfast and escape the stale smell.

Mrs. Miller greeted her with a cheery good morning. Turning from the sink, she saw Myra's swollen eye and pulled out a piece of beef from the icebox. "Here, put this on your eye. It will help with the swelling and the color. You don't look very well. Other than your eye, are you all right?"

"I'm just not feeling well, and I'm so very tired." Myra's voice was small, the fight momentarily out of her.

Mrs. Miller was a wise woman. She'd been watching Martha for the last couple of weeks and had her suspicions on a number of topics. This was clearly a young woman who was used to manipulating men and had met her match with young Daniel and Mr. Brookstone. The girl had been lethargic as of late, and Mrs. Miller had seen no sign of Mrs. Brookstone's monthlies in the five weeks she'd been in the house.

Myra looked at Mrs. Miller. "Can I ask you something? It's personal but I have no one else to ask. My ma, I mean my mother, didn't live long enough to tell me some things that are useful for a woman to know." Myra stopped and took a big breath, "How do you know if you're…if you're in the family way?"

Mrs. Miller felt a pang of pity for young Mrs. Brookstone. "Well now, normally you miss your monthly period. A pregnant woman gets very tired in the beginning, and sometimes your breasts hurt. Do you have any of those signs?"

Myra burst into tears. "I had my monthly curse two weeks before Daniel and I got married. I didn't pay attention to the fact it hadn't come since then." Myra left out the part of deciding to kill Daniel in his sleep, and only when she reached for her gun, realized she might be with child. Her big blue eyes filled with tears. "I have been so tired lately, but I thought it was because Daniel is, well, Daniel won't leave me alone. I'm exhausted. My breasts have been tender, but I thought it was because of him. This morning I threw up. I thought it was the awful smell of stale whiskey in the bedroom, but now I'm not so sure."

"Well now, I'd say you are in the family way. You should be happy. Mr. Daniel and Mr. Brookstone will be very pleased."

Myra grabbed Mrs. Miller's hands, "Please don't say anything to them. I want to wait until I'm positive. Shouldn't I go to a doctor to find out?"

Just as Mrs. Miller was about to answer the kitchen door swung opened. Daniel was on the other side. "Where's my breakfast, and what are you talking about going to a doctor? What's wrong? Are you sick? Surely a little pat on the eye didn't make you sick, did it?"

Mrs. Miller wisely chose to leave the kitchen. Whatever plans Myra had of waiting to tell her news or getting to town to see a doctor evaporated immediately. "It's just women talk, Daniel."

"I didn't ask you for a stupid excuse. I asked you what you were talking about."

Myra tried her best to look excited. Fortunately her lack of excitement looked more like fear. "We're going to have a baby, that's what we were discussing. I was asking about going to a doctor to verify it. Mrs. Miller says I have all the signs."

Despite his hangover and foul mood, Daniel had the decency to at least smile. "Really, a baby? My father will be ecstatic. All he ever talks about is continuing the Brookstone line. When is it due?"

Myra almost laughed. She had absolutely no idea when it happened. It could have been their honeymoon night or sometime during the last seven weeks of nonstop sexual attention from Daniel. "I don't know. I imagine doctors can tell these things. We've been married seven weeks. It could have happened anytime. I know babies take nine months, but other than that, my mother kept my sister and me pretty ignorant about such things."

"Well, keep the beef on your eye, and we'll take you to the doctor when it looks better."

Suddenly Myra was ecstatic. The thought of actually going to town and getting out of this house was worth the horrible news of another Brookstone coming into this world. "Yes, Daniel. Hopefully, I'll be able to go to the doctor soon. Can we not tell your father until we know when the baby will be born?"

In a rare moment of generosity, Daniel decided to grant his wife's wishes. "Certainly, Martha, but let's wait until your eye is better before you go into town. I don't want to answer questions about my clumsy wife falling and getting a black eye."

Myra looked at him incredulously, but held her tongue. She was going to milk this pregnancy for all it was worth, and the first order of business would be for the doctor to forbid any more marital relations. She'd heard of women back home who had difficult pregnancies and the grumble of the men who couldn't sleep with their wives. She didn't understand why they couldn't sleep together until she had married. Myra now understood what "sleep together" really meant. She fully intended to have eight months of marital bliss. For her, marital bliss would be Daniel not pawing at her constantly. And what fiend would hit a pregnant woman? Finally, she felt like she could breathe again.

Chapter 44

Kathleen knocked tentatively on Edward and Lydia's door. It was only nine in the morning, but she knew Lydia would want to hear about the evening.

Edward opened the door and smiled when he saw Kathleen and Bernard standing on their front doorstep. "Come in. Lydia didn't sleep very well, and she's been baking up a storm."

A pleasant cinnamon smell was wafting out of the kitchen. Kathleen called out as she made her way to Lydia. "Something smells wonderful!" When she entered the kitchen, she was astounded at the amount of trays on the countertop laden with sweet sticky cinnamon rolls.

"Aye, I think I got a little carried away. I couldn't sleep." Lydia had dark circles under her eyes, but her smile was as cheery as ever.

Bernard looked at her and immediately asked if she'd had a headache. Lydia wordlessly shook her head no.

Edward walked in behind the group. "All right, I know Lydia is dying of curiosity, and I think by now you've figured out just who the new Mrs. Brookstone is."

Kathleen nodded her head. "I noticed the resemblance immediately. It was such a shock. Then I saw the look on Lydia's face. My heart went out to you, but I couldn't react. When Bernard came in later he noticed immediately. Thank God he's a mind reader and didn't say a word."

"I wouldn't call it reading your mind. Your face said it all."

Smiling, Kathleen continued, "The Brookstones have never met you so there is no way they would make the connection. The evening was a little odd. Daniel wouldn't let your sister out of his sight. She couldn't converse with anyone unless he was right there. In fact it was fairly obvious she couldn't make a move without his approval. He drank very heavily. Oh don't raise your eyebrows at me, Edward. Don't you know Prohibition doesn't apply to the Brookstones?"

"Did they say how they met? How on earth could Myra have orchestrated to marry someone from Little Creek? Why not just come here and try to do whatever she had planned?"

"The story was a little sketchy. They met in New York at the Biltmore Hotel. It's a very swanky hotel. Daniel said he saw her checking in and fell in love with her instantly. Apparently, she gave them both a story about opening a shop on the West Coast in either Seattle or Portland. Daniel accompanied her when she placed orders for stock, but they were very vague when it came down to why she didn't open a shop. Myra was very quiet. Daniel did all the talking. He claimed once he decided to marry her, he didn't want her working. Said he had to do some fast talking to get her to agree to it. Then he exchanged this funny look with his father."

Bernard chimed in, "I'll say this about the girl. She is very pretty, not as beautiful as our Lydia but still very pretty. There are obvious signs of stress. She shrinks back whenever Daniel touches her or makes a sudden move. I don't want to be the one to start false rumors, so I'll just tell you something is not right with this relationship. She looks like she hasn't slept in a month."

"And she's as thin as a twig." Lydia's worry was apparent. "She mouthed the word 'help' to me. She's in danger."

"Please, Lydia, don't upset yourself. You are feeling sympathy for a person who was intent on doing you or me harm. I know she's your sister, but we still need to turn her over to the authorities." Edward was torn between Lydia's desire to protect Myra, and his desire to protect his wife.

Kathleen saw the distress on her friend's faces. "I made a lunch date with her for Monday. Daniel seemed to be OK with it, but said it would be better to have lunch at their house. For some reason, he is very reluctant to let her out of the house."

"If he is being overbearing and Myra is putting up with it, force is involved. Lydia can tell you more, but from what I used to hear from the village lads, she put up with no nonsense."

For the first time, Lydia smiled. "Oh yes, she had quite the reputation as a headstrong girl. Edward, I know what you're thinking, but you have to admit, I'm really not that stubborn."

Kathleen thought back to the Daniel she knew growing up. Their families had always been thrown together. Daniel had been overbearing as a child and always had to win. But, when necessary, he could charm the sun out of the sky. Kathleen didn't want to scare her friends by talking about the old rumors of violent episodes with some of the town girls when they were growing up. "I'll see her on Monday. I promise to come over right after."

Lydia was somewhat placated. "No matter what, Myra's my sister and she needs me."

Edward sighed. He knew the battle was lost, and he would just have to resign himself to trying to protect his wife despite herself. However, he felt he owed it to the Franklins to call them with an update.

Dishing up the delicacies Lydia had made in the wee hours of the morning, the foursome tried to change the subject. Talking about some of the other people at the party and how Brookstone senior had made the comment to Bernard about an employee being in his house. Kathleen laughed about the blatant snobbery, and you could tell she was proud her father had stuck up for Bernard.

Bernard looked at Lydia. "I know we're trying to change the subject, but I must tell you how delicious your cake was. It was magnificent. When your sister tasted it, she got tears in her eyes."

Lydia's own eyes teared up. "Our da used to make the same cake in his bakery. See, Edward, Myra is missing her family."

Realizing he had opened a can of worms, Bernard purposely looked at his watch. "Oh my, Kathleen, we must be going. We told your father we would go to church with him this morning."

Kathleen and Lydia stood up at the same time and hugged each other. "Lydia, I hate to leave you like this. I promise to come over tomorrow right after I see Myra. Oh, I should really stick with Martha in case I slip up in front of Daniel."

Waving goodbye from the front door, Edward thought about how best to broach the subject of telling the Franklins about Myra. As he was about to say something, Lydia turned to him, "We need to call Stephen and Beverly."

Nodding in agreement, they went into the house to place the call. When they finally reached the Franklins, they told what they knew of Myra's transformation into Martha Driscoll Brookstone and her arrival in Little Creek.

The Franklins had already received a call from Michael Tucker alerting them to his suspicions. Stephen was in a quandary. The British authorities had no desire to cross the pond and arrest Myra. The New York police would not be traveling to Oregon to arrest Myra for her battery of Mrs. Hildebrand. If Stephen Franklin had her arrested by Oregon police, he feared the Brookstones would retaliate against Edward and Lydia in some way. After being the ones who put Lydia in danger from her sister, the Franklin's utmost concern was Lydia's safety. With her sister in the same town and now that Lydia was convinced Myra was in danger, Stephen Franklin was unsure of the next move. Edward made the most sense. Wait and see what Kathleen Parrish learns during her visit tomorrow.

One thing was for certain, the Brookstones were not good to their women. The rumors Tucker had been reporting back were too many to be easily discarded. Myra may have met her match on manipulative behaviors and lack of conscience.

Chapter 45

Monday afternoon Kathleen was nervous about going back to the Brookstone house. As she rang the bell, she braced herself for whatever was on the other side. Mrs. Miller answered and looked quizzical for a moment. "Oh, I'm sorry, Miss Parrish, were you expected?"

"Why yes, Mrs. Miller. Mrs. Brookstone and I have plans to lunch together today. Did she not tell you?"

"Please take a seat in the living room. I'll go see if she is available."

A few minutes later, a breathless Myra entered the living room. Her face was not as pale as it had been on Saturday night, and Kathleen was surprised at the amount of make-up the girl appeared to be wearing. Then she spotted the faint blue around her right eye and it looked swollen. Kathleen smiled, "Well, Martha, you're looking chipper today. I was worried you had forgotten about our lunch date."

"No, Kathleen, I've been looking forward to getting together. Would you like to go for a walk around the yard while Mrs. Miller finishes our lunch?" In truth, Myra had remembered the lunch date but was afraid to alert Mrs. Miller until the Brookstones were out of the house for fear Daniel would change his mind and forbid company. Mrs. Miller had taken it in stride when Myra asked for lunch to be served in one hour.

"It's a bit brisk outside but the sun is out. A walk would be lovely." Bundling her coat, hat, and gloves back on, Kathleen opened the front door.

"Oh, I need to tell Mrs. Miller we're taking a stroll in the yard. I'll be right back."

Kathleen looked at Myra's face again. She looked so much like Lydia it was uncanny. If the two of them were seen in town at the same time, there is no doubt people would know they were related. Their eyes were different; same shape and almost the same color, but Lydia's were bright and lively. When Lydia smiled, it reached her eyes. From what little she had seen of Myra, her eyes did not hold the same spark of life as her sister's. She was trying to figure out how she was going to bring up the subject of Lydia when Myra came bounding out of the kitchen. Her step was light, and you could see her enthusiasm over getting out of the house.

Once outside, Kathleen decided the best approach was a direct one. "I know who you are. Your sister is worried to death about you, and she says you need help."

Myra was startled, and then realized Americans were always direct. In her own voice, she answered. "Aye, I was a bit worried about myself too until Sunday, and now it's all changed. He won't be laying another hand on me for quite a while if I have my way about it."

"Did he hit you in the eye?" Kathleen saw no need for the pretense any longer.

"This is a little souvenir Daniel gave me for talking too much with the men at the party. I tried to explain I was with him every moment, but he wasn't in the listening mood."

"Myra, how on earth did you end up married to Daniel Brookstone?" Kathleen couldn't contain her curiosity any longer.

"It's a long story and we don't have much time. I was faced with going to prison for trying to steal investment money from old man Brookstone. I would have married the devil himself to stay out of prison. Little did I know Daniel would actually turn into the devil himself the minute he got a ring on my finger. I know Lydia and my family think I'm a little touched in the head. Maybe I am, but it is nothing compared to the Brookstones. They are sadistic and evil."

"Myra, how are you going to get Daniel to stop hurting you?"

"Oh that will be easy. A little gift I didn't plan on and may I say, a little gift I don't really want, but it will help for now. I'm pregnant. Or at least I'm pretty sure I am. Our mother didn't really talk about such things to Lydia and me."

Kathleen was astounded. "Pregnant? And he hit you?"

"Oh, it was before he or I knew. Now, pregnant with an heir to the Brookstone family, I think the hitting will stop. I just want him to stop his daily and nightly attentions, if you know what I mean." Myra shuddered.

"You need to go to a doctor. You can see Bernard." Kathleen was beginning to get the hint about the daily and nightly attentions. Based on the look of sheer horror on Myra's face, the rumors must be true.

"You're daft. I can't go see a doctor I've met socially and had dinner with. It's just not right. It would be mortifying." It was Myra's turn to be shocked.

"No, you must. He works for the Brookstones so they will assume he'll do exactly what is best for the family. He's a dear friend of Lydia and Edward's. He'll help you as long as you swear you are not going to harm them."

"Them? Which them? I can't swear I won't harm Daniel or his father. The world would be a better place without both of them, but my sister and Edward are safe. I know when I've lost. They won't have any trouble from me. I have my hands full here as it is."

Myra saw Mrs. Miller approaching. "We have to stop talking. She's on their side no matter what happens."

"There you are. Lunch is ready if you'd like to come in." Mrs. Miller quickly took in the scene. Whatever they had been discussing from the look on Kathleen Parish's face it must have been quite interesting.

"Mrs. Miller, I was just talking to Kathleen about my condition. She, too, thinks I should see a doctor. I just want to make sure everything is all right." Myra added a convincing look of fear to her plea.

"I told her she should see Dr. Monroe. He's a good doctor and did his residency in obstetrics in Boston before coming out here."

As a woman, Mrs. Miller could understand Martha's desire to have confirmation of her condition, but her employers would be very angry if she allowed Mrs. Brookstone to go to town. "Would Dr. Monroe do a house call?"

Kathleen realized immediately the older woman was sympathetic to Myra but would not go against her employers. "I could call him and explain the situation. I don't know."

Myra finally snapped, barely slipping back to her Mid-Western voice. "I want a doctor and if he won't come here, then point me in the direction and I'll walk myself. I can't bear not knowing if I am pregnant or not."

Mrs. Miller gave in. "Miss Parrish, please call Doctor Monroe and ask if he will make a house call."

Kathleen entered the house and walked into the hallway to use the phone. She happened to catch Bernard before he left for lunch. She briefly explained the situation and begged him to come. She was no more anxious to have Myra go to town than the Brookstones were. Kathleen was worried someone would notice her resemblance to Lydia and talk would start going around town.

"He'll arrive in about an hour. Martha, let's have lunch before he gets here."

Myra was relieved to have won a minor victory; she needed Doctor Monroe's help with her plan.

The two young women sat at the dining room table and ate the roast pork sandwiches Mrs. Miller had prepared. There was left over cake for dessert.

Myra's face was melancholy when she took a forkful of cake. "It's an old family recipe. It is delicious isn't it? I never thought I'd ever miss anything from home."

Kathleen was surprised at the wistful look on her face. She was still waiting for the look of regret for all the horrible things Myra had done to get to America and for the weeks of worry she had caused her sister. Until she saw some remorse, Kathleen vowed not to fall for Myra's reminiscing.

The doorbell rang and as Mrs. Miller came out to answer it Kathleen ran to the door. "I'll get it. Martha, where do you want Dr. Monroe to examine you?"

Myra turned white. "You'll stay with me won't you? I can't be with him alone. Daniel will have a fit, and I don't want Mrs. Miller in the room."

"Let me talk to Dr. Monroe and explain everything. I won't be but a moment."

Kathleen opened the door and asked Bernard to step outside. "Bernard, this is just awful. She thinks she's pregnant and is scared to death of Daniel." Blushing furiously, she stammered as she tried to explain the problem. "Bernard, Daniel is, well, he is, ah, well he's rather enthusiastic about his husbandly privileges. I think he is hurting her."

Bernard looked at Kathleen and saw her discomfort. "Kathleen, I'll examine her and then I will talk to her, but I won't be manipulated by her."

Going back into the house, Bernard went up to Myra. "Mrs. Brookstone, Kathleen has told me you may be pregnant. Can you tell me the last time you bled?"

Myra's face was so red Kathleen sat next to her and took her hand. "It's OK. He's a doctor. Just pretend like you've never met."

"Well, near as I can remember it was two weeks before Daniel and I married. We've been married almost two months."

"Any other symptoms?" Bernard was trying to keep his dislike for "Martha" out of the interview, but it was difficult.

"I've been exhausted, but I thought it was because of Daniel's demands. He comes home every day for lunch and then makes me do my duty, as he calls it. He had to go to Portland today, or he would have been at me by now. It's the same at night, every night. And yesterday morning I threw up. The smell of Daniel's whiskey breath made me ill. Each time she told of a symptom it was like she was reliving it. "My chest is sore, but I thought it was because Daniel is...." Myra trailed off.

She couldn't tell them what he did to her breasts. It was too mortifying. Plus she really had no idea; maybe all men did the same to their wives.

Bernard was beginning to see where this was going. "Why don't you and Kathleen go into the bedroom. You can undress from the waist down for the examination. Kathleen will stay in the room. It's not a painful examination, and it will be over before you know it."

Kathleen and Myra walked out of the room, and climbed the stairs to the bedroom Myra shared with Daniel. They were quiet until Myra turned to Kathleen. "You've a good man there. I'm sure he's different from Daniel."

"From what you've shared with me today, I will thank God every day for the rest of my life for that fact." Kathleen was appalled by what she had heard.

The women got to business. Pulling a sheet from the linen closet, Kathleen had Myra take off everything as instructed. She covered her with the sheet and pulled a chair up to the side of the bed. A moment later, there was a discrete knock at the bedroom door.

"OK, Mrs. Brookstone, please put your feet on the bed and push your legs apart. I'm just going to take a look here." Bernard looked at Myra's pelvic area and was astounded at the amount of bruising in that region. "Now, you're going to feel my hands for a moment. I just need to get a quick look." As he examined her cervix, he saw the tearing around the vagina. Thinking to himself that Daniel Brookstone was a bastard for what he was doing to his wife, he realized Myra was going to get exactly what she wanted.

"Mrs. Brookstone, you can put your legs down and sit up please. I have some things to discuss I'd rather not say in front of Kathleen, if you don't mind."

"Oh no, Doctor, what you have to say to me you can say in front of her. She needs to know the truth."

"All right, I will reluctantly honor your request. From my examination, yes, you are pregnant. I estimate about six weeks. Your baby will be born sometime in early August."

Myra took the news stoically. She had figured as much on her own.

"What I'm seeing in your cervical area appears to be much bruising and tearing of tissue. This is highly unusual and…" Bernard paused, trying to think of the proper way to phrase it.

Kathleen was beginning to understand where this was going. She knew Bernard was upset over what he had just seen. She had never seen him so angry, and he was having a hard time holding it in.

"I fear for your pregnancy if such strident attention from your husband continues."

Myra's entire body relaxed with relief. "Please, Dr. Monroe, can you tell him? Tell him his baby could die before it's born if he continues."

"Mrs. Brookstone, I am in an untenable position as an employee of your husband and your father-in-law. What I will tell your husband is that you were spotting blood today which is why Kathleen insisted I be called. I will tell him you are in a delicate way, and this will be a difficult pregnancy for you. I will tell him I am recommending bed rest and all marital relations stop until the danger of a miscarriage is past. I will also tell him if you miscarry, it could jeopardize your ability to carry another child to full term."

"When will you see him? Can you come back tonight?" Myra's relief was evident. She was the most animated they had ever seen in their brief association.

"I will speak to him in his office as soon as he returns from Portland. I asked around before I left today. He's expected back later this afternoon."

"Thank you. Thank you, Dr. Monroe. You have probably saved my life." Myra gave her first genuine smile in weeks. At that moment, looking just like Lydia, and knowing the young woman was in danger, a little bit of ice thawed from Kathleen and Bernard's heart.

Myra was resting comfortably when Kathleen and Bernard left the Brookstone home. Mrs. Miller had been given instructions not to disturb the lady of the house and to call immediately if Daniel Brookstone returned home without first speaking with Bernard.

Bernard was glad to have time alone in his car. He was seething with anger. Myra was a despicable person by all accounts. She had a trail of victims on each side of the ocean, but no one deserved what Daniel had been doing to her. What galled him even further was the fact she only suspected it wasn't right. No one had sat down and explained the facts of life to her and the beauty of sex between two people in love. She had all of the horror and none of the love. What Daniel was doing to her was not based on love. It was an obvious form of control. He hoped to God Daniel left her alone for the duration of her pregnancy. He truly did fear the kind of violence Daniel was inflicting on his wife would cause her to miscarry.

He saw Daniel's car was back in the parking lot as he drove to the Mill. His shoulders slumped as he walked into his clinic. He called Daniel's office and told his secretary he was on his way to see Mr. Brookstone and to please make time for him.

Bernard knocked on Daniel's office door. He walked in when he heard Daniel's curt, "Enter."

Noticing Daniel was in a foul mood, Bernard steeled himself for the worse. "Mr. Brookstone, I need to discuss a personal matter with you."

"I've just gotten a phone call from my housekeeper. She informs me you examined my wife today without my knowledge or permission."

"Mr. Brookstone, I received a frantic call from Kathleen Parrish who was visiting your wife. Mrs. Brookstone confided she suspected she was pregnant and was spotting blood. Your wife was very distraught. I did what any doctor would do when called into a medical situation. I examined your wife in the presence of Miss Parrish. Your wife is very definitely pregnant, and if my instructions are followed, your baby will be born sometime at the beginning of August. The bleeding is a concern. She needs total bed rest and the termination of all marital relations until after the baby is born." Looking at Daniel's face, he took a gamble. "Mr. Brookstone, I know what a caring husband you are. I witnessed it myself on Saturday night. I'm sure the safety of your wife and unborn child are paramount in your mind. If you would like, I will continue to take care of your wife throughout her pregnancy. I'll let you and your wife discuss what you would like to do. Congratulations on the blessed event."

After Dr. Monroe left his office, Daniel went into his father's office to share the news. His father was overjoyed. When he told him Martha was already having problems with the pregnancy, his father told Daniel he needed to take care of his wife. "You'll have years of sex with your wife, Daniel. I don't care what you do to her when she's not carrying my grandson, but now is the time to take every precaution to make sure we have a new Brookstone. Understood?"

Daniel was not thrilled his wife was getting out of doing her duty for the next eight months. Resigning himself to finding other ways to release the urges he couldn't control, he left his father's office for home.

Myra was lying in bed. She heard Daniel when he burst through the front door. Seeing Mrs. Miller, he asked, "Where is my wife?"

Mrs. Miller was trying to determine his mood. She had raised him and there were times she could read him like a book, this wasn't one of them. "She's upstairs resting. She hasn't left her room since the doctor was here, and I can't get her to eat."

"Get a plate ready. I'll take it up to her." Daniel realized as he was driving home if anything happened to this baby, there would be hell to pay from his father.

Myra heard him approaching the bedroom and mustered up some tears before he opened the door. She had the good sense to keep the look of triumph off her face. Daniel walked up to the bed with the tray of food and set it on the nightstand. Taking both her hands into his he said, "I talked to Dr. Monroe. He says you need bed rest and need to be very cautious or you'll lose the baby." Showing the first bit of tenderness since prior to the wedding, Daniel took the bowl of soup off the tray and spooned up a mouthful for Myra. This brought true tears to her eyes and, with the raging hormones of a pregnant woman, she started to cry.

"I've never been examined like that by a doctor. I'm so glad Kathleen called him." Falling back into her role of the frail mother-to-be, "Daniel, I was so scared for our baby. Now that I know it's real, I want to do what Dr. Monroe said so our son will be healthy."

Aptly guessing Daniel and his father only thought about a male heir, Myra played her "son" card perfectly. Her cruel young husband folded under the bluff and begged her to eat.

"Martha, you have to keep your strength up. Please eat just a little for me." The new cajoling Daniel was quite a switch from the demanding one that she knew so well, but it did nothing to dissipate her hatred of him.

"Daniel, can Dr. Monroe deliver our baby? I trust him and Kathleen Parrish thinks so highly of him."

Daniel thought it over for a moment. Knowing Dr. Monroe had seen the bruises on his wife; made him hesitate until he realized because the doctor worked for his company, he was less likely to talk than another doctor who didn't have his job in jeopardy. "Yes, if that's what you want, Martha." He was in a very benevolent mood. "And I'll ask Kathleen if she could visit with you and maybe help you get whatever clothes you need while you're in this condition. I guess we'll also need some baby clothes, too."

"Maybe Dr. Monroe will let me out of bed in a month or two, and I can shop for myself."

"Martha, there is no need to overdo. We'll see about it when the time comes. Dr. Monroe says you are very frail. You're carrying a Brookstone and, for now, it is your only priority."

Myra was so grateful to be relieved from her wifely duty she was almost giddy. Smiling she looked at the man she detested and said, "Yes, we'll have to make sure that Mrs. Miller is aware of my needs. I'm just not up to thinking about it right now."

When he finished feeding her the soup, Daniel left giving after his wife instructions to rest. Meanwhile, he was wondering what he was going to do for entertainment for the next eight months. He had an extensive list of "working girls" in Portland. He would have to arrange to be out of town every so often. His father wouldn't care as long as the Brookstone heir was safe. Brookstone men held no illusions of the sanctity of marriage, at least not their end of the marriage.

Chapter 46

Lydia had never been jealous of her sister when they were growing up. But now, knowing Myra had been married only eight weeks and was having a baby; Lydia turned into a green-eyed monster. "Edward, we've been married seven months and no baby yet in our future, and Myra is pregnant after only seven weeks." Tears rolled down her cheeks. She couldn't stop. She wallowed in jealousy and disappointment at her barren womb.

Edward held his wife. "Lydia, good things take time and our time will come. You weren't worried about it before you found out Myra was in the family way. We'll have babies, lots of babies. I'm actually enjoying our time together now. Once babies come, we won't get it back."

Thankful that a knock at the door interrupted their conversation, Edward answered the front door. As on Sunday, Kathleen and Bernard walked into the living room. Edward shook Bernard's hand and hugged Kathleen. Lydia hugged them both. Kathleen noticed Lydia's eyes were red, and her heart went out to her friend.

"Well, sit down and tell us what's going on with Myra and the Brookstones." Lydia did her best to put on a brave front.

Bernard cleared his throat. "There is much I can't tell you. I cannot break the confidentiality of my patient. What I can tell you is she is now safe from her husband, and her pregnancy should progress in a normal matter."

"Safe from her husband, what are you talking about?" The alarm in Lydia's voice was evident.

It was Kathleen's turn to talk. "I'm not bound by Bernard's doctor patient rules. When I went to see Myra for lunch on Monday, she had a black eye. Daniel was jealous about her speaking to men at their party. Myra told me that she suspected she might be pregnant." Kathleen turned red, "I'm embarrassed to say I didn't know the signs, but Mrs. Miller said based on her experience, it sounded like Myra was. Myra hinted rather broadly that Daniel is very rough with her. She was worried about being pregnant and having him hurt her or the baby. I suggested we get Bernard involved. I was in the room when he examined her, and confirmed the pregnancy but I didn't see anything." Kathleen averted her eyes and Lydia knew there was something she wasn't saying. "Before Bernard picked me up tonight, I received a call from Daniel. He would like me to visit Martha and help keep her spirits up. He said I'm the only person she met at the party that she felt comfortable with, and, after yesterday, she considers me her only friend. He asked if I would come take care of her when Mrs. Monroe goes out for errands on Thursdays."

Lydia thought it over. There was much not being said and she was frustrated. "I want to go with you on Thursday. I'll hide in the car until Mrs. Miller is out of the house, but I want to have a conversation with my sister." Edward started to disagree and Lydia quieted him with a look. "I will see my sister, Edward. This has gone on too long. If nothing else, maybe we can help get her out of that monster's house."

"Lydia, we know the Brookstones are prejudiced and hate immigrants, but isn't monster taking it a bit far?" As Edward spoke the words, he glanced at Bernard for support and saw his friend visibly pale and looking down at his hands. Realizing there was more to this than he was being told, Edward threw in the towel. "Kathleen, can you get her in to see Myra? How do you know one of the Brookstones won't come home?"

Kathleen thought for a moment. "Dad and the Brookstones have a meeting in Portland on Thursday. They're even talking about spending the night. Daniel said he was worried about leaving Martha. Maybe I can volunteer to spend the night so someone will be close for her."

All Lydia could think about was seeing Myra. "I don't care if there are risks. Kathleen, please set it up and I'll go with you."

Edward looked at his wife, saw the familiar set of her chin, and gave in. "Bernard, I would appreciate it if you would go with Kathleen and Lydia. I'll feel better knowing you're there."

Bernard nodded and looked at the women. "Kathleen, check with your father and see if they are spending the night on Thursday. We'll work out a plan once we know for sure."

Lydia had the oddest sensation of relief and anxiety. She had no idea what she would say to Myra or what her sister's mood would be, but she knew blood was thicker than water. No matter what Myra had done, she needed help.

Chapter 47

D aniel went to the side of Myra's bed and sat down. "I've asked Kathleen Parrish to come over and sit with you today. Mrs. Miller is going to town and won't be back for several hours. I told her to take the afternoon off. She's been running herself ragged trying to take care of you and the house."

Myra tried to look sympathetic, "Yes I know, Daniel. She has been a dear. I'm happy Kathleen is coming and Mrs. Miller will have some time off."

"You be on your best behavior. No getting up unless it's just to the bathroom. I mean it, Martha. You take it easy."

She would have been touched by his concern if she hadn't overheard him and his father discussing the importance of this baby to the Brookstone family. She was a brood mare to him and nothing more. The fact he had changed so drastically since their wedding proved to her his true nature. The Daniel she met in New York was the aberration. The self-serving, cruel Daniel was the real thing.

"Yes, Daniel, it's so sweet of you to be concerned. I'll be careful." Myra smile didn't reach her eyes, and her sarcasm was lost on him.

As Daniel left, Myra breathed a sigh of relief. She had been afraid he would change his mind about going to Portland for the meeting. She was only two months along. If she had to endure seven months of his hovering, she was going to go mad. Getting Mrs. Miller out of the house was a true bonus. It was time for Myra to do a little snooping around Calvin's study.

Mrs. Miller came and stood in the doorway. "What time is Miss Parrish coming?"

"I'm not sure. Daniel set it up. I haven't spoken to her. I'm sure it will be soon."

"I made a hair appointment and the only time they had is in thirty minutes. It will take me a few minutes to get to town, but I don't want to leave you alone."

Myra jumped on it, trying to curb her enthusiasm. "Mrs. Miller, you've been so kind and have worked so hard taking care of me. I'll be fine on my own for a few minutes. I'm sure Kathleen is on her way. Please go or you'll add to my burden of guilt about all you've done for me."

"If you're sure?" Uncertainty crossed Mrs. Miller's face. She'd been given express orders never to leave Mrs. Brookstone on her own, but she really wanted her hair done. "Please, don't tell either of the Misters I left you alone for a few minutes. I don't want any trouble."

"Mrs. Miller, you have my word I will never ever tell them. Now please go. Get your hair done and enjoy your afternoon off. I'll be fine."

"All right. I've left some cold chicken and a salad in the icebox. Perhaps Miss Parrish can get them out, and put lunch together for the two of you."

A genuine laugh came from Myra. "Our Miss Parrish is quite resourceful. I'm sure she can manage. Thank you for your concern, but I shan't starve while you're gone."

Watching Mrs. Miller from her bedroom window, Myra was relieved when the housekeeper finally drove out the front gates. Not wasting any time, Myra ran to the study, She sat in Calvin's desk chair and looked at the drawers. Pulling on the first one, she discovered it was locked. "Fires of hell, does this man trust no one?"

Getting down on her hands and knees under the desk, she surveyed the top drawer and realized if it was locked, the three drawers on each side were automatically locked too. As she was crawling out, she saw a small envelope taped to the underside of the desk. Carefully pulling it out, she discovered a key. She put it in the top center drawer lock and twisting the key, released the lock. "Now we're getting somewhere."

Rifling through the drawers, she discovered a folder marked "Anna Turner Brookestone." Pulling it out, she held a thick file of reports. The reports detailed a detective's search for Anna Turner Brookestone. Twenty separate reports were in the file. What kind of man searches relentlessly for a woman who doesn't want to be found? Knowing how cruel the Brookstones could be, Myra was sure it wasn't out of love he searched for her. God help the woman if he ever finds her. Myra wondered if that was going to be her fate, too.

The bottom drawer held a tin box. Myra opened it and discovered a cache of money. She was tempted to take some but didn't want to alert Calvin she'd been in his desk. Myra knew if he noticed money missing, she'd be the first one blamed. "I'll be taking this with me when it's my time to escape this mad house."

Myra shut the desk drawer and was careful to put the key back in the same location.

The ringing of the doorbell momentarily startled her until she realized it was time for Kathleen to come. She heard the front door open and Kathleen calling out her name. "Martha, it's Kathleen, I'm coming in."

Myra called out as she came down the hall. "We're alone. Come in, it's good to see a friendly face."

Kathleen was a little taken back by the greeting. She didn't have friendly thoughts towards Myra and she was annoyed at all the stress the girl had caused her friends. "When will Mrs. Miller be back?"

"She's gone for the entire afternoon, had a hair appointment and left a little early. It feels so good to be out of bed and walking around. Playing an invalid is tiring."

"Let me go get Lydia, she wants to see you with her own eyes." Kathleen walked to the kitchen where Lydia was waiting, as planned, by the back door.

When Kathleen opened the door, Lydia burst through it. "Where is she? How much time do we have?"

"I'm right here, Lydia. We have plenty of time."

Kathleen watched as the sisters walked towards each other. Lydia was the first one to make physical contact. She grabbed Myra's hand and held it tightly. "Myra, oh Myra, you've scared years out of me these past few months and now this."

For the first time in her life, Myra felt remorse for the acts that led to her current situation. "Lydia, there's so much to tell you. Let's make a little tea like we used to and sit in the living room. We have a few hours. Daniel and his father are in Portland for a meeting, and Mrs. Miller has the afternoon off."

Myra was unaccustomed to waiting on herself in the Brookstone kitchen but soon managed to get a kettle on and make tea. Mrs. Miller had baked cookies the day before and Myra put some on a plate.

Sitting on the sofa sipping a cup of tea, Lydia had no idea where to begin. Myra saw her dilemma. "Lydia, I'm going to start at the beginning. I was crazy jealous over you and Edward. I was convinced I was the sister he should love. I watched him from the time I got to school to the end of the day. Every day on the playground my eyes followed only him. When you two were ten, I saw him push you into the mud puddle, which was, at that age, a declaration of love. When you wouldn't speak to him for four years, I did everything I could to get him to notice me." Myra stopped for a sip of tea. "He never looked at me, ever. I think that's when I started hating you and doing all the horrible things I did over the years. When Edward left Ireland, I was trying to push you into Tommy's arms and almost succeeded. Then you got word Edward was ill and ran off to America. If only I had gotten to the letter before you. I would have done exactly what you did, and I would have convinced him you were with someone else."

Lydia started to interrupt and Myra waved her silent with her hand. "No, Lydia, I need to tell you everything. I did horrible things to get to America. I know you are aware of them. I hurt our parents. I hurt the Franklins and their employee, Mrs. Hildebrand. But I had to. It's not my fault people are stupid and want to help me. It's not my fault, but believe me, I have been paid back. I was going to come to Little Creek and do I don't know what, but I'm sure it would have been bad. I was crazy with the thought of getting revenge on you for taking

Edward. When I got to New York, I knew Mrs. Hildebrand and the Franklins would try to send me back to Ireland. I enlisted the help of James Vautrin, one of the passengers. I fabricated a wonderful story and he fell for it. I was supposed to meet him at a New York hotel. He was a reporter and wanted to publish the story I told him about the impoverished girl the Franklins were taking advantage of."

Myra saw Lydia clenching her fists in anger. "How could you have done anything to hurt the Franklins? They were only trying to help you."

Myra's eyes flared in anger. "I told you. It's not my fault. I was crazy with the idea of hurting you, and I didn't care what I had to do to accomplish it."

For the first time, Kathleen noted the harshness in Myra's voice and felt concern.

Regaining control, Myra continued, "I switched hotels and names. With the beautiful clothes I had charged to the Franklins, I looked like an affluent woman. I checked into the Hotel Biltmore and that's where I had the unfortunate luck to meet the Brookstones. Daniel pursued me relentlessly. I had no interest in him other than as a charming tour guide while I waited for things to die down so I could catch a train west. Then his father demanded to speak to me, he accused me of having designs on his son. Nothing could have been further from the truth. I made up a story about opening a dress shop in Seattle or Portland. I told him I had East Coast investors and he demanded to know who. Daniel told me of his dislike of Stephen Franklin so, of course, I said the Franklin Bank." Myra let out a hoot of laughter, warming up to her story. "It sent the old man over the edge. I was shocked he could be pulled in so easily. He demanded I take his money. He would not take no for an answer. He kept going on and on about how I should use West Coast investors, not those snotty East Coast bankers as he called them. Well now, what was I going to say? It's not my fault he's vain and stupid. Of course, now I wish it had been 'No' and I had stuck to my plan."

Seeing the stricken looks on Lydia and Kathleen's faces, she continued, "Oh, sorry, I guess it does sound awful, doesn't it? Again Myra laughed. "We left New York five days after I arrived and, traveling with two men in first class, no one even gave me a second look. The only one who noticed me was some old conductor that mistook me for you. It gave my heart a quite a pitter pat, thank God the Brookstones weren't around to hear him. Anyway, we got to Portland and the old man insisted on helping me pick out a storefront. We found one and opened a checking account for the business. He made the initial deposit of one thousand dollars. I was just waiting for them to clear out so I could get the money and head here."

Myra's eyes went blank for a second as she remembered the day she saw Edward and Lydia. "One day my landlady suggested we go to the parade and see the Queen of Romania. I was standing on the street opposite of the hotel the Queen was staying at and I saw you and Edward." Tears came to her eyes as she looked at her sister. "I saw the two of you. Even from across the street I could see how much he loves you and you him. It finally occurred to me he never loved me, never even looked in my direction. It's hard to admit delusions, but I'm admitting to them now. I went back to my room and had a bit of a cry. In the morning, I packed my bags. I was going to withdraw Brookstone's money from the bank and head to Los Angeles."

Lydia couldn't stop the tears from coming. "You saw us in Portland? You weren't going to hurt us?"

Myra became impatient. "Lydia, let me finish. At this rate, Mrs. Miller will be coming home and pulling up a chair. I went to the bank to get the money and had to wait two hours for the bank manager. Unbeknownst to me, the teller alerted Mr. Brookstone. The old man drove to Portland, collected the Sheriff and was at the bank when I returned to meet the manager. He had me arrested and thrown in jail! Can you imagine? Jail! It was frightening. I was sitting in a cell and the guard kept saying he would have his way with me in the middle of the night when no one was looking. The horrible female guard told me everything that would happen to me if I went to prison. I was scared to death. Daniel came in with a lawyer and a judge. My knight in shining armor, all ready to rescue me. However, it came with a horrific price. He told me if I married him, his father couldn't prosecute me. I was so scared I agreed. I had mailed a letter of intent to Mr. Brookstone that morning saying I was leaving town but would honor my debt. Of course I had no intention of doing so, but I wrote it just in case. I told Brookstone and the sheriff about the letter, but when Daniel said marrying him would get me out of trouble, I jumped at it. The thought of prison terrified me, and, for all I knew, Brookstone would destroy the letter. I married Daniel. God help me, I married a monster."

Myra broke down in tears. Her body was racked with sobs. "He's horrible. The minute he put a ring on my finger, the Daniel of New York was gone. He does things to me, horrible things, Lydia. Does it hurt with Edward?"

Lydia hugged her sister. "No, Myra, it doesn't. Edward is good and loving and very gentle. It shouldn't hurt. He would never hurt me."

"He bit me and he hurt me down there. Daniel called it my wifely duty. He came home at lunch and made me do it and every night, too. My body was so bruised and battered from his rutting no wonder I didn't even know I was pregnant. He was hitting me, too. He is insanely jealous. That's why I've never been to town. I can't talk to anyone without him around. It's a miracle Kathleen is here today and Mrs. Miller is not hovering nearby listening to every word."

Kathleen and Lydia exchanged looks of shared mortification.

"Kathleen saved me. She called Dr. Monroe to examine me. When he looked at me, he saw the bruising and the evidence of roughness. That's why he told Daniel I was bleeding and in danger of losing the baby. He explained to him in my delicate condition, intimacy was impossible or I would lose the baby. It worked. Daniel hasn't touched me since and he hasn't hit me. In fact, the bugger has almost been kind. It's so strange to see the New York Daniel emerge again." Myra's eyes darkened with rage, "It almost makes me not hate him so much, almost but not quite. I've a score to settle with that monster before I leave Little Creek."

The vehemence in her voice startled Lydia. "But now there is a baby coming. What are you going to do?"

"I don't want the baby. The minute I can get out of here I'm leaving and never coming back. Something is wrong with these men. They don't care about anything but their own pleasure. I have no doubt Mr. Brookstone is as cruel as Daniel. I won't be the first Brookstone wife to run away from her husband or leave a child behind. He forced me to marry him, it's not my fault."

367

Kathleen looked at the sisters. "I'm going to go make lunch. Didn't you say Mrs. Miller left some food in the kitchen for us? I'll see what I can put together."

Lydia looked at Myra with sorrow and understanding in her eyes. To be married to a man who abused you was unfathomable. Her heart went out to Myra, but the practical side of her still realized Myra had planned on hurting her and Edward, and still claimed none of this was her fault. Looking at Myra she tried to keep her voice neutral. "You can't leave your baby with these men. How can you?"

"It's not my fault that I got pregnant. I didn't want a baby or even a husband. I'm leaving the first chance I get."

Lydia had heard enough for one day and needed to get out of the Brookstone house before she started believing everything Myra was saying. She wanted to talk to Edward who would make sense of this mess and figure out what to do. "Myra, I have to go. I'll talk to Kathleen and figure out a time to come again. Maybe Daniel will let her bring you into town."

Myra grabbed her sister's hands. "Forgive me. Please say you will. I know I was horrible to you growing up, but I promise if you help me get out of this, I will be better. I promise." The words flowed easily from Myra's mouth. Her gift for manipulation was her strongest survival skill.

Lydia rushed out of the living room. She had the presence of mind to grab her tea cup and saucer. "Better wash this. Three cups will look a little suspicious. I'm leaving, I can't take another moment of Myra blaming everyone for her problems. It's never her fault.

Kathleen hugged Lydia. "I know this was difficult for you. I heard her tell Bernard about Daniel, it's horrible but part of me feels like she has shaped her own destiny. That's not a very Christian thing to say, but it's true."

"I've always known Myra was different but to listen to her now I realize my sister is very, very sick inside." Lydia walked out the back door and hurried down the driveway to the street below, running like the devil himself was chasing her.

Chapter 48

Edward was alarmed when Lydia rushed into the restaurant and he saw the grim look on her face. It was obvious her meeting with Lydia had not gone well.

"Edward, we need to talk. Please ask Annie to watch the front of the restaurant."

Her voice was almost curt and very decisive. Whatever was coming was not going to be good.

When Edward walked back into the kitchen, his wife sat in a chair. Her face, void of tears, was a mask of sorrow. "Oh, Edward, she's crazy. I always suspected it, but now I know. You should have seen how glibly she talked about doing us harm. But now she's changed her mind because she now knows how much we love each other and that you never loved her. She saw us in Portland at the parade and decided maybe she wouldn't hurt us after all."

Edward hugged his wife. "Please, Lydia, start at the beginning and we'll figure out what we can do. Lydia relayed the entire story, stressing how Myra kept saying, "It's not my fault" after she told of swindling people out of money or the harm she had done.

Edward took Lydia's hand. "She's manipulative and crazy. Myra has no conscience. She'll accept no blame for her role in any of this. Now that she's in over her head with the Brookstones, she wants her big sister to forgive her and help get her out of the mess she's created." Edward was angry. "We've spent weeks looking over our shoulders waiting for the snake to strike, and now she glibly tells you she's changed her mind and we have nothing to fear. It is the true mark of an insane person, and who's to say she won't change her mind again?"

"She scares me. Sometimes when she was talking her eyes looked dead."

"I know, but at least now Daniel Brookstone has her under wraps and she's confined to bed for the next seven months so we won't have to look over our shoulders for a while." Edward smiled as he said the words. He was trying to find a bright spot in this very dark cloud.

"You should have seen the look on Kathleen's face. She didn't know what to make of her. She slips in and out of her American accent. It really is amazing to watch. Myra is quite the actress. Too bad she didn't get to steal Brookstone's money and go to Los Angeles. She could have been in the movies." Lydia laughed a rueful laugh. "I knew I didn't like Calvin Brookstone when I saw him in the Bank. There was something in the way he looked at me."

Edward swore under his breath and looked at his wife. "The man treats his employees and anyone else he deems as beneath his social status like dirt. Myra better pray he doesn't find out she's just a poor Irish girl. He's bragged all over town about the society lady his son married. A man like Calvin Brookstone will react badly to being made a fool."

"I'm going home to lie down for a bit." Lydia kissed Edward on the cheek and walked out the back door of O'Brien's.

Edward followed her out. He could tell from the look in her eyes she had one of her headaches. "Annie will watch over the place. I'll see you home."

"You'll do nothing of the sort. I'm fine, just a small headache and I need some time to think. Go back to the kitchen. Annie's been a saint and I don't want her worrying about me. Go back sweet husband. I'll be fine as can be in an hour or so."

Reluctantly, Edward returned to the kitchen. Annie came in, concern etched on her face. "Edward, you'd better sit down and tell me what's going on. Johnny and I are worried sick about you two."

"Aye, I'll tell you but you must swear this goes no further than you and Johnny. If old man Brookstone gets wind of it, our lives may be in danger. At the very least he'll figure out a way to run us out of town."

Edward relayed the story to Annie, leaving nothing out. Her eyes widened and, at one point, she actually laughed. "You mean to say a little Irish girl who has never been out of her village has managed pass herself off as a high society woman from Oklahoma? Edward, even you, no matter how dire everything is with this situation, must find humor in the audacity and boldness it took to fool the Brookstone's."

Edward's eyes crinkled at the corners. He was doing his best to be serious and try to figure things out, but the Irish in him couldn't resist a good joke. "Oh there will be hell to pay if he ever finds out and imagine his first born grandson or granddaughter will be half Irish or 'Mick' as he calls us. Maybe if the baby's a boy they can name him

Michael and call him Mick for short." They couldn't help themselves. He and Annie laughed until they cried.

"Serves the old bastard right. He's not a nice man. But what will happen to Myra if they find out who she really is?"

Edward thought for a moment. "From what Lydia said, I think Myra will make a run for it after the baby is born. The question is will it be with the baby or without? She has the maternal instinct of a guppy." Seeing Annie's bewildered look, Edward blushed a bit, "A guppy is a freshwater fish that eats its young. I saw an aquarium in a big hotel in New York and the bellhop explained them to me.

"You think she'd leave her baby at the Brookstones? To be raised by those horrible men?"

"Aye, I'm sorry to say I think she won't even care. She has no conscience. Even Lydia agrees with that. It will kill Lydia if she does because she'll never be able to see the child or help the child for fear it will be worse for it."

"No wonder Lydia has one of her headaches. I notice they are usually brought on by stress. She was getting better until Myra came to America." Annie was upset for her friend.

"Well now, the only thing we can do is wait and see how this unfolds. Myra won't try anything until after the baby is born, of that I'm sure." Edward turned towards the dining room when he heard the restaurant door open. "We just have to do the best we can and take care of Lydia whether she wants us to or not."

The rest of the afternoon was uneventful. Annie prepped the dining room for the dinner crowd, and Lydia returned to the kitchen looking a little more rested and her color was better. Edward saw the set of her jaw and knew she had reached some decisions. He was anxious to hear her thoughts but knew it was best to wait until she was ready.

Kathleen and Bernard came in for dinner. Exchanging looks and sad smiles, Lydia and Kathleen silently agreed not to discuss their morning. Kathleen put up a good front and told funny stories to everyone's amusement. Lydia was watching Bernard who was unnaturally quiet. Fearing the whole Myra situation was awkward for him, Lydia rose and told Edward they needed to let the two have some privacy.

Bernard stood up. "No, please don't go. I need you both to be here for what I'm about to do."

Puzzled, Edward and Lydia sat back down at the table and watched as Bernard got down on one knee in front of Kathleen. Holding a small velvet box he took her hand. "Kathleen, I've known since the moment I saw you trying to hang wallpaper you were the woman for me. I love everything about you and can't imagine not spending the next sixty or seventy years with you. Please marry me Kathleen."

The tears in Kathleen's eyes were at odds with the wide smile on her face. "Yes, yes, yes. I love you, Bernard, and I want to spend the next sixty or seventy years at your side."

Bernard slipped a diamond ring on her finger and cheers broke out from Edward and Lydia and the surrounding diners. Lydia looked at Bernard. "You've picked a wonderful girl. I was worried about you being so quiet tonight, but now I understand the reason. Our best to you both for a long and happy marriage."

Kathleen looked at her ring. "It's my mother's ring. My father gave you my mother's ring?"

"Gave it to me? He insisted if I was going to ask you I had to use what he called a proper ring. I have no idea what he thought I was going to use, a cigar band? He was quite happy for us. He's waiting for us at your house. He said to take our time and he'd wait up."

Kathleen beamed. "He insisted? I'm so happy he approves. Lydia, we need to start discussing wedding cakes. Bernard, I'd love a spring wedding. We need to start planning!"

Bernard hugged her and laughed, "Yes, let the plans begin. I think a spring wedding would be lovely."

Lydia and Kathleen laughed with pleasure. With all the strange issues connected to Myra, it was wonderful to have a happy event to think about. Kathleen and Bernard left to meet with Mr. Parrish, and the good cheer and celebratory mood remained.

Annie was singing in the kitchen as she scrubbed pans. "I love a happy ending. You knew those two were right for each other from the day you met Kathleen."

Laughing, Lydia hugged her friend, "And I knew you and Johnny were right for each other, too."

"And what about Edward? When did you know?"

"Ah, that took a bit of time. I loved him from age eight, and then at age ten, he pushed me into a mud puddle. I was so embarrassed when all of the children laughed at me, I wouldn't speak to him for quite a while."

Edward came into the kitchen as Lydia was speaking. "Lydia, my love, you call four long years 'quite a while'? You nearly killed me with your indifference. It was the worst four years of my life."

"You deserved it, you heathen, for pushing me into a puddle." Lydia's voice was mockingly stern, but her eyes were smiling.

Annie looked at the two of them. "How did you get back together?"

"Oh, I figured he had suffered enough, and I chased him down and let him catch me when we were fourteen. I knew he was the one for me." Lydia gave Edward a quick kiss. "Now, Annie, my dear friend, we need to get on with the plans for your own wedding. We only have a month left before the big day."

Annie and Johnny had decided to have a small wedding after the New Year.

"It's going to be such a small wedding the final plans will be easy. Johnny's family can't afford to come out for the wedding and there's only my aunt and me for my family. With you, Edward, Kathleen, and Bernard, we'll barely fill a booth in the restaurant!"

Lydia smiled to herself. Annie had no idea how many people had already asked to be invited to the wedding. In her quiet way, Annie made an impact on Little Creek. She never failed to help a person in need. Annie took all the leftovers from the restaurant and distributed them to families she knew were having a hard time. Many of those people had asked how they could help with Annie's wedding.

"Well now, it works out well because you're getting married in the sacristy of the church and there is not a lot of room. We'll come back here for a nice dinner and reception."

Lydia looked forward to her best friend's wedding, a bright spot on her stormy horizon.

Chapter 49

The weeks continued to drag by. Myra's only reprieve was once a week when Mrs. Miller had a day off and Kathleen came to watch over her. Myra was incensed Lydia had not come back to visit.

"She's busy at the restaurant and her best friend is getting married. Lydia is planning the wedding." Kathleen patiently explained this fact every week.

"I'm her sister. It's me she should be helping, not some stranger." Myra's cool façade had broken weeks ago.

Kathleen tried to overlook the fact that Myra had become a screaming shrew. Even Mrs. Miller would raise her eyebrows and wish Kathleen luck with the missus as she literally ran out the door for her few hours of freedom. Kathleen wanted so badly to stop coming every week, but she knew the only connection Lydia had to her sister was through her. Kathleen hadn't planned on telling Myra of her engagement and always took her ring off before going into the house.

"Oh my, what have we here? You're engaged? Are you marrying that nice Doctor Monroe?" Myra produced a sinister laugh and grabbed Kathleen's hand for inspection.

Kathleen silently cursed herself. She was late this morning and, in her haste, forgot to take off her ring.

"Yes, Bernard and I are getting married on May 28." Kathleen was silently praying Bernard would keep up the ruse of confining Myra to her bed, so there would be no chance of her attending the wedding with Daniel.

"Well now, at the rate I'm going I'll be as big as a house by that time. I do hope that I'll be able to attend. Is Lydia going to be there?"

"Of course Lydia will be there. She's one of my dearest friends."

Myra pinched up her face. "Well, she certainly has shown how she prefers her new friends to her family."

Kathleen almost bit her tongue in half at that pronouncement. She managed not to say what was on her mind and settled for, "I understand you two were not very close growing up."

Myra's eyes went dead as she looked back to Ireland and her life. The voice that came out was not hers but the voice of Martha Driscoll as she recounted Maryanne Driscoll's tales of growing up with her sister. "We were extremely close. We shared everything, and we lived a charmed life. Our parents were among the wealthiest people in Oklahoma. We had everything and loved each other dearly."

Kathleen looked at Myra in astonishment. She had never seen a mentally ill person but recognized Myra had lost touch with reality. Cautiously, she asked, "Where is your sister now, Martha?"

"She and her husband, Jonathon, are home in Oklahoma. They are living in our parents' house and Jonathon has taken all of our parents' money. They left me penniless. It's not my sister's fault. She loves me. It's his fault. He took her away from me. He took everything from me."

Just then the back door opened and Mrs. Miller walked in from the kitchen and looked at Myra. "Mrs. Brookstone, are you all right? What's happened?"

Myra snapped out of her fugue. "Mrs. Miller I'm fine. What are you doing back so early? Did you come back to spy on me?"

Kathleen and Mrs. Miller exchanged stricken looks. "Why of course not Mrs. Brookstone. I just wanted to let you know I'm back. I'll be in the kitchen getting dinner started."

Kathleen helped Myra back to the bedroom. "There you go, Martha. I'll see you next week."

Myra whispered frantically, "Please help me. I don't know who I am anymore."

As soon as Myra's head hit the pillow she fell into a deep sleep. Kathleen looked at her with a mixture of concern and fascination. She was fearful of Myra's rambling, and when she started blaming her Oklahoma sister's husband for all her problems, a shiver of fear went through Kathleen. Something bad was going to happen, and Kathleen prayed she could help keep Lydia safe.

Kathleen was relieved to be on her way. Spending time with Myra was draining. As she was walking out the front door, she saw Daniel approaching. Even from a distance she could see the scowl on his face. He stormed by her barely saying hello. Kathleen was so anxious to leave the Brookstone house she decided not to comment on his lack of manners.

Daniel went into his bedroom and stood at the foot of the bed staring at his sleeping wife. Daniel couldn't hit her. His father had made it very clear that he was expected to produce an heir, and his wife was to be treated with kid gloves until the birth. Daniel had to content himself with verbal attacks aimed to mentally wound.

"Wake up. Who knew I would marry a frigid virgin bitch that got pregnant at the drop of a hat. Well at least my father is happy with the outcome." It was the same refrain Daniel said on a daily basis.

His barb always missed the mark. Myra could care less what he said to her. Her eyes followed him as he paced the room. She could see his frustration. His fists would clench and unclench. Myra knew if not for this pregnancy she would be on the receiving end of those fists. *There's nothing I can say back to him. I should never have tried to steal money from the Brookstones. It's the old man's fault for being so stubborn and stupid. It's his fault Daniel is so violent and angry. It probably started in the womb when his mother fought off his father's abuse. I hate them both. They'll be sorry.*

Myra laid there, her hand on her stomach, the slight swell beneath her hands. An observer would think she was dreaming of her baby. In actuality, her only dreams were of sweet revenge.

Daniel looked over at his wife. He saw the set of her jaw and realized her silence meant his little game was over for the evening. She would not respond to his taunts. His need to hurt was throbbing and he longed to strike out. Daniel was already frustrated by her pregnancy. His only wish was for it to be over so he could resume the sexual assault on his wife.

Chapter 50

The O'Brien's were excited about celebrating their first Christmas as a married couple. Lydia and Edward had a small gathering of friends over to celebrate the holidays. Kathleen presented the O'Brien's with Christmas stockings to hang from their fireplace mantle. Their first Christmas in their new house, surrounded by friends, almost made up for not being with their families.

Lydia made the best of the fact Myra was in the same town even though she was unable to see her. Kathleen told her Daniel, in a display of cruelty, decided Myra needed to rest more and could not have visitors. From the gleam in his eyes, Kathleen knew it was just one more way of showing control over his wife. Lydia knew Kathleen was relieved because sitting with her every week had become difficult. Housebound, Myra was becoming more and more unstable. She had not been off the Brookstone property since Daniel brought her home from their honeymoon. Lydia thought to herself *it would make anyone mad as a hatter. Add to the fact that Myra was already unstable. It's a deadly combination.*

Edward and Lydia were thankful for the distraction and to have a day with friends. Sitting around the living room, the three couples exchanged small gifts and ate a sumptuous meal prepared by Lydia and Annie.

The couples bantered around the table about Johnny and Annie's upcoming nuptials. Several times Edward snuck a look at his wife. He saw the finely etched lines of worry around her eyes and knew that she was thinking of Myra, and he damned the day that Myra set foot on American soil.

On the other side of town, Myra was experiencing an entirely different Christmas. No callers had come over for Christmas cheer, and no invitations had been received to join other families. Her first Christmas away from home and Myra was in tears.

"You never let me out of this house. I've no Christmas presents to give, not even two nickels of my own to rub together. This is the worst Christmas of my life. I hate you."

Myra was breathing fire and wasn't expecting Daniel's slap. Her tirades had grown stronger thinking she was safe from physical abuse, but Daniel had reached his limit.

"See what you made me do, you stupid bitch. If you go running to my father, I swear I'll hurt you even more. It's not my fault you're too weak to carry a baby properly and the doctor confined you to bed. It's your fault." Daniel's face was red with anger and, for a moment, Myra likened him to a squalling child.

Shock at being hit stopped her tears. Her mouth hung open as she stared at the man she loathed. Survival instinct kicked in and she managed to stop herself from saying what was on her mind. "You're right, Daniel. I'm sorry."

"You're damned right I am. Now dry your stupid tears and let's go down to Christmas dinner. Remember, you shut up about this. No tattling to my father."

Myra meekly shook her head yes and accepted his arm as he walked them down the stairs.

Calvin Brookstone watched as they approached the table. Myra looked uncharacteristically subdued and Daniel looked a bit contrite. If he were a betting man he'd bet that his son had lost his temper. He didn't give a damn about his daughter-in-law. His opinion of women would never change, but he wanted to make sure the grandson in her womb was safe.

"Everything all right?" He addressed the question to Myra.

Myra nodded her head and sat down. She saw a small package on the plate in front of her. Her mood changed in an instant as a smile spread across her face. "Is this for me?"

Calvin Brookstone had a fleeting feeling of pity for the girl in front of him. "Yes, it is Christmas, you know."

"Open it up. It's from both of us." Daniel got a cross look from his father but he wasn't about to admit he hadn't bought his wife anything for Christmas.

Opening the package, Myra looked at the contents. Inside were two tortoise shell hair combs with a beautiful carved design. They were rather old fashioned, but still quite beautiful.

"Your hair is getting longer. I thought, I mean, we thought you might like the combs."

Myra looked up with a calculating eye. She saw no hint of malice or deception in either of the two men's faces. "Thank you both very much. I do have presents for each of you. Mrs. Miller gave me some yarn and, well, let me go get them."

Myra went back to the bedroom and fetched the two packages. Daniel had been so terrible to her all day she had decided to just forget giving them their presents. As she approached the dining room she saw Daniel and his father talking earnestly. When she entered the room, they stopped abruptly.

"Here you are. Merry Christmas." Myra grew shy suddenly, feeling a bit petty she thought to withhold their gifts.

Both men opened their packages at the same time and smiles broke out on their faces. Daniel fingered the knitted scarf. "Martha, this is lovely work, you've done a wonderful job." He actually looked at her and smiled. The first she'd seen in over a week.

Calvin looked at his scarf. He recognized the yarn as some that his wife had stored away. He carefully folded it back and did his best to maintain a steady temper. It's not Martha's fault that Daniel's mother was a whore, he thought to himself. Looking at his daughter-in-law, he smiled. "Thank you, Martha."

For the first time since entering the Brookstone home, Myra felt a little bit of kinship with the two men. She recognized there was something basically wrong with both of them. Their cruelty to women couldn't be overlooked by one kind gesture, but she realized there was a tiny bit of humanity in the father. Myra sat and thought for a moment how she never fit in with her own family. In an odd way, knowing what kind of twisted souls she was living with made her own personality defects not as hard to bear.

Chapter 51

Daniel Brookstone called Kathleen and asked if she would come visit his wife once a week to give their housekeeper a break. Kathleen relayed the news to Lydia saying, "He actually begged me to come over and apologized for his earlier rudeness."

Visiting Myra held a fascination for Kathleen. She had never seen someone who could change like a chameleon at will. Her speech pattern, hand gestures, and expressions changed, depending on whether she was playing the well bred society woman or the poor little Irish girl who really hadn't done anything wrong.

Lydia and Kathleen discussed the situation and agreed sneaking Lydia in for a visit every week was very risky, and was mentally exhausting for Lydia. Invariably, she left with one of her headaches. The constant refrain of "It's not my fault" reminded Lydia her sister was without remorse or a conscience. Her sense of entitlement knew no bounds.

In April, Daniel Brookstone and his father took another trip to Portland. By then, Myra's pregnancy was quite obvious. She had kept up the ruse of a dangerous pregnancy, and her only release from bed was when Mrs. Miller was out for the day. She was weary of her self-imposed invalid status but was scared to death of Daniel being allowed his husbandly rights again.

Kathleen rang the front bell and Mrs. Miller eagerly answered it. "I'm so glad you're here. She's in a particularly foul mood this morning. She is going stir crazy. Is Dr. Monroe coming this afternoon?"

"Yes, he's going to check her out and see if she can start getting up for a few hours each day."

"I hope so. Being bedridden has made her time being pregnant stretch out, and, with four months to go, she's not going to be able endure it."

Kathleen was touched by the concern on Mrs. Miller's face, "You've been so wonderful to take on all that you have. I'm sure the Brookstone's appreciate it.

"Well, they are at their wits end, too. She's not easy to get along with, but these two men have no idea what she's going through. I feel sorry for them all and hope the next four months pass quickly."

Mrs. Miller left for her afternoon off and, after a few minutes, Lydia knocked softly at the back door. "Is it safe?"

Kathleen looked at the strain on her friend's face, "Yes, all clear. Come in. I guess Myra is in a state right now."

Lydia clutched a parcel to her chest. As she entered the bedroom, she saw Myra sitting in a chair. Her pregnancy was obvious and her stylish clothes were replaced by a tattered robe that didn't hide her protruding belly. Her eyes were flashing fire as she turned to the two women. "Is the old bat gone? I'm so sick of her hovering around me I could scream."

Lydia went to her sister and hugged her. Myra sat, not moving and not returning the hug. "Well, it's about time you showed up. Where have you been all these months?"

Taken aback, Lydia looked at her sister. Her sleek bob had grown out and her hair was unkempt and dull. "You know I can only come when your husband and father-in-law are out of town. It's too dangerous otherwise. What do you think would happen to you or your baby if they discovered who you really are? Now calm down. I've brought you a present."

Myra's temper evaporated and, with childish excitement, she exclaimed, "A present! Really? For me?"

Lydia and Kathleen sat on the bed and watched Myra open the package. Inside was a maternity dress Lydia had made for her sister. The turquoise color matched Myra's eyes and the fabric was soft to the touch.

"Oh Lydia, it's beautiful. Thank you so much. I haven't been out of the house since I got here. Prison would have been better. Who knows, maybe I'd be out by now. But at least now I have something I can wear around the house other than Daniel's ratty robe."

For a moment, Lydia gazed at her younger sister and enjoyed the childish pleasure her present had brought. Then, in a moment of clarity, she saw the sister who would have tried to harm Edward or her. Sitting a little straighter, Lydia attempted to harden her heart a bit but was finding it difficult. She looked at her sister's swelling belly and her felt a pang of envy. "Have you thought of any names for your baby?"

"Daniel's father wants the baby named after him. I was thinking of naming him Calvin Patrick Brookstone so he would at least have

Da's name if he has to have Calvin's first name. Of course the baby could be a girl. I really don't care. I just want it over."

Lydia almost cried at her words. How could she not enjoy the most beautiful gift in the world? Swallowing her personal sorrow, she held her little sister's hand. "I know you'll give the baby a beautiful name."

Myra looked at her Lydia and laughed out loud. "I don't care what the brat is called. I won't be around to worry about it."

Lydia looked at her sister. "It's your baby. You can't just leave it."

Myra shrugged her shoulders. "I can't stay here. Living with Daniel is like being in hell, and it will only get worse once this baby is born. I'll kill him before I let him lay another hand on me."

"Myra, it's OK. I'll help you get out of Little Creek if you promise not to hurt Edward, but can't leave your baby with these monsters."

Lydia watched her sister's face and saw a flicker of malice. "Oh, all right. I'll think about taking the baby with me. I already said I wasn't going to hurt you or Edward. Why don't you trust me?"

Kathleen noted the tension between the two sisters and intervened. "Myra I think you've been housebound too long. We need to talk to Bernard about letting you take some small trips to town."

Myra's lifeless eyes brightened immediately. "Do you think he'll let me? Will he be able to tell Daniel I'm still too fragile for, you know, my wifely duties?"

Kathleen colored slightly. "He'll be here in an hour. Let's visit with your sister. She can't stay very long."

Lydia tried to make small talk. Failing to find a subject that didn't upset Myra, she was relieved when the doorbell rang.

"That will be Bernard. I'll be right back." Kathleen rushed to the front door.

"I'll leave you now. Kathleen will keep me posted on how you're doing. I'll come back as soon as I can." Lydia hugged her sister, receiving a small hug back.

Bernard walked into the bedroom as Lydia was exiting. He noted the distraught look on her face, and was about to stop her when Kathleen gave a slight shake of her head indicating no.

Myra, as usual, was overjoyed to be the center of attention. "Dr. Monroe, I need to get out of this house. Please tell Daniel I can go out on short trips. The walls are closing in on me here."

Bernard looked at his patient. Her color was good, but the look in her eyes was wild and a bit frightening. "Kathleen, why don't you get the sheet and help Mrs. Brookstone prepare for the examination. Once I see how things are going, we can discuss outings."

Kathleen got Myra ready and opened the door to let Bernard back in. Myra scrunched down in the bed and Bernard proceeded with the examination. He was relieved to see no signs of bruising or vaginal tears. Obviously, Daniel had taken his advice to heart and left his wife alone.

"Everything is progressing nicely. The baby seems to be doing well. Have you had any pains or any unusual symptoms?"

"No, but sometimes I feel something catching in my stomach."

Bernard was surprised at her naïveté. "Your baby is kicking, letting you know he's going to want out soon."

Kathleen looked at Myra, expecting to see excitement. Her odd eyes held none. Kathleen was relieved Lydia wasn't there to witness how cold blooded and uninterested Myra was in the entire process.

"Well, it's annoying. Sometimes it keeps me awake."

Bernard looked at his patient realizing she had absolutely no idea what to expect. "It is all part of the birth process. I delivered quite a few babies in Boston. While it was hard work, all of the mothers forgot the pain the minute they saw their new baby."

Myra was appalled but tried to keep her face neutral. Kathleen watched in fascination as she saw the emotions flooding Myra's face before she spoke. "Doctor, I am not going to think about it. When the time comes I'm sure you have some sort of drug that will help. For now, I just want to get out of this house. Please, I'm begging you to tell Daniel to take me out for short outings, but tell him I'm still too frail for anything else."

Bernard noted the near hysteria in her voice. "Mrs. Brookstone, I will speak with your husband tomorrow. I believe there would be no danger to your baby if you were allowed out of bed a few hours a day, provided, of course, you do not tax yourself."

A look of satisfaction came over Myra's face. She needed to get out of the house and start learning the area. She was under no illusion she'd be able to manipulate the good doctor or Kathleen when it was time to make her escape. They were too close to Lydia. A hard glint came into Myra's eyes, *At least getting out of the house opened up possibilities of finding other people willing to help a woman in distress.*

Chapter 52

Kathleen and Lydia were visiting at the Parrish Hardware Store when the door burst open with a loud bang as it hit the wall behind. Daniel Brookstone walked in and with him was Myra. Kathleen and Lydia exchanged panicked glances as the couple approached. Kathleen walked forward to greet them, and Lydia crept to the back of the store, exiting to the outside through the stockroom door.

"Well, what a nice surprise." Kathleen was trying to appear calm belying her beating heart. "Have you two been shopping for the baby's layette?"

"Oh yes. My little wife has spent a fair amount of money today. She's bought some dresses and managed to pick up a few things for the baby, too. Martha seems to think my pockets are stuffed with money."

Daniel's tone was hard to read, and Myra was getting a tense look on her face.

"Oh come now, Daniel. I for one know your pockets are stuffed with money. I'm sure everyone is impressed with how generous you are to your wife and unborn son."

The satisfied smile on Daniel's face told Kathleen she had said the words that played to his ego. He puffed with pride thinking that his largesse had been noticed.

"I just don't understand why she needs more maternity dresses. The baby will be here in two months. Why can't you just wear what you already have?"

"Daniel, all women have the desire to look nice for their husbands. Surely as a man who has been married for seven months understands women?" Kathleen forced laughter into her voice, aiming to lighten his dark mood.

"I guess so. I'll just be glad when all of this is over and our life can go back to normal." Daniel flashed a lewd look at his wife.

Myra shivered involuntarily. She looked at Kathleen and said with a plaintive tone. "Kathleen, will you come visit me on Thursday? Mrs. Miller will be off all day, and Daniel and his father will be in Portland again. Please say you'll come. It gets so lonely in that big house."

Kathleen could read between the lines. Myra was desperate to see her sister. It had been over two months since their last visit, and Lydia was also anxious to check on Myra.

"I would appreciate it, if you could stop by. I hate to leave her by herself, but these people in Portland keep on insisting on meeting with my father and me. We've almost nailed down the deal. Hopefully, this will be our last meeting. Mrs. Miller has volunteered to forgo her day off, but she really needs a break. She's been running herself ragged waiting hand and foot on our little princess."

As he said that, Myra's smile faltered. "Please say you'll come."

"I'd love to. I imagine you've been working on a nursery for the baby. I'm excited to see it."

Daniel looked embarrassed. "Well, we haven't started yet. Martha has bought plenty of baby items, but we haven't picked out wallpaper or paint."

"Martha, I'll bring some samples over when I come on Thursday. Daniel, leave this to us. I can't imagine you'd want to do women's work anyway. We'll need you when it's time to paint and hang wallpaper."

At the mention of women's work, Daniel looked appalled. He recovered by smugly stating, "I've already done the man's work on this little project." He leered at his wife and had the temerity to pat her protruding stomach in public.

Myra blushed to the roots of her hair and instinctively batted his hand away. Without thinking, Daniel grabbed her by the wrist and squeezed until Myra let out a little yelp.

Michael Tucker was in the hardware store and was watching closely. He thought Myra looked beautiful, but when he heard her yelp in pain, it was all he could do not to run over and slug his boss in the face.

Kathleen looked at Myra's face. "Daniel, stop being so rough with your wife, she's very delicate."

Daniel had the decency to look ashamed before he ruined it by stating, "She hit me first. Come on, Martha, we need to get back home so you can rest."

Myra turned to walk out the door and spotted Michael Tucker in the next aisle. The shelves were not very high and, for a second, their eyes met before he directed a look of such intense dislike at her husband, Myra was momentarily stunned. Smiling on the inside, she realized her knight in shining armor had just appeared.

Myra was pacing in her room. She'd thrown a tantrum this morning about what was served for breakfast. She almost hated being mean to Mrs. Miller, but it got her out of the house earlier and Myra needed some time alone. Entering her father-in-law's study, she crawled under his desk to retrieve the key. Her bulk was not making it easy, and by the time she got the key, she was breathing hard. Unlocking the desk and opening the bottom drawer, she was relieved to see the tin box of cash was still full of money. This time she took a few minutes to count it and was pleased to see $425 in the box. She knew the box contained household money old man Brookstone doled out to Mrs. Miller, and prayed when she was ready to make her escape it would be full.

Replacing the key, she couldn't stand being in the vulgar house a second longer. She decided to walk out into the yard. There was no one around to watch her, and she figured Kathleen and Lydia wouldn't arrive for another hour. Shutting the door behind her, Myra breathed in the May air. At some point in time, gardeners had laid out beautiful flower beds, now lush with colorful flowers. Myra looked at all the color and, standing back, realized the plan must have been to distract the eye from the mismatched style of the house. Looking at the flowering trees and azalea bushes, Myra's mood calmed down. She sat on a wooden bench and looked at the street through the wrought iron fence. Feeling like a bird in a gilded cage, she wondered for the thousandth time what would have happened if she had just taken prison as an option. Her body was swollen with a child she didn't want. In just over two months, the much anticipated birth would take place. Then she would be back where she started. Myra could tell by Daniel's mannerisms he was just itching to hit her. Anger had always been inside the small abandoned boy and was now being directed at her. She knew once the baby was born, he would resume his assaults on her body, both physically and sexually. The thought of it, partnered with her out of control hormones, made her burst into tears. Sobbing her heart out in the quiet yard, she didn't hear the footsteps until they were directly in front of her.

"Mrs. Brookstone, are you all right?" Michael Tucker knelt in front of her with a look of such sweet concern it ignited another racking sob out of Myra.

"Should I call someone? Do you want me to get Dr. Monroe?" Michael was getting panicky. He didn't have the slightest idea what to do.

"Please don't call anyone. Why are you here? Did Daniel send you?"

"No, your husband is in Portland. I was on my way out to the logging site to drop off some paperwork. I saw you sitting here and you looked so upset I had to stop." Michael didn't want to admit he had been driving by very slowly, hoping to catch sight of her. "I saw what he did to you at Parrish's Hardware store last week. He should be shot for treating you that way. You're his wife and the mother of his unborn child."

Myra wanted to play this new fish, but she felt so utterly defeated by the circumstances she just told the truth. "I fear he will kill me one day."

Michael looked at the broken angel sitting before him and knew she was probably right. In all the talk around town about the Brookstones, their cruelty to women was a whispered fact that couldn't be ignored. Knowing this woman had been accused of doing horrible things, and was said to be unbalanced, couldn't stop Michael from asking, "How can I help you, Mrs. Brookstone?"

"I don't have much time. Kathleen Parrish and my s…" Catching herself she went on, "Kathleen is coming to watch over me today while Mrs. Miller is gone and Daniel is out of town. He rarely leaves me unattended. He thinks I'll run away. He's right. I would if I could, but he took all my money and watches me like a hawk. I know if I try to leave with his baby, he will hunt me down and kill me. I don't know you, but I'll have to trust you. Once this baby is born, I will have to leave town before he…." Myra couldn't go on. She couldn't tell a stranger what her husband had in store for her.

"Does Mrs. Miller go into town every Thursday?"

"Yes, she does shopping and then takes the afternoon off. That's when Kathleen comes over. Although for a while Daniel refused to allow her to come because he knew she was my only friend here, and he had to show me he controlled everything." Myra couldn't stop the tears. "I've done some terrible things in my life but nothing makes me deserve what is happening to me now."

Michael was torn. There was so much he wanted to ask her, but to do so he would have to admit he knew all about her. Seeing her tears, he couldn't believe she was the monster everyone made her out to be. Michael had worked at the Franklin Bank for six years. He was often sent off on assignments where he worked in a company Mr. Franklin wanted to keep an eye on. The things he had seen the Brookstones do in business were dirty and, in most cases, illegal. They had shown over and over again they were bullies who went for their opponent's jugular. He knew what Daniel Brookstone was capable of and he would inflict pain on anyone who got in his way.

Choosing his words carefully, "Mrs. Brookstone, is there anyone you can trust, anyone who could get a message to me if you're in trouble? I won't be able to stop by here unless your husband is out of town, and we can't rely on that. He's wrapping up the business in Portland and may not be going again in the near future."

Myra knew he was friends with Lydia but was not about to admit they were sisters. "Maybe Kathleen. Do you live close to here? If I were to make a run for it, how would I find you? Will you really help me get out of here? If I could just get to Portland, I could catch a train and get far away."

Michael explained his location, finding it hard to believe she had lived in town for seven months and had scarcely been out of her house. He silently cursed Daniel Brookstone and his obsession to own and control people. Once Myra realized her new rescuer lived only a few short blocks away, she began to relax. Now she had to get him to leave before Kathleen arrived. "Please, Mr. Tucker, go before Kathleen gets here. I don't know yet if I can trust her."

Michael walked back to the street and got into his car. He'd taken the precaution of parking a three blocks away, not wanting word to get back that his car had been near the home. The corner of the Brookstone's property had lush trees and bushes and it was from there that he had entered and exited, leaving Myra sitting in the garden. He hadn't been able to get her off his mind. Listening to the fear in her voice and, remembering his mother, he knew he had to help her.

Kathleen arrived twenty minutes later to find Myra sitting on a bench in the front garden. Lydia was beside her in moments, rushing from the car to embrace her sister. Myra's eyes were swollen from crying and she made no effort to disguise her distress. Kathleen eyed the bruise on her wrist and knew it was from Daniel manhandling her in the store.

Myra clutched at her sister like a woman adrift in a troubled sea. She held her so tightly when the baby kicked, Lydia felt it. Sitting back with a look of amazement, she exclaimed, "That was the baby! Oh, it must be a boy. It was a big healthy kick."

Myra didn't even smile. "Aye, he's a kicker, all right. I'm sure he's going to be as evil as his father, judging by the way he's battering me from the inside."

Kathleen cried out, "Myra, it's just a baby. From what I've been told, that's what babies do. It's a wonderful sign of the life within you."

Shrugging her shoulders and regaining her composure, she contemplated her sister and Kathleen. She decided not to share her conversation with Michael Tucker. She still had some plans to make and decide what to do about her violent husband. He was not going to get off without some kind of punishment before she left.

Kathleen tried to lighten the mood by pulling wallpaper samples out of her satchel. "Look, Myra. We can pick out the wallpaper for your baby's room."

Myra stifled a hysterical laugh. She could care less what kind of a room Daniel Brookstone's brat slept in. If she had her way she wouldn't be around to see it. Trying to look interested, she turned to her sister, "What do you think?"

"I think these animal pictures are very cute. They have both pink and blue in the pattern, suitable for either a boy or a girl."

"Go ahead and order it. Daniel will hire someone to paint and hang the wallpaper. Is there a handyman in town that does that sort of thing?"

Kathleen looked at the sisters. She could see Lydia was trying to contain her enthusiasm for the project based on her sister's disinterest. "Yes, I'll find someone to do it and have it finished within the next two weeks.

Myra nodded disinterestedly and rose from the bench. "Come in, I'll show you the room we're using as the nursery. You'll need to measure, right?"

Lydia and Kathleen followed her into the house and up the stairs. Entering the nursery they were struck by the coldness of the room. It was on the north side of the house and there was no morning sunshine. The ceiling was high and seemed cavernous. Lydia looked at her sister, "How did you settle on this room?"

"It's the farthest from our bedroom. I didn't want to be disturbed if the baby cried."

Lydia looked at her sister in shock. "You are the mother of this baby. Once it is born and you hold it in your arms, you'll barely be able to let it out of your sight. Now show us some other rooms to choose from."

There were two other bedrooms. One faced east and rays of morning sunshine were shining through the windows. The walls were a pale yellow and the ceiling was only about eight feet high. The two windows faced the garden.

Kathleen looked at her friend and knew Myra would resent it if her sister stepped in again. "Myra, this is a perfect room for the baby. It's much cheerier than the other room. The view is quite nice. When you're feeding or rocking the baby, you'll have something nice to look at."

The look on Myra's face said it all. Lydia looked at her sister and knew that she had no intention of being around to raise her child.

Sorrow gripped her, knowing she would never get to know her nephew or niece. Lydia was torn between the selfish desire to have Myra out of Little Creek and the knowledge that a part of her family would grow up not knowing her and Edward.

Lydia couldn't stand Myra's indifference to her unborn child. "I need to get back. We have a big party tonight." Once the words were out of her mouth, she could have bitten her tongue off.

Kathleen also looked embarrassed. Looking at her sister and Kathleen, Myra figured it out. "Oh, so it's a party for your wedding, is it?"

Kathleen slowly nodded her head. "It's not really a party, just a few close friends getting together before the wedding this Saturday." Trying desperately to change the subject, she asked, "Will you and Daniel be attending the wedding?"

Myra hadn't realized an invitation had been issued. She was momentarily ashamed by how much of her life was controlled by Daniel. Looking defeated, she sat down hard on the nearest chair. In a small voice, she admitted, "I don't know, he hasn't brought it up. I'll ask him when he comes home tonight."

Lydia was hoping that none of the Brookstones would attend her friend's wedding. She was nervous they would see her face and notice the close resemblance to Myra. Looking at her sister and seeing how dejected she was, Lydia went to her. "I'm so sorry he's cruel to you. I promise we will figure out a way to get you out of this mess, but you have to promise me to take your baby. I couldn't bear to have one of my family members raised by those immoral men."

"But don't you understand, Lydia. This baby is going to turn into his father. Just like Daniel turned into his. It's like a curse of each generation. I'll not be able to stop it."

"Love will change it. I know it will." Lydia looked at her sister imploring her to listen, but looking into Myra's dead eyes, she knew it was useless. Myra's mind was made up and only a miracle could change it.

Lydia walked to the door of the bedroom. "This will make a fine room for the baby. I hope you choose it. Kathleen, I'll see you this evening."

Leaving the house, Lydia's heart was heavy. She wanted this baby to be born into a house of love. She looked at the coldness of her surroundings on this beautiful spring morning and knew her prayers wouldn't be answered.

Chapter 53

The party at O'Brien's consisted of Kathleen's closest friends. It was an eclectic group. Kathleen included girlfriends from college as well as two girls from grade school, who were from the other side of town. Two of Bernard's friends had come all the way from Boston. Lydia and Edward were the matron of honor and best man. Pleased to be asked, they took their duties seriously, making sure all the arrangements were perfect and their friends were comfortable. Kathleen realized she had more in common with Lydia and the girls from town than her fancy college friends who were married and already had two children each.

Mr. Parrish looked dumbfounded at the group. Part of him wanted to be put off by this group of people that weren't in his social circle, but he was having such a wonderful time, he laughed at himself for his own snobbery. He was sorry Mary couldn't join him for occasions like this. He sighed, thinking how Kathleen's mother would have loved to see her daughter about to be married and so happy. Parrish was pleased to be welcoming Bernard into his family. Bernard had demonstrated on many occasions his devotion to Kathleen and had a good head on his shoulders. Who could ask for anything more in a son-in-law? Sitting back, Parrish observed Lydia and her husband Edward. He remembered his prejudice against the couple when they came in for the bank loan. He had heard through many sources they were a hardworking couple who cared deeply for the people in town, helping out wherever needed. He couldn't take his eyes off of Lydia. He couldn't place it, but she reminded him of someone, and it was driving him crazy. Seeing his consternation, Kathleen walked up to her father. "This is a glorious party, Father. Thank you so much for agreeing to have it at my friends' restaurant."

"Well, the least I can do is to try and make my only daughter happy. I have to admit, I'm having a wonderful time. What a lively group of friends you have."

"Yes, they are! And Bernard has some lovely friends, too."

"I keep looking at Mrs. O'Brien. She reminds me of someone. I just can't place her. She's a beautiful woman and your wedding party will be quite spectacular."

Kathleen tried to keep her face neutral. "Yes, Lydia is quite beautiful, and the nice thing is, she's as beautiful on the inside as she is on the outside. It's funny how people can remind you of someone. I guess we all have our doubles somewhere."

The next two days were filled with preparations for the wedding. Kathleen realized how much her mother was missed on this special day. She wished her father had someone special in his life to share the occasion with. Stopping at the bank for a quick visit with her father, she stopped at Mary Hanson's desk for a moment. "Mary, it's so good to see you. Will you be coming to the wedding tomorrow?"

"Kathleen, I wouldn't miss it for the world. I've known you since you were a little girl. I'm pleased you've met such a nice young man. I know you'll be happy together."

Kathleen was glad Mary was joining them. Her father must think she was deaf, dumb, and blind not to have noticed the relationship between the two of them. She was happy her father had someone in his life. Kathleen couldn't figure out why he kept it such a big secret and why Mary put up with it. She looked at Mary and asked innocently, "Will you be bringing a guest, Mary?"

Mary was sure no one knew of her relationship with Harold but could see a twinkle in Kathleen's eyes. "No, Kathleen, I'll be coming alone. Not too many bachelors in this little town, and, if there are any around, I'm sure they couldn't put up with a woman as stubborn as me." Laughing, she nodded towards Harold's office door. "Go on in. He doesn't have anyone with him, and I'm sure he'd appreciate seeing a smiling face."

Kathleen walked into her father's office. "Dad, have you heard from the Brookstones? I'm curious if they'll be at the wedding. They've become even more reclusive than usual."

"Calvin stopped by earlier today to express his regrets. Seems like Daniel's wife isn't feeling too well, and they don't want to tire her out."

"Really, she was fine when I saw her yesterday. I'll bet Daniel just doesn't want anyone seeing how mean he is to her. He is out of control. He bruised her arm when we were talking in the hardware store. He's a bully and a brute."

"Kathleen, calm down. I know Martha is your friend but surely you're exaggerating. I don't think Daniel would harm his pregnant wife."

"Dad, you're wrong. Something is not quite right with him. He's hurt her before. He gave her a black eye after the party his father had for them. He's insanely jealous."

Harold Parrish knew his daughter was probably right, but in his heart he really hoped she wasn't. The Brookstone men had issues, there was no denying it. Part of him was relieved they wouldn't be at the wedding tomorrow. He wanted the day to be about his daughter and her fiancé. Parrish knew the Brookstones were never happy unless they were center stage at any event.

The day of the wedding was perfect. The spring showers were taking a break and the church was decorated with bowls of exotic flowers that Kathleen's father had flown in. Kathleen was in the brides' room in back of the church and Lydia was helping her with the final touches on her dress. The other two bridesmaids were chattering about their children and husbands. Lydia felt a twinge of jealousy over their good-natured grousing about the mischief their young ones got into. She and Edward's first anniversary was quickly approaching and still no baby in their future. She tried not to think of it and concentrated on her friend's wedding; there was so much happiness to celebrate today. She could worry about babies later.

There was a soft knock at the door. Mary Hanson poked her head in. "Do you need anything? Can I help at all?"

Kathleen got up, her long train trailing behind her. Hugging Mary, she shook her head. "Have you met my friend Lydia O'Brien? She is a model of efficiency. Everything is done. We're just waiting."

Suddenly Lydia remembered her broach. "Kathleen, you shared the wonderful American tradition of something borrowed, something blue with me…I was wondering if you would consider using this for your something borrowed something blue?" She held out the sapphire and diamond broach the Queen of Romania had given her as a wedding present.

"Oh Lydia, this is lovely. I would be honored to wear it. It's beautiful."

"Aye it is and it comes with a wonderful story." She told them the history of Queen Marie of Romania and how she had been given the broach as a wedding present. She had them all laughing as she relayed the story. It was just the thing they all needed to put them at ease before walking down the aisle.

Kathleen hugged Lydia. "You are such a dear friend. I'm so lucky to have you in my life."

Lydia blushed with pleasure. "We best be going or I'll have an angry bridegroom to deal with. I think Bernard is very anxious to have this all over. Edward said he's never seen him so eager."

Now it was Kathleen's turn to blush. "I love him very much." Lowering her voice for Lydia's ears only, "We're both lucky to have found good kind men. It makes me sad to see what Martha is going through. I know she's done some things, but she's being paid back in spades."

Lydia's eyes teared up for a second. "Aye, but I know she'll be all right. The girl is nothing, if not resourceful."

A soft knock and the door opened. "It's time, Kathleen. Are you ready to go?" Harold Parrish was exceptionally handsome in his suit. He looked at his daughter with pride and once again wished her mother was here. He said a silent prayer that she was looking down.

"I'm ready." Kathleen took her father's arm as the bridesmaids lined up for their procession down the aisle.

Bernard stood at the altar with his best man and groomsmen, a smile of anticipation on his face. The wedding march started and all eyes were on Kathleen as her father proudly walked her down the aisle. She was beautiful in her lace gown and flowing train. Edward noticed his wife's lovely diamond pin on her wedding dress and smiled. He stole another glance at Bernard and almost laughed at his expression. Bernard was struck dumb by his bride's beauty. Bernard only had eyes for Kathleen and knew that it would hold true for the rest of his life.

When they finally stood side by side, Bernard willed the ceremony to go quickly. He was anxious to kiss his bride and start their life together.

The ceremony was blessedly quick. The vows and rings were exchanged and the final pronouncement of "man and wife" brought smiles and tears from the people watching in the pews. Walking down the aisle arm in arm, the couple hurried to the reception in the church hall.

Edward followed them down the aisle with his wife on his arm. Thinking back to their own wedding, he wondered if he should offer some honeymoon advice to his friend. He remembered how he had been given the best advice by Stephen Franklin and knew he would find a quiet moment with Bernard to share it with him. Smiling to himself, he recounted Stephen's advice to not "break" his wife. He surely had not. She was stronger than he ever suspected, and he knew, as trying as the situation with Myra was, Lydia would survive. He would stake his life on it.

Chapter 54

Lydia sat in the kitchen drinking a cup of tea as she watched the sun come up. She could hear Edward's soft snores coming from the bedroom. Smiling, she thought of all that had happened in the past few months. Her life was so different from what she had known in Ireland. Life without her parents made her a bit lonely, but the fullness of life with Edward made up for it. She heard Edward stir from the bed and went to the stove to heat up water for his tea. The kettle began to whistle as he walked into the room.

"Darlin' how long have you been awake? Are you not sleeping well?" Worry creased his forehead as he looked at his wife. Edward tried to determine if she was having one of her headaches.

"No Edward, I'm fine. It's so peaceful here, watching the sun rise and thinking about how blessed we are."

Edward wouldn't call it blessed with Myra still lurking about. He knew Lydia was worried about her. The Brookstones were finished with their business meetings in Portland and Lydia had not seen Myra in a few weeks. He hadn't seen Myra in all the months she had lived in Little Creek and he thanked his lucky stars. He feared what he would do if he came face to face with her. Daniel had limited Kathleen's visit to once every other week. Edward was relieved Lydia wasn't able to see her. Contact with Myra gave his wife the headaches she tried to hide from him.

"Edward, you have a horrible frown on your face. What are you thinking about?"

He knew he was caught. "I was just thinking I will be relieved when Myra leaves and our life can go back to normal."

Lydia looked at her husband. She knew he was worried and tried to choose her words carefully. "Edward, there is no such thing as normal. There will always be challenges in our life. We will just face them as they come. It breaks my heart Myra is in this situation. Kathleen says Myra is very lonely and is starved for conversation. I keep asking if Myra talks about her baby but Kathleen avoids my questions. I know in my heart there is not a maternal bone in Myra's body. There's only a few weeks left. I keep praying when the baby is born Myra will have a change of heart and love her child.

"Lydia my love, don't get your hopes up. Myra has never shown interest in anyone but herself and probably won't be changed by the birth of her child."

"Aye, you may be right, but for the baby's sake, I'll not give up on her. This afternoon I'm going over to Kathleen's and give her a cooking lesson. Bernard is examining Myra today and I want to hear what's going on."

Edward sipped his tea and kept his thoughts to himself. He learned long ago, painful as it was, holding his tongue on matters he couldn't change was a wise course of action.

Chapter 55

Bernard walked slowly to Daniel Brookstone's office. He had examined Mrs. Brookstone and he was expected to give her husband a detailed report.

"She's progressing nicely. The baby has some very lusty kicks. Your wife is still terribly thin and I'd like her to gain a little more weight."

Daniel puffed with pride. "Can you tell if it's a boy?"

Bernard tried to hide his frustration. "No, Mr. Brookstone. As I've said, it's all a mystery until the baby makes an appearance. You've got about two weeks to go. Please try and get her to eat more. She's going to need all her strength to deliver this baby."

Daniel thought about how sick he was of his wife's pregnancy. It had been a long eight months without sex with her. Fortunately, his sporadic trips to Portland had given him a few hours of the kind of pleasure he enjoyed. At least the prostitutes put up a good act of pretending to enjoy sex with him which is more than Martha ever did. He knew she would try and weasel out of sex once the baby was born but he was not going to allow her to say no.

His thoughts were interrupted by Dr. Monroe. "Mr. Brookstone, I feel I need to remind you that after women give birth it is at least six weeks before they can resume marital relations. Your wife will need time to heal. Giving birth is very hard on a body."

Daniel flushed slightly. The doctor was a mind reader. He was just thinking his wait was almost over, but now he was supposed to wait another six weeks after the birth. "Dr. Monroe, I'm sure every woman is different. I think my wife will definitely heal faster than the type of women you usually deal with."

Bernard was unsure what type of woman he was referring to but decided not to belabor the point. "I'll be going back to the infirmary now. Your wife is getting close to her due date. Babies have a mind of their own, so please let me know the minute she goes into labor."

Leaving the office, Bernard thought how heartless Daniel Brookstone was. He wanted his heir, and he wanted his sexual demands fulfilled as soon as possible. Bernard realized Myra was going to have her hands full trying to take care of a new baby and fending off advances from her husband.

Kathleen and Lydia sat in the Monroe's kitchen sipping tea. They were waiting for Bernard to come home and give them an update on Myra. When Bernard walked into the kitchen both women started talking at once.

"How's she doing? How much longer?" They asked in unison.

"At least two more weeks. Myra's overall health is ok but she's very thin and I'm a little worried about her being anemic. I asked Daniel to try to get her to eat more."

Lydia chewed her lower lip. "Is she in any danger? Our ma always said she never had any trouble having her babies. I hope Myra is the same."

"We'll see. It won't be much longer." Bernard didn't want to share the details of his conversation with Brookstone so he changed the subject. "And what fabulous meal has my wonderful wife prepared for dinner tonight."

Kathleen looked sheepish. "Well, I did get a lesson today from Lydia. We made a lovely chicken. It should be ready in an hour or so."

Bernard tried to keep the smile off his face. He loved the days that Lydia came over to give Kathleen a cooking lesson. "Lydia, you are my salvation. Without you I would wither away."

Kathleen swatted Bernard with a kitchen towel. "My father says we can come for dinner any evening. I think he's worried about you wasting away, too."

Lydia stood up and carried her cup and saucer to the sink. "I've got to get back to the restaurant. Please keep me posted about my sister."

Kathleen hugged her friend. "I know how hard this is for you, Lydia. It will be over soon and things will get better."

Lydia returned the hug but couldn't return the sentiment. She knew it would never be better. That no matter what happened; Myra's baby was lost to her.

Chapter 56

Myra felt the first pains in the middle of the night. She was afraid to wake Daniel. He and his father drank quite a bit of bootleg booze the night before, and she worried he'd wake up swinging. She lay there gritting her teeth and thinking of all the swear words her father would say in Gaelic.

She was afraid if the pain got to be too much to bear she would inadvertently revert to her own accent, instead of the cultured accent of Martha Brookstone. Myra needed to hang onto Martha's persona just a few weeks longer. As soon as the baby was born she would focus on escaping.

At 6 a.m. Daniel stirred. Myra forced herself to get up and try to act as normal as possible. She wanted Daniel out of the house before she sent for Dr. Monroe. She had quizzed Dr. Monroe over and over again about what to expect. Her water had not yet broken, and the pains were still far apart, but they were definitely low and her back hurt. Dr. Monroe had cautioned her it could take many hours.

It was Mrs. Miller's day off. Myra knew the housekeeper wouldn't leave if she knew her labor had started. She forced a bright smile on her face as she walked into the kitchen.

"My, you're up early. Are you feeling all right?" Mrs. Miller looked her over noting her pale face and a light sheen of perspiration on her face.

"I'm fine. Daniel was snoring so loudly I couldn't sleep and decided to get up. I want you to take some time off today. This might be your last chance for a while. Once the baby get's here, we'll both be busy. Mrs. Monroe is going to come over today so you won't have to worry about me."

Mrs. Miller looked skeptical. The young woman standing before her had not been cheery or kind in the last few months. That in itself was suspicious, and the way she was holding her protruding belly was unusual.

"I have no plans for the day. I've instructed the grocery store to deliver my order so I think I'll just stay in my room and do a little reading today after the men have their breakfast."

Myra knew she couldn't make a scene so she just smiled and asked for a cup of tea. Holding her tea cup and saucer, she went to the sun room facing the garden. Myra settled into a comfortable chair and tried to appear relaxed as she sipped her tea.

Daniel stumbled into the sun room, "What are you doing out here? My God, look how huge your stomach is. I certainly hope you have this baby soon. You look ready to explode."

Myra tried to look at her husband, but was so disgusted by him all she could do was stare straight ahead and hope her face did not give away the fact she was having another one of those things Dr. Monroe called contractions. She wanted Daniel and his father out of the house before she called Kathleen to come over with her husband.

Daniel walked out of the room, more interested in breakfast than he was in trying to antagonize his wife.

Calvin Brookstone walked by without comment. He was anxious to get to work and was trying to hurry his son along. "Daniel, can't you get up early enough to have your breakfast and be ready to go out the door by 7a.m.? You know I like to get an early start."

Daniel had a piece of toast in one hand and a cup of coffee in the other. "Give me five minutes and I'll be ready to go. Let me go give my loving wife a kiss goodbye."

Calvin and Mrs. Miller exchanged quizzical glances. It was obvious the young couple had no love lost for each other.

The men left for work and Mrs. Miller went to check on Myra. "Mrs. Brookstone, do you need anything? Are you all right?"

Myra shook her head. "I'm fine. Go ahead and relax for the day. I'll call you if I need anything."

The contractions were getting closer but still at least fifteen minutes apart. She sat staring at the grandfather clock in the corner of the sun room trying to figure out when she should call Kathleen. She knew Kathleen would tell her sister. Myra wished she could see Lydia. She had no idea what would happen after the birth of this wretched baby. One thing for sure she needed to make her escape before Daniel reclaimed his marital rights. The last thing Myra wanted was to end up pregnant again with another spawn of the devil. She'd kill him if he touched her again.

An hour later, her water broke. She felt the warm gush of fluid between her legs soaking her nightgown and robe. Resigning herself to the inevitable, she walked out to the hallway to call Kathleen.

Kathleen was running late. It was almost 9 a.m. and she wanted to get to the store. The ringing phone sent a wave of irritation through her. Picking it up and snapping out a hasty "Hello" and she was startled to hear Myra's voice on the other end.

"Kathleen, can you get your husband over here without alerting the Brookstones? I think it's my time. My water just broke, and I've had pains all night."

"Oh my, oh my." The usually unflappable Kathleen was at a loss for words. Finally, getting herself on track, she tried to sound reassuring. "I'll call Bernard right now. He'll be there soon. Can Mrs. Miller let him in?"

"No, I don't want her hanging around because she'll call Daniel. Can't the two of you come and we'll just call it an examination? I'll let you in. I've been sitting in the sun room. I'll be able to see your car come up the drive."

Kathleen swallowed down her fear. She'd never been to a birth before and really didn't want to see it. However, she knew Lydia would be very anxious about her sister's care in the house of heathens as she called it. "Yes, we'll be there as soon as we can."

"Make sure Daniel doesn't find out yet. Please, I couldn't stand it if he was here."

Hanging up the phone, Kathleen wondered if Bernard would agree to her requests. Working for the Brookstones and treating Daniel's wife put him in a precarious position. He also detested Daniel so maybe he would go with Myra's plan.

"Bernard, Myra is in labor. You need to stop by home and pick me up. I'll be ready." Kathleen could feel a light sweat break out on her brow as she said the words.

"I'll be there in fifteen minutes." Not wanting to ask any questions to give away what was going on, Bernard hung up the phone and grabbed his coat. "My wife needs me. I'll be gone the rest of the day." He abruptly walked out the door before his nurse could say a word.

Pulling up to the front of his house, he saw Kathleen rushing down the walkway. "Oh Bernard, she sounded quite calm but she's such an actress who would ever know. I can't believe she wants me there."

Bernard reached across the car and grabbed her hand as he drove. "You'll be fine. You said she mentioned before she didn't want Mrs. Miller in the room and who else does she know other than you or Lydia?"

Myra was sitting in the sun room when she saw their car come up the driveway. She was thankful Mrs. Miller's room was on the opposite side of the house. She hoped to get them in the house without alerting the housekeeper that her labor had started. Painfully getting out of the chair, Myra walked to the front door.

Bernard looked at Myra. "How far apart are the pains? When did your water break?"

"Pains are about ten minutes apart and my water broke an hour ago. How long does labor normally last?"

Bernard didn't want to frighten her. He had assisted in deliveries lasting forty eight hours and some as fast as four hours. "It depends on the person. Did your mother ever talk about her deliveries?"

"Good heavens no. We didn't talk of such things. Although now I wish we had. Oww, oh, there it goes again."

"Let's get you to bed and I'll take a quick look." Bernard took her elbow and Kathleen walked behind them. As they started up the stairs, Mrs. Miller came rushing behind them.

"Is it time? Is she in labor? I'll call Mr. Daniel."

As she turned to make the call, Myra pushed past Bernard and Kathleen. "You'll do nothing of the kind. This is not your business. You'll call him when I say to call him and not until." Seeing the shock on Mrs. Miller's face, which was quickly replaced by a defiant look, Myra tried another tactic. "I don't want to worry him until the doctor confirms that I'm in labor. Surely you can understand how upsetting that would be to him if it turns out a false labor."

Mrs. Miller's defiant look quickly changed to one of agreement. "Yes, Mrs. Brookstone." Not to lose face, she turned to Bernard to assert the remainder of her authority. "Doctor Monroe, you need to inform me immediately when it is time to call Mr. Daniel. He will be quite upset if he misses the birth of his child."

Bernard nodded and turned back to Myra. "Mrs. Brookstone, please, let's get you to bed and we'll see how things are progressing. And, Mrs. Miller, you might as well get some towels ready just in case."

Kathleen pulled the covers back and, as she had done before, put a sheet on top of Myra. She held her hand as Bernard raised the sheet and examined the mother to be.

Myra let out a yell. "Oh my God, don't you have drugs or something? I thought you put women to sleep. I feel like it's breaking me in two."

Bernard looked at his patient. "Mrs. Brookstone, you are doing very well. Just relax until the next contraction starts. Please trust me. You don't want to be put to sleep. It's harder for the baby and it makes your recovery harder."

"I don't care if it's harder for the baby. I can't stand this pain."

Kathleen grabbed her hand. "Martha, from what you've told me about Daniel, you're going to want to be awake and in control after the baby's born. Please, just do as Bernard says. It will be better for you both."

Myra looked at Kathleen. She understood the logic in what she said but, as another pain racked her body, she was tempted to demand a shot.

The next four hours went by quickly. The baby was in position and crowning when Kathleen gently suggested, "Martha, you need to let Mrs. Miller call Daniel. He's missed most of this, but the baby is coming and he'll be upset with you if he's not here."

"Fine, just keep him out of this room." Myra's voice was pure Irish. She was having difficulty maintaining her Martha voice. "Keep Mrs. Miller out of here, too."

Kathleen left the room quickly to find Mrs. Miller and have her place the call. She knew Daniel would be here within minutes and braced herself for the verbal attack sure to come.

When she reentered the bedroom, Myra was mid-screech. "Make it stop. Oh my God, make it stop."

"You're doing great, Mrs. Brookstone. One more big push. The shoulders are almost out."

Myra was exhausted. The last four hours had been the most painful of her life. She did as he asked. She wanted it to be over with before Daniel came home.

At last the wracking pain stopped. Kathleen still held her hand and when she peeked over the sheet, she saw a look of wonderment on her husband's face as he held the baby. He took a moment to clear the mouth before a large lusty cry filled the room.

"Oh thank the saints it's over. What is it?"

"It's a boy, a beautiful boy with glossy black hair like his mother." Bernard cut the umbilical cord, wrapped the baby in a blanket, and laid him in Myra's arms.

She took a look at the baby and waited for the maternal moment everyone had predicted. It didn't come and she was relieved, thinking how much easier it is to leave when you have no ties.

As she drifted off to sleep, she heard Daniel burst into the room. "Why didn't you call me sooner? Is it a boy? Where is he?"

Bernard took the tiny bundle from Myra's arms and handed him to Daniel.

Looking down into the face of his son, he too waited for the clutching of his heart or the overwhelming love he was supposed to feel. Instead he only felt relief his old man would be happy and off his back about the continuation of the Brookstone line. "Why did you wait to call me?"

Kathleen stepped in, "Your wife thought it would be easier for you if we waited a while to call. She knows how busy you are and thought it would be hours and hours before the baby came. Once we realized it was happening faster, we had Mrs. Miller call you immediately."

"Just as well. We are busy and sitting around listening to her scream would have driven me nuts. How long will she be out?"

"Mr. Brookstone, your wife is exhausted. She'll probably sleep for hours. The baby is going to want food before long. Kathleen and I will go home for a bit and come back in the afternoon."

Calvin Brookstone came into the room. He stopped the minute he saw Daniel holding the baby with a smug smile. "Here dad, come and take a look at your grandson."

Calvin's smile stretched ear to ear. He looked almost feral as he took the baby and stared down at him. The newest Brookstone stared back with eyes as green as his father's and grandfather's. He then let out a throaty cry as if he already knew the struggle ahead of him.

As Kathleen and Bernard got into their car, tears came to Kathleen's eyes, "She barely looked at the baby and Daniel wasn't much better. I hope to God that someone in that house comes to their senses."

Bernard took her hand, "I think the new grandfather was pretty pleased. Maybe he'll be the guiding hand for the new baby."

They drove slowly to O'Brien's. Kathleen was steeling herself to break the news to Lydia that Myra's baby boy had been born. She wanted so badly to bring Lydia to see her sister, but knew it was an impossible dream.

As they walked through the front of the restaurant, they caught Edward's eye. He rushed towards them. "What's going on, have you some news?"

"Yes, Myra's had her baby. It's a healthy boy. Mother and baby are doing fine."

"Well no doubt the Brookstone's are pleased. I wish I could feel something for Lydia's sister, but I think of all the terrible things she's done, and I just feel anger. It would have been better if she had died while giving birth."

As Edward spat out the last word his wife came up behind him. Seeing Bernard and Kathleen together at this time of day she knew something was up. "It's early for you two to be here. What's going on? I can see by the look on Edward's face there is news."

"Yes, Myra had a baby boy. As I was just telling Edward, he's healthy and Myra is doing fine." Bernard looked at her with concern.

"Oh thank God. Is she happy? Did she hold her son?"

As she looked into her friend's eyes she already knew the answer. Myra did not fall in love with her baby. A tear fell down Lydia's cheek. She mourned for the baby she would never know and for the love she couldn't give him.

Chapter 57

M ichael Tucker was worried sick about Myra. He knew she had given birth to a son when Daniel walked into the office handing out cigars.

"Congratulations, on your baby boy. And how is your wife doing?" Michael kept his voice light.

"Yes, a big boy, weighed in at over eight pounds, Calvin Patrick Brookstone. We're calling him Cal." Daniel beamed with pride but ignored the question about his wife.

Michael smiled broadly and clapped Daniel. "It's a fine name. I bet your father is pleased, too."

Daniel's smile faltered for a moment. He and his father hadn't been getting along lately. Calvin's obvious pleasure at having a new grandson irritated him. He could see his father already attaching himself to the child and pushing Daniel aside. "Yes, he's a proud grandfather. I'm surprised he can tear himself away to come to work."

Picking up on the resentment in Daniel's voice, Michael made a hasty excuse and walked back to his desk. He was racking his brain for some way to check on Myra. He gambled she would not be making her escape until she recovered from the birth of her child. He would wait and pray it was soon. Michael didn't like the look in Daniel's eyes, realizing he was jealous when the attention shifted from him to his wife. Vowing not to make that mistake again, he returned to working on the payroll.

Chapter 58

The baby cried incessantly. Daniel would push at her in the middle of the night, "Go take care of him. I can't sleep with his constant screaming."

Myra would get out of bed and go to the nursery. Feeding the baby was a chore and not one she enjoyed. It had only been a week and Myra was already making her escape plans. She was still weak from giving birth, but knew she had to make it soon. Daniel was already talking about resuming his marital rights.

In the morning, she sat at the breakfast table, fatigued beyond words. She looked at her father-in-law. "A family as prominent as this one would have a nanny in Oklahoma. Is it so different here?"

Calvin was ready to make a glib comment, but he noticed the exhaustion in his daughter-in-law's eyes and how she barely had the energy to put food into her mouth. A rare moment of compassion engulfed him. "I want the best for my grandson. You look like death warmed over. You can't give quality care in the state you're in. Mrs. Miller knows a lot of women in town. Why don't you get her to help you find a nanny?"

Just then Mrs. Miller came into the breakfast room with a plate of toast and some homemade jam. "Mrs. Brookstone, try and get some toast down. I have your favorite strawberry jam."

Myra looked at her. "I'm going back to bed. Can you see to the baby if he wakes up? I fed him at 2 a.m. and 5 a.m. He should be good for an hour or so. Also, do you know a woman who could be hired as a nanny?"

Mrs. Miller nodded her head. "I'll put the word out and we'll see who comes around."

"Thank you, Mrs. Miller." Myra dragged herself up from the table and back to bed. She felt wretched, so weak she could barely put one foot in front of the other. She collapsed into a deep sleep only to be roughly shoved awake by Daniel.

"You're worthless. You sleep all day and now the old man is getting you a nanny? Well at least you'll have some energy for sex in a couple of weeks. The doctor said six weeks, but I think three is enough."

In her exhaustion, Myra let her mouth speak before she had time to think. "Leave me alone, I'm not having sex with you ever again. I need some sleep. I've been up half the night feeding and taking care of your son."

She shouldn't have been surprised when he slapped her. The blow stung but what frightened her was the murderous look on his face. "You do nothing around here, and now, you can't even take care of your own child. The one thing you will not deny me is sex whenever I want it. Think of it as payment for the roof over your head and the food you eat."

"Is that what I am, Daniel? No better than a whore to you? I must pay for the privilege of being your wife with my body?"

"Martha, don't you know all women are whores." Daniel spun around and walked out of the room.

Too tired for tears, Myra curled up and quickly fell asleep. It seemed like only moments later that Mrs. Miller lightly knocked at the bedroom door. Myra almost didn't hear the knock over the insistent roar of the baby crying.

Mrs. Miller walked to the side of the bed, "Mrs. Brookstone, it's been three hours. This little guy is very hungry. Can you prop yourself up a bit and feed him from bed?"

Myra wished herself to be anywhere but this time and place. She couldn't block the dark thoughts that none of this would have happened if only Edward had loved her, instead of her sister. It was his fault she was in this mess. Silently reaching for the baby she pulled open her nightgown and watched as he hungrily nursed. She looked down at the baby. His eyes were open and staring at her intently, as if he knew the time with his mother was almost at an end.

Chapter 59

Lydia was smiling again. It had been over a week since Myra's baby was born and Edward had lost sleep worrying about his wife. Standing in the dining room of the restaurant, Lydia rushed in the front door.

Edward watched her walk across the restaurant, a wide smile on her face and a bounce in her step. It had been months since he had seen Lydia this happy.

"You're awfully cheery this afternoon. I've missed seeing your beautiful smile." Edward hugged Lydia to him and thanked God the ordeal with Myra would hopefully soon be over.

"Edward, I've been so upset and distracted the last couple of months. I'm sorry, but I think I have news that will make up for it." Lydia couldn't hold it in any longer. "We're going to have a baby."

Edward's jaw dropped and he finally understood when Americans said they were thunderstruck. "A baby? Are you sure? Quick sit down. Let me get you some tea. Are you tired? Put your feet up."

His rapid fire questions and instructions had Lydia in a fit of laughter with tears of joy streaming down her face. "Edward, calm down. You have seven months of taking care of me. Don't wear yourself out the first hour!"

"Seven months? Why didn't you tell me you suspected you were pregnant?"

Lydia got a sheepish look on her face. "I didn't know, hadn't a clue. I was so tired, but I thought it was because I wasn't sleeping well worrying about Myra. I am embarrassed to admit for all the months I wanted to get pregnant I watched my monthlies like a hawk. Then all of the drama with Myra, I was so distracted I didn't think about it. I went to see Dr. Groves. I just couldn't go see Bernard. I would have been mortified. I hope he understands."

Edward started to chuckle. Two months ago was their anniversary and he had planned a romantic evening at home. He managed to get a bottle of wine from a friend who owed him a favor. He set candles out and Annie cooked a delicious dinner for two and left it in the kitchen for him.

After a glass of wine before dinner and one with, Lydia had declared she was no longer interested in food and attacked her husband with vigor. The fact the wine left his young wife without inhibitions was a surprise and added to their evening. He hoped their child was conceived on that wonderful evening.

Edward put his hand on his wife's belly. A look of amazement lit up his handsome face. "To think our baby is growing in there."

Annie walked out of the kitchen and stopped in her tracks. She looked at her dear friends, and a smile spread across her face. Not wanting to interrupt their moment together, she quietly walked back into the kitchen. Annie knew Lydia would confirm her suspicions as soon as she finished talking to Edward.

Annie didn't have long to wait when the kitchen door burst open and her friend grabbed her in an enormous hug. "Annie, you're not going to believe it but we're having a baby!"

Returning Lydia's hug, Annie could finally share her own news. "I'm so happy for you and Edward. You'll be a wonderful mother. I know our babies will be dear friends."

Lydia was about to tell Annie about Edward's reaction when the words registered. "Dear friends? Annie, are you pregnant too?"

"I didn't want to upset you. I know how much you've been hoping and praying for a child, and I felt so guilty I got pregnant first. I'm due the middle of March. I'm so glad we can talk about it. Johnny was going crazy wanting to tell everyone."

"Oh, Annie, our babies are going to be better than dear friends. They'll probably share a birthday. Our baby is due the same time as yours." Lydia giggled. "The doctor thinks the baby was conceived on our anniversary. That was also when your aunt went to visit a friend. You know what they say 'when the cat's away the mice will play!'"

The two best friends hugged again, tears of joy mixing together, just as their lives had inextricably mixed.

Chapter 60

The nanny had been with them for two weeks and Myra refused to breastfeed any longer. Her breasts were so sore she could barely wear clothes and the baby never seemed to get enough. Daniel was very unhappy until she told him the baby bottle would give his son more food than she was able to produce, and he'd grow better. Heartless as she was, even Myra couldn't conceive of leaving a baby without weaning him off her breast.

As a nanny, Claire Sefton was efficient and self assured. She was in her late twenties and unmarried. Claire was tall for a woman and broad. Her crowning glory was the beautiful thick blonde braid that cascaded down her back. Her face was plain and she wore no make up. Her size made her movements slow, but her eyes were quick to take in details. Physically, she was the exact opposite of the slender, petite Myra. Her physical presence was intimidating to most people, but Myra ordered her around without compunction.

Claire lived in fear of Mrs. Brookstone who she believed actually breathed fire. On Claire's first day when she had dared to bring the baby to be fed, Myra screamed at her to leave her alone and feed the baby with a bottle.

It didn't take long for Claire to realize that Mrs. Brookstone wanted nothing to do with her baby. She feared her employer was suffering from the new mother's sickness. She had seen it before and tried to step carefully around the lady of the house. The baby's room was so close to the master bedroom their paths kept crossing. Claire would sit in the rocker and sing songs to the baby as she cuddled him after his bottle. Myra would walk by without even stopping to look at her baby.

After a week, Claire approached Mrs. Miller. "I can't get Mrs. Brookstone to even look at her child. I think she has the new mother sickness. She seems so sad."

Mrs. Miller had seen much during her years in the Brookstone household. She knew the cruelties the men had inflicted on their wives and was powerless to stop it. The new Mrs. Brookstone was undoubtedly feeling trapped with a new baby and a husband with a quick hand. "Give her time. She's had a lot to deal with these past few months."

Claire looked at Mrs. Miller and knew she would not say more. She shrugged her shoulders and commented, "I don't know how she can resist her sweet little baby. He is beautiful with her dark hair and his father's green eyes. His eyes are the exact same color as his father's and grandfather's. What a handsome baby."

Myra walked into the kitchen. "Claire, go look after the baby. He's crying."

Claire ran out of the kitchen faster than a scalded cat. She had no desire to endure the wrath of Mrs. Brookstone.

"Your color's better. How are you feeling?" Mrs. Miller looked at her and was relieved to see Mrs. Brookstone no longer looked like death warmed over.

"Still weak." Myra couldn't admit she was feeling better. Daniel had been insinuating for days she was faking and it was time for him to reclaim his wife.

"I'm feeling guilty about Claire and me going out tonight. Will you be all right? The church is having a dinner to welcome the new minister. We're both on the welcoming committee. Claire volunteered before she accepted this position and can't back out."

Myra's heart started beating rapidly. Daniel hadn't told her the help would be gone for the evening. Trying to keep her demeanor calm, she smiled at Mrs. Miller. "Have a wonderful evening. Thank you for all you do for this family."

Mrs. Miller looked at Myra oddly. She had never been thanked by a Brookstone before.

Myra knew she had to make a break for it now if she was ever going to get away from Daniel before he "reclaimed" her. She'd been wracking her brain on how to get Mrs. Miller and Claire out of the house at the same time. She had almost been ready to put some of the sleeping drugs Dr. Monroe had left her in their tea. Finally, an opportunity had presented itself.

"No, I'm better really. Daniel will be home and he can help me with the baby. Claire has been here two weeks without any time off and probably needs a reprieve and, you too. We'll be fine."

Mrs. Miller couldn't help but notice Mrs. Brookstone never called the baby by name. She was anxious to go to her function tonight. She needed a break from this insane household. "We'll be leaving about 5 p.m. I'll serve you and Mr. Daniel dinner before I go. Mr. Brookstone has plans for the evening and indicated he won't be home until late."

"I'll just go tidy up. Daniel should be home soon." Myra turned and tried not to run wildly back to her bedroom. She sat on her bed trying to organize her thoughts. She needed to get the money out of the desk and try to find a small satchel to pack some necessities. She wouldn't be able to run with a large suitcase. Carefully making her way to her father-in-law's study, she snuck in. She immediately went under the desk. Shielded from anyone who might walk down the hall, she quietly unlocked the desk drawer and pulled out the money tin. It was full of bills. Relief flooded through her body; one less thing to worry about. Grabbing the bills, she smoothed them out and put them in her pocket. As she scooted out from under the desk, she saw an old leather briefcase sitting by the hat rack. She pulled the money out of her pocket and stuffed it into the briefcase. Myra made her way back to her room and put the briefcase under the bed.

Pulling the dresser drawer open, she grabbed Mrs. Hildebrand's gun. A steely look came to her eyes as she thought of the last eleven months of abuse from Daniel. She put the gun in the pocket of her dress. The Derringer was small, but it made a noticeable bulge. She got down on her knees and put the gun on top of the briefcase. She stood up just as Daniel opened the bedroom door.

"There you are. Mrs. Miller is ready with dinner. She and the nanny are going to some damn church function. Come on, let's get dinner, and then it's just you and me all alone tonight." Daniel gave her an unmistakable leer. The undercurrent in his voice alerted her that as far as he was concerned, tonight was the night.

An involuntary shudder went through her body. She'd kill him before letting him touch her again. Stalling for time she looked at Daniel. "Go ahead. I'll be there in a minute. I need to go to the bathroom."

"Hurry up."

Myra walked into the bathroom and splashed cold water on her face. She needed to get through dinner. Mentally she walked herself through the directions to Michael Tucker's house and prayed he would be home. The thought of escaping Little Creek and the Brookstones was making her shake.

A loud knocking at the door startled her out of her reverie. "Hurry up, Martha, before I come in there and get you."

Opening the door, she tried to give Daniel a neutral smile, "Sorry, my stomach has been upset all day."

"Well, we sure as hell know you're not pregnant. You're like the Virgin Mary, but that's going to change soon."

Myra was about to remind him of Dr. Monroe's instructions, but knew it would be a waste of time. Instead she walked down the stairs to the dining room. Mrs. Miller saw them approaching and hurried into the kitchen to get their food.

"We'll be leaving now, if it's all right with you, Mr. Daniel."

Daniel waved his hand dismissively. "Go ahead, Mrs. Miller. You two have a good evening. Martha, go get me a glass of scotch. It's been a tough day."

Myra was beginning to see the light at the end of the tunnel. If she could get Daniel drunk he would pass out, and she could make her escape. Picking up the bottle of scotch she saw there were only about two jiggers left. She cursed Prohibition, knowing this is all they had on hand until Daniel's supplier came by next week. Putting the glass of scotch in front of his plate she tried to be nonchalant. "How was your day?"

"My, my, aren't we being the nice little wife tonight. I wonder what your alternative motive might be. I bet I know. You're just dying to have sex with your husband. It's only been almost an entire god damn year!" Daniel's voice was rising.

"Shhhh, you'll wake the baby. Please, Daniel. Let's just have a quiet dinner." Myra did not want to deal with the baby. She didn't want to see baby Cal again.

Daniel rushed through his meal. He finished the second glass of scotch and pushed his chair back from the table. "Come on, it's time."

Myra stood and looked at his face, "Daniel, please you know what Dr. Monroe said."

The punch in her stomach knocked her back into her chair. The air left her lungs and she struggled to breathe. The pain was overwhelming and she felt wetness between her legs. Hot tears coursed down her cheeks and she vomited her dinner. Daniel grabbed her roughly by the wrist and pulled her out of the chair. "Hurry up. Mrs. Miller said the kid will probably only sleep for two hours, and I want what's mine right now. You can clean your mess up afterwards."

Dragging her feet only angered him more and he punched her in the face. "Damn, see what you've made me do. If there's a mark on you, the old man will have my ass. He's getting soft now that he's a grandfather."

He flung her on the bed and ripped at her clothing. Myra kicked and screamed but he shoved the pillow on top of her face and held it with his left arm. Pushing her panties aside he didn't even bother pulling them off. He rammed himself in her and tried to hold her arms down as she scratched at his face. He raised his fist to defend himself from her nails and the pillow slid from her face. Myra gasped for air. Daniel was quickly spent and rolled off her.

Myra survival instinct kicked in. Ignoring her pain, she got off the bed and reached down and grabbed the gun. Daniel was lying flat on his back, a self satisfied smile on his face. His pants were halfway down, and he still had his shoes on. Myra looked at him with a visceral loathing that steeled her courage. She had heard whispers of a girl in the village who had been violated by some British soldiers. Her mother had whispered the word "rape" but wouldn't explain the unfamiliar word to her daughters. Myra, battered and used, now understood what it meant. Her hands shook as she put the gun to his head. Daniel started to turn towards her, with a sneer on his face, and she pulled the trigger.

Her hand jerked back and she saw the look of surprise on Daniel's face. Myra watched as the light went out of his cold, calculating, emerald green eyes. She felt no remorse or sense of loss. She looked down at him. "You deserve this you bastard. You'll never hurt me again. It's your fault, you made me do it."

She went into the bathroom and stripped off her dress. It smelled like Daniel. The bodice was ripped, and there were stains on the front. Her face was a mess, one eye was swelling, and there was an angry red mark on her jaw that would bruise. She filled the basin with hot water and painfully washed herself. She was bleeding profusely and knew it wasn't from her monthlies. Myra walked back into the bedroom, studiously avoiding looking at Daniel, dead on the bed. Changing her clothes, Myra realized she could now pack a small suitcase. There was no one to stop her.

She hastily repacked, adding some clothes and other items to what she had previously thrown together. As she walked out of the bedroom door, the baby let out a howl. Myra turned away from the nursery and from the insistent cries.

Carrying the small valise under the cover of night, she walked the eight blocks to Michael Tucker's house. She had memorized the instructions and strode down the unfamiliar streets with purpose. Feeling like a prisoner on parole, the taste of freedom was bitter. She could still taste the scotch on her lips from Daniel's brutal kisses. She almost gagged at the thought.

She turned down Pine Street and counted houses. Michael's was two doors away. A car came down the street, and Myra tried to turn away so they wouldn't see her. The black ford stopped in front of Michael's house. She saw a tall man get out of the car. Relief flooded her body as he turned to look at her.

"Oh, my God, Mrs. Brookstone?" Michael rushed towards her and took her valise. "Are you all right? Come in."

Myra wasn't going to tell him all that transpired in the Brookstone house. He could see the evidence of violence. Her face was starting to swell and her eye was black. Michael rushed to the kitchen and brought back a cold cloth. "Here put this on your face. It will help with the swelling."

Myra gratefully took the cloth. "I need to see my sister."

Michael saw no use in keeping up the pretense he didn't know who she was. "I can take you to her home. It's close. Then I'll drive you to Portland and get you on a train."

"We have to hurry. They'll be after me as soon as they realize I've run away. There's not a lot of time. I need to say goodbye to my sister."

Getting into his car, Michael drove to the O'Brien's home. Myra instructed him to drop her at Lydia's house and wait around the block. "No one can see you with me. The Brookstones will stop at nothing to find me."

Michael did as she requested. Myra walked up to her sister's front door and knocked urgently.

Lydia was laughing as she opened the door. "You two are early…." Her eyes widened with shock when she saw her sister instead of the Monroe's. "Myra. Oh my God. Look at you. What happened?"

Myra hurried into the house just as Edward walked out of the kitchen. The look he gave her was one of pure hatred. He could not be as forgiving as his wife. He wanted Myra as far away from his Lydia as possible.

"What are you doing here?"

"Well, that's a fine way to start the conversation after not seeing me for almost four years. We're family now, Edward. I'd think you'd speak more kindly to me."

"After the grief you've caused, you should be glad it's only speaking that I'm doing and not hauling you off to jail. Or, better yet, killing you with my own two hands."

Lydia couldn't stand it any longer. "Quiet both of you. Myra, why are you here? Where is your baby? Are you running away?"

Myra ignored her sister. She had eyes only for Edward. "Do you see my face? Do you know what's happened to me all these months? Do you even care?" As she spoke, Myra reached into her pocket and pulled out her gun. "None of this would have happened." Myra raised her voice. "Do you hear me? NONE of this, if you had only loved me, instead of her."

Lydia's eyes grew wide when she saw the gun pointed at her husband. "Myra, you promised. You promised you wouldn't hurt Edward. What are you doing?" As she spoke she tried to get closer to her husband.

Edward was thankful the gun was trained on him and not Lydia.

Myra stared at Edward, "It's all *your* fault. You have no right to be happy."

She raised her arm, and as she fired, Lydia screamed, throwing herself in front of Edward.

Myra looked in horror as a red stain spread across her sister's chest. Edward grabbed his wife as she started to slump to the floor.

"It was supposed to be you, not her. It was supposed to be you."

Myra pointed the gun at Edward. She wanted him dead. Edward covered Lydia with his body. Myra squeezed the trigger and nothing happened. She squeezed again and finally threw the gun at Edward hitting him in the forehead. Myra turned and ran out the door.

Edward was powerless. He couldn't leave Lydia to chase after Myra. He screamed Lydia's name and turned her over looking at the blood soaking her dress.

As Lydia faded from consciousness, she thought that Stephen's friend was right, no good deed goes unpunished. And now, because of her actions, Edward's life would be changed forever.

Chapter 61

Myra rushed down the street. Opening the car door, she forced herself to be calm. "Drive. We need to leave now. I've said my goodbyes."

Michael was unaware of what had gone on. The sound of the shot had not reached his ears. He looked at Myra's battered face and knew he had to rescue her from the Brookstones. As he sped off into the night, his only thought was if he could save Myra, perhaps it would help make up for his inability to save his mother from his brutal stepfather.

Myra sat in the passenger seat and began to shake. She was trying to wipe the tears from her eyes. She had only wanted to say goodbye to her sister. She hadn't planned on using Mrs. Hildebrand's gun, but she was so enraged Edward couldn't see her pain, she snapped. It was *his* fault she shot Lydia. He would have to live with that fact, not her. Myra couldn't stop her thoughts. *Oh God, I shot Lydia. It was Edward who deserved to die. It's not my fault.*

Michael Tucker continued to drive. He could see his passenger was upset but realized saying goodbye to her sister and leaving her baby must be devastating to her. He knew the poor woman had been vastly misunderstood, and he would worry about the wrath of his employer's later, not realizing the series of events his inadvertent betrayal had set into motion.

Chapter 62

Calvin Brookstone walked in the front door of his house only to hear the hysterical crying of his baby grandson. Cursing, he ran up the stairs and pulled the baby out of the crib. He kicked open the door to his son and daughter-in-law's bedroom, ready to berate them for their neglect. He stopped when he saw his son lying on the bed. At first glance, he thought Daniel had passed out drunk and felt embarrassed his son would be caught literally with his pants down. Calvin turned up the lights and saw the scratches on Daniel's face. Slowly he took in the rest of the scene. Then he saw the bullet hole on the side of his son's head, with the pool of blood on the pillow. Finally, he looked into his son's dead, lifeless eyes. It only took a moment to realize what had taken place.

He stumbled towards his son and fell to his knees. Tears blinded him. He held his grandson close, poisoning yet another Brookstone generation, as he whispered into the baby's ear, "See baby Cal, all women are whores."

THE END

Acknowledgements:

I am blessed to have my wonderful husband Gary Arnold, who is supportive and encourages my writing. Thanks so much to friends and family that read the book during various stages and gave me great feedback and encouragement....Kitty Burnett, Lily Gunn, Kim Robey, Sue Berard, Bev Franklin, Val Walser, Kathy Pierce, Julie Wasson, Patty Songstad, Terry Moffat, Soni McKiernan and Greg Tuttle. I am fortunate to have strong female and male friends whose positive personality traits made it into the book. Thinking of my friends made developing various characters easy, I drew on their strength, their sense of purpose and most of all their sense of the right and wrong. My writing group, Kathleen Lawrence, Ed Nichols, Mark Bowman, Bart Bardeleben and Susan Schrieber, thank you for your feedback and thoughts.

I hope you enjoyed my book. Researching this time period made me realize what strong determined people our ancestors were. So many things make the 1920's a special time in our history.

If you enjoyed my book, please leave a review....even if you didn't, please let me know why.

11036511R00256

Made in the USA
San Bernardino, CA
04 May 2014